TRIALS

Of

Horse & Human

By Juliet Chambers

Published by

Serendipities Ltd

ISBN 978-0-9926379-6-5

CHAPTER 1

Chloe Marcus paused to gaze out of her office window. She took in the sweeping vista of the city below her. The view stretched across to the far side of the river as it wound its way through the Capital. The traffic hummed away busily below. She smiled to herself. What a place. Who would want to be anywhere else?

Chloe paused briefly as she caught a reflection of herself in the window. Her dark hair fell around her shoulders it still had a curl in it that she had taken time to add that morning. She could make out her slender form. Everything appeared to be in the correct place. She nodded to herself she'd seen a lot worse thirty year olds.

She turned back to her P.A. Chloe stared at Jade for a moment, taking in her bottle green tights and grey tweed suit and sensible flat shoes. She really ought to have words with her. Image was so important in this game, especially in a youthful PA. Chloe noted Jade looked uncomfortable, but when did she not? Chloe had hoped that Jade would come out of her shell more if she took the tough approach with her, however it seemed to be having the opposite effect.

Jade looked back at Chloe with a feeling of unease. She suspected that Chloe was going to give her another reprimanding for some minor misdemeanour. She felt herself cringing in anticipation.

Chloe saw Jade's apprehension. Jade seemed to shrink behind those bright red glasses that clashed dreadfully with her overly bright short red hair. Chloe sighed. "Jade, how many times do I have to tell you not to book my appointments at the far reaches of the City in the same day, I spend most of my time travelling when I should be closing bookings."

Jade squirmed visibly, she didn't want to say that she'd had no choice as the Martell Group were jetting back off to Paris the next day. She was sure that Chloe knew this and it would only make her more annoyed if she dared to contradict her. She pursed her lips in an apologetic smile. "Sorry, it seemed a good idea at the time," she murmured.

Chloe sat back in her chair and observed her for a moment. Jade started to feel even more uncomfortable as the office became filled with a heavy silence. She braced herself waiting for Chloe's backlash.

The sound of the telephone ringing made Jade jump so hard that she nearly left the ground. Chloe regarded her with slight amusement, "Jade you should really take a chill pill. I'll get it, why don't you get us some coffee."

Jade scuttled from the office feeling an overwhelming sense of relief. She couldn't make out that woman, one minute she would seem like she was so angry and the next she was nearly normal.

Chloe picked up the telephone, watching Jade hurry away as she did so.

"Chloe Marcus," she answered. Chloe listened to the voice on the other end of the phone. The last thing that she had expected was a call from her Solicitor's office. As the voice on the other end of the line continued to talk, Chloe slumped slightly in her chair. When she finally put the phone down she sat in silence for a few moments.

Finally she got up from her chair and walked over to the large window. She gazed at the view before her as she had done only moments ago. How things could change so much in a matter of moments?

Chloe was highly successful in her role as Marketing Executive. She had worked all of the hours she could to get to this level and to prove to some of those sexist pigs around her that she could do a damn good job. It had taken her three years to work her way up from an Assistant to this and those years had been tough. She'd had to use every opportunity to prove her abilities and commitment and now just when she thought that she might be taking another step further up the ladder, this had to happen.

Chloe folded her arms and leaned back to sit on the edge of her desk. The last thing she needed was to be called away from her work. The phone call had been short and to the point. Her Aunt had died suddenly and Chloe had, for some reason, been named Executor of the will. It seemed that there was no money in the estate, it was mortgaged to the hilt apparently, but there were some issues that needed addressing and she was required to go to the house to sort them out. It would appear that there was no other way for things to be tied up.

Chloe had not seen her Aunt Sophie for years they had once been close. She reflected for a moment on their last meeting. Unfortunately, it had not been pleasant. She sighed. This was a major inconvenience. She had more bookings than she could handle and she was in the process of winding up two major deals that would be quite lucrative for the firm. If only she could get out of it but the Solicitor had insisted that the matter required her urgent attention. What could be so important? Surely it would be just a simple matter of finalising a few financial matters.

Chloe wandered out of her office and into the corridor. She walked down the corridor and stopped in front of Carl's office. She could see him on the telephone through the window. She waved and smiled. Carl gestured her in.

Carl smiled back and waved his head from side to side to her as she walked in, he was trying to wind up his phone call, he was pretty sure that the representative on the other end was wasting his time and would not pay for their services. Finally, he hung up. He looked at her curiously, "Chloe, to what do I owe this unusual pleasure?" Normally you have far more important things to do than wander into my domain."

Chloe raised an eyebrow. "Carl, I have a problem."

Carl observed her serious demeanour. Her bright blue eyes were wide and serious. Her dark hair sat levelly below her shoulders and he detected the faint hue of Chanel. He tried not to stare at her slender legs that were enhanced by a pair of killer heels that God only knew how she managed to walk in. She was ever the professional.

Carl swallowed. "It's not some kind of "women's problems" thing is it? Because I just can't deal with that kind of stuff. Just take some time off to sort it out, or ask Jade to find you some counselling. Maybe, yes, that might be the best option. I'll tell you what I'll ask my Sandra to look someone up, she's really hot at all of that kind of stuff..."

"Carl." Chloe interrupted him. "It's not that kind of problem." Chloe observed him for a moment. Carl was only 38 but sometimes he had the demeanour of a much older person. Perhaps that's why he had been so successful. He had previously been an entrepreneur, with a variety of rather lucrative web based companies. Then he had decided to set up Kismet Marketing, which had taken off in leaps and bounds.

Carl ran a hand through his short dark hair. He stared back at her. He looked pale and vulnerable as always. His exterior gave the totally wrong impression of his real character. Chloe gave a slight smile. "I have had a telephone call from my Solicitor. There has been bereavement and I am needed on urgent business."

Carl widened his eyes slightly. "Oh. Well I'm sorry about your bereavement, what sort of business? Er, if you don't mind me asking, that is," he waved at the chair in front of his desk.

"Why don't you sit down for a minute Chloe, you're straining my neck."

Chloe pulled out the chair and sat opposite him. She still had a slight smile on her face. She always found it slightly amusing that Carl became so deferential when she was around, yet he was a different person when dealing with anyone else, and was positively intimidating when he needed to be. She observed him for a moment. He sat back in his chair and picked up a pencil and started flicking it around between his fingers.

Chloe took in a deep breath. "My Aunt has died and I'm the Executor of the estate. There are no other relatives you see" she gazed at the corner of the desk distractedly. She looked back at him. He was looking at her intently now. The pencil was now still in his hand. "Unfortunately there appears to be an urgent need for me to go to my Aunt's house and sort out some financial problems or other."

Carl put down the pencil. "Well then you'll just have to go then. Where is it?"

Chloe rolled her eyes. "Oh it's a good hour and a half drive away I suppose."

Carl nodded, "well that's not too bad, you could probably commute if you still wanted to fit in your work." Carl knew how driven Chloe was, although personally he thought that sometimes she was perhaps a bit too work obsessed.

Chloe gave him a grim smile. "I mean it's a good hour and a half there, and a good hour and a half back."

"Ah." Carl nodded again. "Perhaps not so commutable then. Well you will just have to take some leave and see how you get on."

Chloe's eyes widened even more as she glared at him. She was taken aback and a little irritated by his attitude. He didn't seem bothered that she would be leaving her work. She felt a prickle of annoyance, she was clinching bigger and bigger deals for him and all he could say was that she could go on leave just like that.

Carl noticed her icy expression. Oh dear, what had he said? Chloe was sitting in the chair giving him a disapproving look. Chloe was good at her job. That's why he had promoted her from Assistant to Marketing Executive after she had helped out on a few contracts. Giving her a chance to prove herself had proved to be rather lucrative for the company. She was however, rather cold at times and seemed to have tunnel vision in life. The only thing she seemed concerned with was to be the number one at her job.

Carl realised that he really didn't know anything about Chloe socially. The only things he knew about her private life were those that she'd disclosed on her application form when she first came to his firm. She never discussed her private life and rarely attended any Social events that were arranged. Only if she absolutely had to, and then she only discussed work ensuring that she wasn't veered off topic to any personal matters. Shame, she was an attractive woman. She should get out more.

"You know that I need you here," Carl said diplomatically, wondering how he could lighten her mood. "But you need to get your personal house in order too. You're no good to me if your mind's not on the job," he added. Carl saw that her expression lifted immediately. Thank goodness. "Any idea how long this will take?" he ventured.

"I would like to think that I could wind things up pretty quickly. Say a week. I suppose it depends on what state Aunt Sophie had let things get into." Chloe paused, she pondered for a moment on what she would have to do if her late Aunt's

Estate really was in a mess it didn't bear thinking about. She would just have to work nights on it if that were the case.

Chloe shook her head slightly. Carl regarded her with a mild amusement now. She had suddenly looked as if she were a million miles away. He had seen her like that once or twice before. He wondered where her mind went.

Chloe sharpened her focus as she became aware of his gaze. "Carl, I have quite a schedule this week."

"I know. I can do some of your bookings and I'll share the rest between Simon and Matt."

Chloe bristled at the sound of Simon's name. He had been trying to muscle in on her success ever since she'd been promoted. He had started as an Executive at the same time that she started as an assistant. Simon was well versed in dropping snide comments implying that her success was only down to cherry picking and luck and not to her skills or hard work. She really would have to get back here as soon as possible.

Carl raised an eyebrow. "I'm sure they'll manage. Perhaps not quite as well as you though?" He smiled at her. Chloe stared back at him. Carl looked down at his desk briefly. He could tell that she still wasn't happy. He had a sudden moment of what he felt was pure genius. "Why don't you take Jade with you? She can help with any admin. You can wind things up quicker then."

Chloe widened her eyes, "why on earth would I want Jade dragging along with me?"

Carl started fiddling with his pencil again perhaps he shouldn't have mentioned it after all. Still, he thought that it might do both Jade and Chloe some good to spend some time together that wasn't work orientated.

He had given Jade a job partly because her father had been a friend of his own father. They had hoped it would bring her out of her shell the girl was so overly timid and shy, mainly due to her being bullied at school. Her long red hair had made her stand out and she wasn't allowed to forget it by a certain few. Unfortunately, being with Chloe had seemed to make her even more of a mouse.

Carl thought for a moment, no he really did think it might be good for Jade and besides it would give her a change of scenery and a break from her well meaning but over protective mother. "Well, she is good at paperwork and she's very organised. Besides, it will keep her out of my hair for a while. I'll keep her on the salary, she can have a working holiday with you." Carl picked up his telephone and punched in Jade's number. Chloe made a slight movement towards him then sat back in her chair with a resigned look on her face.

Carl smiled at her. "Jade, come here for a minute please, I need to discuss something with you."

A few moments later Jade crept into the office. She glanced from Carl to Chloe nervously. "Is everything all right? Do you need some coffee too?"

Carl observed her for a moment. He was trying not to stare at those awful bottle green tights. Maybe she might get some dress sense from Chloe as well, if she spent some more time with her. Carl smiled warmly at Jade, who now looked like she might have a nervous breakdown at any minute. "Jade, Chloe has to go away for a little while and I thought that it would be a good idea for you to go with her. She will need some help with some paperwork and stuff." Carl waved his hand in the air.

Jade gaped at him in horror. "What? You want me to go away? With her?" Jade looked like she may take a running leap out of the window. Carl now waved his hand up and down at her whilst Chloe observed them with a slight feeling of amusement.

Carl was worried now. Jade was looking quite pale. "It's just to sort out Chloe's relative's Estate. You won't need to do anything unsupervised. Chloe will just be giving you some admin work to do. But it will include weekend working."

Jade didn't look convinced. "Where are we going? I'll need an overnight bag then?"

Chloe rolled her eyes. "We're going to the wretched provinces so you'll need a suitcase and we're going today so you'd better go home and get your stuff. I'll pick you up in an hour."

Jade lurched sideways as her ankle collapsed. Carl winced and frowned. Fortunately, she managed to remain upright. Chloe stared at her. "Oh and by the way. This was not my idea," she turned and glared at Carl. Who gave her a small smile He glanced back at a sweating pale faced Jade. Perhaps this wasn't such a good idea after all he thought as she fled from the office.

Chloe continued to stare at him now with a slight smile on her face. "You do realise that this could finish that poor girl off. She will have a heart attack if she sees anything that's not from the City."

Carl smiled apologetically and shrugged. "It could be the making of her. I'm sure you'll sort her out." He paused for a moment unsure whether to continue, then ploughed on. "Chloe, you know you could be a bit nicer to her."

Chloe stared at him with a look of amazement on her face. "Why?"

Carl looked down at his desk, why did Chloe have this effect on him? He always felt like he didn't want to upset her. He didn't have this problem around anyone else. "Because she could learn a lot from you if didn't terrify her so much."

Chloe raised an eyebrow. "Carl, you know this is not a popularity contest. Besides, she needs to learn that the world's a tough place and she'll never survive if she carries on acting like such a weak little school girl."

Chloe stood up. "I suppose I'd better be off then. I'll let you know as soon as I'm done," she turned and left the office.

Carl watched her go. He felt a strange pang as she left. A sudden fleeting thought that he might never see her again. He turned around in his chair and stared out of the window. The pencil was back in his hands now and he twiddled it around from one side to the other. Dam why did he think that he was going to miss her so much?

CHAPTER 2

Steve Bradshaw was fed up with that awful racket. It was supposed to be his day off. In fact it was his first day off in two weeks and he had been woken at six o'clock in the morning by that bloody alarm continually going off. Why the hell couldn't that idiot next door just get up and shut the dammed thing off? The walls in the static caravan were paper-thin and Paul knew that. Paul also knew that this was Steve's day off, inconsiderate sod.

Steve finally gave up and sat up in his small bed in the tiny bedroom. He rubbed his hands against his eyes and then ran them through his golden blonde hair. He yawned and stretched, feeling the opposite wall of the caravan with his feet. He just about managed to fit his six feet two frame in to the bed. If he lay in the recovery position that is. At just about the same time the alarm was finally silenced. Great. He might as well get up now.

Steve supposed he should count his blessings. He was lucky to have got this job. He'd never really managed to hold down a decent job. Things always seemed to go wrong, that's why he was glad to work here. Working with horses meant that at least some of the time you had nice natured creatures around you.

Steve dressed, managing not to bang his elbows on any of the walls in the room. He fished out a jersey from the pile of clothes that he had left on the floor beside the bed. He didn't see the point in trying to put them away. There was barely any room for his underwear in any of the caravans' bedrooms draws let alone anything larger.

He moved to the window and pulled a curtain to one side. Steve peered outside into the dim light. Seemed pretty fine, a dry spring morning and no rain yet. He left the bedroom and went in to the caravan's kitchen. Paul was already sitting at the small table chomping on cereal that looked decidedly unappetising. Probably contained more sugar than cereal by the looks of its day glow orange appearance thought Steve.

Paul observed him, continuing to chew on his food. "You're up early, thought it was your day off," he said after a moment. Steve paused. He had one hand on the fridge door and in the other he had a carton of milk. He briefly considered throwing the milk at Paul. He could see by his slight smirk that he knew that he had woken him up. Steve turned away and continued to make his coffee. He looked back at Paul for a moment, "Well, someone had an orchestra playing in their room and didn't seem to want to turn it off," he said, giving him a harsh stare.

Paul leaned back in his seat and smiled back at Steve. "Well now you're up you might as well give me a hand, I need someone to groom for me."

Steve stopped and turned back to his coffee. He looked over the small kitchen sink and out of the window. He had a wonderful view of a rather large muckheap just across the way from here and it was steaming gloriously in the morning sunrise. How very apt, he thought. He turned back and looked at Paul. Paul stopped chewing for a moment, his eyes widened slightly. Steve was looking at him rather intently. He hoped he hadn't gone too far this time. Steve was six feet two and looked well toned, much to Paul's annoyance, as he was five feet six and skinny as a rake.

Steve observed Paul's brief look of fear and turned back to stir his coffee. He shook his head and walked away to take a seat in the caravan's small lounge.

There was a sudden loud knocking on the caravan door. "Hey guys, are you decent? Hopefully not!"

Steve sighed. It was those girls again. They had plagued him since he started here two weeks ago. Always trying to rope him into one of their activities. So much for him getting some peace and quiet.

The caravan door was flung open and Ella stepped in. Her long blonde hair was tied back in a ponytail. Her slim frame was briefly surrounded by a halo of sunshine and indeed she did look like an angel. Paul stopped chewing for a moment as he stared at her. He felt a sudden pang of longing. He quickly looked back at his bowl and continued to devour the remains of the toxic feast.

Ella watched him for a moment then continued into the caravan. "You'll be hyper after eating that crap."

"I need the energy. Got a full day in the saddle ahead, it's tough at the top you know," said Paul with a smirk.

A slightly chubbier face suddenly appeared in the doorway. "Make us a coffee Ell. I'm going to have to eat something even if you don't." Joanne said and marched up the caravan steps and into the kitchen. She looked around, noting Paul had a slight dribble of milk on his chin. Paul looked back at her and rolled his eyes She was shorter than Ella and considerably larger. Her auburn hair fell to her shoulders in an unruly bob that she didn't even bother trying to tie back.

Ella and Joanne had started at the yard at the same time. They had known each other from school and had always been horse mad. Although Paul gathered that their parents had not been too happy about them avoiding college to come to work here.

Joanne moved towards Ella. They both paused for a miniscule moment as they noted Steve in the corner of the room trying to ignore them. Paul felt a stab of irritation as he watched the way that they looked longingly at Steve. It was obvious that they both fancied him.

Ella and Joanne exchanged looks and both grinned. "Hiya Steve. How's it hanging?" Asked Joanne.

Ella stifled a giggle. "How about a coffee?"

"I have one thanks ladies." Steve said without looking at them. Perhaps if he gazed out of the window they might take the hint.

Ella and Joanne made their drinks and then plonked themselves down on the sofa in the living room. Ella sat in the middle of the sofa next to Steve. She pushed back a piece of her blonde hair that had escaped from her ponytail. "What are you up to today Steve?"

Joanne was sitting on the end of the sofa next to Ella. She gave Ella a slight nudge and raised her eyebrows at Steve.

Paul observed the girls as he sipped on his coffee. He was feeling more annoyed by the moment. Couldn't they see how childish they were being? Steve wasn't stupid he saw the looks that they gave each other. Ever since he had been here they had been throwing themselves at him. It was embarrassing. Surely the novelty should have worn off by now?

Paul glowered at them over his coffee cup now. He supposed that the girls would always be after the likes of Steve. He was different to most of the other lads around, being taller and more solidly built. But God, he was so obviously good looking, didn't those girls have any class? Paul had heard Ella describe him as "Our own answer to Brad Pitt" when she had been having one of her silly swooning sessions over him with Joanne in the yard one day.

Paul rolled his eyes as he looked up and saw their mooning looks, what a stupid pair. Steve did have the looks, thought Paul but he was a loser. He may be all muscle bound but he was too tall to be a jockey so he'd never amount to anything.

And he had such a quiet personality, almost moody. He would never get on in the world. Steve had all the charm of a dog turd stuck to your shoe mused Paul. He was sure that Steve had only got the job here because Celia was desperate. Either that or he'd let her shag him.

Steve had been sitting on the sofa with his eyes firmly on the window. However, these two just couldn't seem to take a hint. Finally, he looked at Ella and then Joanne who were smiling at him from the sofa. He looked further across the caravan and saw that Paul was looking daggers at him. He felt a faint flush of pleasure at Paul's obvious irritation and casually rested his hand on Ella's knee smiling warmly at her. "You girls doing anything today? " He asked.

Ella beamed back at him, enjoying the warm sensation of his hand on her knee. "Oh, we've got to work today, but we can always pop back here later in our lunch break." Joanne nodded enthusiastically in agreement.

"Sorry girls, have to go out in a while. Anyhow, you'll be lucky if you get a decent break today I hear Mrs S is taking delivery of some new hopefuls."

Ella's face slumped with disappointment. "Oh bugger. We were hoping for a quiet day too."

Joanne nodded in agreement. She had noted Steve's hand on Ella's knee and was wishing that she had sat next to him first. "More cannon fodder I suppose."

Paul stood up and threw his breakfast bowl and cup in the sink loudly. "Well, I'm off. Some of us have to bear in mind we have a future in this industry," he looked pointedly at Steve and shook his head. He paused, "you two will be for the high jump if you're late again, you know what Celia's like."

"Yeah, a miserable old harridan," said Joanne. She looked at Ella and they both started giggling again. "Still, suppose we'd better go." Joanne looked at Steve "Later," she said with a wave of her hand.

Ella paused for a moment before taking Steve's hand. She removed it gently from her knee and placed it high up on his thigh, giving it a soft squeeze as she let it go. She stared into his eyes briefly as she rose. "Yes Steve, definitely later."

Steve observed them as they left the caravan. He supposed he should be pleased with the female attention but he just found them rather childish. They were like two annoying little schoolgirls. Although, he did enjoy the obvious irritation that it caused Paul.

Steve found Paul more even annoying than the girls. He was so full of himself. Paul was just five feet six and could eat just about anything he wanted without putting on any weight and he was an okay horse rider, although a bit too hard for Steve's liking. But this seemed to be everything that Paul needed to succeed in the racing game. Unfortunately, Paul took every opportunity that he could to remind everyone around him that he was the one going places and was in with a shout at becoming a professional jockey, unlike the rest of them.

Steve sighed and finished his coffee. He suddenly wished that he could get a break in life He really wanted to go somewhere and be someone but so far his life had been a catalogue of disasters. He had planned to use this day off to try to research some way to get himself a new career. He had decided to venture into the village library and see if he could look up anything on the Internet. Unfortunately, Steve wasn't exactly a computer whizz so it was something that he wasn't looking forward to. That was part of his problem- he wasn't well versed in all things educational.

Steve had spent most of his time bunking off school after his father had left home when he was ten, declaring to Steve and his mother that he "wanted his freedom back". His mother had then decided to work her way through as many men as possible in order to find a "keeper" which meant that she was out of the flat more often than she was in. She had staggered from one useless relationship to another and had never had the money, or the inclination for that matter, to get a computer. In fact she had rarely been at the flat after a while. This turned out to be a blessing as when she was in the flat, she had been more interested in sucking up the last dregs from any cheap wine bottle that she could find in order to render herself comatose, than advising Steve on his school work.

Still that had been a while back and Steve was twenty-five now it was about time he got himself a decent job. Steve rose from the sofa. He had better do something before he started to feel melancholy. He rinsed his cup and grabbed a fleece before starting out of the caravan. He didn't bother locking it, as far as he was concerned there was nothing worth pinching inside.

Steve walked around the muckheap and strolled across the yard. It was too early to go to the library yet. He heard the clatter of horse's shoes, as the string were led out from their boxes ready to go to the gallops. He paused and watched for a moment.

He noticed that Joanne was struggling to mount a particularly flighty horse. He had better go and help her. She tried several times and before he could get to her,

finally managed to mount by flinging herself across the horses back from the mounting block. Luck was on her side as her mount span around towards her rather than away and she managed to scramble aboard. Oh dear, thought Steve, she really wasn't cut out for this type of thing.

Ella gave him a wave as they jogged off away towards the gallops. Joanne was still having problems as her horse, not content with travelling sideways, was also throwing a few small bucks in just for good measure. Steve watched as she bobbed around on its back.

Steve pondered on this for a moment. Then shrugged, surely Paul would have checked who he put her on. That was supposed to be his job.

Steve wandered around the yard and loose boxes for a while. He stopped at the occupied stalls to check that the inhabitants were all happy. They seemed pretty cheerful. They all had hay and water so they were munching away peacefully.

Steve walked back outside and wandered further away from the yard. He walked along the track that led away from the stables. He had not been up here yet. He had hardly had time, since he'd started there it had been constant work, work, work. There always seemed to be something that needed doing. He hadn't complained though. He liked being here. He had only managed to get the job by chance.

A few weeks earlier Steve had managed to hitch a lift in the back of a builder's van and the village of Diddlecot was where the builder had terminated his journey. Steve had been making his way further north. He had been laid off from his job in the warehouse where he had been order picking, due to the slump in business. He'd only been there on a temporary contract so he'd known that it was on the cards. After much searching without success, he'd decided to try further north to see if he could get some work vegetable picking. He thought that it would at least see him through to the end of summer and he knew that you could make some extra cash with the overtime with that kind of work.

Steve had been parched when he got out of the builder's van and decided to get some water from the local shop before continuing with his journey or rather with trying to get another free lift. If that failed he would just have to catch a bus. Steve was trying to hang on to his cash for as long as he could though, just in case he struggled with work at the next stop.

Steve had wandered into the shop and there had been Celia Stone complaining loudly about how she was struggling to get staff. Apparently, another groom had left her yard. Joanne was carrying her shopping basket for her. She had been thinking that if Celia didn't treat her staff like dirt and work them into the ground without paying them overtime then Celia wouldn't be in this predicament.

Steve had been unable not to listen to Celia's loud voice as she went on about how no one wanted to work for her. Joanne had seen him look over at them. Joanne had smiled at him the moment she saw him. She wondered who the fair-haired good looking guy was. He looked well fit! Couldn't be a local she would definitely have known this one. Celia had stopped briefly and stared in the direction of Joanne's gaze. Celia sucked her ample stomach in suddenly and grabbed a piece of her overly long, overly curly hair that she started twirling absently around a finger. That was when Steve had taken the opportunity to volunteer his services. He had been quite involved with horses in his youth.

Steve had discovered that local stables were a great place for bunking off as a teenager. He just told them he had a free period or lied about his age and would muck out or groom some horses in exchange for a free riding lesson. He hadn't minded the walks into the country that took him to the stables and riding schools. It had always been a pleasant escape and that was when he learned that horses were the nicest people to be around.

Working for a yard would certainly be better than digging around in the dirt for vegetables he supposed. He had turned on the charm for Celia and fortunately it had worked. So here he was.

He carried on up the track that ended in front of a large brick building. The large doors were drawn shut. Steve pulled at one and it opened a short way, dragging along the floor. He pulled again until he had enough of a gap for him to step inside.

The building had some makeshift stables inside. It looked like they had been thrown carelessly together. Parts of the wooden panels were secured to the walls with baling twine. The place was filthy. There were piles of rotten straw in the narrow walkway down the middle of the building and a few full bin bags dumped at the side of the stables. He counted four stables in all. He stepped forward. Suddenly a bay horse's head appeared over a door. Steve walked towards the farthest stable.

Steve stopped in front of the stable door and peered over it at the horse. It was a tall bay gelding who looked as if he could use some feed. You could see his ribs quite clearly. The horse looked back at him hopefully. Steve wrinkled his nose in disgust at the condition of the horse's stable. It was appalling the animal was fetlock deep in filthy manure and pee covered straw. His hayrack was empty and there was no sign of any water anywhere.

Steve opened the door and stepped inside. "Hey there fella," he stroked the horse's head who moved his head down into Steve's hand.

Steve looked down at the horse's legs. His left front leg was considerably larger than the right from the back of the knee down. Looks like he'd had some kind of tendon injury thought Steve.

Steve patted the horse and went out of the stable. After searching through the rubbish he finally found what he needed; A bucket, wheelbarrow and a dusty pitchfork. He rinsed out the bucket and filled it with water from the tap at the end of the building that fortunately worked at the first attempt. Then he went back into the stable and set to cleaning the box out. All thoughts of going to the library had left his head now. This poor horse needed looking after.

Steve had just finished cleaning out the stable. He had found an ancient muckheap at the back of the building, which he had increased to nearly double its size. He was just about to find some hay and straw for the poor creature when he heard a voice behind him.

"What the hell do you think you're doing?"

CHAPTER 3

Jade was quite relieved when they finally reached the Solicitors office. Chloe's driving had terrified her. She had been doing ninety-five miles an hour down the motorway in her X5, flashing her lights at anybody who dared to slow her progress by overtaking in front of her. Jade's left hand knuckles were permanently white as she gripped the side of the car seat.

Chloe finished parking the car and looked across at Jade who looked her usual terrified self. In fact she looked a little paler than normal. She left Jade biting her nails in the X5 and went in to the Solicitor's office.

After telling the receptionist who she was Chloe sat down in one of the over sized sofas and picked up a copy of Country Life. Typical she thought, still she might as well get into the swing of things she mused and started leafing through its pages.

A few minutes later a forty something dark haired man appeared. He was wearing a tweed jacket and waistcoat and peered at her from behind his small glasses. He smiled. "Chloe Marcus?" I'm Robert Morecom, how do you do. Please accept my condolences for your loss," he held out his hand to her.

Chloe rose from the sofa, holding out her own hand. "How do you do," she looked him up and down, taking in the tweed jacket and corduroy trousers. Very Countryside she thought. She really was getting closer to her destination.

Robert showed her through to his office. "Take a seat Ms Marcus," he said gesturing to the chair on the other side of his desk. Robert sat down and opened a side draw in the large desk. He pulled out two large envelopes, which he placed in front of him. Chloe looked at them curiously.

"The funeral arrangements have already been made. The details are in the envelope as are the keys to the property." He said tapping one envelope with his finger. "

Chloe looked back at him. "Well Mr Morecom, I'm hoping that I can wrap this all up pretty quickly."

Robert peered at her over his glasses. "Quite," he said. "However, you will need to read the contents of these envelopes to make you fully aware of the situation."

Chloe stared back at him. "Is there something you need to tell me? She asked him her eyes narrowing. He placed his hands together and looked thoughtfully back at her. Chloe was beginning to have an uncomfortable feeling that there was more to this than he was telling her.

After a moments silence Robert spoke, "everything is explained in the paperwork." He suddenly smiled brightly at her, "oh dear, how remiss of me. Actually there was one more thing. Just before your aunt passed away she left you this note. I understand that it was the last thing she wrote." Robert pulled another smaller envelope from his draw and handed it to her.

Chloe stared at the envelope and then looked back at Robert who was still smiling at her. She opened the envelope quickly and pulled out the paper that was folded

inside. She stared at it for a moment and then looked back at Robert. "What on earth does this mean?"

Robert raised an eyebrow. "I'm afraid I don't know what you're referring to."

Chloe frowned and read out the note. "It says "Don't give up on Sam, use the formula." Are you sure that this was her last note for me?"

Robert nodded solemnly back at her. "Well your aunt and uncle were always quite eccentric weren't they? Anyway, you have the property address in the envelope so I won't delay you any further," he stood up suddenly and walked around his desk. He was opening the door before Chloe even had time to get up from her chair. She rose quickly, "oh, well if that's it then yes. I suppose I'd better be of," she said as he made a sweeping gesture with his arm guiding her towards the door.

She walked out of the office and left the building. Pausing as she closed the door behind her. What the hell was all that about? She held the envelopes up in front of her. Why did she have a feeling that this was going to be nothing but trouble?

Robert shut the door of his office and sat back at his desk. He clasped his hands together in front of him placing them on the desk. He shook his head. If only she knew.

Chloe flung open the door of the X5, throwing the envelopes onto Jade's lap who almost exited through the roof of the car. Chloe glanced across at Jade. She fired up the engine and tapped the postcode in to the Sat Nav ignoring Jade's questioning gaze.

Jade held on to the envelopes on her lap, she didn't dare look at them, Chloe didn't seem in a very good mood. She wondered what had gone on in the Solicitor's office. Chloe hadn't been gone long.

Chloe drove on, she finally gave Jade a sideways glance. Why did the girl always look so scared? She'd hardly said a word all the way here. Chloe had nearly fallen asleep driving along that tedious motorway. "According to the Sat Nav we're nearly there. There's a shop up ahead I'm going to get some provisions. Just in case, I've a feeling we may need them."

Jade kept her gaze fixed straight ahead. She didn't want to look at Chloe as Chloe would only look back at her and they might end up driving into a ditch. "Okay," she squeaked. "Haven't you been to the house before?"

Chloe didn't look at her this time she kept her eyes on the road. "No, not to this house," she said quietly.

Chloe pulled up outside the village shop. "You can come and help with the shopping," she said to Jade.

Jade clambered out of the car and trotted after her. Chloe paused and looked at the sign hanging on the door of the shop. Jade almost ploughed into her. She looked at

Chloe nervously, "are they shut?" Chloe gave a small smile and shook her head. "No," she said and pushed open the door and marched into the shop.

After filling a shopping basket with a variety of supplies that they stashed in the boot of the car, they continued on their way. After negotiating a few lanes that seemed to become ever narrower Chloe finally stopped outside a large gated drive.

They both stared silently at the gates. Chloe looked at Jade and inclined her head sideways. "There are some keys in one of those envelopes." She said pointedly.

Jade opened an envelope and pulled out a handful of keys that were all secured on a large key ring. She opened the car door and stepped out almost falling out of the door. She just wasn't used to vehicles this big. Jade started fumbling with the keys, trying to find one to unlock the padlock that was holding the chain around the gates. Finally she found the right one and managed to pull open the gates. She returned to the car clutching the padlock and keys to her chest with one hand. She climbed back in to the car whilst Chloe observed her. Chloe was wondering if Jade was going to cope out here in the country, she just wasn't made to deal with anything more advanced than a doorstep.

Chloe drove along the drive and pulled up in front of the large house. Jade observed it with wide eyes. "Wow, it's massive," she couldn't help but state the obvious.

Chloe was also looking up at the house, it certainly was a lot bigger than the last house that her aunt and uncle had owned and that one hadn't been small. "Come on," she said to Jade. She pulled the keys from Jade's grasp and got out of the car. "Let's have a look at the place before we unload anything. Just in case we need to book into a Hotel."

Jade followed her up the stone steps. She paused and looked up at the house again. Suddenly she shivered. It reminded of her of something from a horror film it looked so large and desolate and the fading light gave it a grey look that screamed creepy.

Chloe fiddled with the keys until she found the right one for the door. Finally she pushed the large door open that gave a small squeak of protest as it swung ajar. She peered around the door into the house.

Chloe pulled the door back towards her and looked at Jade. "I don't think I should let you go inside there," she said, her eyes wide.

Jade put a hand to her mouth, she felt a surge of dread well up inside her. "Oh, no is there something awful in there?"

Chloe looked at her sternly now. "No I'm just concerned about all of those ornaments in there. I know how accident prone you are, you'll have something broken in no time." Chloe gave a small smile and turned and walked into the house.

Jade lowered her hand and rolled her eyes at Chloe's back. "That wasn't funny," she mumbled quietly as followed Chloe in to the house.

Jade looked around the hall. Her eyes wide behind her over sized glasses. "Wow, it's amazing," she whispered.

The vast hall had a variety of ornamental pieces, which had been subtly placed around it. There was something of interest where ever you looked. Jade approached a beautiful bronze horse that was rearing up on top of a column.

"Don't touch it!" Chloe shouted making Jade jump out of her skin. Jade paused and approached the horse cautiously stopping a few feet away. She stared at it, admiring it from a safe distance.

Chloe looked around the hallway. There were several corridors leading away and a large staircase in the middle. Chloe looked back at Jade who was peering around the hallway at the other pieces of art. "Come on, let's see that everything is in working order," she said marching up to a brass light switch and giving it a flick. The hallway was flooded with light from the chandelier hanging in its centre. Both Chloe and Jade now looked up to admire it.

"Well the power's not been turned off, at least we don't have to go and find a circuit box," said Chloe brightly. "Right, let's see where everything is then," she continued, glancing at Jade who was still gaping around her. "You'd better stick with me. I don't want you getting lost and knocking things over."

Jade nodded and followed her as she started to walk along a corridor on the left from the hall. Yes, unfortunately Chloe was right. Jade was terribly clumsy. She often knocked cups off her desk and had dropped her laptop on more than one occasion. The last time she had broken the laptop screen and had to creep into Carl's office in tears to confess. Fortunately Carl had been very understanding and had it fixed straight away managing to hide it from Chloe. It had been their little secret.

They walked around the length of the house. Jade lost track of where she was after a while. She was too engrossed in all of the ornaments and lovely old decor of the place.

Eventually they were back in the hallway. "We'd better get our stuff, it's getting dark outside. Put the food in the kitchen Jade." Chloe said as she headed for the car. Jade was trying to remember the way to the kitchen as she carried the bags Chloe handed her into the house.

Chloe switched a few lights on as she walked up the stairs and deposited her suitcase in the large master bedroom. It had a lovely view of the fields outside. Chloe paused in front of a picture hanging on the wall. It was of her aunt and uncle, obviously painted from their younger days. They were embracing each other whilst looking lovingly into one another's eyes. The air of love and energy radiating from the scene was almost tangible. Chloe swallowed and turned away, she stopped in front of the window and gazed out at the fields beyond. She felt a sudden pang of sadness. She took a deep breath and turned away. She took a few things from her suitcase and placed them on the bed for later. She didn't think that she would need to unpack fully just yet. Hopefully they wouldn't be here that long.

Chloe returned downstairs and paused in the hallway to witness Jade dragging her case up the stairs. Clunk! Clunk! Clunk! The sound resounded around the hall. "Jade, do be careful," she scolded.

"Sorry, I'm trying to," said Jade trying to grab the bottom of the case to pull it up.

Chloe watched as she carried on up the stairs clutching at the case. Clunk! Clunk! Clunk! She was relieved when Jade finally made it upstairs. There was a brief moment of silence and then the clunking was replaced by a loud squeaking from the wheel of the case. The wretched thing obviously hadn't seen the light of day for years.

Chloe sighed and turned away and headed for a sitting room. She had some reading to do. She would have a look at that paperwork the Solicitor had given her and try to tie things up here.

Jade returned a while later and hovered in a corner for a moment, surveying the large room. Chloe was sitting on the sofa with the envelopes next to her. "Why don't you make us some dinner Jade," she suggested. "Perhaps you'd better make a fire in here first, though it's bound to get chilly at night in such a large house."

Jade nodded enthusiastically and marched towards the large stove She knelt down in front of it and stared at its doors. Chloe observed her, looking over her papers. She watched as Jade moved from one side of the stove to the other, looking all around it in an effort to understand its alien workings.

Chloe couldn't help but laugh. Jade turned around suddenly at the sound of her laughing. She frowned in puzzlement. "I've no idea how this works, I can't even see the "On" switch."

Chloe put her papers to one side. "Why don't you just see what you can sort out for dinner, I'll fix the fire." Chloe went over to Jade and opened the doors on the stove. She was foraging around the hearth for firelighters and kindling as Jade left the room. Jade hurried out. Perhaps this wasn't going to be as bad as she had dreaded thought Jade as she started opening all of the drawers in kitchen trying to find the cutlery. Chloe hadn't shouted at her about the fire.

After a dinner of lasagne and salad with some cheesy garlic bread, both Jade and Chloe sat in the lounge warming themselves in front of the fire. After a time, Chloe picked up the papers that she had been reading. She glanced at Jade.

"You can go and watch telly in one of the other rooms if you like?" She suggested.

Jade had been perched on the chair trying to get as close to the fire as she could. She really didn't fancy sitting alone in one of those other large rooms, she felt incredibly tired. She was finding all of this change very stressful. "If you don't mind Ms Marcus, I'll have a shower and go to bed, I mean if you don't need me for anything else that is?"

Chloe looked heavenward. "Jade, for the umpteenth time, call me Chloe and no I don't need you to do anything. You can go and relax."

Jade smiled nervously. She took a big breath and walked steadily away and up the stairs. She managed not to jump in fright when a floorboard creaked beneath her foot.

Chloe resisted the temptation to bang on a table just to make Jade jump as she heard her creeping away and left her to go to bed. She turned back to the papers. She paused momentarily and picked up the envelope with the note in, she still had no idea what that was all about She placed it on the table next to the sofa and continued reading

Jade plodded along the landing and into the bedroom. The bedroom was a beautiful spacious room overlooking the drive and grounds of the house. She felt exhausted as she drew the curtains. She still had such a feeling of apprehension over this whole assignment. Chloe made out it would just be a short-term job but looking around at this place Jade couldn't imagine how much sorting out would be needed to finalize things. There were a lot of rooms in the house and one had just been full of books and paperwork that they hadn't even looked at. The only plus was that Chloe wasn't being as bossy as normal. Jade's main concern, however, was the amount of breakable items around the house. She was always breaking things. She didn't mean to it just seemed to happen wherever she went. She pondered for a moment as to how long it would take her to pay for something if she did break it. She shuddered at the thought and decided to have her shower.

She showered and put on a pair of thick pyjamas and her bed socks. She gave a slight smile, her mother had put those in the suitcase for her, good thing too. It was rather chilly in the room. Oh God her mother! Jade fumbled for her mobile, finally finding it on the dressing table. She had switched it to silent, as she didn't want Chloe to tell her off if it rang.

She checked the screen to see eight missed calls from her mother and one from Carl. Oh no, her mother had probably called Carl to see where she was. She pressed, "return call" quickly and waited for the barrage.

Finally Jade managed to end her call. She had relayed the entire events of the afternoon and all of the details of the house and assure her mother that she was not going to be kidnapped by locals or sold into some kind of debauchery. For goodness sake they weren't that far from the City.

Jade felt cold. She fiddled with the knob on the heater and then realised that it was already on its highest setting. Chloe had put the heating on as soon as they had arrived but it was taking al long time to have any effect in the vast house. Jade jumped into bed, switched off the bedside lamp and wrapped the duvet around her. She hardly had time to worry about what tomorrow would bring before she was asleep.

Jade open her eyes. For one moment she thought that she was in her own snug bedroom at home. Then she realised that she was lying star shaped in bed. That would not have been possible in her single bed back home. She remembered where she was. It was pitch black. There was no distant light from the street lamps filtering into the room. Jade had a sudden feeling of apprehension. The silence was cloying.

She took a deep breath then paused, listening. She thought that she had heard something. She kept perfectly still. Yes, she had heard a noise, a soft creak of a floorboard from the corner of the room. Jade felt herself start to tremble. She started to sit up, very slowly. She needed to reach for the light. She almost made it then she felt it. Something had just landed on her bed with a thump. She was terrified she shot upright and screamed in fear.

Chloe must have dozed off she realised as she awoke on the sofa. The papers were resting on her chest. The house seemed quiet with only the embers of the fire crackling slightly in the room. Chloe went to sit up, then stopped. She had a sudden strange feeling. She moved slowly upwards and looked slowly around the room. All seemed as it was, yet she still felt as if something was not quite right. What was wrong? It dawned on her then, she felt as if she was not alone, as if she were being watched.

Chloe sat upright on the sofa then got to her feet. She looked around again. What was it? She glanced downwards. The envelope, it was gone, hadn't she put it on the table? She couldn't see where it was. She was about to throw the sofa cushions off and start searching when a loud scream came from upstairs.

CHAPTER 4

Sarah French looked up as she heard a car pull on to the drive. Staring out of the kitchen window, she saw a grey Mitsubishi being parked outside. Sarah rolled her eyes here comes Harvey Smith she thought. She turned back to the flat screen in the kitchen and flicked a switch on the box beside it switching it to the CCTV. She could have a nose at what Mr Know it all was up to as she washed the saucepans from last night's dinner.

Sarah put on her marigolds and started chiselling at the congealed spaghetti that was stuck to the bottom of the saucepan. Mark always shoved everything in the dishwasher as it was and she always ended up having to wash things again as they never came out clean. She sighed she should have given them a good soak.

She glanced at the screen to see Rory scratching his backside as he walked towards the tack room. She looked back at the pans. Sod it, she thought and rammed them back into the dishwasher. She shoved in a tablet and switched the machine on. She decided it was time to go for a check on the yard. It was Saturday morning and they would all be arriving soon to start their weekend workouts with their beloved steeds.

Sarah ran her fingers through her short dark hair tweaking it in different directions as she walked to the outhouse to put on her wellingtons and coat. She struggled with the zipper of her coat as she fastened it. She really was going to have to think about going on a diet. Since she'd stopped doing the mucking out she had started putting on weight. Even riding the horses didn't seem to be keeping her in trim. Then again, she was doing less of that too these days. Still, weight gain was to be expected at the age of forty-five as was being allowed to slow down a little.

She heard another car pull up. Here we go. Sarah took a deep breath, preparing herself for the usual irritating banter that would now be shouted around the yard. These people just had no consideration. How would they like it if some people started walking around their garden shouting to their friends at the top of their voices while they were trying to relax in their living room? She often wished that she didn't have to run a stupid livery yard but it was the only way that she could afford to keep the place on. Mark's salary as an architect just didn't cover the maintenance. She supposed it had seemed a good idea at the time and it had been supposed to fund her competing with own horses but she till hadn't quite got around to doing that yet either.

She marched outside and started to do a check on the yard. She always had to keep an eye on that useless groom Kelly. No doubt she would be leaning over a stable door staring at the horses in her usual dreamy way instead of doing something useful like cleaning Sarah's tack. That was the trouble with these young girls, no work ethic, still she was cheap Sarah supposed.

She glanced up at the new car arriving. It was a Volvo estate. Big Jayne had arrived. She was glad that she'd left the CCTV on she could have a laugh later watching Big Jayne screeching at her wimp of a daughter in the manege. Sarah smiled to herself as she walked across the yard, a quick check and she'd soon be back in the house.

"Morning Sarah." Rory smiled at her as she approached. "Looks like a good day for some schooling eh? Are you going for a whizz round the paddock?"

Sarah gave him a slight smile back "Maybe later, I have a few things to do in the house yet," she paused for a moment taking in Rory's curly red hair which already had a significant bald patch in its middle, even though Rory was only thirty five. Rory maintained that this was due to the constant wearing of helmets. She noticed that his boots were polished to distraction and his dark grey jodhpurs looked like they were fresh from the saddlers shop

Rory continued smiling at her, "Well I've got some serious schooling in mind today. Need to polish up Ted's flying changes."

Sarah nodded at him as she walked away, poor bloody Ted she thought. Rory would be hammering him round that manege for an hour and a half now until he was satisfied that the horse was up to scratch. Everyone knew that Ted wasn't really a dressage horse he was much better at show jumping.

She walked into the stable block to see Kelly grooming a dark brown horse of about seventeen hands. Kelly didn't hear Sarah approach as she was singing quietly to the horse as she groomed him. The horse had his head lowered and her eyes half closed, enjoying Kelly's soft brush on his withers.

Sarah rolled her eyes, soppy girl. "I hope you finished the stables and swept the yard before you started messing about with the Rory's horse," she said sternly.

Kelly jumped as she heard Sarah's voice. Sarah always seemed to be moaning at her. Kelly was only eighteen and had always wanted to work with horses so she had ended up at Sarah's after dropping out of College, much to her parents annoyance. They just didn't understand. Kelly wished that Sarah wasn't' so miserable it would be so much nicer here if she were more cheerful.

Kelly smoothed back her hair tucking it behind an ear. She had been daydreaming that she was show jumping around the Hickstead Derby. They had just gone down the Derby Bank and had a little stumble at the bottom. Kelly had picked up the reins and Ted had made an amazing recovery, putting in a huge leap to clear the fence at the bottom of the bank causing a huge roar of approval from the crowd as they headed on towards the Devil's Dyke. "Oh, yes, I just said I'd give Ted a brush for Rory."

Sarah rolled her eyes and looked at Kelly. She was a skinny rake of a girl considering she didn't do anything. Sarah felt a pang of annoyance, "you really don't have to do that. They can groom their own horses. You know you don't get paid for those sorts of things, they're supposed to be extras. They need to book you in properly."

Kelly said nothing as she patted Ted. She liked being with the horses and she knew that Ted loved being groomed. She also knew that Rory would be drilling him in the manege soon. Rory was aiming high in dressage with Ted. Kelly also knew that Ted was not a dressage horse and that Rory had got him on the cheap. Ted's sire was a horse that threw either dressage horses or jumpers and Ted had inherited the jumping line. His previous owner had won several hundred pounds on him. Unfortunately, she then had got into financial difficulties and had needed a quick sale so he had been sold for peanuts to Rory who always had an ear to the ground.

Rory thought that he'd got a bargain and was convinced they could turn Ted into a dressage champion and finally become a "name" in dressage.

Kelly sighed as she stroked Ted's nose, she would give him a carrot later. "Oh, Sarah, before I forget..."

"Not now, if no one's dying you can tell me later." Sarah said. She had heard Big Jayne starting to raise her voice to her daughter in the distance and another car had pulled up. She decided that a quick health and safety check would do and then she would be out of here, before it became bedlam.

Sarah turned back to Kelly, "Give my horses a go round the manege would you, I don't know if I'll have time to ride them today, not with all the paperwork I need to sort out. Oh, and make sure the yard stays tidy and for goodness sake clean some more tack. Don't forget to try and get some of the hairs off those travel rugs as well. They're in a terrible state. What on earth do you do all day?" She said over her shoulder as she marched away.

Sarah nodded across at Lyn as she walked across the yard towards the tack room. Sarah couldn't wait to get back to the house. She went back inside and removed her coat and wellingtons. She lit up a cigarette as she went inside the kitchen, opening a window on the other side of the room to try and waft the smoke out of. She flicked on the kettle, pulled up a stool and sat down looking up at the TV.

Sarah studied the cctv. Rory was in the table throwing on Ted's dressage kit while Ted stood perfectly still with his eyes still half closed. Probably saving his energy for the work out. She could hear Rory talking enthusiastically to Kelly, "I know what to do to get this horse up to a good enough standard. I'm sure he could even do Grand Prix. He's got the breeding. It's just a question of him never having the right rider before."

Kelly gave a slight nod and cleared her throat, "I heard that he was a good show jumper, don't you want to do that instead?"

Rory froze for a moment as he bent down to pull the girth around Ted's stomach. He wondered for a moment if Kelly knew something. Had she found out that he was scared to death of jumping anything more than a pole on the ground? He pulled up the girth and gave her a smile. No, she still had that stupid enquiring look on her face. "Oh, he'd be wasted as a show jumper. Besides I much prefer something more technically challenging from a point of view of teaching a horse something. Show jumping's all about ability, you just need the basic flat work sorted and that's it. Now dressage, that's different. There are so many different factors involved, you need to be so much more skilled to train a horse to a decent level." He neglected to add that doing anything else set the fear of God into him.

Kelly nodded and looked longingly at Ted. She wished he were hers. They wouldn't be wasting their time on dressage she thought. They'd be in training for show jumping, trying to qualify for The Horse Of The Year Show or the Hickstead Derby.

Kelly walked away down the stable corridor. She supposed she'd better ride one of Sarah's horses. Sarah had two horses. One was a rather sweet welsh cob cross of about fifteen hands called Billy that Sarah had intended to do some small hunter classes with but as far as Kelly knew, he hadn't set foot from the yard since she'd been there which was over twelve months. The other was a very quiet thoroughbred of sixteen hands called Chester that Sarah had acquired from Celia Stone with the intention of showing him or even eventing him if his legs were up to it. To date, Chester hadn't done either.

Kelly had noticed that Sarah didn't seem to be bothering with either of her horses very much these days. Mind you, she had put on rather a lot of weight lately. Perhaps it was a good thing. Billy was a bit on the small side for her and Chester was no weight carrier.

Kelly went in to the tack room to find Jayne and her twelve-year-old daughter, Heather in there. She knew that Jayne's nickname was "Big Jayne". Partly because of her rather large frame and partly because there was also another lady named Jane on the yard. The other Jane was a pale nervy lady who was in constant fear of her own daughter being hurt or falling off her mount.

Big Jayne was strapping Heather into some body armour as Kelly walked in. Heather looked at Kelly dismally as her mother spoke to her, "Don't worry Heth, Foxy will look after you." Big Jayne said briskly "and besides every good rider has to fall off now and then, at least you'll be in the manege where the landing is soft."

"But I don't want to do jumping schooling, I want to go for a hack. Kelly will come with me, won't you Kelly?" Heather looked at Kelly pleadingly.

Kelly smiled back at her "Yes that's fine I can do that if you like, " she said wondering if Sarah would moan at her if she did.

Big Jayne shook her head and put her hands on her hips as she inspected Heather. "Kelly has other things to do. Now stop whinging and go and get on your pony."

Big Jayne rolled her eyes as Heather trudged out towards the stables. "Bloody kids, eh, don't know they're born." She nodded firmly to herself as she marched out the tack room.

Kelly picked up a grooming box and headed for the stables. She went to the end of the line of boxes and found Chester wind sucking in the corner of his box as usual. This was why he was hidden away on the end of the line. Sarah didn't want people complaining about his vices and fearing that their own horses might start to copy him.

"Oh, Chester, I wish you'd stop that," said Kelly as Chester grabbed the manger and took in a long gulp of air. He was like a smoker who couldn't kick the habit. Kelly had hung toys up in the stable for him that she'd made and she tried to get him turned out as much as possible. Trouble was, at weekends Sarah always wanted him ready to be ridden, even though she usually changed her mind and had Kelly ride instead. Kelly thought that if he were hers he would just live out in the field all the time then he'd soon forget his vices.

Kelly put the grooming box down and grabbed a brush. She didn't bother with a headcollar she knew she didn't need one.

She started working on Chester's bright bay coat. Chester stopped his wind sucking and stood quietly for Kelly. He enjoyed his massages.

Kelly heard footsteps and someone humming to themself. She looked over the box door. "Morning," she said as Lyn walked towards her horse who was stabled next to Chester.

"Hello Kelly. Are you riding again today?"

"Yes, she's given me my instructions," answered Kelly.

"Well I'm going to see if Rory can give me a jumping lesson with Quicky. Might find out where I'm going wrong." Lyn said, looking rather sadly at the bay gelding standing sleepily in the box next door.

"Oh, right. Well I suppose it might help. I'm sure it'll come together soon," said Kelly trying to be bright. Lyn had already had a series of dismal attempts at trying to get the inaptly named Quickstep around a few classes at show jumping shows recently in an attempt to prepare him for his eventing debut. Unfortunately Quickstep had other ideas. He was probably the laziest horse Kelly had ever seen. As soon as Lyn took him into the ring he just turned into a complete swine and refused to even attempt to jump decently. They knew that he could jump as Lyn could get him flying around a course of one metre twenty at home when he was in the mood. That was just the problem; Quickstep was rarely in the mood for anything when he finally got to a show. After all the travelling and fussing he just couldn't be bothered.

Kelly turned back to Chester. She gave him an ear rub and finished grooming him. She was careful not to brush his slightly bowed tendon too hard, although he was sound he could be a bit sensitive there. Kelly also arranged the fur on his neck to cover the small scar on his throat from his wind operation.

Chester was so quiet you'd hardly believe he was an ex race horse, mind you if he'd been any other way Sarah probably wouldn't have bought him. He'd been too slow to be a success in racing. They'd operated on his wind, giving him a hobday, in the hope that this would improve him as he had good bloodlines for National Hunt racing. Unfortunately he had broken down in training shortly later hence the bowed tendon. Although Kelly had heard that this had been more due to the fact that Celia had trained him too hard and too fast in an effort to improve his form.

Still, Chester had found a reprieve when he ended up at Sarah's. Apart from the box boredom he had been gently worked and Kelly felt his flatwork had really improved. He was a sweet horse and very quiet to ride. Plus, being an ex-racehorse you could pretty much do anything with him around the stable without any drama.

Kelly tacked up Chester and was about to lead him out of the stable when a man's head appeared over the door. "Hiya Kells, are you going for a hack? Do you fancy some company? I want to try out the new boots on Gatsby." Ben smiled at her over the door, eyes twinkling with excitement from behind his round glasses. He looked like a middle aged Harry Potter.

"Blimey, Ben where the heck did you get those?" Kelly said looking in amazement at the over reach boots emblazoned with the Welsh national flag that he was waving at her.

"Oh you can get anything if you know how these days," said Ben with a wink. "I'm going to show these to Gatsby and brush off his furry bits before we ride."

"Oh," said Kelly, the sight of the boots had momentarily taken her aback. "I'll go in the manege first and do a bit of flat work but I'll see you later." Kelly hoped that Sarah wouldn't be cross at her if she went in the manege first.

"Well you won't miss us in these beauties," said Ben flicking a wave at her as he strolled off to find his steed.

Kelly smiled to herself as she led Chester out. Ben was really sweet and he adored his piebald cob Gatsby. Fortunately the yard had a huge arena to ride in. Kelly always thought that it was quite fun seeing what everyone else was up to in their own corners. Dam! She had a sudden thought. She really ought to tell Sarah about the call she took on the yard mobile earlier Sarah always left the yard's mobile out for her first thing so she didn't have to take any calls. Mind you, she had tried to tell her but Sarah had said it could wait. Kelly shrugged and carried on into the manege.

Sarah sat on her stool watching the TV. She was on her fourth Hob Nob. Cheeky cow that bloody Kelly she thought. Instructions indeed. Oh look at that Welsh twit Ben what the fuck were those hideous boots in aid of. Sarah felt sorry for that poor horse having to wear those, as if having Ben bumping around on his back wasn't bad enough.

She lit another cigarette. She had been trying to call Celia to see if she wanted to come around later but hadn't been able to get a reply on her mobile. That was unusual for Celia who was normally glued to the phone.

She took a long puff on her cigarette and switched the camera to the manege. Oh, there was Rory forcing poor Ted to tuck his head into his chest whilst he demanded that he take the biggest strides he could in order to get his extended trot perfected. Stupid twit.

Sarah switched across to the other camera across the manege. Big Jayne was yelling at Heather. She was trying to get her to jump a cross pole. Every time Heather turned the pony towards it the pony started to jump up and down with excitement and leapt forwards resulting in Heather dragging her away from the fence in terror.

"For God's sake just let her jump it! Stop pulling her away!" Big Jayne yelled.

"But what if I fall off? I might break something." Heather wailed.

"Well don't bloody fall off then! It's only a sodding cross pole! Firefox knows what to do. Show some back bone girl!"

Heather turned the pony around once again. She pointed her towards the fence and hung on to her mane in fear. Firefox locked on to her target with delight and cantering rapidly towards it. She barely had to do more than a canter stride to clear the obstacle. Heather had shut her eyes just before she reached the jump. She opened them just in time to swerve Firefox out of Ted's path and avoid Rory's glare.

"Bloody amateurs." Rory muttered.

"Where the hell are you going now?" Shrieked Jayne. "Oh for goodness sake!" Jayne strode over to the cross pole and to Heather's horror she made it into an upright fence.

Rory slowed Ted to a walk, this should be interesting he thought, seeing Heather's terror stricken face. Rory was momentarily distracted however at the sight of Ben's arrival. What in the name of sweet Jesus Christ had he got on that horses feet? Rory was all for a bit of bling for the dressage arena but those were just plain tat.

Ben nodded to him as he trotted past grinning with pride. His round glasses were steaming up already as he manoeuvred Gatsby over to the other end of the manege. Gatsby plodded along. His hairy feathers poked out from beneath the boots. They were still green from the stable stains and his black and white coat was dusty on the black bits and poo stained what should have been his white bits. Gatsby trotted gaily along, he could sense his owner was in high spirits and decided to humour him.

Sarah flicked on the kettle and poured herself another coffee. She reached into a drawer and pulled out a hip flask dropping a slug of brandy in to the coffee. She needed it with this lot.

Sarah grabbed another Hob Nob and dunked it into the coffee. She sucked on the biscuit drawing out the brandy laced coffee closing her eyes in delight. Thank God Mark wasn't here she thought.

She made herself comfortable as she saw Big Jayne moving the cross fence in to an upright. This should be a laugh. Sarah was watching with interest when she heard another vehicle pull up outside. She looked towards the window distractedly. She almost dropped her Hob Nob as she saw that the car was towing a trailer. If she wasn't mistaken it was one of Celia's.

Sarah's jaw hung agape as she saw the trailer ramp open and a horse being led, hobbling down the ramp. What the hell? She knew that horse. She left the coffee and cctv as she scrambled for her coat and boots.

Who the hell were these people and what were they doing with Celia's trailer and more importantly, with her horse?

CHAPTER 5

Chloe flicked on the light switch as she threw open Jade's bedroom door. She stopped and stared at the bed where Jade was sitting bolt upright with the bed sheet clutched to her chin. She took in a deep breath and walked over to the bed. "Looks like we have a lodger," she said as she sat down on the bed next to Jade.

Jade looked at her and smiled weakly back, "I'm sorry I thought there was someone in here, I just felt something land on the bed."

Chloe managed to stop herself from laughing and turned back to look at the grey cat sitting on the end of Jade's bed. He observed them with an air of superiority that always surrounds a cat. He had the deepest amber eyes Chloe had ever seen. He seemed unfazed by the sudden attention and flood of light in the room. Chloe looked back at Jade, "Handsome devil isn't he?"

"Or she," observed Jade reaching across to the bedside table for her glasses.

The cat continued to sit on the bed looking at each of with interest. He didn't appear to want to move. Jade leaned forwards and reached out to stroke him.

"Watch he doesn't scratch you!" Warned Chloe. Jade stopped for a moment and looked back at Chloe, then she looked back at the cat and stroked his head gently. She smiled as he allowed her to stroke his head and neck and the smile turned into a huge grin as he started purring loudly and closed his eyes in enjoyment.

Chloe laughed "Oh what a sweetie," she also reached forward and started to stroke the cat who continued to purr with enjoyment. After a moment he lay down on the bed with his paws folded neatly beneath him.

Chloe stood up, "Well thank goodness it was a friendly burglar. Can I go to bed now you've got a guard cat?"

Jade nodded back at her still stroking the cat. "Yes, could you turn the light off please."

Chloe smiled again as she turned off the light and shut the door, hopefully Jade would be a little more settled with her feline friend to keep her company. She realised how exhausted she felt. Probably because she had so much going through her mind now. They would be busy in the morning she thought as she went to her room.

The following day was bright and sunny. Jade smiled to herself as she opened the curtains. She had slept so well now she had a new friend to keep her company. The cat was now sitting up on the bed fastidiously cleaning his tummy.

Chloe was at the large kitchen table drinking coffee when Jade descended with a grey companion walking along beside her.

"My you have found a friend," she said.

Without hesitation the cat trotted forwards and jumped on the breakfast table seating himself in front of Chloe. He looked at her meaningfully for a moment and then uttered a croaky miaow. Jade and Chloe both laughed.

"He wants his breakfast," said Jade and started searching in the cupboards for something for him. "I can give him this can of tuna for now, if that's all right? I was going to use it for sandwiches."

"Yes, give him that, we can get some cat food for him later if he's staying, answered Chloe.

Jade smiled with delight and started to decant the tuna into a breakfast bowl. The cat watched her with interest as it caught a waft of the fishy smell. Jade brought the bowl over and was about to serve the cat its breakfast when there was a loud knocking on the door. She looked at Chloe with wide eyes. Chloe looked back at her, "I'll get it." Chloe sighed as she rose from her chair.

Chloe opened the door to see an elderly lady who had the height of a dwarf standing in the doorway. She was wearing a raincoat and had her hair was neatly arranged in a hair net. She smiled up at Chloe. "Hello, you must be Chloe. I'm Anne Radcliff. I was your aunt's cleaner. So sorry about your aunty she was a lovely lady," she paused for a moment and then thrust her hand out towards Chloe.

Chloe clasped the tiny hand and was surprised by the firm grip and vigorous shake that the old lady gave her. She smiled politely, "Well you'd better come in, I suppose." Chloe didn't recall anyone mentioning a cleaner. She stepped back as the lady walked in to the house and headed off to the kitchen.

"I wanted to make sure that everything was all ship shape for you." Anne said, pausing briefly in the hallway. She turned back and walked on into the kitchen. She smiled at Jade, "Hello..." she stopped as she saw the cat on the table eating his breakfast and laughed. "I see you've met Jerry. That's another reason that I came here, I've been feeding him since... well you know."

"Jerry, what a sweet name," cried Jade. Anne smiled at her and looked at Chloe. Chloe looked back at her and then understood, "Oh, this is Jade, she's my assistant. Jade this is Anne." Anne nodded, smiling at Jade.

Chloe paused for a moment and looked back at the cat, "You mean that this is, was, Auntie Sophie's cat?" She asked looking at Jerry with interest.

"Yes, young Jerry was Sophie's best friend," said Anne, as she pulled several sachets of cat food from the pockets of her raincoat placing them on the table. She leaned across and tickled the back of Jerry's neck fondly. "Well, he was your Uncle's cat too. He was here when Harry was alive. They were best pals as well." Anne raised an eyebrow. "Oh dear he's lost his collar again," she tutted at the cat. "Naughty boy. He's always losing it, it'll be around somewhere," she looked back at Chloe, "Your Aunt liked him to wear his collar."

Chloe frowned and stared at Jerry curiously. Anne sniffed and looked back at Jerry, "Goodness Jerry your breath will smell nice after that little treat." Anne turned back to Chloe, "Would you like me to carry on with the cleaning?"

Chloe paused "Well, I'm not sure, everything's a bit up in the air at the moment, I don't have any money to pay you yet."

"Well, don't worry, we can sort out the money later. I'll just get on with it." Anne said giving Chloe's arm a pat. She turned and marched towards a cupboard where she pulled out a can of polish and some worn out dusters. "It's all right, I can let myself out when I'm done. If you need to know where anything is, do ask me. I assume you will be able to sort yourselves out tomorrow so will see you Monday," she smiled, straightened her hair net and set off purposefully.

Jade looked up at Chloe who shrugged. "Jade, we have things to do. There is something that we need to sort out. This estate isn't as straight forward as I thought it would be."

Chloe couldn't see that Anne was smiling broadly as she marched away.

Jade looked at Chloe with a worried frown on her face. "What is it?"

Chloe sighed. "I'll show you. Come on let's get to the car. You'll need to get your wellies on though." Chloe thought that

Jade could also do with changing out of that dark blue suit but refrained from adding this, she didn't want to have to wait all day for her.

"Oh, do you think it's going to rain then?"

Chloe laughed suddenly "I really have no idea," she said as she went to find her coat.

As Jade sat in the car she had a mild feeling of excitement, she had no idea where they were going but it was certainly far more interesting than sitting in an office, even if it was a weekend. She had already called her mother so hopefully she wouldn't have to worry about losing her signal either.

Chloe gave Jade a quick look. Jade had taken her sensible shoes off and was wearing a pair of bright pink wellingtons adorned with butterflies. They clashed dreadfully with her purple tights. Chloe managed to stop herself from smiling as she started up the car.

As they drove along Chloe decided she should have a talk with her P.A. "Jade, as we are in the country for the time being. I think it would be sensible if you dressed a little more, casually shall we say."

Jade looked back at her questioningly. "What do you mean by casual?"

"Well, for the time being, I think you'd be better off in a pair of jeans with a nice little top. I just think that wearing a three piece suit, albeit with wellingtons, is perhaps not suited to the current working environment into which you've been

placed." Chloe said thinking that Jade could have got away with the dark blue suit but the bright purple tights were the deal breaker.

Jade looked away, "I haven't got any jeans," she said quietly.

Chloe almost crashed the car as she looked at Jade in amazement. "How can you not have any jeans? What do you wear on your days off?"

Jade looked sheepish, "Well, just a skirt and jumper. I suppose," she mumbled.

Chloe stared at the road ahead. "Jade you're only twenty five, I can't believe that you don't have a pair of jeans."

"I don't really go anywhere, so I've never bothered buying any. Besides, I'd never know what to buy. I don't go shopping. Mum likes me to be with her when I'm not at work, now that Dad's, well..." She tailed off and stared out of the window.

Chloe bit her bottom lip. She had forgotten that Jade's father had been taken into a home due to his Alzheimer's. "Well, we'll sort something out for you. We can put it down to work wear." Chloe said nodding to herself.

Jade said nothing, continuing to stare out of the window. She suddenly wondered how her mother would be coping without her, she had called her enough times. But knowing her mother, she would just carry on as normal and then end up crying in the kitchen over a bowl of ice cream and then phone Jade to sob down the phone to her.

Chloe clutched at a piece of paper she had left by her side and read off the directions from the paperwork she had been looking at the night before. She turned off and drove down a narrow lane. She slowed down and then stopped before a large house. "This must be it." She said looking at the sign at the front of the house.

They got out of the car and jade stared around her. "This is a horse yard?" Asked Jade in surprise.

"Yes and we have a horse here. Apparently." Chloe looked around. There wasn't a soul in sight. "Hello." She shouted loudly. No one appeared so she walked towards the stables. Jade followed her from a distance, looking nervously around. She wasn't sure about horses. They looked so big and scary, one end could bite you and the other could kick you. She hoped that they were all locked away in their dens.

Chloe marched back from the stable block. "No one's here." She looked around. "Look, there's a track there, perhaps there's someone up there," she walked away. Jade took a deep breath and followed her.

They walked up the track and saw the brick building at the end. Chloe walked towards it. Jade now followed closely behind. She had decided that it would be safer to hide behind Chloe if any of the beasts were free.

Chloe pulled open the large wooden door and stepped inside. She stopped suddenly at the sight of the young man leaning on the stable door with his head in his hands. He looked in despair.

He turned around as he heard her enter. For a fleeting moment both Chloe and Jade froze as they saw the look of sadness on his face. It was heart wrenching to see such a beautiful face filled with such sadness. His expression changed quickly into a suspicious glare. "What the hell do you want?"

Chloe immediately felt a sense of irritation. "Is that how you normally speak to your customers?"

"It's not my yard and you should have made an appointment," said Steve who had no idea if that was correct or not.

"My name is Chloe Marcus and I am here on behalf of my late Aunt; Sophie Clayton. I believe that she has a horse stabled here? He is now under my ownership!" Chloe replied, although she knew that last bit was not technically correct. "Oh, and this is Jade," she added gesturing at Jade who smiled shyly.

Steve raised an eyebrow "Well you're in luck." Steve stepped back from the stable and gesture with his arm. "This is the luxury living which your horse has been enjoying at your aunt's expense."

Chloe and Jade stepped forward. Chloe peered over the stable as Jade edged slightly back. Jade smiled nervously at Steve who gave her a rather intense stare, sending her shrinking back even further.

Chloe threw open the stable door. "He's in an awful state, he's far too thin. What on earth have you done to him?"

Steve gave a half smile. "You will have to ask Celia Stone that. "

Chloe glared at him. "Well, aren't you one of her staff? Why did you let him get in this stat?"

Steve held the cynical smile. "I am no longer one of her staff. I found this horse this morning and she was none too happy that I had cleaned out his stable so she sacked me. The only reason I know that it is your late aunt's is because she said, something to the effect of "who cares what happens to him she's bloody dead now and Sophie Clayton wouldn't know a good horse if it kicked her in the arse, it should be called Saddo not Seven." Steve paused as he remembered "She has a way with words does Celia."

Chloe glared at him furiously. "Where the hell is she?"

Steve had stopped smiling, "I'm afraid there was an emergency. One of the staff has had an accident on the gallops. She had to take her to hospital. In fact, you've just missed her." Steve stopped, remembering how Ella had suddenly appeared at the stable door. Shortly after Celia had appeared looking furious and telling him to clear off. Ella had looked ashen. She had said that Joanne's horse had bucked her off, twice! She had re mounted after the first time and it had done it again and this time she had been in agony clutching an arm that had a bone protruding unnaturally beneath the skin, just by her shoulder joint.

Ella had dragged Celia away to take Joanne to hospital. She had looked fleetingly at Steve and smiled weakly, the horses were still at the gallops and they had to sort them out she'd said. Steve had nodded back at her.

Chloe looked at Steve who seemed distracted. "Well, we need to remove this horse, this is just appalling. Where else can we take him?"

Steve looked back at her, "I don't think that there are any more local racing yards. You'll have to find a livery yard. You can't travel him far. His leg is in a bad way."

"So I see, " said Chloe looking at the horse's swollen front leg. "Where is the nearest yard?"

Steve pondered for a moment trying to remember if the girls had mentioned anything about yards."

Jade looked at Chloe, "Can't we take him back to the house. There's lots of grass for him to eat?"

Chloe rolled her eyes. "No, it's all lawn and the rest is rented out to a farmer for haylage, he'd do his nut if we stuck a horse on it."

Steve looked at Jade. "There is a yard actually, one of Celia's friends owns it though so they might not take him. Her name's Sarah French."

Chloe also looked at Jade, "Call her, I want him out of here now! Go back to the car we'll bring him out in a while. We need to bandage his leg up."

Steve watched Jade as she plodded away, taking in the pink wellingtons and purple tights. He turned back to Chloe who looked pristine in her designer jeans and short boots. He wondered if they were related, no, surely not. Jade looked too meek to be related to Chloe.

Steve spoke to Chloe who was inspecting the horse's leg. "I'll sort his leg out." He said, " It's the least I can do for the poor guy. I should have found him sooner."

Chloe watched as Steve bandaged the horse's leg, he obviously knew what he was doing. He paused to pat the horse as he finished. "Good boy Seven," he smiled.

"Strange name." Chloe muttered.

They led the horse slowly down the track towards the yard. Jade was sitting in the car with the passenger door open. She jumped out as they approached and walked over to Chloe, her eyes bright. "You'll never believe it but they have a vacancy, the girl said we could come today and she would let the owner know. The only thing is you have to pay a months livery in advance."

Chloe sighed. This horse might need a lot of care. She thought for a moment, Jade was too scared to be much use with the horse. Chloe looked over at Steve who was gently stroking the horse's neck.

Chloe made a sudden decision. She turned to Steve. "How do you fancy a temporary job looking after this horse and doing some house maintenance and being the head gardener?"

Steve took a deep breath. He tried not to smile, he didn't want to appear too keen but he had been wondering what on earth he would do now that Celia had given him the sack.

Chloe frowned, "You could stay at the house, there are enough rooms, as long as you're not too untidy mind."

Now Steve did smile, "I'm not a horse you know. I suppose it's the best offer I'm going to get round here though."

Chloe smiled back at him, "I'll take that as a yes then, in a back handed way." She looked back at the horse "I have a slight problem though, I have no transport for him."

Steve nodded, "Oh don't worry, I see you have a tow bar and I know someone who's got a trailer," he marched off giving Jade a wink as he left.

Jade felt a sudden tingle of excitement in her tummy. She smiled with delight. She had a feeling that things might just be improving around here.

CHAPTER 6

Celia was fuming. She had spent far too long at that bloody hospital and had been asked far too many questions. Those idiot Doctors seemed to be implying that Joanne's accident might be her fault. The stupid little cow should never have fallen off in the first place.

She parked in the yard and got out. Joanne clambered out from the passenger side. Celia didn't bother trying to help her from the Range Rover she didn't deserve it.

Joanne looked pale. Ella and Paul came from the stables to greet them. Ella gave Joanne a hug, avoiding touching her left arm, which was strapped up against her chest. "What did they say? Will it be all right?" She asked looking at Joanne's pale face.

Celia spoke before Joanne could open her mouth, "No, it's not all right. She's got to go back to have a pin put in it. The useless bunch couldn't do it before next week. The overpaid fools were moaning that they were short staffed. Can't be bothered to do any extra hours more like."

Ella looked from Joanne to Celia, her eyes wide. Joanne nodded back at her. She pulled her mobile phone from her pocket. "My arm's snapped in two, look I've got a picture of the X Ray. You should have seen the nurse's face when she saw it. She turned tail and ran off for a Doctor, she said with a proud smile.

Ella gazed at the picture of the snapped bone. She began to feel quite queasy and couldn't help but stare at the bulge under Joanne's immobilised arm where the humerus was snapped in half.

Paul appeared and sauntered over to Celia. He gave Joanne a look of distaste. "Where's that waster Steve? He can help with the horses now she's out of action. No doubt he'll need the extra cash."

Celia's eyes narrowed. "I sacked him. "

Ella looked around in surprise. "You sacked him? But he was so good with the horses." She remembered how angry Celia had looked when she had finally found her Ella had ran up the track in desperation as she hadn't been able to find Celia anywhere. Ella hadn't even realised that there were any stables up there. Mind you, the horse in that shed had looked in a pretty poor way; perhaps Celia was trying to hide him?

Celia glared at her, "He was not looking after the horses. I found him beating that horse with a pitchfork and he hadn't lifted a finger to take care of it properly." Celia shook her head, " You are so gullible Ella. Sucked in by a handsome face no doubt." She turned back to Paul. "Come with me. I need you to help me sort something out." She glanced back at the two girls. "And you two go and get some work done. I don't pay you to stand there sucking air like a goldfish."

Joanne looked at her in alarm, "But my arms sooo sore."

Celia rolled her eyes. "All right, don't milk it. Ella, find her something she can do with one arm or improvise. She needn't think she's free loading from me!" With that Celia turned and walked away with Paul at her side.

Ella looked at Joanne, "Evil cow. It's her fault that you're in this state. I overheard Paul saying to her when she came to pick you up, that the horse you were on should have been turned out before any one rode it cos it gets so hot. She said she knew that and thought that he would have known to do that anyhow so she didn't bother to mention it. Apparently, it's already decked five people from the last yard. That's why it ended up here."

Joanne frowned at Ella. "Bloody hell. She was lecturing me all the way back on how I should try to improve my riding and learn to ride out a buck. It's not like I didn't try. I'd already been chucked off it once and I got straight back on."

Ella nodded in agreement. "You should sue her if she doesn't start treating you better.

Joanne gave a small smile at last "Yes, I might just do that. I wonder how much I could get."

Ella shook her head "And I can't believe that Steve would be cruel like that. He always seemed so gentle with the horses, even the stroppy ones. They all seemed to like him."

Joanne nodded "It doesn't seem like him, maybe they had a row."

"Perhaps she made a pass at him." Said Ella.

The girls both looked at each other and started giggling. Ella paused for a moment "I wonder where he's gone. There's not much going in the way of work around here."

Ella noticed Joanne's pale face again and looked at her with concern. "You don't look good. I don't care what she says you go back to the caravan and rest. I'll get on with the horses."

Joanne looked at her with a relieved expression on her face. "Thanks Ell, I don't feel so hot."

Ella watched her walk away and shook her head again. This was not turning out to be a good day.

Celia and Paul walked up the track and entered the brick building. Celia stared around the shed her eyes widening in amazement. "The bloody horse, it's gone. What the fuck's going on."

"Perhaps Steve let it out," volunteered Paul.

"The dam thing was lame as hell! What in fuck's name do you think it would do? Advanced dressage round the fucking yard and then cross country across the frigging fields?"

Paul looked away. He daren't say anything else, Celia looked so furious.

Celia turned back to him "That tosser must have taken him. Well he can't get far with him and that loser's penniless. So where the hell could they have gone?" She glared at Paul as if expecting him to provide the answer to the question. Paul shifted on his feet uneasily. He wished he could go back to the yard.

Celia turned and marched quickly back down the track. Paul walked after her, he had to almost jog to keep up with her. Celia paused as she arrived at the yard she could see Ella sweeping the yard but there was no sign of Joanne. "Where the fuck is Joanne? She'd better not be skiving off!" She shouted across at Ella.

Ella stopped sweeping and stood up, she paused briefly and swallowed. Celia looked in a rage. "She's cleaning tack, do you want me to fetch her?" She answered quickly, praying that Celia would say no.

"No, as long as I know where she is." Celia answered, she had other things to deal with. "Just keep an eye on her," she muttered as she turned away" I don't want any more accidents."

Celia waked on and then stopped. She surveyed the far side of the yard where the horse lorry was parked and next to that the horse trailer. Her eyes widened in disbelief. "Where's the fucking trailer?" She shouted.

Paul looked over to where she was staring. There was no doubt about it. The trailer was gone. He smiled and barely managed to stifle his laughter. That arse hole Steve must have taken it.

Celia turned and looked at him angrily. Paul managed to recompose his expression to one of horror. "Looks like Steve may have borrowed it. God knows what he towed it with though. And where the hell would he go?"

Celia's eyes narrowed, "Jumped up shit, I knew I shouldn't have trusted him. What the hell is he playing at?"

"We should phone the Police." Paul said suddenly. Celia gave him a look, which if he wasn't mistaken was one of alarm. "We should wait." She said quickly. "He must be bringing it back. Even he isn't stupid enough to steal something like that. Anyway he can't go far with that horse."

Celia didn't want the Police involved unless they had to be. The horse was in poor condition and the last thing she needed was news of a poor sickly horse being on her yard leaking out.

" What the hell did he use to tow it? He hasn't even got a car." Celia said with a frown. She glanced around quickly. Ella was still sweeping fastidiously. Celia hoped that Ella hadn't heard their discussion. She turned around as a car pulled up on to the yard and parked next to the lorry.

Ella continued sweeping whilst keeping Celia and Paul in her sights. She threw a few quick sidelong glances in their direction whilst maintaining an apparent

concentration on her broom. Celia always had a loud voice, which carried well, and this sounded interesting. From what she could gather Steve had taken the horse in Celia's trailer. What a blast! It was getting more intriguing by the minute. She continued sweeping as the car pulled up on the yard.

She saw the tall man turn towards Celia and Paul as he closed the door of the Volvo. It was Celia's partner Duncan returning from the bank where he worked as Manager. This should be fun thought Ella. No doubt Celia was going to be giving him a bollocking too shortly. They had often heard them rowing from the yard, or rather Celia screaming at him. She made her way closer to Paul and Celia with the broom, trying to get into a better place to hear them.

Duncan Morcross had felt his shoulders sag as he pulled on to the drive. The sight of Celia's face was enough to tell him that she was absolutely furious about something – again. He noted Paul was also looking rather serious standing next to her. He'd had enough aggravation at the Bank that morning without having to come home to even more fuss. He sighed. He was getting too old for this. Sometimes he wished he had settled down with a normal woman who just worked nine 'till five in an office and didn't have all of this horse business to deal with. He supposed he'd better see why she was looking so angry.

Celia looked at Duncan as he walked slowly towards her with his brief case in one hand. He was tall and rather skinny, with a significant receding hairline, which seemed to have receded even more since he had been with Celia. He peered at her warily from behind his glasses. She glared at him. "Everything all right dear?" he asked cautiously.

Celia glared at him, "Are you taking the piss? No, everything is not all bloody right. I've been stuck at the hospital for Christ knows how long because some stupid little cow can't ride and now I've come back to find that low lifer has taken off with a horse. In my bloody trailer!"

Duncan paused for a moment as he took all of this in. He assumed that she meant that new lad, the good looking one with no money. "Oh dear, you have had a busy morning. How did he take the trailer, I didn't think he had a car?"

Celia gave him an even blacker look, "How the fuck should I know? You're supposed to be the brains around here, you tell me!"

There was a moment of silence as they all stared at the empty spot where the trailer should have been. Duncan swallowed before he spoke, "We'd better call the Police then."

Celia rolled her eyes, "No, I don't want the Police involved, not yet anyhow. He can't have gone far."

Duncan pushed his glasses further up his nose, "Celia, that boy could have sold it to his gypsy friends by now. They'll have it repainted and sold on before the end of the day." Duncan looked at Celia trying not to flinch away from her savage gaze. She was still fuming, trying to decide what to do.

Paul turned his gaze to Ella trying not to smirk. He was enjoying this now that Duncan was here for Celia to direct her anger on. Ella turned away and started sweeping in the other direction. Paul admired her slender backside as she bent over the broom. He was feeling decidedly cheery. Now that prick Steve was out of the way, those silly girls wouldn't keep fawning over him like bitches on heat. He could get back to how things were before he arrived on the scene. He was the one that was going places around here and it was about time that those girls realised that and showed him some respect and hopefully a lot more. It was time to show Ella what she'd been missing while she was fawning over that loser.

Duncan's stomach was churning. He was too scared to say anything in case Celia started screaming at him. He wished he could escape back to the Bank.

Celia turned back to Paul, "Any idea where he'd go? "

Paul stared at Celia, momentarily taken aback, "Well, no actually, to be honest. I suspect that he'd probably do just what Duncan said. He's probably sold the horse and the trailer to travellers. In fact I wouldn't be surprised if he stole a car to take them away with, " he paused for a moment and then added, " he was such a loser he'd shaft anyone."

Celia looked at Ella and then marched over to her. Ella stopped sweeping and looked at Celia nervously. Celia gave her a crooked smile, "You're friend, that waster Steve. He's taken off with the horse he had beaten, probably trying to hide the evidence. Any idea where he'd go?"

Ella swallowed, she still didn't believe that Steve would be cruel to any animal. She looked back meeting Celia's angry stare, "No I haven't a clue, I don't think he had any money and he never mentioned he knew anyone." Ella shrugged, "But you never know..."

Celia turned on her heel, "Useless! The bloody lot of you!" She said as she marched towards her car. She opened the door of the Range Rover and pulled her phone from the side pocket. She stared at it as she closed the door. "Shit!" she snarled and started punching at her phone. Celia had switched her phone to silent when she had been at the hospital and completely forgotten to switch it back on.

"What now?" Asked Duncan.

Celia glared at him, "Loads of bloody missed calls from Sarah. Shut your trap, I'm trying to pick up my voicemail." Celia turned away from Duncan who looked around at Paul and smiled uneasily. He really thought that he should push off and leave Celia to sort this out. After all, the yard was supposed to be her responsibility. He shifted from one foot to the other wondering if she would notice if he sneaked off now.

Celia suddenly turned around and glaring at Paul and then at Duncan. "That shite, I don't believe the nerve of him!" She snapped.

Paul exchanged a confused glance with Duncan. What a complete Duncan was, thought Paul. He was obviously too scared of Celia to say anything. "What is it?" He ventured, pausing, waiting for Celia's backlash.

Celia walked back over to where Paul and Duncan were standing and looked at them both with a steely gaze. Duncan felt himself shrink back into himself. Paul managed to meet her stare.

"That piece of trash. He's only gone and taken the horse to Sarah's yard."

Paul's eyes widened, "What Sarah French's?" He stared in disbelief as Celia nodded back at him.

"Of course, Sarah, bloody French's. Who the fuck else called Sarah has a yard around here?" Celia spat rolling her eyes.

Paul shook his head "But how could he take him there? He hasn't got a bean? How's he going to pay for him?"

Celia turned away and stared angrily into the distance. "Apparently some woman is with him. She claims to be the new owner of the animal." She turned back to Paul. "That shit Steve must have conned her into doing this. He has the charm of the devil."

Paul stared back at her and frowned. "What are we going to do?" He looked back at Duncan who shrugged. "Well at least we know where the trailer is." Duncan muttered looking back at Celia. Thank God. She seemed to be in a calmer state now that she knew where they had taken the horse. Duncan's only worry was that it might be the eye of the storm and she might explode again later, possibly over dinner. He really should try to get them out of the house this evening. Anything would do to avoid one of Celia's rants.

Celia gave a small tight smile. "I'm going to have a word with Sarah and find out exactly what the hell is going on." She turned and started to walk away towards the house. Paul and Duncan stared after her. Suddenly Celia paused in her tracks and looked back over her shoulder at Paul, "Don't just stand there. Get those horses sorted out, I don't pay you to ponce around admiring the frigging view!" Celia gave Duncan a disapproving stare and then continued walking away towards the house.

Duncan suddenly sprang into life, "I'd better go and help sort things out," he said giving Paul a nod he turned and scurried off after Celia. He would throw some coffee and chocolate digestives at her, hopefully it would quell the worst of the ranting.

Paul turned away. He was feeling irritated. What had that shit Steve managed to swindle now? He was desperate to find out what he was up to. He took a deep breath then gave a small smile to himself. One thing was certain. Celia would not let Steve get away with this. She wouldn't tolerate being shown up by her staff and if anyone got wind of this she would be the laughing stock. Paul knew that she would be aware of this. That was why she was so angry.

Paul turned back to walk towards the stables. He paused for a moment to look at Ella who was gazing after Celia. She looked at him uneasily, his salacious stare made her feel uncomfortable. Her blue eyes widened as he looked back at her. Paul suddenly smiled warmly at her. "Aren't you supposed to be doing something?"

Ella turned around to continue sweeping. Paul admired her backside once more, for a moment and then walked on to the stables smiling to himself. He did not hear Ella's phone ring as he walked away.

CHAPTER 7

Chloe sat down at the desk in the large study. She needed some time to think by herself. It had certainly been an eventful day and she was wondering if she had taken on more than she could handle, what with all that was going on around her.

She had felt a sudden pang of nervousness shortly after hiring Steve. That was unlike her, questioning her own judgement was not something she did these days. She pondered on why she had hired him like that. Well it had just felt right and Chloe always trusted her instincts, they never let her down. That's why she had done so well in business.

Chloe rose from the desk and walked around the room admiring the bookcase. She went outside and paused in the corridor. Jade was in the kitchen feeding a delighted Jerry, who was on his umpteenth sachet of cat food. Steve was upstairs "moving in" to one of the bedrooms. Steve had called someone at Celia's yard that was going to bring his things over for him. Chloe gathered that they would be waiting for an opportune moment to collect Steve's things.

They had left Celia's trailer at Sarah's yard. Chloe would take it back tomorrow. Chloe hadn't liked the way the owner of the yard had looked at her, or rather had avoided looking at her. Sarah had kept looking away and chewing on her bottom lip. Chloe could see that she was not entirely comfortable with something, and, after all this was a small village.

Chloe walked on around the corridor and into the large sitting room that she had been in last night. It felt chilly in here now. She shivered slightly and walked around to make up the fire. She paused as she passed the coffee table where the papers that she had been reading the evening before lay.

Chloe picked up one of the sheets of paper and sighed. She'd had no idea that things were going to be so complicated. She had thought that she could just put the estate on the market and leave an estate agent to sort out the rest. A few letters to the creditors and that should have been it. But no, her aunt had her owns wishes and she wanted them to be adhered to. One of her wishes had been that the horse was not to be sold. Apparently she could loan him or lease him, but who the heck would want a clapped out ex racehorse?

Chloe suddenly wondered if she could find out how old the horse was. She walked up the stairs and onto the landing. She wandered further up the corridor. "Steve," she called. She paused and a door suddenly opened. He'd chosen the green room at the back of the house that overlooked the rolling open fields behind.

Steve peered around the doorway, he looked like he'd just woken up, his hair was tousled and his eyes were tired. "What is it? " He asked

"Steve, what do you know about the horse?" Chloe enquired. " How old is he? What happened to him? I would like to get hold of his paperwork."

Steve moved out from behind the doorway. He'd been admiring the view across the fields from the bedroom when he had suddenly felt overwhelmingly tired. He'd laid on the bed hoping that a brief stretch would re charge his batteries and the next

thing he'd known was hearing Chloe calling his name. He'd awoken and for one moment had no idea where he was. He took in the sumptuous large room and thought that perhaps he'd won the lottery and was in a Hotel. Then it had all come flooding back to him. He'd jumped up quickly to answer Chloe's call.

Chloe observed Steve as he gave a slight stretch, which pulled his top across his taut torso. He really was rather attractive she mused. He probably had all the girls after him. "I'm sorry, have I woken you?" She asked with a small amused smile.

Steve looked sheepish, "I must have nodded off," he muttered. He looked back at her. She didn't seem to be angry with him fortunately. He thought for a moment. "I didn't know about the horse until today." he paused "to be honest I'd only been there a couple of weeks," he looked down for a moment, "I can ask if one of the girls could find out what was going on with him though."

"Yes, do. That would be very helpful. I'm going to ring that vet that Sarah said Celia would probably have used and find out what's wrong with his leg." Chloe turned and walked back towards the stairs. Steve watched her go for a moment. He hoped that he wouldn't blow this job, she seemed like a good person to have on your side and she seemed very businesslike and practical. He sighed and closed the door to look for his phone.

Chloe paused as she walked past the kitchen. Jade was feeding Jerry on the table, stroking him and chattering away to him, telling him how handsome he was. Jade smiled at Chloe as she paused in the doorway.

"Jade you really shouldn't encourage Jerry to get on the surfaces like that." Chloe sighed. She looked enquiringly at Jade. "Everything all right?" Jade blinked back at her, eyes wide behind her red glasses.

Jade remembered her phone call to her mother who had spent half an hour telling her rambling on about the price of bread. Which apparently was the root of all of the world's problems. "Yes, Jerry's got a tummy full of food now," she smiled stroking him again. Chloe observed the cloud of grey cat hairs as they fell on to the table and clung to Jade's suit.

"Jade, will have to get some casual clothes. We'll order some on line for you later." Chloe said with a nod. Jade gave a small nod as she left and turned her attention back to Jerry. It was a good job that Chloe hadn't walked in earlier.

Jade had been telling Jerry all about what a handsome chap Steve was and how she wished that she looked like Chloe so that he might ask her out on a date. She wouldn't tell her mum though she'd only start to fret. Jade sighed and turned to look in the cupboard to see what they could have for dinner. She would just have to try and impress Steve with her cooking. She wondered if Chloe's aunt had left any cookbooks lying around the place.

Chloe put her phone back into her pocket with a sigh. She had called the vet and

managed to find out that the horse's leg had been damaged in a training accident and it might heal. Unfortunately, the vet seemed to think that it could take a long time and a lot of money for the medicine and therapy.

They had left the horse in a stable at Sarah's. Chloe had to leave a month's rent in advance and also a damage deposit. She had also needed to buy hay, feed and bedding from Sarah that had cost her an arm and a leg. Not to mention the bandages she had also bought from Sarah for him. Chloe had written a cheque from her own bank account. She would need to keep a close record of all of these expenses. The horse had been left happily munching between two large hay nets, knee deep in straw bedding.

Chloe took in a deep breath and looked around the sitting room. Why did she have a feeling that something was different in this room? Chloe turned around. She felt a sudden chill again. She walked towards the fire and then the coffee table on which her papers were lying. She picked them up again. She was about to have another look through them when she heard a knock at the door.

Chloe went to answer the door but surprisingly Jade had beaten her to it. Jade opened the door as Chloe arrived behind her. They both observed the young blonde girl standing in the doorway. An old bicycle lay on the ground behind her. The girl smiled and looked at them with her bright blue eyes. "Hello, I'm Ella." She smiled. "I've got Steve's stuff," she added holding up her arms showing them the carrier bags she held in each hand.

Chloe stared at the bags. Was that it she wondered? She moved over to stand next to Jade who was looking at Ella with a slightly dazed expression on her face. "Jade would you give him a shout." Chloe said giving Jade a nudge. Jade nodded and hurried off. Chloe looked back at the slim pretty girl who was smiling back at her. She wondered if she was Steve's girlfriend. "Come in, I'm Chloe and that was Jade." Chloe waved her in and Ella stepped through the door into the hallway.

Ella gazed around at the large hall, "Wow, this is some pad," she said as she looked around with wide eyes.

"Yes, it certainly is quite something," said Chloe dryly as she closed the door.

Steve appeared at the top of the stairs with Jade in tow. "Hi Ella," he said as he descended towards her "Thanks for doing this." Ella turned around quickly at the sound of his voice. Chloe noticed how her eyes lit with excitement up at the sight of him and managed to restrain a smile.

"I hear you've been beating up horses and stealing them. Not to mention stealing trailers." Ella said to Steve with an enquiring smile. She thrust the bags towards him. "There you go. I raided your room and assume that these are all your worldly possessions. Talk about travelling light."

Steve took the bags from her with a slightly embarrassed smile. "Thank you. I

gather all is not well at Stone Towers?"

Ella's grinned back at him, "She's mad as hell. She really went off on one at Paul and Duncan. Then I got Joanne to go crying about her arm to her saying that she had to do an accident report. That soon distracted her. She made Paul go to her office No doubt trying to put the blame on to him. That's how I managed to sneak in and nick the keys to the van from the tack room and get your stuff. They were still having a conference." Ella paused, she hoped that Joanne hadn't had too much of a grilling she had looked rather pale when Ella had left her knocking at Celia's front door. She looked questioningly at Steve "You didn't really hit the horse did you?" She asked.

Steve stopped smiling and rolled his eyes. "Oh, please Ella. What do you think?"

Ella smiled again, "I thought not, lying old cow."

Steve put the bags down then turned back to Ella. "What do you know about the horse?"

Ella looked enthusiastically back at Steve. "Oh yes." She grinned again "Did you really take him to Sarah's? That was hilarious. I'd love to be there when Celia gets hold of Sarah, she's supposed to be her best buddy!"

Chloe shook her head. She didn't think this girl was going to be much help with providing any information on the horse. She glanced at Steve who noticed her expression and turned back to Ella. Chloe frowned as she saw that Jade was standing behind Steve looking as if she had the weight of the world upon her shoulders. Chloe stared at her but Jade continued looking sadly at Ella. Oh no, surely Jade didn't really have a crush on Steve?

"Do you know if Celia has any paperwork for the horse?" Chloe asked Ella.

Ella dragged her gaze away from Steve and looked back at Chloe. "Oh yes she probably would have his passport. She usually wants to keep stuff like that at the yard. But I couldn't get hold of it she must keep it in the house. I've never seen any official papers around the yard. She doesn't like us seeing anything like that. Secretive old bat."

"Right," said Chloe. "I'll take this trailer back before she gets us arrested and I'll get his paperwork while I'm there." Steve, Ella and Jade all stared at her. Jade and Ella's eyes were wide. Chloe managed to stop herself from smiling at them. Jade now looked terrified.

"Don't worry. You lot can stay here. Unless you want a lift back?" She asked raising an eyebrow at Ella. Ella shook her head vigorously. "Oh no way! I mean thanks but she'll bury me if she knows I've been fraternizing with the enemy. I'll make my own way back in a while if that's ok."

Jade's expression had gone from one of relief to one of bleakness again. Surely this

golden beauty wasn't staying? She stared at the floor wishing she were somewhere else, preferably with Steve.

Chloe noted the change in Jade's demeanor and mentally rolled her eyes. Yes, she definitely had the hots for young Steve. "All right. Behave yourselves." Chloe said as she turned to leave. Chloe shook her head as she left the house.

Things just kept getting better. Now she had a love sick Jade to look after as well as everything else. Must be all of this fresh air she mused.

Chloe wondered how things would pan out as she drove into Celia Stone's yard. She had no qualms about confronting Celia, despite what she had heard about her. In fact, she was looking forward to it. She was annoyed that the horse was in such poor condition and the woman sounded like a right little bully. Chloe had long since lost any fear of dealing with characters of Celia's ilk. Gone were the days when she shied away from confrontation. Better to grab the bull by the horns. She smiled at how apt that phrase was, She'd heard that Celia certainly had the build of an Ox.

Chloe parked in the middle of the yard and unhitched the trailer. She saw a skinny looking young man stop in his tracks across the yard and turn to observe her with an expression of stunned surprise on his face. She looked back at him and gestured for him to come over. "I could do with a hand with this," she called, pointing at the trailer. Paul paused, undecided for a moment and then walked over. Chloe noticed the stony expression on his face. His lips were stretched tautly in a thin smile, or was it a grimace? Chloe stifled a grin as he helped her push the trailer back into its usual parking space.

Paul said nothing as they moved the trailer. This was going to be interesting he thought. No Doubt Celia would be here any minute. He wasn't sure whether he should hang around and watch the fireworks or make himself scarce. This attractive woman may be younger than Celia but she had an air of confidence about her that made him feel that she would give Celia a good run for her money if they had a set to.

Chloe stood back when they'd finished and dusted her hands off on her jeans. "So where's Celia Stone? I want a word with her."

Paul stood back and looked at her levelly. He gave her a small smile now. "She wants a word with you too and here she is now," he said pointing behind Chloe.

Chloe turned around to see a short plump woman striding towards her. She looked around forty five. Her long unkempt tightly curled hair flopped around her shoulders. She had a fixed look of annoyance on her face as she marched towards Chloe.

Paul shifted back slightly from Chloe. He was beginning to think that he should have made himself scarce after all, as he backed further away around the trailer. Celia looked pissed off as hell.

Celia stopped and glared at Chloe. "You're lucky you haven't been arrested!" She shouted. "How dare you take my property without my consent! What the hell do you think you're playing at?"

Chloe gazed back at Celia. "My name is Chloe Marcus, I am the new owner of the horse which I removed from your yard. I've come for his passport and any other paperwork that you have. I expect to receive all of the information which you hold on him."

Celia blinked at Chloe. "Are you deaf or just fucking stupid?" She spat "You cannot remove animals from this yard without my consent. That horse was in my care!" Her voice was creeping higher with every word that she spoke.

"Care? Is that what you call it? Now, you can either run along and get me his paperwork or I can call the Police and the RSPCA and show them how you treat horses in " care". You have been paid to look after that animal and you have nearly killed him. I think the racing authority will also be interested to see the photographs of him."

Celia stopped and blinked. She looked as if she had been slapped in the face. Her eyes flicked sideways briefly as she pondered on Chloe's words. She looked back at Chloe who was smiling warmly at her. Celia felt surge of rage well up inside her. She glared at Chloe for a moment and then turned around and marched back to the house without a word.

Chloe raised an eyebrow and turned back to Paul. He seemed to be hiding behind the trailer. "Your boss seems a nice lady," she said.

Paul looked at her with wide eyes and then turned around and shot back across the yard and into the stables. That was it. He was out of here.

Chloe was beginning to wonder whether she should go and bang on the front door of the house when Celia came marching back. She thrust some papers into Chloe's hands "Now get off my yard! I'll be sending you a bill for everything and that includes the hire of my trailer!" She snapped.

Chloe made no move to leave but looked at the paperwork. It appeared that the Passport was there. She glanced back at Celia who was as red as a beetroot. "Send it to my Solicitor," she said, "I'm sure you know him, he's Robert Morecom." Chloe turned around to leave and then paused, turning back to Celia. "Oh the rear left indicator is out on your trailer. You really should get that fixed you know."

Celia stared at her in stunned silence. Her mouth fell partly open. This was unbelievable.

Chloe was smiling to herself as she drove out of the yard. "What a nasty little person that woman was. She paused as she turned the car to leave the yard and pulled out the passport form the paperwork Celia had given her

Chloe looked at it for a moment. The horse was only five. Her eyes widened suddenly as she saw his name. It wasn't Seven it was called Samson VII. She stared at it in disbelief. His name was Samson! She remembered the note her aunt had left. The last thing she'd written: "Don't give up on Sam, use the formula". Chloe's heart suddenly picked up a beat. She'd been talking about the horse.

CHAPTER 8

Sam stood in his stable and let out a contented sigh. He was enjoying the sweet haylage that had been left for him and the fresh clean water felt refreshingly cool as he dipped his muzzle into it and took a long drink. He was also enjoying the attention that he was receiving from the yard liveries.

Sam stretched his head down so that the young girl could stroke his soft nose a little easier. Heather smiled and continued making a fuss of him. Her mother observed Sam. Big Jayne stood outside the stable in her usual pose; legs apart hands on hips. "Heather you shouldn't touch that horse, he could be carrying anything. My God what a state that horse is in, poor thing ought to be put to sleep. He can't even walk properly."

Rory, who was standing next to her, nodded in agreement. "Is it some kind of rescue case perhaps?"

Kelly appeared in the stable block. She had finally managed to escape from Sarah who was berating her for allowing the horse on to her yard. Sarah had been so annoyed at her, "You can't just let anyone move here. This is a small village and we don't want to upset anyone. This was supposed to be one of Celia's clients and we've taken her business from her." Sarah had said, with a roll of her eyes.

Personally, Kelly thought that Celia should be taken to court if that was how she looked after her client's horses but she'd bitten her tongue. She liked her job here on the yard and it was the only way she could get to work with horses and remain living at home. Unless of course, she risked life and limb by going to Celia's yard and taking a chance with her. Kelly didn't fancy that idea. Celia seemed worse than Sarah and she'd heard that she could be a right mad old cow as well.

Sarah had continued to glare at her shaking her head, until Kelly had finally said quietly, "I did try to tell you, earlier on…"

Sarah had ignored her, " and not to mention that Celia is a close friend of mine. How am I supposed to explain this to her?" She had shook her head at Kelly again and then turned and marched back to the house giving a dismissive wave of her hand as she left.

Sarah suddenly paused and turned back to Kelly, "Oh and put a rug on that bloody horse will you, I don't want the wretched animal on display. People might report us otherwise. Tell the owner he was cold." Sarah nodded to herself. She could add that on to his livery costs. It was a shame the horse was from Celia's yard, she'd made a nice bit of profit already from it."

Kelly had smiled at the pretty dark haired woman as she opened the trailer door but couldn't help but take a sharp breath when she saw how thin the poor horse was. No wonder they'd moved him from that Celia's place. She'd taken another deep breath when she saw the handsome young man leading the horse from the trailer. Fortunately she had managed to quickly look away before he saw her wide-eyed gaze. Kelly had helped them prepare the stable and showed them where everything

was before they settled the horse in and went off to pay Sarah. She wondered what the nervous looking girl in the pink wellingtons was doing with them. She looked completely out of place alongside the other two.

Kelly smiled to herself as she walked back to the stable block. At least there was a good looking bloke around here now. It would be nice to have a someone attractive to watch riding in the manege She hoped that he was a good rider that would put that stuck up twit Rory's nose out of joint too. She'd noticed that Rory and Jayne had quickly finished their sessions in the manege upon seeing the commotion with the new arrival. No doubt they wanted a nose at the new livery. Mind you at least it had given poor Heather a reprieve from having to jump Firefox again, the poor girl looked so scared Kelly thought she might just pass out.

Jayne had decided that Firefox was a little stuffy today and so they would put her away until next time she was saying to Heather as they strolled past. Kelly smiled Firefox was the most unstuffy animal on the planet. In fact she was positively crackers. She wondered if Heather had finally realized that she was going to have to jump over fences whether she liked it or not. The moment Heather so much as turned Foxy's head towards a jump she lost all hope of doing anything but sailing over it.

Rory had declared that Ted was also not forward going enough to continue with his intensive dressage schooling. He'd hoped to have a laugh at Heather's attempts at trying to stay on Firefox but they'd gone back in so that had spoilt that. Anyhow, he'd also seen the new arrival pull up. Or rather he'd seen the attractive dark haired woman that had accompanied the new arrival. He couldn't wait to introduce himself to her. He was getting quite excited at the prospect of having a chat with her. Finding out how much she knew about horses and whether she might be worth having a crack at.

Big Jayne looked up as Kelly entered the block clutching a stable rug that she'd pulled from the tack room. "Where on earth has this horse come from? It looks like a rescue case. Those owners should be reported."

"Oh, It's not them, he's been at Celia Stone's yard." Kelly said, pulling open the stable door. She gave Sam a quick pat on the head before placing the rug on him. He stood quietly grabbing at his hay as she pulled it over him and tightened the straps up.

"Oh dear." Rory said with a shake of his head, "Looks a tad large." He exchanged a glance with Big Jayne who also shook her head.

Sam continued to munch on his ha. He was, still savouring the attention that he was receiving. Sam liked to be the centre of attention and that was something that had been missing in his life for a while.

Kelly stood back and observed the rug, which hung loosely around Sam's shoulders. She had tightened up the straps as much as she could but the rug was still too big

for him. "I thought this would fit, it looked his size," she muttered.

"It would fit if he wasn't a walking skeleton." Rory observed. "You'll have to tie some knots in the straps and put another surcingle around it. He'll step out of it in his sleep otherwise."

Kelly started adjusting the rug, wondering why Rory was always stating the obvious. Perhaps he thought she was an idiot. Or perhaps he just liked the sound of his own voice. Probably both.

Sam lifted his head and gave a small whicker as he heard a horse approach. A smiling Ben led Gatsby into the block, walking him past Sam into his own stable. Sam watched them with interest.

Rory exchanged a glance with Big Jayne and pointed down at Gatsby's new boots as he walked past. Big Jayne rolled her eyes and shook her head. Kelly saw their looks from inside the stable and sighed. Those two could be a right pair of bitches when they got together. Ben was all right. He may not be the best rider in the world but he took great care of his horse and he always had a smile for everyone on the yard.

Rory turned back to Kelly who was looking at the rug on Sam which now had several knots tied into the straps. She would have to get a surcingle or it might still not be on him in the morning.

Big Jayne also turned back to observe Kelly and Sam. She shook her head before saying "Personally, I don't think it's right that Sarah would allow a horse in this state to come on to the yard. He should be quarantined, he could be riddled with lice, or have something contagious. Especially in that condition."

"Well, she could hardly turn him away," said Kelly looking at Sam and smoothing his mane down on the side of his neck. "I mean she couldn't let him go back to Celia's when she's the one that got him into this awful state."

"I blame the owner," said Big Jayne. "How could they allow this to happen?"

Rory said nothing, he was hoping to meet the dark haired woman sooner rather than later. He didn't want to say anything bad about her yet in case she didn't turn him down.

Kelly stood up "It wasn't the owner's fault. She was ill and she died. That's what they said before they left anyway."

Big Jayne blinked in surprise. "Oh, so who was that woman and who was the dopey looking girl in the suit? Not to mention that young man that was helping them out."

Kelly wished she'd kept her mouth shut now as Rory also looked at her with interest, wondering who the man was and whether it was the dark haired woman's boyfriend. Ben's face also appeared around the stable door. "What's this? Are you having a meeting?" He asked.

Big Jayne gave a tight-lipped nod. "Perhaps we should."

Rory was still waiting, hoping to find out more about the dark haired woman, "So, Kelly. Who were those people?"

Kelly turned back to Sam's mane. "All I know is that the girl in the suit: Jade she said her name was. She was the one who rang and asked if they could bring a horse. She said it was an emergency and that her boss had inherited it and needed a place to keep it. So I said that It would be okay as I knew we had a place now that Jackie had left and the dark haired woman said they'd rescued him from Celia Stone's yard."

Rory laughed suddenly, "You mean you didn't ask Sarah if they could bring him here? She must be livid. Celia's supposed to be her best friend. No wonder she looked so pissed off."

Big Jayne glared at Rory, "Do you mind, there are children present," she said covering Heather's ears with her meaty palms. Heather started to wriggle away and then thought better of it. Life was always easier if she didn't protest.

"Sorry, mum," said Rory raising his eyebrows at Big Jayne still smiling. He was imagining what would happen when Sarah and Celia next met up.

Ben was still standing in the doorway with a grin on his face. "He looks like a sweet horse," he said observing Sam.

Kelly smiled back at him, 'Well he's been pretty laid back so far," she said giving him a pat. She still had to take Billy for a ride and time was getting on. She didn't want to give Sarah any more reasons to moan at her.

Lyn suddenly appeared behind Ben "Oh what a lovely head that horse has. Shame about that leg though, wonder what happened?" She was peering at Sam with interest.

"It's not just his leg that's the problem. The poor creature's thin as a rake," said Rory trying to give Lyn a charming but professional smile. Lyn glanced back at Rory. Why was he looking at her with that idiotic grin on his face? She turned back to the horse. "I'll bet he'll look lovely when he's all better and fed up though," she reached out to touch Sam's nose who obligingly leaned his head towards her.

Kelly walked out of the stable closing the door firmly behind her. She thought that she had said too much already. "We'd better leave him in peace so he can enjoy his hay."

Big Jayne frowned, "I still don't think she should allow a horse in this state to just turn up here."

Rory smiled as he had an idea, "Well, maybe we should have a talk about this over a drink. Let's say we meet up at The Arms?" He said glancing around, his gaze lingered slightly longer on Lyn's face.

Ben nodded enthusiastically. He enjoyed their liaisons in the Pub. "Well yes, that sounds terrific," he said glancing across at Lyn with a smile. She didn't look too keen though she was giving Rory a rather stern look.

"It's none of our business really." Lyn said "But I'll come along for a drink," she added

Big Jayne nodded, "Count me in. There's nothing on the box tonight anyhow," she glanced across at Kelly, "You can come too, if you like now that you're just about old enough for more than an orange juice." Big Jayne suspected that Kelly might be able to enlighten them some more on the horse's owners.

Lyn noticed Rory roll his eyes at Big Jayne, he was probably worried that Kelly would blab to Sarah about their liaison she thought.

Kelly nodded, "I'll see what I'm doing," she said as she walked away. Kelly wasn't sure if she wanted to spend that much time with some of these people, she would have to think about it.

Rory smiled back at Lyn, "Right see you all about seven then," he said and strode away to finish Ted off.

Kelly headed off to Billy's stable. She still had to ride him. She'd better get a move on before Sarah came out and started moaning at her. She walked back across the yard, turning as she heard a car pull up. Kelly quickened her stride. She decided she was going to go for a hack she needed to make herself scarce. Celia had just arrived.

CHAPTER 9

Chloe practically ran up to the steps of the house. She quickly opened the door and hurried inside. She found Steve and Ella sitting on the sofa in the large sitting room. Jade was perched on the edge of a chair looking slightly uncomfortable.

They all looked at her as she stood breathing slightly rapidly, in the doorway of the room.

Steve raised an eyebrow, "Everything go all right?" He asked tentatively. Jade's eyes widened, "You didn't have a row with her did you?"

Chloe paused for a moment then shook her head. "What, with that daft old bat? I wouldn't waste my time," she stepped forward into the room and stood in front of the sofa. She waved Sam's passport in front of Steve and Ella. "Got his papers," she said triumphantly. "We've got his name wrong." she continued and thrust the passport into Steve's lap.

Steve looked at her curiously. Chloe's face was alight she looked positively radiant. He wondered what she was so excited about as he opened the passport and inspected it. Finally he spoke, "Samson VII. Oh, well it's not completely wrong, they called him Seven."

Jade stared across at Steve. She wished she'd been brave enough to sit next to him before Ella had done so. She sighed, "What difference does it make what his name is, as long as you've got his paperwork?"

Chloe walked across the room and sat on the arm of Jade's chair. "Well, it doesn't make much difference technically. But I was left a message by my aunt and until now I had no idea what she was talking about. Come to that, I still don't have much of an idea what she was talking about, but at least I know who she was talking about."

Jade stared at Chloe in confusion. Steve and Ella both turned and looked at her questioningly. Steve cleared his throat, "I'm afraid that we also have no idea what you're talking about."

"I know," said Chloe. "Well, the last note my aunt left before she died said, "don't give up on Sam, use the formula," she smiled at them as she finished.

Steve stared blankly back at her. "Right, so now we know who Sam is. Now we need to know what is the formula and why do we have to give it to him?"

"I've no idea," smiled Chloe. "Maybe it's something for his leg. His leg went just before she went into hospital. We need to try and find out where the formula is."

"How are we going to find out what something is when we don't even know what we're looking for?" Said Jade shaking her head.

"I'm not sure. We'll just have to look around the house," said Chloe firmly. "If we go through everything, surely eventually we must find something here that will give us a clue"

Chloe looked at Steve and then Jade who stared blankly back. "Look, you two just go through everything in here and I'll start in the study," she looked at Ella meaningfully. "Well, I'm afraid that these two will be busy for a while."

Ella reluctantly rose from the sofa. It was a shame that Jade had been here, she was pretty sure that she could have developed things further with Steve if she hadn't been playing gooseberry. "Actually, I'd better get off. The wicked witch of the west might notice I've disappeared," she also thought that she'd better check that Jo wasn't in screaming pain. She smiled at Steve, "I'll be in touch." She said as she walked away.

Chloe raised an eyebrow, "Looks like you've got an admirer," she said staring at Steve.

Steve gave a small smile and shrugged, "It's always handy to have a friend of the enemy," he said. He looked across at Jade who was standing in front of the chair staring blankly into space. She caught his gaze and he winked at her. Jade felt a fluttering in her tummy and turned away to pretend to fluff the cushions on the sofa as she felt herself turning bright.

Chloe didn't notice she was frowning thoughtfully to herself, "Do you think that Celia woman is the enemy?"

Steve looked at Chloe, his expression had become serious "From what I've heard, she doesn't like to be crossed. Besides, she struck me as a bit of an evil cow. She certainly didn't treat Sam very well did she?"

Chloe nodded, "I suppose I'd better keep an eye out for her then," she glanced over at Jade, "right, well, let's get started then," she clasped her hands together and marched off to the study.

Steve looked back at Jade who smiled shyly back at him. Jade was glad that Ella had gone. She had felt like an old crone compared to Ella's obvious beauty. Ella had not stopped talking about Celia, the yard and horses the whole time Chloe had been out. As Jade knew nothing about any of those subjects she had felt completely inadequate and spent the whole time wishing that she could contribute to the conversation so that Steve wouldn't think she was stupid. Still, she had decided to remain in the room with them. She might as well put a damper on Ella's obvious flirting with Steve.

Jade pushed her bright red glasses further back up her nose.

"How are we going to find something if we don't even know what it looks like? She's asking the impossible," she muttered, looking around the room with a shrug.

"Well, she's the boss. Just go through everything and see if anything of interest crops up. You never know, we might find some useful information about the estate for her," said Steve.

"I suppose you're right," admitted Jade, picking up a large cushion and giving it a shake. She started kneading it and then clutched it to her chest with a sigh, "this could take forever".

Steve started smiling, "You take you're job very seriously don't you?"

Jade smiled brightly back at him, her face expression suddenly lifted. "Oh, yes I like to do a good job, otherwise why bother?" She nodded as she knelt down and peered underneath the sofa.

Chloe was in the study. She gazed around at the masses of books and files in the room. She took a deep breath as she realised the enormity of the task that she had set herself. She walked over to pull a file from one of the shelves. It was crammed full with paperwork. She sat down at the desk and opened the file. She frowned as she looked at the writing. This was way beyond her comprehension.

She stared at the equations on the page in front of her. This must have been part of uncle Harry's work. He had been a physicist. Quite high profile apparently. Chloe realised that she had never really known what he did for a living. It was something that had never really been discussed.

Chloe sighed and put the file down. She picked a book from the shelf instead and looked at it. "Lucinda Lilac's Eventing

Extras", she smiled to herself, remembering that this had been one of the books that aunt Sophie had bought for her all of those years ago. When she first had come to live with them. She sat down and at the desk and gazed out of the window It looked a little misty outside. She was momentarily distracted as her thoughts turned to the time that she had first come to live with her aunt and uncle.

It was after her parents had died. She'd only been ten and she hadn't really known what was happening, except that she would never see her mother and father again. The memory made her feel a sudden chill and she felt the goose bumps as they rose on her arms. One moment she had been so happy, it seemed that the world was such a lovely place and the next moment everything had changed.

She had been at her aunt and uncle's when she had heard the news. Her parents had left her with them as they had been going out to make some last minute preparations for their annual holiday. They had planned to take Chloe camping in Wales. It would have been by the seaside. Her parents liked to take her camping despite the fact that the weather was not always reliable and the tent often rocked sideways as the wind and the rain assaulted it.

They liked to sing songs and cook breakfast on the little camp stove that they took. Chloe remembered that she usually took a friend along and she had been looking forward to paddling on the beach with her.

She remembered how her aunt had commented on how misty it looked outside and that her parents had better be careful when they came to pick her up. At that time her aunt and uncle lived in another house on the other side of Diddlecot. It had been much smaller than this one, but still had lovely views. No wonder they'd chosen to stay in the village.

She remembered how her aunt had been telephoning her parents, trying to find out where they were but getting no reply. As the evening drew on even Chloe had been wondering where they were.

Her aunt had finally turned to her uncle and told him that he would have to take Chloe back home himself. It was an hour long drive back to the City but he would have to go. They had thought that perhaps Chloe's parents had had a problem with the car. Chloe had remembered being worried that they wouldn't be able to go on the holiday now. She'd been so looking forward to it.

Her uncle had said that they would give it a while longer. They would have some dinner first as they might still on their way and that would just be a waste of his time. Chloe had smiled at the thought of aunt Sophie's dinner. She always did such yummy puddings.

It had been while Chloe was finishing her second helping of aunt Sophie's sticky toffee pudding that they had heard the banging on the door. Chloe noticed the way aunt Sophie looked at uncle Harry. A wave of concern had crossed her face. It was only later that Chloe had understood that the only people who bang on the door like that are Policemen or criminals. This had been the Policemen.

Chloe suddenly inhaled sharply as she remembered the look on her uncle's face as he had returned from answering the door. She had been so shocked that she stopped eating. Her mouth hung open and her spoon fell from her hand, clattering into her bowl splashing sticky toffee bits around her.

Uncle Harry had taken aunt Sophie aside and murmured in her ear. Aunt Sophie had made a strange noise – a kind of gargling sigh and she had clasped her hand to her mouth. She turned and stared at Chloe, her face pale and drawn. That's when Chloe had known that her parents were dead.

Chloe blinked as she looked around the study and felt a sudden shiver travel along her spine. Apparently her parents had been on their way to pick her up. They had been almost there when it happened.

Her father had been driving slowly along and suddenly a car was heading straight towards them. Some young fool and his friend had decided to overtake the village bus. The bus was the last one of the evening and had been plodding carefully along in the mist with its one solitary passenger. They youth couldn't even see properly but he'd still overtaken. Her father had swerved across to the other side of the road to avoid them. Unfortunately, he had seen the bus too late to avoid a collision. The bus driver slammed on his brakes causing his passenger to head butt the seat in front of him. It was not enough though. Even at their low speeds the bus had ploughed straight into the car. So there it was. Killed by the 501 to Diddlecot.

Chloe slumped back into her chair and took a deep breath. She was gazing into space when Jade entered the room. "We haven't found anything at all." said Jade brightly "What should we do? We could ….," she tailed off as she saw Chloe's expression. Jade's eyes widened in concern, she had never seen Chloe look like that before she looked so desperately sad.

"Are you all right?" Jade asked quietly. Steve walked in and looked across at Chloe who was still gazing into space. He walked over and touched her shoulder. Chloe jumped visibly. Steve looked at Chloe's pale face. "You were miles away, everything okay?" He asked.

Chloe blinked and looked at Steve and then at Jade, she had lost all track of things, then she remembered. "Have you finished looking in that room yet?"

Jade frowned and nodded "Oh yes, we did that and we've done all the rest of downstairs practically."

Steve gave a slight smile. "Why don't we have a coffee and then we'll start again. Come on Chloe," he nodded at her and she rose from the chair. She gave a final glance out of the window as they left the room.

They sat at the kitchen table and Jade peered out of the window. "It's getting misty out there," she said as she handed out the coffee. Chloe said nothing and started to sip at her drink.

Steve was sitting opposite Chloe. He eyed her with interest from over his coffee cup.

Jade was peering inside the kitchen cupboards, "Wonder if there are any biscuits I could do with a snack," she said as she inspected their contents.

"They'll probably be stale if there are," Said Steve.

"You never know," answered Jade, "perhaps Anne likes a nibble when she's cleaning," she continued to look around. Finally her gaze rested on a large jar next to the Aga. She marched over to it.

Steve watched her, "That's probably where the spuds live," He smiled.

Jade ignored him and opened up the jar. She stopped and blinked as she looked inside. Her eyes widened suddenly and her mouth dropped open.

"What is it?" Asked Steve. He put down his cup and waked over to her whilst Chloe watched them with interest.

Jade handed him the jar. He put his hand inside it and grabbed at something. He pulled it out slowly and held it up in front of him for a moment gazing at it intently as he turned it around in his hand. He turned and placed it on the work surface, string at it again. It was a glass bottle type container. The glass had a dark blue tint to it and it had a rustic silver lid screwed on to it.

He brought it over to Chloe with Jade following him. He placed it in front of Chloe. He looked at her for a moment. "It has something inside it and there's something written on its side."

Chloe looked up at him, her eyes wide and curious. "What does it say?"

Steve gave a small smile, "It says formula 12," he paused and looked at Jade and then at Chloe, "I believe that we've found our formula."

CHAPTER 10

Celia sat in cold silence as Duncan drove to Sarah's yard. She was furious. She would be having serious words with Sarah when they arrived. Duncan had given up on trying to engage her in conversation as everything he said only resulted in her snapping at him or responding with a sarcastic quip. He now kept his eyes firmly on the road and hoped that he could just leave Sarah and Celia to it when they arrived. With any luck Sarah's husband Mark would be there and they could slope off for a crafty drink and leave them to it.

Sarah was in the kitchen when they arrived. Celia knew that was where she would be and marched straight to the back door giving it three loud knocks. Sarah opened the door quickly, with a feeling of trepidation. She paused for a moment in anticipation of Celia's barrage of shouting which she had been expecting.

Celia gave her a small tight smile and walked past her into the kitchen. She turned and looked back at Sarah. "I think we have a few things to discuss, don't you?" She punctuated the sentence with a severe glare.

Sarah nodded as she turned away to close the door. She was relieved when she saw through the window next to the door that a black Audi had pulled up. It was her husband Mark.

Sarah turned to see that Celia was standing leaning against the kitchen unit with her arms folded. She was looking at Sarah with an intense stare that made her feel like running for the stables.

Duncan walked in giving Sarah a quick nod. He and stood next to Celia wringing his hands uncomfortably. He daren't say anything in case Celia kicked off. A heavy silence penetrated the room. Fortunately it didn't last long as Mark breezed into the kitchen with a big smile on his face.

Mark paused momentarily his smile froze and a frown settled on his forehead. He looked from Sarah to Celia and then at Duncan. Duncan's bald head was shining in the light as a few beads of perspiration settled upon it. He pushed his glasses back up as they started to slide down his nose Mark almost burst out laughing. Duncan looked like even taller and more ungainly than normal as he and sweated and fidgeted next to Celia.

Mark smiled returned to his face again, "I say, Celia, Duncan have you come for dinner? Or are we going to have a little party? It is Saturday night after all."

Celia momentarily removed her gaze from Sarah and glared at Mark. He stood by the door smiling. His dark eyes twinkled mischievously. He knew that something was going on. Sarah looked guilt ridden and Celia had a face like thunder.

Celia stared at him. He was so annoying, facetious twat. How different he was to Duncan. He had an air of quiet confidence and always remained composed. But it wasn't just his attitude. Mark was shorter with a full head of short dark neatly cut hair and a perfectly proportioned physique. She sometimes wondered how Sarah had managed to bag such a fit bloke.

Celia took a deep breath and looked pointedly at Sarah. "I think we should have a chat," she paused "in the Snug," she added. Sarah swallowed and nodded at her. She glanced at Mark who grinned and winked back at her.

Mark turned to Duncan. "Well, we might as well have a Brandy eh?" He said and pulled open a cupboard containing a variety of glasses. He poured two glasses from a bottle that was sitting in the corner of the kitchen. Celia paused and turned back around. She picked up the glasses and smiled at

Mark. "I think we need those, more than you two, eh?" She turned back to Sarah and they both left the kitchen and walked out into the hall.

Mark raised an eyebrow and smiled at Duncan. "Well, it looks like they're off for a girlie chat. Looks like they had things to discuss. We'd better keep an eye on them," he smiled as he poured out more brandy and handed a glass to Duncan who had now slumped against the kitchen unit. The relief of not having Celia there to berate him was a huge weight off his shoulders. He hoped to God that she would be in a better mood when she came back.

Mark nodded at him, "Let's go and make ourselves comfortable. You look like you could do with sitting down. Has the old girl been picking on you again?" He managed not to laugh as they headed off into the sitting room of the cottage.

Sarah opened the door to the snug and glanced around. The room was not really a snug, more of an extra sitting room. It was pleasantly large with a stove set against the far wall. The room was in the corner of the house and had two windows. It was furnished with two large sofas that sat in an L shape in front of the stove. A dark cream rug was placed in front of the stove over the oak floorboards.

Sarah sat on one of the sofas and Celia sat down next to her handing her a glass of brandy. Celia looked at Sarah as she did so and then stared turned away staring at the stove. Celia spoke quietly, "Sarah, do you know the aggravation that you have caused me?"

Sarah sniffed and took a swallow of her brandy, she as also staring at the stove. "I didn't know it was one of your clients. That stupid girl took the call and told that woman that the horse could come. You know I would never do anything..."

"Shush," said Celia still in that same quiet tone. She took a large gulp of her brandy and put her left hand on Sarah's thigh. "It's not just the annoyance. It's the embarrassment. If this gets out people will think that I can't control my staff," she started to stroke her hand along Sarah's thigh now Sarah bit her bottom lip as she felt herself start to tremble.

Celia finished her brandy in another gulp as she moved her hand further up Sarah's leg. She could feel that Sarah had started to tremble. She leaned across Sarah to place her glass on the table that was on beside her. As she put it down she placed her hand on Sarah's other thigh and looked at her. Celia's face was barely an inch from Sarah's and her voice was a whisper.

"You know that I have to punish you?"

Sarah said nothing. She was clutching her brandy glass just below her chin. Her eyes were wide and her lower lip was trembling slightly as she nodded at Celia.

Celia touched Sarah's forehead with her own and turned away. Sarah downed her brandy as Celia walked over to the corner of the room. She paused at the saddle rack that was standing there.

The saddle rack had a saddle on it with a bridle hung over the cantle. Celia was not interested in those items. Instead, she leaned over and inspected the variety of whips that were propped against it.

Sarah's eyes widened even more as she watched Celia reach towards the whips. "No, not the schooling whip!" Sarah said, her voice rising to a squeaky trill.

Celia paused and looked back at her with a grim smile on her face. Celia's voice was little more than a whisper as she spoke

"You know, I really should use the schooling whip after the way you've behaved today. But I've decided that I will be kind." She pulled out a jockey whip and held it up in front of her. "Think yourself lucky." She muttered as she stroked the whip along its length. She raised a hand and beckoned Sarah over to her

Sarah sat up and moved slowly towards her. Celia breathed in deeply. She poked the end of the whip at Sarah's chest and glared at her. "Strip off and get on your knees. You need some serious re schooling.' she snarled pushing Sarah towards the rug.

Sarah nodded and peeled off her clothes slowly. She could not meet Celia's gaze. Celia watched her with a slight smile on her face. Her breathing started to become shallower as Sarah removed her underwear. Sarah heard Celia's shortness of breath and felt surge of excitement. She stepped forwards and knelt down on the rug looking up at Celia.

Celia walked slowly around her. She caressed Sarah's chin, pulling it briefly into her crotch as she stepped past her. Celia admired Sarah's large breasts and comfortably large thighs as she paused behind her. "Get on your hands and get that fat arse in the air!" She barked.

Sarah moved forwards placing her hands in front of her on the rug and thrusting her backside upwards. She bit her lip as she felt a tremor of longing well up inside her. She let out a small gasp as she felt Celia run her hand across her buttock and the whip in her other hand rest on her other buttock. Celia ran her hand over her skin, keeping the whip resting against her other side. She circled her hand around Sarah's buttock and then moved it further across and down between her legs, Sarah let out another gasp and pushed her backside against Celia's hand. Celia smiled to herself and pushed her index finger inside Sarah who let out a slow moan as she felt it enter her.

Celia leant over Sarah and started moving her finger gently inside her. She took the whip from Sarah's buttock. Celia spoke quietly in her ear "You needn't think you're getting a reward, you have been playing up too much," she murmured. She moved her finger harder inside Sarah and suddenly brought the whip sharply down on her behind.

Sarah cried out as the whip cracked down hard on her backside. Celia smiled to herself and thrust her finger harder inside Sarah again, simultaneously giving her another sharp thwack with the whip. "That's for shitting in my trailer! Bad pony!" Celia paused for a moment and then pushed her finger forward again as she brought the stick down hard across Sarah's behind. "And that's for slobbering on my clothes. Mannerless beast!" Sarah cried out again feeling her eyes beginning to water.

Celia was breathing heavily now. She paused and stroked the whip across Sarah's behind, smiling as she heard her wince at the pain. She slipped two more fingers inside Sarah and continued massaging her inside. She caressed her outside with her thumb, delighting in the trembling that she felt arise in Sarah. Sarah shut her eyes and exhaled gruffly making a noise that sounded uncannily like a horse whickering. Celia sighed to herself and murmured into Sarah's ear "If you misbehave like that again you know that I will have no choice but to use the schooling whip, don't you?"

Sarah gave a small moan and nodded frantically, her eyes were shut and her face was flushed. Celia continued to caress her with the whip whilst her other hand moved rhythmically between Sarah's legs. Celia leaned on Sarah and sighed, "And if you're really bad, I might have to get out the lunging whip," she muttered.

Sarah's eyes opened suddenly, "No! Please, you mustn't!" she gasped!" Her lips were trembling. Celia smiled again and moved her hand further inside her. She felt the intensity of Sarah's trembling and quickened her movements. Sarah let out a long moan and Celia brought down the whip once more, this time with more force than previously and giving a deep thrust with her other hand as she did so. Sarah let out a cry as she climaxed and then dropped sweating, to the floor.

Celia stood up and observed Sarah's shaking sweat covered body. The final whack of the whip had left a deeper red mark across her buttocks. Celia nodded. "Now get yourself dressed and get me another drink." She said and turned to return the whip to its place next to the saddle. She paused for a moment to touch the schooling whip. She ran her finger along its length and observed it's thin sharp end. Yes that would have to be used if Sarah played up again she thought.

Celia turned around to see Sarah had dressed quickly and was just pulling her socks back on. She sat on the sofa and tugged at the sock, her face was still flushed. Celia tutted at her, as she saw that one sock had a large hole on the heel.

"You must be in need of some more liveries if you're wearing socks in that state." she said flatly. Sarah glanced down at her socks and then back up at Celia. "I didn't notice," she said quietly.

Sarah jumped up quickly and grabbed the two empty glasses. She strode past Celia who was still watching her with a small smirk on her face. Celia ruffled Sarah's hair casually with one hand as she walked past her. Sarah blinked and walked quickly to the kitchen.

Celia walked out of the snug and into the sitting room where Mark and Duncan were sitting on the sofa. Mark looked up as she walked into the room and sat down on one of the chairs.

His eyes narrowed and he gave a small smirk, "I suppose you two have had a good chat, you certainly look a lot more cheerful than earlier on," he looked up as Sarah entered the room with two more glasses of brandy. She handed one to Celia and sat down on another chair. She avoided Mark's stare and gazed out of the window.

Mark now had a grin on his face, "My dear you look a little flushed. Has Celia been berating you? Wish I'd been a fly on the wall," he said giving a sharp laugh. Sarah took a deep breath and continued to avoid his gaze. Mark grinned even more, "Is there something that you should be sharing with Duncan and I?" He asked with a raised eyebrow.

Duncan licked his lips and looked uncomfortable. He wished that Mark would shut up and talk about something else. He didn't want Celia getting wound up again. Not when she seemed to have calmed down so much.

Mark shrugged. "Oh well, I'm sure I'll find out later. Why don't we go down the Pub and have a swift half. We can have some chips, save you cooking Sarah, eh Sarah. Seen as how you look a little overheated."

Celia looked at Duncan and nodded. "Yes why not," she said as she took another drink of her brandy, she was feeling much more relaxed now. She looked at Sarah who glanced back at her, "Might be wise to change those socks first." Celia said to her firmly.

Mark smirked again, "Oh, she's not wearing holey socks again," he said Celia raised an eyebrow at Mark and they both laughed as Sarah got up and hurried out of the room.

Duncan sighed, Celia was definitely a lot mellower now. He looked at Mark and Celia laughing and felt a pang of annoyance. They always seemed to have some private joke going between the two of them. He gazed out of the window and took a sip of his drink.

Mark glanced up as Sarah came back in to the room. She had put a clean pair of jeans on and a fresh top and had added some lip balm for good measure. Her backside was throbbing but at least Celia had been placated.

Mark stood up, "Okay girls let's party," he said with a grin and marched out of the house. He paused as he stepped outside, "My, it's getting misty out here," he turned and grinned at the others, "Better watch out for the werewolves," he gave a mock growl then marched off towards the Pub with Duncan trailing along behind him. Celia looked at Sarah who was biting her lip. Celia smiled with satisfaction. She needn't think that this was over yet.

CHAPTER 11

The Diddlecot Arms was a traditional old pub with wooden beams and a carpeted floor that looked like it had seen better days. It was a large expanse of a room with just a small separate dining area that you accessed through the main room.

Rory was sitting in a corner of the large room wondering whether anyone else would be turning up as he sipped on his pint of beer. He was also hoping that Lyn would arrive before anyone else so that he could test the water with her as to whether she might be inclined to spend some more time with him on a more physical level.

His prayers were answered as Lyn walked in to the pub. She paused to look around the room. There were a few locals at the bar gossiping and drinking beer. They stopped briefly to inspect her as she walked in. Lyn saw Rory and gave him a small wave before ordering a drink.

Rory smiled as she walked over with her diet coke. She was wearing faded blue skinny jeans and a fitted cream top. Her hair was fair with a hint of pale brown and it lay around her shoulders neatly. Rory swallowed quickly, she looked delightful. Lyn sat down beside him, not quite close enough for his liking. She eyed him for a moment and then spoke. "I'm glad that I got here before any one else, I wanted to ask you something."

Rory smiled back at her and managed to restrain himself from edging closer to her. He took a swallow of his beer and licked his lips turning back to her. Lyn also took a sip of her coke before she started, "It's a bit embarrassing really. That's why I wanted to talk without anyone else around."

Rory raised an eyebrow and said nothing, this was going

better than he could have expected. She must have a crush on him. He nodded at her and continued smiling. He'd better let her come out with it. He didn't want her to realize that he was quite happy to take their friendship one step further. It would be better if she did the running, then she would be much more eager to please him. He quickly took another swallow of his beer.

Lyn paused and stared at him, he looked like he'd just taken a shot of something a lot stronger than the beer. His eyes were wide open with a slightly glassy look and he had a strange smirk frozen on his face. Lyn wondered momentarily whether she should continue. She was still not one hundred percent sure as to whether Rory was the right person to speak to about this. She took another sip of her coke and mentally shrugged, oh well she supposed he was the best option she had at the moment.

"Well, I'm really fed up with getting nowhere with Quickie. I'm in a dilemma really. You see I think that I'm just not a good enough rider for him. He just doesn't seem to want to jump anything for me," she looked at him earnestly. Her eyes were wide and questioning. Rory blinked, was that it? She just wanted to ask him about her useless bloody horse? He stared back at her.

Lyn sighed, "I know that you're busy, but I was wondering if you'd have a go on him for me and just see how he goes for you over some fences. It's the only way I'll find out whether it's me or not. I really want to compete and I need to know if I'm good enough or not. At least I will know whether I'm wasting my time or not if someone else has a go on him," she looked at him again his mouth was slightly open. "I'll pay you, obviously," she added.

Rory blinked and took a deep breath to suppress his sudden feeling of irritation. He nodded at her slowly, "Yes I have noticed that you don't seem to be having much luck over the poles. But I really think that it might be better to just have a lesson first. A one to one perhaps, then I can really assess what's going on. "

Lyn nodded at him, "If that's what you think is best then I suppose we could give it a try..."

Rory patted her gently on the shoulder and nodded again. "As a professional, I can tell you that having someone get on your horse and sort it out for you is not the answer. The problem with doing that is that it doesn't address the real problem," he gave her a knowing smile. Lyn blinked at him, wondering why he suddenly looked a little flushed. She took another sip of her coke. "Yes I guess you're right. If I'm really no good then there's no point in anyone else riding him, as soon as I get back on he'll just grind to a halt again," she said with a sad nod.

Lyn was beginning to feel completely fed up. She hated her job in insurance and had been hoping that having a horse again would give her something to aim at outside of the office. Instead, it just seemed to be making her life even worse. She didn't even have a boyfriend to help comfort her.

Rory gave her shoulder a gentle stroke now. She looked as if she might burst into tears. "Hey, now don't worry I've seen you ride and I know that you are doing well, it's just a case of ironing things out between you and Quickie."

Lyn looked back at him and gave a small smile. "It sounds like you're talking about my boyfriend," she said and gave a short sad laugh. Rory stroked her shoulder for a moment more. Maybe this would be a good time to put forward the idea of a more physical liaison.

"I say this looks rather serious."

Rory turned around with a start only to see Ben grinning at them like an idiot. He had a pint in one hand and was fumbling to replace his wallet in his back pocket. Lyn smiled warmly at him, "I've just been discussing my equestrian failings." She said.

Ben widened his eyes "You don't have any failings, you're great," he grinned again as he plonked himself down next to Lyn. "You are still going to the horse trials?"

Rory rolled his eye. He wished this twit would push off. He should have been more careful about who he asked to the pub.

Lyn shook her head, "Oh Ben, I don't know, I'm beginning to think that I'll just make a complete fool of myself. I bet Quickie will just stop and we'll get eliminated after the first fence."

Ben shook his head, "You'll have to give it a try. Look on the bright side, he should get a good dressage test, he seems to enjoy doing that sort of thing."

Lyn nodded glumly "Yes he does seem to like his dressage."

Rory glared at his pint as he took another mouthful. Of course the horse liked dressage, he was a lazy beast and the dressage test only took a few minutes and hardly any effort on his part. Rory suspected that Quickstep was just plain bone idle and couldn't be arsed to make the effort to clear a course of jumps. He wondered which fool had christened him Quickstep in the first place. Someone had really taken the piss there.

Rory scowled sulkily at his pint as he listened to Ben encouraging Lyn to compete in the horse trials. The competition was only a few weeks away and most of the yard had decided to attend. This had been a decision following a similar meeting in the same pub. They had left in a flurry of enthusiasm, deciding that they would all go to the competition and give each other morale support. Rory wondered if it would be worth taking a video camera to film Heather cringing in fear as the show jumping started. He pondered as to whether she would ever decide which was worse - getting a bollocking from her mother or jumping a fence. He had a small smile on his face as he looked up to see Big Jayne standing in front of him with her hands on her hips. "Have I missed anything?" she asked with a slight smile.

A slender frail looking woman with short dark hair crept along behind her and placed two halves of lager on the table. Big Jayne nodded at her "I texted Jane and she said she'd come along for the ride," she said gesturing with her thumb as Jane sat down opposite Rory. Big Jayne pulled a chair out and sat on it with a large thump. She turned back to Lyn and Ben "Are you two talking about the trials? I can't wait, it's going to be so thrilling."

Lyn and Ben both nodded at her. Jane felt her stomach do a back flip. She was so worried that her daughter Britney was going to fall off. Britney seemed to have no fear and would probably fly around the cross country taking all the shortest most terrifying routes. Jane took a quick gulp of her lager.

Lyn and Ben nodded at Big Jayne and Jane, "Yes," said Ben with a smile "It'll be great. I'll bet your two girls are looking forwards to it too?"

Big Jayne pressed her lips together and nodded. Truth was, Heather seemed scared to death. Big Jayne swallowed some lager as she wondered why Heather was just so dam scared of leaving the ground on horseback. She had invested a considerable sum of money on purchasing Firefox and all Heather had to do was point and steer. Firefox could get her out of the trickiest of situations, if she just had the nerve to have a go.

Jane gave a weary smile "Britney can't wait. It's all she talks about. She just needs to get Whitney a bit more fired up," she glanced at Rory who seemed to be engrossed in his pint. ""You're still coming aren't you?" She asked him.

Rory glanced up, momentarily shaken from his reverie. He leaned back with a smile "Of course, I'll be on hand to help you all out."

Ben grinned at him, "You should be taking part, you can show us how it's done."

Rory rolled back his shoulders, "There's no point. I've evented and show jumped to a high level. I need a bigger competition really, one that qualifies for an important final. I just don't feel motivated otherwise, plus it wouldn't be fair on all the real novices to have a pro competing against them."

Rory sat back looking smug. It wasn't strictly the truth. Ted had done all of the jumping and cross country before Rory bought him. As well as winning in show jumping he'd also shown promise as an eventer. That silly cow who'd sold him could have got loads more money for him if she hadn't been in such a hurry to get rid of him. Still, it had been Rory's gain. Ted had the breeding to be a great dressage horse and as he'd had the basics of dressage already instilled in him Rory's just needed to refine him.

Ben took a swallow of his beer and nodded. His face suddenly lit up. "Oh did anyone see that notice in the Horse and Hound last week about the clinics?" Big Jayne and Lyn both looked at him eagerly. Rory took a deep breath, he felt like strangling him. Lyn's eyes were wide, "What clinics? Are they local?"

Ben swallowed "Oh yes, Lucinda Lilac is holding a clinic at Berryford. It's the only one that's within traveling distance of here. Perhaps we should see if we could go. "

Big Jayne's eyes widened "Lucinda Lilac? Are you sure?"

Ben licked his lips and nodded keenly, "Yes definitely and when I checked on line there were still some places left."

Rory was glowering at his pint again. Lyn was glowing with excitement she looked ravishing. Rory wished he could ditch the others off.

Lyn sat upright looking at Ben enthusiastically " Oh could you let me know the details?"

Jane's face had gone a shade paler, "No doubt Britney will want to go." She murmured. Big Jayne grinned. "This could be the making of Heather. Lucinda Lilac is amazing."

Rory had had enough. "We were supposed to be discussing the new livery," He said looking around sharply. "That was the point in us meeting here, remember?"

Ben was grinning happily and Lyn was gazing into space dreamily. Big Jayne was smiling to herself and Jane looked like she was about to have a nervous breakdown.

Rory rolled his eyes. "Well, what about the new horse then? Should we be reporting them to someone about the state he's in?" He said looking at each one of them in turn.

Ben shrugged, "We don't know enough about him really. There could be stuff we don't know that's gone on that explains everything"

Lyn blinked and came back to earth. She nodded, "Yes, perhaps we should ask Sarah about him?" She said and took a gulp of her coke. She couldn't stop thinking about the clinic.

Big Jayne folded her arms and stretched her legs out underneath the table. "Yes, perhaps we should mention to Sarah that we're not happy," she said, gazing into space. She wondered if Lucinda Lilac could fit in a private lesson for Heather while she was at Berryford.

Rory stole another glance at Lyn and sighed. It was no good now. She was in a dream world. Probably imagining herself flying over fences with that stupid creature Quickstep. If only she realised, she'd be better of selling the animal and getting something decent. She was too soppy though. She worried about selling the wretched beast. No doubt she would stop jumping and switch to dressage rather than sell him.

Rory smiled to himself. Yes, if she switched to dressage he could give her lessons and then they could spend some time alone together. Maybe he should persuade her to do that instead. He licked his lips. Perhaps that was the way to go. He must give her a lesson that would be the way to start things off.

Jane sipped her drink and then said quietly, "Who's going to ask Sarah about the new horse then?" She looked around quickly eyebrows raised.

Big Jayne patted her hand' Oh don't worry Rory can ask," she smiled at Rory who stared at her. "Well you've been at the yard the longest. You get on with her best and you're such a pro. You've dealt with things like this before I'm sure."

Rory managed not to choke on his drink. Cheeky cow, how did she manage to do that? She always weaseled her way out of doing crappy stuff. He swallowed and nodded quietly. "All right." He said looking heavenward. "I'll sort it out," he wished he had never suggested the meeting in the first place he thought as he leaned back in his seat.

Ben nodded at him happily, "That's great. Well, here's your chance," he said nudging Lyn and looking at Rory. "She's just walked in!"

Rory felt his stomach lurch as he turned to see Sarah, Celia, Mark and Duncan stroll into the pub

CHAPTER 12

Chloe stared at the bottle. It seemed to glow dimly in the light from the kitchen. Jade was standing behind Steve gazing at it and Steve also stared at it in silence.

They all jumped suddenly as Jerry leapt up on to the table. He strolled across to Chloe and sat in front of her regarding her with his amber eyes. Jade let out a sigh and smiled. Steve pulled out a chair and sat down opposite Chloe again.

Jerry looked at Chloe unblinking and for a moment she stared back at him, admiring his smiling face and golden eyes. She gave a slight smile as he stretched out his nose and sniffed at the bottle. He started purring loudly and tried to rub the side of his face against it. Chloe reached out quickly to stop it falling over. Jade laughed delightedly and sat down next to Steve without thinking.

Chloe smiled and touched Jerry's head. He closed his eyes and sat back, purring loudly. Chloe opened the silver lid and peered inside the bottle. It had some kind of powder inside. She shook a little out on to the palm of her hand.

Steve frowned, "Be careful, you don't know what's in that. It could be something toxic."

Chloe paused for a moment and then sniffed at the palm of her hand. "It doesn't smell of anything."

Jade reached over to rub Jerry's head as he continued purring. He lifted his head to push it further into Jade's stroking hand. A misting of fur was wafting over the table, as if in sympathy for the weather outside. Chloe shook her head at it and stared back at the powdery substance in her hand.

Steve looked at her "Where would this come from? Is it something from the vet do you think?"

Chloe shook her head. "No the vet didn't give my aunt this. He just gave her some bute for Sam and said he needed resting and possibly some expensive therapy," she looked back at Steve. "The prognosis wasn't very good though, even with the extra therapy," she sat back in her chair and took a deep breath still holding the substance carefully in the palm of her hand.

"My uncle was a physicist. He had some high profile job with a Global company. I'm not sure what he did, it wasn't really ever mentioned."

Jade's eyes widened and she looked at Chloe curiously, "You mean he was some kind of scientist?"

Chloe smiled, "Yes, something like that. My aunt was a horse person though. She infected him with her passion and he became interested in their bloodlines and breeding too. She used to have a horse of her own."

Steve looked at her curiously, "Did you used to ride it?"

Chloe's stared back at him and paused for a moment. "Yes," she stopped and then took a deep breath, she might as well tell them, they'd find out sooner or later. "I lived with my aunt and uncle. After my parents died," she said staring at the powder in her hand.

Steve glanced at Jade who was staring at Chloe with a shocked expression on her face. She had stopped stroking Jerry. Chloe had never talked about her past, come to that, Chloe had never talked about anything except work. Jade saw Steve looking at her and tried not to blush. She had sat next to him without thinking and now she realised how close to her he was. She looked down and smiled to herself.

Jerry continued to sit in front of Chloe as she spoke. He had stopped purring when Jade stopped stroking him and he was now looking over at the cupboard where his food was kept.

Chloe took another deep breath, "Yes, I was with them for a while," she stared at the table, "They were very good to me. Even after I left and…," she stopped and looked up quickly. "Anyhow, that's why I'm sorting this lot out. There is no one else now. "

Steve and Jade now looked at her intently. Chloe continued, " this place is a bit of a mess by all accounts and we need to sort this horse out."

Steve was intrigued, "What do we need to do?"

Chloe sighed, "Well, under the terms of the will, I can't sell or remove any animals from the care of the estate."

Jade blinked at her, "Well what happens to the horse then if you can't put him in one of those holiday homes?"

Chloe managed not to laugh. "I have to use any funds available from the estate to keep him under its care until he's lived out his life. I'm only allowed to re home him if he competes and shows enough promise for someone to want to carry on competing him and look after him properly. And that's not going to happen with that leg."

Jade smiled "Oh well then you can just let him stay at that yard then."

Chloe gave a cynical smile, "It's not that simple. Unfortunately there's hardly any money left in the estate to pay for him."

Steve licked his lips, "I know this is harsh but he may not have much longer if his legs that bad. The vet may say he has to be put to sleep anyhow."

Jade's eyes widened in horror, "Oh no, how could you say such a thing, poor horse."

Chloe smiled at Jade's outburst, she was such a sentimentalist, "It's okay Jade, the vet said he might recover and be able to carry out light duties. Under the terms of the will that means that he won't be put down. That's only allowed to happen if he's suffering or he has no quality of life and all that, you know what I mean," she finished looking at Steve who nodded back at her.

Jade smiled "That's fine then, you will have to give him some of that stuff and see if he gets better then," she said pointing at the bottle.

Chloe rolled her eyes, "Jade I don't even know what's in it. It could be nothing. "

"But your aunt wouldn't have left a message to give it to him if it would hurt him would she?" Jade ventured.

Steve nodded. "From what you've said Jade's right. It must be the same formula that she was referring to, so we'll have to give him some of it and see if it helps."

Chloe sniffed at the powder again and then stuck her other finger into her palm and moved the sandy powder around. Jerry now watched her with interest. He reached his nose forwards and sniffed at her hand. He paused and then raised his front paw and gently touched her hand. Jade grinned with pleasure, "Look Jerry says it's fine," she smiled.

Chloe gave her a stern look, "Jade, Jerry is a cat. Besides, I think that Jerry wants his tea," she said getting up from the table and walking over to the sink. She dusted the powder from her palm and rinsed her hand under the tap.

Jade jumped up to get a sachet of food out for Jerry who

leapt off the table to follow her. He landed on the floor with a small squeaky meow. Causing Jade to let out a short laugh. "Oh Jerry, you need oiling," she smiled.

Chloe turned around, observing Jade. She watched as Jade gave Jerry his food, stroking him fondly as she did so. Jerry was purring loudly again. Jade stood up and turned around. Chloe couldn't help but smile. Jade's suit was now covered in grey fur. Jade looked back at her and raised an eyebrow' "What?"

Chloe shook her head, "Nothing," she really was going to have to sort out some clothes for Jade. She leaned against the sink. "It's getting late, we really should have some dinner."

Steve nodded realizing that he was also famished. Chloe opened the fridge and started rummaging around and then stopped, shutting it with a sigh. "I don't think I can be bothered to cook anything. Can we get a take away around here these days?" She asked Steve.

Steve laughed, "Nope. You'd have to drive into town. There's always the pub though, they do basic food."

Chloe pondered on this for a moment and then walked back to the table and sat down again. She suddenly felt incredibly tired. "I don't know if I can even be bothered with that."

Jade jumped forward, "I'll sort us something out," she said brightly. She had noticed Chloe's drawn expression. She had not seen her look that way before. She switched on the oven and opened the fridge. After a short while she turned around triumphantly. "Pizza and salad," she smiled, "we still have our supplies."

"How about a glass of wine too," said Chloe, "I could do with one."

Steve looked at her. She did look tired. He turned to see that Jade was busying herself with the salad, "Do you want a hand with that Jade?" He asked.

Jade smiled to herself, "No, I can manage."

Finally Jade finished her food preparation. She took off her jacket and sat down to wait for the Pizza to cook. She glanced at Chloe who appeared to be in deep thought. Chloe looked back at her, "We need to try to find out what's in that formula. There are lots of files with codes and stuff in the library. We must have a look through them and try to find out what it's in it."

Jade blinked "But I don't know what to look for," she said.

"But you're still going to give Sam some of it?" Asked Steve.

'I don't see that I have much choice," said Chloe with resignation. "But I just think we should try to find out what's in it."

Jade stole a worried glance at Steve who smiled reassuringly back at her. She felt herself blushing and looked down at the table. Chloe saw the exchange and rolled her eyes but she was smiling as she took another sip of wine. She suddenly got up from the table, "I'm going to get that paperwork about the will. I need to have another look at it," she announced.

Jade looked at her as she rose from the table, "What will we do if Sam doesn't get better?"

Chloe paused. "Jade, I really have no idea. To be honest I think the house will have to be sold anyhow, it's just too expensive to run and there's hardly any money left to pay any of the bills."

"Why don't you have the house? You could run it." Jade

smiled at her with wide expectant eyes.

Chloe frowned at her, "what on earth would I do with a place like this?"

"You could keep Sam here until he's better. When you can use the field you'll have lots of space for him. You could even get him a friend." Jade said beaming excitedly. Steve smiled at her and nodded.

Chloe looked heavenward, what was she going to do with these two dreamers. "It's not going to happen. It's just not practical," she said as she left the room.

Chloe entered the sitting room and fired up her laptop. She looked around. Where was that paperwork? She looked again. She thought she had left it over there on the coffee table. She wandered over and then looked around the room. She couldn't see the paperwork anywhere. She paused to glance out of the large window. The night had drawn in but she could still see the thick fog billowing outside. She shivered. Everything seemed so quiet.

Chloe jumped as she heard a sudden noise. What was that? It sounded like a thud but she couldn't tell where it had come from. She walked over to the window and peered outside. She couldn't see anything. She turned back and stopped.

There were the papers. They had been on the chair by the fireplace. She frowned to herself. How could she have missed them? She picked up her laptop along with the papers and walked back to the kitchen with them tucked under her arm.

Steve and Jade were chatting. Jade was glowing a warm shade of red. Chloe sat back down at the table and put her laptop on top of the papers, opening its cover. "Did you hear a funny noise?" She asked them. Steve and Jade both looked at her questioningly.

"What sort of noise?" Steve asked.

Chloe stared at her laptop. "A kind of a thud."

Steve and Jade both shook their heads slowly.

Jade's eyes were widening, "Why? Did you hear something strange?" She asked. Chloe raised an eye to her, and looked quickly back at her laptop. Jade had an expression of fixed fear creeping across her face.

"It was nothing," said Chloe dismissively, "must have been me, hearing things."

Jade shook her head. Chloe wasn't the type to imagine things. "You don't think this place is haunted do you?" She asked. She looked horrified.

Chloe shook her head and looked up. Steve was staring at her curiously. She didn't think she could pull the wool over his eyes. Steve turned to Jade. "It's an old house, there's bound to be creaks and stuff. There's probably mice in the attic too."

"Mice!" Jade was mortified "They won't come into my room will they?" She paused staring helplessly at Steve who managed not to laugh at her horrified expression.

There was a sudden thump and Jade nearly screamed as she leapt back in her chair.

Jerry was on the table again. He sat down and started purring loudly.

Chloe and Steve both burst out laughing. "Oh Jerry," said Chloe reaching out to stroke him, "You're a star." Jerry closed his eyes and purred even louder.

Chloe sat back in her chair and once more she observed the blue bottle. "I'd better keep an eye on this." She said and pulled it across the table next to her laptop. "How's that pizza doing?" She asked Jade who was stroking Jerry. Jade got up, "Should be done I'll serve up," she answered through a cloud of grey fur.

Steve exchanged glances with Chloe. Chloe gave a wry smile. Steve sat back in his chair. He wasn't sure what he was getting involved with here but it certainly looked like it was going to be interesting.

CHAPTER 13

The morning was bright and sunny without a trace of fog in sight. Kelly paused to enjoy the warmth of the sunshine on her face as she swept the yard. She looked up as a car pulled up by the house.

Kelly had decided not to bother going to the Pub to meet the others, No doubt Rory would probably just spent his time running down the new horse. Kelly got sick of hearing him barking on sometimes, he could be so bitchy. She finished her sweeping and piled all the rubbish into the wheelbarrow, ready to cart it to the muckheap.

Lyn wandered over from her car as she saw her, "morning Kelly," she smiled.

Kelly smiled back, "nice day. How did the team meeting go?"

Lyn laughed. "Rory's been delegated to speak to Sarah about the new arrival," she shook her head, "you know Sarah came in to the Pub, but he said he'd speak to her here. He said a pub wasn't the "appropriate place" to discuss these types of matters."

Kelly nodded she wasn't the least bit surprised. The more she saw of Rory the more she thought that he was all talk.

They both looked up as the black X5 pulled up. Lyn raised an eyebrow. "Looks like the new arrivals are wanting an early start." Kelly and Lyn watched as Chloe, Steve and Jade got out of the car.

Kelly grinned at Lyn. "He's a bit of all right isn't he?"

Lyn looked at her in surprise and then laughed again. "Oh Kelly!" She exclaimed and tried to stifle her smile.

Chloe gave them a quick nod. "Morning."

Kelly looked at Chloe. "I've given him some hay and feed," she said.

"Thank you," said Chloe. Steve smiled at them as they walked past. Jade was walking next to him. She was feeling slightly apprehensive about being around the horses again but Chloe had insisted that she come along. Chloe was hoping that Jade might overcome her nerves if she were made to spend more time with the horses. She had also insisted that Jade borrow a pair of jeans from her. Unfortunately this had only added to Jade's nerves. Jade was walking carefully trying to avoid any mud or dust. She had noticed that the jeans were designer and must have cost a huge amount. She was now terrified of getting any dirt or horse muck on them or even worse ripping them.

Lyn avoided looking at Kelly as the others walked past. She knew that she would only start laughing again. Lyn composed herself and followed them into the stable block. She saw that they had gone straight to the horse's stable. As she entered Quickstep's box she turned an ear towards them curiously but couldn't catch what was being sad as they were speaking in rather hushed tones.

Jade stood behind Steve and Chloe inside Sam's box. Sam turned to them and nuzzled Chloe happily as he chewed on his mouthful of hay. Chloe stroked him and turned to Steve "Go and get some food and we'll give him some of the formula." She said quietly. She was holding the bottle close to her side, hiding it under her coat.

Steve nodded and waked out of the box. Chloe looked at Jade. "He won't hurt you. Here, give him a stroke. Jade was standing against the wall of the box trying to avoid a pile of droppings. She moved a pink wellington clad foot slightly closer to Chloe and looked at Sam. "He's so big," she said, staring at him in awe "How do you know he won't bite me?"

Chloe rolled her eyes. "Because I just do, now come here and give him a stroke," she ordered grabbing Jade's arm and pulling her closer to Sam.

Jade took a sharp intake of breath as she realised that she was now standing right next to this enormous creature's shoulder. Chloe smiled at her. "Go on, stroke him," she commanded raising her eyebrows at her.

Jade swallowed and tentatively reached her hand out towards Sam. She cautiously stretched out two fingers and touched his withers. She stopped and pulled her hand back quickly. Sam looked at her for a moment, still chewing on his hay and then turned back to his fodder to pull out another mouthful.

Jade gave a small smile and reached out her hand again. This time she carefully placed it on his withers and ran it down across his shoulder. Her smile broke into a grin that made Chloe smile too.

"See, that's not too bad is it?" Asked Chloe.

"He feels so soft," said Jade, continuing to run her hand up and down his shoulder.

Chloe moved across to Sam's head and gave him a rub behind his ears. He leaned into her hand and cocked his head to one side his lips started flapping about in enjoyment.

Jade laughed. "He likes that."

Chloe nodded, "You see, he's just like a big cat," she rolled her eyes at herself, "Well, perhaps not, don't get too carefree around these animals."

Jade looked at her in alarm. "But I thought you said they were safe?"

Chloe stopped rubbing Sam's ears. "Well most are most of the time but you still need to be careful. Oh and watch they don't step on your feet. They'll quite happily stand on your feet without budging."

Jade's eyes were wide again. "What? No! Why would they do that?"

Chloe shrugged, "I suppose they don't notice and they have hooves so they probably think that we can't feel anything."

Jade was looking at Sam in wonderment as Steve came back into the box. He glanced at Jade and frowned, "Is she all right?" He asked Chloe.

Chloe nodded. "Yes, she's been fussing Sam."

Steve nodded back, "of course."

Sam had homed in on the feed bowl as soon as Steve came in to the stable. With a small whicker he thrust his head into the bowl. Steve put it down on the floor in front of him.

Chloe glanced quickly around to check that no one was watching and took the bottle out from underneath her coat. She held it up for a moment and then took the lid off. "How much should I give him?'

"Did your aunt not say how much? Asked Steve.

Chloe shook her head. "No she just said to "give him the formula"."

"Then perhaps you should give it all to him?"

Jade nodded in agreement.

"No." Chloe said shaking her head. "I'll give him half of it," she looked at Steve, "We still don't know what it is. I don't want to overdose him," she stepped forwards and sprinkled the powder into Sam's feed bowl.

Sam paused briefly and stopped eating the food. He lifted his head up slightly and sniffed at the powder.

Jade opened her mouth in dismay. "Oh no, he's not going to eat it."

Sam sniffed again at the powder. This time he inhaled its smell deeper into his nostrils. After the sniff he thrust his head back into the food and devoured the remaining mix, powder and all.

Chloe let out a sigh of relief and slipped the bottle back under her coat as she watched Sam lick the bowl clean. Jade watched Sam with wide eyes as if expecting him to suddenly turn into some magical beast. Sam turned around and looked at them. His ears were pricked, he was checking to see if they had any more food for him.

Steve looked at Chloe and raised an eyebrow. "Well now we'll have to wait and see if it has any effect."

Jade turned to Chloe. "What if it doesn't do anything?"

Chloe glanced at her, "I'm not getting my hopes up anyhow, but we'd just have to see what the vets can do. If we can afford to pay for anything that is."

Steve nodded. "I'll get a wheelbarrow and clean out his box," he said walking off outside to find some mucking out tools. He wandered out across the yard, glancing across at the manege as he went. He looked up in time to see a horse sliding into the bottom of a small fence. The horse dropped his shoulder to the right as he stopped, depositing the girl riding him firmly on the ground.

Steve jumped up and ran across to the manege. He ducked under the fence and across to where she was. She was sitting up rubbing her arm. Steve looked at her. "Are you all right?" He asked.

Lyn looked up at him. It was that good looking guy with the new horse. She felt herself flush with embarrassment. Typical. The first time she'd spoken to him and it was just after being dumped on the ground.

Lyn nodded. "Yes, I think I'm all right. Thank you."

Steve held out his hand and she held on to it with her free arm as she got to her feet. Her right arm was aching and she let go of his hand to give it another rub.

Steve was looking at her with concern. "Is that arm all right? Let me have a look."

Before she could protest he took her right arm and pushed her sleeve further up to inspect it. He studied it for a while and gently manipulated it around. Lyn was rendered speechless as she felt his touch on her. He looked at her again, "does it hurt when I move it at all?"

"No," she managed looking back into his blue eyes. She swallowed. Steve smiled, "Hopefully nothing's broken then, it's just bruised. But you should still get it checked, especially if it gives you any more problems."

"Thank you Doctor." Lyn managed a small smile.

Steve looked at Quickstep who was trying to eat the grass on the other side of the manege. "You should never jump by yourself. Just in case."

Lyn nodded, "yes I know, I'm not supposed to. To be honest it's not allowed, but Sarah's not about," she looked back at Quickstep and then glanced at Steve who was looking at her questioningly. She swallowed again, "I just thought I'd have a go while no one was here. I'm sick of being laughed at," she said glumly.

"Does he make a habit of dumping you then?" Steve asked.

"He could make a career out of it," said Lyn with a cynical smile. "I don't suppose I help though, I must be doing something wrong for it to happen so often."

Steve shook his head. "Would you like me to give you a hand for a minute? If you're up for getting back on that is."

Lyn nodded. "Yes I'd better get on now before I start to think too much about it," she gave her arm a final rub and they both walked over to Quickstep who lifted his head and regarded them for a moment before continuing on his quest to eat the grass on the other side of the fence.

Steve gave Lyn a leg up and watched her for a moment. Lyn managed to compose herself and cantered Quickstep around on both reins before bringing him back to a walk in front of Steve.

Steve shook his head, do you always have to boot him like that?"

Lyn nodded, "oh yes, pretty much all of the time."

Steve walked over to the show jump and moved the poles so that it was a sharp angled cross pole. "Ready to have another go?"

Lyn took a deep breath and nodded. She headed off and cantered back around to the cross pole. Quickstep cantered happily around until he was just in front of the fence. He ground to a halt in front of it with his head virtually on the floor. Lyn had already been holding on to his breastplate, just in case, so she managed to stay on board.

Suddenly Quickstep jumped forward over the fence. He did an over exaggerated leap over it and landed with a grunt on the other side. Lyn was thrown out of the saddle but managed to stay on again as he landed on the other side. She pulled him up and walked back to Steve who was standing watching with eyebrows raised.

Steve cleared his throat. "My, you weren't kidding," he looked at Quickstep who had his eyes half closed. Steve shook his head. "Perhaps I could have a ride on him?" He asked Lyn.

Lyn's expression brightened. "Do you have much experience of these things?"

Steve nodded. He wasn't going to bore her with the time that he had spent at a show jumping yard or grooming at eventing stables. He'd always managed to find some work on horse yards, even if it was usually temporary. He'd also discovered that he seemed to have a knack for reschooling the difficult horses.

Steve mounted and rode Quickstep around the arena, putting him through each gait. Steve brought him back to a trot and then asked him to canter. Quickstep continued with his listless trot. Quickstep had decided that he'd had enough exercise for one day. Steve picked up the stick that Lyn had shoved down the middle of the saddle and pulled it into his hand.

He gave Quickstep three sharp whacks on the backside.

Quickstep shot forwards into canter. He was completely shocked he hadn't been whacked like that for years. He cocked an ear on Steve suspiciously.

Lyn bit her lip as Steve smacked Quickstep. Rory had told her she must use more leg on him. Still, he was certainly looking a lot livelier with Steve on board. Lyn looked up as she heard a car arrive. She saw the grey Mitsubishi and gave an internal groan. It was Rory. No doubt he'd have something to say about this.

Lyn watched as Steve cantered around the manage and then popped over the fence, Quickstep showed no sign of refusing and flew along with an ear continually flicking backwards towards his new rider.

Steve pulled Quickstep up in front of Lyn just as Rory sauntered over to the manege. Steve smiled at her. "He's a cheeky beggar this one. Lazy too, he's just trying it on with you, he knows you'll be soft with him."

Lyn sighed, she had suspected as much. It just made her feel miserable now that Steve had confirmed that she was rubbish.

Steve noted her expression. "Hey, it doesn't mean you're no good. It just means you're too soft with him. Maybe you should think about moving him on to someone who just wants to plod around the lanes and getting yourself something with a bit more energy and less attitude."

Rory rolled his eyes. "Do you have much experience in teaching? Are you qualified? I'm an AI, by the way. Have we met before? You're not setting a very good example, you know, you should be wearing a hat," he snapped from behind the fence.

Steve smiled at Lyn again and jumped off Quickstep handing

him back to Lyn. He looked at Rory who looked suddenly uncomfortable. Steve also gave him a warm smile. "I'm surprised you haven't helped her to sort this out before now. Seen as how you're qualified and obviously so knowledgeable."

He turned back to Lyn and gave her a wink causing her to grin. Her face started to redden and she bit her lip. She noticed Rory's expression darken as Steve hopped over the fence and went back to finish his mucking out.

Rory looked back at her angrily. "That's it! I'm going to speak to Sarah about this and they needn't think that they're staying on this yard!" Rory turned on his heel and marched towards the house. It was about time he got this sorted out. There was only room for one expert on this yard and that was him.

CHAPTER 14

Paul was leaning against the tack room doorway with his arms folded watching Ella cleaning tack. Joanne was propped on a chair in the corner of the tack room trying to clean a bridle with her good arm.

Ella glanced at Paul. "You could help you know," she said glaring at him.

Paul smirked and regarded her with his head on one side. "That's girls work."

Ella rolled her eyes and looked back across at Joanne who had one end of the bridle's headpiece in her mouth and the other wedged between her knees as she tried to clean the dirt from it. She shook her head. "You're just getting saddle soap everywhere, you might as well leave it."

Joanne sighed and looked at Paul who was still smirking in the tack room doorway. He looked so smug. She wasn't sure about Paul he had an air of slyness about him. It was a shame that Steve had left, he'd been so good looking and he seemed a lot more honest than Paul. On the other hand, Paul had his jockey licence and would be going places, by all accounts. Joanne ran her good hand through her unruly bob and stared at the floor. She was fed up already with being partly incapacitated.

Paul licked his lips. "You fancy a fag?' He asked looking at each of them in turn as he reached into his pocket and pulled out a packet of Marlboro lights.

Ella looked at him and shook her head, "you know that's not allowed!'" She said, a bit too sharply for Paul's liking. "What if Celia catches you? You'll be given the push."

Paul shook his head and gave her a knowing smile. "Celia

didn't get back until late last night, she won't be up for ages. Any how, she wouldn't sack me, she knows that I'm going to get some winners for her," he said giving Joanne a wink.

Joanne gaped at him as he lit up a cigarette and took a long puff. Ella turned back to her tack, "Those won't do you any good for competing either. Don't forget the horse trials are on in two weeks."

Pal took another drag on the cigarette. "What a waste of my time that crap is."

Joanne frowned at him. "But I thought it was good for improving the horses jumping?"

Paul leaned further against the doorframe of the tack room. "That was the idea but it seems that she wants to use it as a marketing exercise now. She's going to try and sell some of the horses on for eventing that won't make it in racing."

Ella stopped for a moment and swallowed, she looked at Paul. "Do you think Celia would let me compete in the trials? She hasn't mentioned anything yet but I've been doing enough schooling with the horses on their flat work and over jumps," she looked quickly back at the tack and gave it another wipe.

Paul smiled at her. "Has she not said your going to compete yet?"

"No, and I thought that she wanted Mary to go there, that's why I've been doing extra work with her," she added as she rubbing furiously at the tack. She didn't want Paul to know how much she wanted to compete at the trials. He was far too smug for his own good already.

Joanne looked glumly at them. "Well, I certainly won't be going anywhere," she said waving her broken arm in the air.

Paul gave a derisive laugh. "Did you seriously think that you were going anywhere anyway?" He said nastily. He looked back at Ella and winked.

Ella frowned at him as she saw Joanne's downcast face. "Jo, " she said, "Why don't you make us a coffee I could really do with one, and bring some of those biscuits out. The ones with the nuts and chocolate chips in."

Joanne nodded. She was feeling rather peckish herself. She pulled herself up from the chair with a sigh. She walked out of the tack room giving Paul an evil stare as she passed him. Sometimes he was so nasty.

Ella waited until she'd gone. "Why did you have to say that? Don't you think she's down in the dumps already without you adding to it?"

Paul took another drag of the cigarette and threw his head back to exhale the smoke. "Oh please, that dumpy little cow's never going to be any good on a horse. She's hopeless and she's nervous as hell. She's lucky she hasn't had a worse injury before now."

Ella scowled at him. "You could at least give her a chance."

Paul laughed. "What? Give her a chance to kill herself? Or worse still someone else. She needs to be told, she should go and get a normal job and go and find a bloke and have a few kids. That's what she was made for."

Ella stared at him in disbelief, "I can't believe that you just said that. You sexist shallow pig!"

Paul laughed again and threw his cigarette on the floor crushing it under his foot. He looked at her for a moment. Her blond hair cascaded around her shoulders like a waterfall and her skintight jodhpurs showed off her slender physique. He felt pleasant warmth begin to quell inside him.

Paul had only had a couple of girlfriends but he had made sure that he had plenty of sexual experience by sneaking off into the City and paying for the services of hookers. He had found this most beneficial and rather educating, particularly when the only available women had been a bit older than him.

Ella glanced back at him. He was gazing at her quite salaciously. She turned back quickly to her cleaning.

Paul moved from the doorway and into the tack room to stand beside Ella. He reached out a finger to touch her hair. Ella moved her head away. "What are you doing now?" She asked warily.

"You've got some straw in your hair." Paul lied, pretending to flick something on the floor.

"Oh." Ella said. She removed the bridle from the hook and hung it back on its bracket on the other side of the tack room. She turned around to find Paul standing in front of her.

Paul was smiling at her, but his smile was not filled with warmth. "You know if you really want to compete in those trials and other things, come to think of it, I could help you do that. Celia is always asking me who I think should be doing what around here. You just need to do a few things for me in return," he said quietly. He was enjoying this, and she hadn't tried to move away from him yet.

Ella looked at him, considering his words. He was staring at her with that strange smile still on his face. She had a feeling that he wanted more than just his tack to be cleaned.

Ella really wanted to get on and do something with horses that was a bit more fulfilling than just shoveling muck or cleaning tack. Although she thought that Paul was a weasel

Celia did seem to look upon him as her head lad. He also had his jockey licence and would probably be riding in some real races soon.

Paul felt his stomach lurch as he saw Ella's expression soften. He reached out his hand and touched her neck beneath her hair, running the outside of his finger downwards slowly. "I could really help you get on if you were just bit nicer you know," he said.

Ella stopped and looked at him. Her blue eyes regarded him softly. "I really do want to get on, perhaps you could help me," she said quietly.

Paul a tingle of excitement, he moved towards her swiftly, putting his other hand behind the other side of her neck he ran both hands down her neck together. She leaned her head back and closed her eyes. Paul leaned forwards to murmur in her ear. "There's no one about and that dopey cow will take an age to get the coffee, maybe you could show me how willing you are to learn".

Ella swallowed. She had only had two previous sexual encounters and they had both been a disaster. The first was with the school heart throb behind the bike sheds. She had thought that he would whisk her off her feet and show her how to make passionate love for the first time. He had simply had a quick snog and a tweak of her breast then span her round, shoved her skirt up and thrust his cock inside her. A few thrusts later and he had slumped over her with a cry as he ejaculated. She had wondered what all the fuss was about as he flicked his condom into the corner and dragged her back to classes.

The next encounter had been on holiday in Wales with her parents. She had sneaked off with Joanne and two local lads to the beach while her parents were playing crazy golf. This time he had been so eager that they had barely got down in the sand and he was pumping away like a rabbit inside her gasping with every thrust before he finally gave a squeak and threw his head back shouting "I've fucked a goddess!" while she lay back waiting for something to happen. It had taken an age to get the sand out of everything and Joanne couldn't stop shrieking with laughter when she told her about it.

Ella looked at Paul who gazed back at her. The lust in his eyes was tangible. He licked his lips in anticipation and planted a kiss gently on her neck. She didn't move away.

Paul felt elated. Christ, she might actually go through with this. He decided to take charge. He turned around and shut the tack room door, sliding the lock across. He looked back at Ella who was gazing back at him with those big blue eyes of hers. He rolled back his shoulders and gave her his most steely gaze, "First of all, take off your top and those jodhpurs." He moved back and sat in the chair to watch, as she did as he asked.

Ella swallowed, a little nervous now, she paused and then pulled her top over her head. She pulled off her wellies and then dragged off her jodhpurs. She was glad that she was wearing decent underwear. That was more by luck than judgement. Fortunately her greyed out undies were in the wash so she was wearing a pale pink bra with matching knickers.

Paul smiled at her, admiring her slender body and the way hair fell around her shoulders in appealing blonde waves. He had a sudden thought. "Put your riding boots on," he ordered.

Ella always wore her boots to ride in and she left them in the tack room. She didn't favour chaps, much preferring her long black leather boots which zipped up along the back of her calf

Her parents had bought them for her two Christmases ago and she had looked after them well, polishing them to distraction. She saw Paul smiling as she slid them on.

She turned back to him. He was still staring at her with a predatorial smile. He got up and picked up a sponge from the water that she had been using to clean the tack. He walked over to her, his gaze never left her face. He placed the sponge on her head and squeezed some water from it. She gasped as she felt the cold water run from it down her head and neck and across her shoulders. The water ran down her body in rivulets. He reached into the bucket and poured more over her, enjoying the sound of her gasps as the cold water covered her.

He stepped back and looked at her, standing in front of him in her boots. Her underwear was soaking now. You could see her nipples protruding from her bra and the darkness of her hair through her knickers. Paul felt himself grow hard as he looked at her. He walked over to her and grabbed her firmly by her hair. He pulled her head back and kissed her roughly. He grasped her bra and dragged it down quickly, grabbing her breast and pulling at her nipple. He stopped kissing her mouth and turned to her breast. He started sucking and chewing on her, delighting in the feel of her breast in his mouth and the sound of her moans as he bit her lightly.

Paul stopped and moved back from her. He turned and pulled a lead rope from a hook. He grabbed her arms and pulled her wrists towards him. He looked at her. She was watching him with an expression of curious anticipation. He gave a small smile and bound her wrists together with the lead rope. He pulled her towards him and pointed at a saddle rack. "Sit!" He ordered and pushed her on to the saddle sitting on the rack. Ella obeyed feeling a rise of excitement inside her.

When she had seated herself on the saddle Paul pulled her

wrists above her head with the lead rope and fixed the end of it around the bridle hook above her. With her arms stretched upwards her breasts were pulled provocatively upwards. He stood back and grinned wickedly. This was just how he wanted her.

He undid his trousers and pulled them off revealing his erect penis trying to escape from his underpants. He pulled down his underpants and threw them aside. Ella noted with surprise, that he was rather well endowed for one so slight in build. No wonder he always looked so smug.

He pulled off his jersey and stood in front of Ella who was trying squirming around on the saddle in anticipation. He grabbed her hair again pulling her head back, enjoying the sound of her squeal. He kissed her roughly on the lips and then started sucking at her breasts again, chewing and biting, savouring the hardness of her nipples.

Ella leaned back and started to groan. She was quite stunned to find that she was actually rather enjoying this, Paul was very toned from all the horse riding and his biceps were rather inviting. She leant back and closed her eyes as she felt a warm tingle start to develop inside her.

Paul paused and smiled at her. She was begging for it. "Quite a little slut aren't you," he murmured. Ella opened her eyes to berate him but he planted a kiss over her mouth before she could reply. He parted her legs with his hand, feeling her moistness down there, "you really want me to fuck you don't you. Well, let's give you a ride you won't forget then," he muttered, massaging her breast with his other hand.

He pulled her towards him and stepped over the saddle. He leaned forwards to kiss her and pushed himself inside her as he did so. She gasped as his penis slid into her. Paul moved himself slowly in and out of her, going deeper inside with each thrust. He kissed her and massaged her breasts as he did so. Ella threw her head back and

started to moan. She could feel a pleasant warm feeling down below and that delicious tingle was becoming stronger. She didn't want him to stop. She widened her legs, trying to get him further inside her. Paul moved a hand beneath her buttocks pulling her closer towards him and thrust himself deeper into her, relishing her look of longing and delighting in her moans. He started to move quicker now. He saw the water trickling down her body and her hair cascading around her breasts. He closed his eyes in ecstasy. "You really needed a good fuck Ella and that's just what you're getting," he muttered as he picked up his speed.

Ella could feel the hardness of the saddle banging at her behind as Paul pushed away in her. She moaned as she felt herself shaking more with each thrust. She spread her legs wider and tilted herself towards him with a gasp. She wanted him as far inside her as possible.

Paul pushed again and smiled as Ella let out a long low cry as she had her first orgasm. Finally he could let himself go, he took one more look at her beautiful body, now consumed in the throes of ecstasy and closed his eyes as he gave a final push and ejaculated inside her.

He stopped. He was breathing heavily Paul looked at Ella, she was also breathing heavily, her eyes were wide and she was positively glowing. Finally she smiled. "That was amazing," she gasped.

Paul narrowed his eyes as he slid out of her. He wasn't going to tell her how electric his own orgasm had been. He dressed quickly and turned back to Ella. He untied the rope setting her free to rub her wrists. He picked up her underwear and threw it at her. "Get dressed before fatso gets back," he paused as he turned away, "no wait." He grabbed a whip. "Stand over the saddle and put this in between your teeth," he said handing her the whip.

He grabbed the sponge and doused her with more water. She squealed in protest. "What for?"

"I want a picture of you."

"I don't know about that. You could show it to anyone." Ella frowned as she stood over the saddle rack.

"I promise I won't show anyone." Paul said gently, "It's just for me to look at when you're not around."

"Oh, all right then," said Ella, who was finding this all rather enjoyable. She straddled the saddle rack and held the whip at each end in her hands and put it in between her teeth. She gave the most provocative pose she could muster as Paul snapped the picture.

He grinned as he looked at the photograph. Ella walked over to him, "show me," she demanded. Paul did and she giggled as she looked at the picture of herself. "That

looks like something out of some sleazy magazine," she said.

Paul smiled at her, "if the cap fits."

Ella scowled at him. Paul was about to grab her again when there was a sudden thud as as the door of the tack room was pushed from the other side. Joanne was back. She knocked on the door as Ella dressed quickly and Paul put everything back in its place.

Joanne knocked again. "Why is this locked? Let me in?" She asked pushing again at the door.

Paul opened the door and Joanne nearly fell inside. She almost flattened the tray with the coffees and biscuits that she had been carrying in her good hand.

She looked at Paul who was sitting back in the chair and at Ella who was cleaning tack again. Her eyes narrowed. "What have you two been doing, you're wet Ella."

Paul frowned at her, "that's because I whacked her with her sponge because she's useless at cleaning tack," he sneered, "a bit like you really."

Joanne gave him a filthy look, "I don't know why I bothered making you a coffee, you're an animal."

Ella nodded at her, "Oh yes, he definitely is an animal," she said with a smile.

CHAPTER 15

Chloe stood in front of the French doors and sipped her coffee. Jerry watched her lazily from the arm of the sofa where he was lying with half closed eyes. She looked outside to see Jade and Steve in the garden. Steve was starting to tidy it up and Jade had gone out to help him on Chloe's instruction. Chloe wanted some quiet time to check her lap top. The sun was shining brightly and it looked like it would be a lovely morning. Chloe turned back to her laptop and checked her e mails. Once she had filtered out the junk she sat down and read the rest.

There was a message from Carl asking how things had gone over the weekend and how long she thought that she would need to wind things up there. Chloe smiled and sent him a text:

Re. the e mail: Taking a bit longer than I thought will let you know ETA to finish shortly.

She pressed the send button and looked back to where Jade and Steve were pulling up weeds in the garden. Jade was smiling brightly. It was the happiest that Chloe had ever seen her looking. Chloe was glad that Jade seemed to be coping. She had heard Jade on the phone to her mother she had been saying how nice it was here and how peaceful it was in the countryside.

Chloe finished her coffee and grabbed her coat and car keys, pausing to give Jerry's head a stroke as she walked past him. As she went outside she shouted across to Jade and Steve, "I'm going to the yard you two carry on, I'll be back in a while. Don't forget Anne is coming."

They both stopped and looked at her, Jade's eyes were wide in surprise but Chloe had already jumped into the car and started it up before she had time to say anything. Steve just watched as Chloe pulled away.

There were no other cars on the yard as Chloe arrived up at the yard. The other liveries that took care of their own horses had either come first thing before work and would arrive again later for their evening chores and possibly a ride. She parked and went to Sam's stable to find him dozing in the corner. He looked up as she entered and gave a low whicker. Chloe gave a small smile. She reached forward and ran her hand softly down the front of his nose. "Morning fella, how are you today?" She turned to see that he had eaten his hay. "My you're certainly making up for lost time aren't you?" She said as she went off to fill his hay nets.

Chloe returned a while later carrying a hay net over each shoulder. She pushed open the stable door to hang them up. Sam came over and started pulling at the hay eagerly. Chloe laughed. "All right, I've still got to get your other food too, don't worry," she stopped suddenly as she realised that Sam had moved swiftly across the stable and not done his usual careful hobble.

She stepped back and stared at Sam's leg. She blinked and continued to gaze at his limbs with widened eyes. No, she wasn't imagining it, his leg was not swollen and it looked the same size as the other one.

She knelt down and ran her hands up and down both of his legs. She did this again and then moved her hands to run them around both sides of his legs. She stood up and looked at him again. She couldn't feel any heat or swelling in the bad leg. She took a deep breath and went outside to pull out Sam's headcollar. She put the headcollar on Sam and led him out of his stable. He took another quick swipe at the hay before he let her drag him away into the stable block corridor.

Chloe walked him up and down the corridor observing his every movement. She couldn't see any sign of pain in his gait. She took him further down the corridor where there was enough room to trot him, much to the interest of the other horses who popped their heads over their doors to see who was there.

After trotting him twice along the corridor Chloe stopped and returned him to his box. She took out her phone and rang the vet's number. She wanted him out to check this. Chloe wanted to make sure that she wasn't mistaking this apparent return to normality from Sam for something else.

Chloe tied Sam up outside his stable and gave him a bowl of food whilst she cleaned out his box. Her mind was racing. Surely this wasn't right? He couldn't have made an overnight recovery like that. Chloe thought about the powder, what the hell had been in that stuff? It must have been that which had made him feel better?

Chloe was fortunate in that the vet had a rare quiet Monday and would be driving right past the yard on his rounds so she didn't have to wait long before he arrived. She strolled outside as she heard a car pull up.

Chloe walked outside as Leon Connor stepped out of his car. He turned to her. "Ms Marcus? You requested a vet?"

Chloe observed the slightly older, bearded man who was smiling at her, his eyes twinkled warmly behind his glasses. "Yes, call me Chloe, thank you for coming out so quickly." Chloe showed Leon to where Sam was still standing outside his stable. He was leaning inside trying to eat his hay now that his feed bowl was lying empty beside him. She quickly undid his rug and removed it so that he could have a good look at Sam.

Leon raised an eyebrow at Sam's lean frame. "He could do with some more weight on him."

Chloe nodded, "I know, I'm working on that. I've only just managed to remove him from that awful yard."

Leon gave a small smile and examined Sam who tried to nuzzle Leon's shirt curiously, looking for treats. Chloe held on to Sam's head chiding him softly to be still.

Finally Leon stood up. "My word, he's leg's looking so much better, I remember when I first visited him. It looked pretty grim," he beamed at Chloe. "Could you walk him up and trot him too."

Chloe did as she was instructed and Sam executed a prefect gait. He even started his trot with a toss of his head.

Leon shook his head. "Remarkable," he stated and looked at Chloe who stared back at him unblinking. "When did the swelling start to go down?" Leon asked.

Chloe swallowed. "Well I suppose it seemed to have happened all of a sudden, almost overnight."

Leon smiled and gave a short laugh. "Well, perhaps you didn't notice it had gone down until today." Chloe smiled back. "Perhaps," she decided that it would be best not to mention the formula. He probably wouldn't believe it had anything to do with curing Sam's leg anyhow.

Leon turned back to observe Sam. "Well, apart from his poor condition he's looking one hundred percent better," he nodded at Chloe. "I would recommend that you had an x ray though, just to be sure, before you start doing any serious ridden work with him."

Chloe nodded, "I'll arrange that then," she said also staring at

Sam. She was feeling quite dazed at his sudden improvement.

Leon left and Chloe finished cleaning out Sam's stable. She sighed. Now she would have to decide what to do with him. She decided that he should be turned out as soon as possible. She didn't want him cooped up in the stable any more now that his leg was so much better. In fact that was an understatement she pondered, he actually seemed to be sound.

She turned around to see Sarah standing looking at her from the entrance to the stable block. Chloe walked towards her, "good morning, I was just about to come and see you," she said as she strode towards her.

Sarah gave her a half smile as she approached. "Yes I need to have a word with you too," she said quietly.

Chloe looked at Sarah's face as she stood n front of her. She looked slightly uncomfortable. Chloe smiled at her, "Sam appears t be sound so I'd like to turn him out now."

Sarah blinked and widened her eyes. "What? But he was lame as hell yesterday."

Chloe's smiled widened. "Yes, I know, amazing isn't it? It must have been that food we gave him, it said it was good for their limbs."

Sarah gaped at her. "They said he was done for," she muttered glancing at Sam.Chloe frowned. "Who said that?"

Sarah looked quickly back at her. "Oh, er the vet, That's what I heard anyhow."

Chloe stared at Sarah intently for a moment and Sarah wilted beneath her penetrating gaze. Chloe suddenly smiled again. "Where shall I turn him out then? Preferably somewhere with good grazing, we need to get him back to top condition." Chloe sighed, "I can't believe that woman let him get in such a poor state, she should be shot."

Sarah started to chew her bottom lip. She had been going to tell Chloe that she would have to leave. She didn't want to upset Celia again. On the other hand she could do with the money from the livery. She looked back at Chloe and took a deep breath before she spoke. "One of the liveries has complained about you, well not you exactly, more the horse."

Chloe raised an eyebrow. "Really? Why what's he done? He's only been here for a minute and he hasn't even been out of the stable."

Sarah looked at Sam. "It's because he's so thin and ill, he can't even walk. They thought that the RSPCA should be called. Perhaps it would be better to see if you could rent a field for him. Perhaps somewhere out of the way. " Sarah looked back at Chloe and started to chew her lip again.

Chloe rolled her eyes. "Oh well, I hope you told them that I didn't get him in that state. Anyhow, that's all sorted out now. He's back on his feet and we'll soon get him in good condition. Besides, I need somewhere that has a manege so that I can get him going."

Sarah stared at her. Chloe gave her a warm smile. "Don't worry, it'll be fine. Who complained by the way?"

Sarah swallowed and then thought what the hell? "It was Rory but he said that the other liveries all felt the same."

Chloe nodded thoughtfully. "So, where shall I turn him out then?" She asked brightly.

Sarah gave a big sigh. "Follow me."

Sarah watched as Chloe turned Sam out. She had endured Rory's complaints about the new livery and him trying to order her to throw them off the yard. Sarah suspected it was more to do with the fact that Steve was so good looking and could obviously ride a horse that probably rattled Rory. Sarah had watched Steve riding Quickstep in the manage on the cctv and he seemed quite competent. Rory was just not happy that he had some competition, if you could call it that.

Sarah smiled to herself, fact was there was no competition Steve was better looking and a better rider than Rory. Sod Rory she thought and made her way back to the cottage, time for a coffee and a chocolate biscuit. She'd worry about Celia later.

Chloe smiled as she watched Sam in the small paddock. The first thing he did was to get down and have a good roll. "Oh Sam." Chloe called, "you're filthy now."

Sam ignored her and suddenly leapt in the air and span. He gave a large buck and shot off across the paddock. Fortunately it was a small paddock and he couldn't get build up too much speed. But Chloe felt her heart lurch, what if this damaged his leg again? Perhaps she should have waited and limited him to just being walked out on lead rope rather than just throwing him out like this.

She watched nervously as he trotted across the paddock looking for any potential friends but they were all further away in the larger fields. He had another trot around and then put his head down to graze. The lush grass was just too tempting.

This paddock was hardly used as it was so small, which was why the grass was so rich and Sam was soon tucking into it giving the occasional swish of his tail. Chloe smiled, relieved that he had calmed down so quickly. He looked so contented now that he was out in the field, her aunt would be pleased she thought suddenly. Chloe frowned to herself, she felt so sad for her aunt and uncle. She really wished they were here.

Chloe felt tears prick against the back of her eyes and touched her hands to her face to stop them from flowing. She swallowed the rest of her tears back, she mustn't dwell on such things, what was done was done. She would telephone the vet again in a while to arrange that x ray for Sam and get back to sorting out the paperwork for the estate.

She paused as she turned to leave and looked back at Sam. He was still grazing contentedly by himself. She stared at him for a moment remembering what Sarah had said – she thought that he was "done for".

Chloe wondered why she would have said such a thing? I sounded as if Sarah had been speaking to someone about Sam. Perhaps she had been discussing him with Celia? She wondered if Sarah knew more about Sam than she was letting on. Chloe shook her head and headed for the car, she had things to do and she wasn't going to dwell on this, not yet.

Chloe drove away from the yard. She didn't realise that she had been watched the whole time. Sarah took another puff on her cigarette and switched off the cctv as Chloe left. She reached for her mobile phone frowning. She pressed dial when she found Duncan Morcross's number. He had some explaining to do.

CHAPTER 16

Sarah stared out of the window for a moment and observed the morning sunshine. She looked up as she heard a car pull up on to the drive. She gulped down her coffee as she saw Celia get out of the Range Rover and march towards her door.

She quickly tried to clear things away as she heard Celia walk in through the back door. Celia walked in to the kitchen and looked around. "My this place could do with a tidy up. What have you been doing in here for heaven's sake?"

Sarah glanced around, "I've been trying to stitch up some rugs. You know how rubbish I am at sewing."

Celia frowned, "why don't you get that little girl of yours to do it?"

"Oh she's worse than me." Sarah said with a sigh.

Celia sat herself at the table. "Are you going to make me a drink or do I have to help myself?" She asked, giving Sarah a sidelong glance. "Make sure you move those stinking rugs first, I don't want horse hairs in my hob nobs," she added as she rummaged through the various horse magazines lying on the table.

Sarah switched the kettle on again and made Celia a drink, handing it to her along with a packet of biscuits. Celia helped herself to a biscuit and munched on it loudly, spilling crumbs all over the table. She looked at Sarah who was leaning against the kitchen unit. "So, what's happened with that horse then?" She asked taking a sip of her coffee. Sarah looked away uncomfortably. Celia put her cup down and widened her eyes. "Oh, for goodness sake, don't tell me they're still here?"

Sarah nodded. "They hadn't anywhere to go and now the horse is sound, I couldn't say that he should be put down or anything," she said, avoiding Celia's steely gaze.

Celia let out a big sigh. "How did that horse come sound all of a sudden?" She asked narrowing her eyes.

Sarah shrugged. "God only knows. She couldn't even explain it herself, but the vet was out to x ray him this morning and apparently he's had the all clear."

Celia frowned. "How odd that is." She stopped for a moment, deep in thought as she took another sip of her coffee. "You know, maybe it's better that he does stay here. At least you can keep an eye on what they're up to."

Sarah nodded feeling a sudden rush of relief. "Yes, that's a good point."

They both looked up as they heard a car arriving. Sarah rolled her eyes, "oh here we go. It's the after work thrashing for Ted," she said as they watched Rory's Mitsubishi pull up.

Celia shook her head, "put the cctv on. We can have a laugh at the silly fool." She helped herself to another hob nob as Sarah switched on the screen in the kitchen.

Celia smiled to herself for a moment. "Have you got anything good on there for us to watch?"

Sarah shook her head. "It's just been the usual rounds of them trying to get their horses to do stuff that they don't want to." Sarah decided that she would keep the tape of Steve riding to herself. She didn't think that Celia would be too impressed if she put that on.

Celia rolled her eyes, "you know your really going to have to find them doing something interesting. We haven't had a Friday night film show for a while."

Sarah nodded. "Yes, that's true. What about you?"

Celia smiled slyly, "Well as a matter of fact, I do have something rather interesting that I caught recently. It certainly was a good idea of yours, to put those cameras about the place."

Sarah looked at Celia's smug expression and raised her eyebrows. "What? Do tell." Sarah said and sat opposite Celia at the table looking at her keenly. She certainly looked rather pleased with herself.

Celia put down her cup and leaned towards Sarah confidentially, as if suspecting they might be overheard. "Well," she said quietly "my lad Paul and one of the grooms were at it in the tack room."

Sarah's eyes widened, "No way!"

Celia nodded smugly, "oh yes and they were going at it like rabbits and he had her all tied up. You should have seen her face, she was loving it."

Sarah licked her lips, "you must bring it."

Celia smiled at her, "I shall and we can watch it at our leisure in the snug. By ourselves." Celia said lowering her eyes and then looking intently back at Sarah. Sarah returned her gaze licking her lips again.

They both turned as another car arrived at the yard. This time it was Big Jayne. They both watched as she clambered out from her car followed by a nervous looking Heather.

Sarah let out a sudden shriek of laughter. Heather was wearing the latest in body protection. "Does Big Jayne seriously think that buying a new body protector will turn that nervous wreck of a daughter of hers into a fearless rider?"

Celia smiled as they walked across the yard. Heather was struggling to keep up in her new armour.

Celia's face darkened suddenly as Chloe's BMW pulled up. Sarah turned back to the monitor and swallowed. They watched as Chloe and Steve got out of the vehicle and walked away to the small paddock that Sam was turned out in.

Chloe glanced across at the house and then looked at Steve with a small smile on her face. Steve raised an eyebrow. "Do you think we're being watched?" He said with a smile.

Steve had been quite stunned when Chloe had told him of Sam's sudden recovery. They watched as he grazed in the paddock. "The vet said he was okay then." Chloe nodded. "Yes his limbs are fine." Steve shook his head "Amazing," he murmured.

Sam saw them and lifted his head giving a gentle whicker. He strolled casually across the paddock to them as they watched. Both Chloe and Steve were smiling.

Chloe stroked Sam's face as he stood in front of her. She glanced at Steve. "I've decided that he must be brought back in to work. We need to do something with him then maybe we can rehome him."

Steve looked at her intently, "you aren't going to keep him?"

Chloe looked away shaking her head. "I have to get back to work, this is no place for someone like me. Besides, there's not enough money in the estate to maintain him." She looked back at Steve now, "we need to get cracking with him as soon as we can. "

Steve raised an eyebrow questioningly, "what do you mean by "Somebody like me"?" He ventured.

Chloe frowned back at him. "This kind of country stuff just isn't me, not any more," she said firmly, turning back to look at Sam.

Steve nodded and also looked at Sam, "we'll need some tack for him."

Chloe smiled, "we already have some. Guess what my aunt and uncle had stashed in their garage? There's enough tack in there to clothe a herd let alone just one horse."

Chloe nodded towards the car. "I happened to bring some of it along with me. Shall we?" She asked tilting her head to one side. Steve smiled. "Why not, Ms Marcus" They both headed back to the car.

Sarah and Celia watched, as Chloe and Steve brought Sam into the stable block to fit the tack on him. Celia was scowling at the screen. "I can't believe that horse has come back sound so quickly." Celia turned her gaze to Sarah, "give us a ciggy then," she ordered.

Sarah reached into a draw and pulled two cigarettes out and handed one to Celia. She pulled out a lighter and they both sat down, puffing at their cigarettes watching the TV.

Heather was struggling to mount Firefox in her new body protector. She was finding it difficult to move in. Firefox danced in a circle around the mounting block while Heather tried desperately to reach the stirrup.
Big Jayne rolled her eyes. "For goodness sake. Can't you even get on her? Pull the right rein round then she will move towards you."

Heather did as she was bid and finally managed to collapse onto Firefox. Big Jayne watched as Firefox jogged across the yard with Heather clinging on, trying to get her self properly in the saddle. Big Jayne rolled her eyes again. Why couldn't the child just vault on like all the other kids at Pony Club did? She was really exasperated with Heather, she just didn't seem to have any aptitude for riding and she was the most nervous rider she had ever seen.

Big Jayne struggled to come to terms with this. Her husband had once been a keen huntsman and had been quite renown for being rather a thruster. Big Jayne had also had her own horse and been competing in horse trials before she had become pregnant. After having Heather she had never seemed able to lose that baby weight so had not had another horse.

Big Jayne sighed she had decided that the only way to try to give Heather some confidence was to force her into doing things that scared her. That way she would have to face up to her fears and thus conquer them and move forwards. Unfortunately, Heather seemed to be ending up on the ground rather a lot lately, hence the new body protector. She had managed to persuade her husband to invest in the latest protector on the market in the hope that it would instill some confidence in Heather.

Sarah and Celia were both giggling at Heather's attempts to mount. Celia shook her head, "that stupid woman, why on earth has she wasted her money on such a good pony for that useless child. She should be riding a hairy cob not an eventer."

"A Shetland pony would be safer." Sarah smirked.

Big Jayne opened the gate to the manege, giving Rory a wave as he approached on Ted. Heather managed to steer a jogging Firefox into the manege. Firefox had not been turned out that day. Big Jayne had wanted her in the stable for when they arrived, so that Heather could ride her early on, as she had an a music lesson that evening. Big Jayne waited for Rory to enter the arena before closing the gate behind them. She turned around to see Heather cantering around the manege briskly with a grin on her face. She smiled, "Heather you should have warmed her up first but I'm glad to see you cantering so early on." Normally it took Heather a while to work herself up to faster work.

Heather's grimace widened. She was too scared to open her mouth and shout back that she had no choice as Firefox had taken off around the school upon entering it and she had absolutely no brakes. She hoped that Firefox would wear herself out and then perhaps she could slow her down.

Rory strolled around on Ted, forcing the horse's nose as far into his chest as he could. He observed Heather from the corner of his eye as she flew around the manege, completely out of control. He rolled his eyes the poor kid was hopeless.

Chloe and Steve had found some tack that fitted Sam nicely and tacked him up quietly in the stable. When they had finished they stood back to observe him.

"He looks very smart." Chloe said.

Steve was staring closely at Sam, "is it me or has he put some weight on?"

Chloe nodded. "That's what I was thinking, mind you he's getting enough food shoved at him. Or maybe something in that powder helped?" She said quietly.

"I wondered that too. It just shows how much that cow Celia was starving him though." Steve said.

"Yes. Evil woman." Chloe paused for a moment, "well, now he's all tacked up..."

She looked back at Steve and raised an eyebrow. Steve looked back at Chloe and then back at Sam. "I suppose you want me to ride him then?"

"Well I am rather out of practice and goodness knows when he was ridden last."

Steve smiled, "actually, according to Ella he was in full training until he hurt his leg, which was only a couple of weeks ago. It happened before I got to the yard. Ella thought that he'd been sent back to his owners," he said reaching out for Sam's bridle.

Chloe opened the stable to let them out. "Do you know what happened to his leg?" Steve shook his head, "no, apparently the lad; Paul was riding him and they didn't say what went on."

Chloe put a hand on Sam's nose as Steve went to get on him. Sam stood with his ears picked as Steve gently mounted from the mounting block.

Steve and Chloe both paused, Sam also remained immobile until Steve gave him a gentle squeeze and he stepped forward politely. Chloe gave a cautious smile, "well would you like to try a walk around the school?" She asked Steve who nodded back at her.

They walked across to the school and Chloe stopped. "Do you want to go somewhere else as there are people in there? I don't want him getting excited."

Steve shook his head, "no, it's fine it's big enough we'll just go into a corner over there. I'd like to see how he is with stuff going on around him anyhow." Chloe nodded. Steve certainly didn't seem bothered to go in there, which she was glad to hear. They walked over to the school and Chloe opened the gate for Steve, they smiled at Big Jayne and Rory as they made their way across the school, avoiding Heather and Firefox who were cantering rapidly in circles at the top of the arena.

Heather had managed to make the circles smaller and smaller and was hoping that she might be able to bring Firefox under control before she fell over.

Rory was furious. They shouldn't be riding that horse, he thought, he was only barely sound and he still needed weight putting on. He was still seething that Sarah had ignored his request to order them to move. He couldn't believe that she took the side of these new liveries over someone who had been on the yard much longer and also was far more knowledgeable on horses than she was. He forced Ted's head tighter into his chest and sent him across the manege demanding he extend his trot as he went.

Chloe watched as Steve walked around quietly on Sam. After a while he did started trotting and then had a short canter on both reins. Steve rode beautifully he was totally in balance with Sam and after a short time Sam had relaxed into a lovely rhythm holding himself in a soft outline.

Steve gave Sam a pat and walked him over to Chloe. "He's a real softie, he really listens to you and he's very balanced," he smiled. Chloe nodded "Yes he looked lovely."

Rory trotted past them scowling, he was hoping to spook Sam into misbehaving but Sam just stood quietly half closing his eyes. Chloe laughed, "he looks like he's going to sleep now. Yet he doesn't look sluggish to ride."

Steve shook his head, "no he's very responsive he's just smart. He knows when to save his energy," he smiled.

Chloe laughed again as they headed off back to the stables.

Big Jayne nodded as they left. Steve certainly looked like he could ride. She wondered if she should get him to give Heather a lesson. A bit of new blood might give her some confidence Mind you she'd been quick off the mark today, perhaps that new body armour was doing the trick. Big Jayne watched as Heather finally managed to bring Firefox to a halt and collapsed across her neck in exhaustion. Big Jayne smiled, Firefox was also drenched Heather had certainly given her a good work out.

Sarah and Celia observed the monitor. Sarah could feel the loathing emanating from Celia as they watched Steve and Sam trotting harmoniously around the manege. Celia frowned and turned to Sarah. Sarah felt herself wilt beneath her malicious stare. Celia gave an evil smile and spoke quietly, "I am going to make sure that shit pays for making a fool out of me. Oh yes, he'll wish he'd never met me."

CHAPTER 17

Jade stood in the garden gazing dreamily at the flowerbeds that she and Steve had been weeding. Chloe had asked her to continue with the weeding while she and Steve were out. Jade wished she could have gone with them though. She was missing Steve already. Jade pondered morosely for a moment on what she would do when she had to go back home and wouldn't see him again. She sighed, she would just have to make the most of her time here she thought sadly.

She looked up as she heard a peculiar squeaking from further up the drive. She felt a tug of disappointment as she saw the long blonde haired figure cycling along towards the house. Jade supposed that she had better go and greet Ella as she had no idea where Anne was, or even if she was still at the house.

Anne would appear with a smile and then vanish like a ghost, to do whatever cleaning she thought necessary. It seemed that she must be letting herself out of the house, as she hadn't been seen yesterday since her arrival in the morning.

Jade made her way over to the front door where Ella had left her bike propped against the steps to the house. Jade managed a small smile. "Hello, there's only me here. Steve's gone with Chloe to see the horse," she said.

Ella frowned "Oh," she said.

Jade felt her heart sink as she saw the look of disappointment on Ella's face. No doubt it was only a question of time before Steve was with her. How could any man resist someone so beautiful?

Jade shifted her weight form one foot to the other uncomfortably. "Would you like a cup of tea?" She asked finally. It was the only thing she could think of to say. She instantly regretted it. If Ella said yes then she would only have to spend more time with her and she really didn't think they would have much to talk about. They really wouldn't have anything in common.

Ella looked at Jade standing there in her green woolen suit with a respectable calf length skirt and bright yellow blouse underneath, topped off with tights in a hideous bright yellow colour. She was also wearing pink marigolds. Ella suddenly felt like giggling. She bit her lip. "I might as well. Seen as how I've come all this way now," she said nodding.

Jade mentally rolled her eyes as she led Ella around the back of the house and into the kitchen, peeling off her marigolds as she went. She gestured to the table as she put the kettle on. "Take a seat," she said. She brought out the biscuits and placed them on the table in front of Ella. "Help yourself," Jade said, trying to smile.

Ella stared at the biscuits, she was feeling decidedly sick. She needed to escape fro Celia's yard. She had not been able to look Paul in the eye since their sexual encounter in the tack room. She had noticed him looking at her though and he always had a slight smirk on his face. She was going to have to talk up to him about what had happened, she was beginning to think it might have been a big mistake.

Although, deep down, a part of her still wanted to experience that feeling of excitement and pleasure again. Ella had decided to come over to see Steve to try to get her head back in the right place. She was sure that once she saw him again she would put all thoughts of having sex with Paul from her head.

Jade made the coffee and placed the mugs on the table. Just as she was about to sit down there was a loud knocking on the front door. Saved by the bell, thought Jade as she hurried off to answer it.

Ella sighed as Jade walked away. Ella had also been too embarrassed to tell Joanne about her sexual encounter with Paul and she was glad that Joanne hadn't been able to come here with her. Joanne was unable to cycle with one arm disabled and was too heavy for Ella to have on the seat of her bicycle. This was fortunate, as she would only have been asking Ella probing questions. She had already noticed that something was on Ella's mind and it was only a question of time before she ended up dragging the details from her.

Jade returned to the kitchen, she was clutching several large bags and frowning deeply. Ella smiled at her. "What's up?" Jade shook her head, "I don't understand. This has just arrived," she said holding up the bag. "It's addressed to me! Care of this house," she continued to frown at the bag.

Ella looked at it with interest. "Ooh, it's a 'Vexed" bag. Open it and see what's inside." Jade glanced at Ella. "I suppose I should be all right to. After all it is addressed to me," she put the bags on the table and pulled some scissors from a draw to make a large incision across each one. She turned each one on their side and pulled out the contents.

Ella's eyes widened. "Oh wow look at all of those!"

Jade stared at the items on the table in disbelief. Vexed was a large clothing manufacturer and it appeared that most of their store was now lying in front of her.

Jade continued to frown at the items. "I didn't order these. Why are they addressed to me?"

Ella took a sip of her coffee and looked Jade up and down. Perhaps your mum sent them?"

Jade shook her head. "No she definitely wouldn't order anything from Vexed. Besides she wouldn't even know how."

Ella nodded then she had another idea. "Perhaps your boss decided you needed updating?" She regretted the comment immediately, as she saw Jade's hurt expression. "I mean, perhaps she thought you needed some more appropriate work clothes as you're not in the office now," she added quickly, waving a pair of jeans from the table at Jade.

Jade looked at the jeans remembering Chloe's earlier comments on her clothes. She sat down next to Ella fingering the jacket of her cheap woolen suit. "Yes she did say something about me needing some jeans," she muttered.

Ella was still holding the jeans. "These look good. Oh look at that top, that colour would suit you," she said holding up a dark olive top.

Jade stared at the top. "That's a nice colour," she agreed. She surveyed the mountain of clothes. "I've never really taken much interest in clothes," she said with a sigh.

Ella laughed. "You'd never know," she said smiling at Jade.

Jade looked quickly back at Ella to see if she was making fun of her. She saw Ella's expression and Jade felt herself smiling too. "Well they always seemed too expensive and I just couldn't be bothered," she said taking a drink of her coffee and reaching for a biscuit.

Ella was ruffling through the clothes, "Oh you must try this on!" she said holding up another item this time in a turquoise colour.

Jade looked at the blouse. "Oh that looks nice," she paused and then took it from Ella. She held it up observing its rich turquoise sheen.

Ella looked at it with wide eyes. "Put it on! And these jeans, let's see what they look like. You can give me a fashion show," she said, reaching for a biscuit.

Jade bit her lip and then nodded. She picked up the jeans and disappeared into the cloakroom to change.

Ella sighed as she left. It was nice of Chloe to get all of this stuff for Jade she thought. She wished she had a boss like her.

Ella nearly choked on her biscuit as Jade emerged from the cloakroom. She stared at her with wide eyes. Jade felt her heart sink as she saw her expression. "I look awful, don't I?"

Ella laughed. "No! You look lovely."

Jade tilted her head on one side and raised her eyebrows. "Why are you looking at me like that then?"

"Because you look so different. In a good way I mean. That turquoise top looks so good on you and so do those jeans. That look really suits you. Check it out in a mirror." Ella answered with a grin.

Jade managed a small smile as she marched into the hallway to inspect herself in the mirror. She observed the pale red haired girl looking back at her. She had to admit she certainly looked a lot better than when she was wearing her suits.

Ella waited for her to return. She was relieved to see that Jade had a smile on her face. "Well?' She asked.

Jade's smile widened. "Yes I do look better."

"Great, try something else then." Ella said holding up another bag.

Jade rolled her eyes but took the bag from her.

Jade tried on a variety of outfits becoming more delighted with each one. Finally there was only one left. A large bag which Jade pulled open to reveal a shimmering knee length off the shoulder dress with different shades of gold layered across its width.

Ella widened her eyes. "Wow! That's gorgeous!"

Jade nodded in agreement and then trotted off to the cloakroom. When she emerged Ella was rendered speechless for a moment. Finally she spoke, "you look stunning."

Jade shook her head. "This is far too nice for me. You should be wearing something like this not me."

Ella snorted. "Don't be daft. I'd only end up doing something stupid like tearing it or staining it. I'm always doing stupid things."

Jade gave a small laugh as she walked over to her. "You can't be as stupid as me. Believe me."

Ella shook her head. "I don't believe it for a minute."

Jade sat down again smoothing out the dress carefully. "I'm always making mistakes. I have to check everything at work all the time to make sure I haven't messed up."

Ella stared at her. "Okay then, what's the stupidest thing you've ever done?"

Jade stared at her nails and chewed her lower lip for a moment before turning back to Ella. "Well, I wore odd shoes to work once. I didn't even notice until I got there and then it was too late to go home and change."

Ella gave a shriek of laughter. "Ha! That's a good one."

Jade looked back at her hands. "The worst thing was, that nobody even noticed."

Ella stopped laughing and looked at Jade, she felt a sudden pang of sympathy for her. Jade continued. "You see that sums me up. I'm just a useless nobody."

Ella shook her head. "No you're not. You've live in the City and you've got a good job, with prospects."

Jade sighed. "I live with my mum and I only got this job because my dad was a friend of Carl's dad. Carl's the big boss."

Ella stared at Jade. "Well at least you've got a chance to progress. The only way I can get on is by sleeping with the head lad."

Jade looked at her, shocked. "That's terrible, it's harassment if he's threatening you with that, he should be reported."

"He's not threatening me with anything, I just did it with him the other day." Ella said looking away. "You see what I mean about doing stupid things."

Jade sat back in her seat, not knowing what to say. Finally she muttered, "well I just hope you used a condom, you should be careful with these flings."

Ella gave a derisive laugh. "I hadn't even thought about that," she said

"What? You mean you didn't use protection? You could be pregnant!" Jade said.

"No!" Ella cried. "Oh shit Jade what should I do."

"When did you do it?" Jade asked.

"Yesterday."
"Well you should get the morning after pill. Quickly."

Ella was beginning to feel a rising panic in her stomach. "Where can I get it?"

Jade chewed her lip in concentration. "Go to the Doctor."

"I can't do that. Not in this village. Everyone will know about it in five minutes. There's always some gossip getting out from that practice."

"Well go into town."

"By the time I've got there on the bus, everywhere will be shut." Ella answered trying to fight back a tear.

Jade saw the look of sorrow on Ella's face. Suddenly she had an idea. "I know, we'll get it on line," she said triumphantly.

Ella looked at her, feeling a tear slide slowly down her cheek. "Can you do that?""We'll find out." Jade said, getting up. "I'll just get changed and then I'll fire up the lap top."

Jade emerged a while later wearing jeans and an emerald green blouse. She put the laptop on the table and sat down next to Ella. Jade started tapping away on its keyboard, a frown of concentration on her face. After a while she smiled. "See there's one here. It says it's next day delivery and you'll be within the three days needed for it to work," she said.

Ella's expression brightened and then she sighed. "I haven't got any money with me and I don't have a computer at home."

Jade looked at her for a moment before replying. Ella did look really upset. "Don't worry, I'll order it. You can pay me back later," she said and went off to get her purse.

Ella was starting to feel much calmer now and her tears had stopped. They had another coffee as Jade placed the order for her. They finished in time to hear a car arrive outside.

Jade looked at the laptop that was sitting on the table surrounded by a sea of clothes. "Oh dear, I'd better clear this lot up, I'm supposed to be working." She switched off the laptop and hurriedly put it away. She turned back to help Ella who was rapidly folding up the clothes.

They exchanged glances as they heard Chloe and Steve enter the house. They finished tidying the clothes away just in time and were both sitting back at the table as Chloe came into the house.

Ella winked at Jade who managed not to laugh. Perhaps Ella wasn't so bad after all? Jade wondered.

CHAPTER 18

"You should move that bike before someone falls over it," shouted Chloe as she walked into the house. Steve strolled along behind her. He was pleased with how Sam had gone today, he seemed to be a nice balanced young horse and he certainly had a lovely temperament. Perhaps there was hope of finding a good home for him yet.

Steve stepped into the kitchen behind Chloe who paused briefly to observe the clothes mountain on the table. Jade was standing in front of the table looking guilty.

Chloe gave her a small smile, "I see your work clothing has arrived," she nodded and walked across the kitchen to put on the kettle. She turned around to see that Steve was staring at Jade in surprise.

Chloe's smile widened, "suits her, don't you think?"

Jade was turning a lovely shade of beetroot as Steve glanced back at Chloe and nodded. He walked over to help with the coffee whilst Jade turned back to a grinning Ella.

"You girls like a drink?" Chloe asked from across the kitchen. She had noticed that Ella had puffy eyes and looked as if she had been crying, although she was smiling now.

Ella and Jade both shook their heads in unison. Chloe narrowed her eyes, "what have you two been up to?" She asked.

"Nothing." Jade said quickly "and thank you so much for the clothes, they're wonderful," she added, trying to change the subject.

Chloe shook her head. "No problem. You need something practical whilst you're here. Although I'm hoping we won't be stuck here for too long. Have you tried the dress on?"

Jade nodded enthusiastically, "oh yes, it's lovely."

"I thought it would be. You never know when you might need a decent frock." Chloe said as she poured out drinks for herself and Steve who had wandered back to the table and pulled out a chair. He sat opposite Ella observing her puffy eyes with interest.

"How's the horse?" Jade asked him as she piled the clothes into a corner of the table.

"He's very well and very good to ride."

Chloe nodded in agreement. "We need to get him out competing as soon as we can."

Steve looked at her in surprise. "Is this your plan? What would you compete him in?"

Chloe leaned against the kitchen unit, mug in one hand. "Well I was thinking, maybe he should be evented. We don't want to send him back to racing, besides we couldn't afford it. If we could find some horse trials competitions to try him in and he was any good then he will easily be re homed."

Steve raised an eyebrow. "We haven't jumped him yet."

"You can pop him over some poles in a few days and we'll see how he goes."

Steve shook his head. "He'll need to be fit, that will take a while."

Chloe shook her head. "It won't take long, remember he was in National Hunt training before he hurt his leg," she said looking at Ella.

Ella had been looking doe eyed at Steve as he sat in front of her. He was so good looking she wished that she could have an encounter with him in a tack room. He probably wouldn't boss her about like Paul did either.

Ella blinked and nodded. "Yes he was supposed to be raced. Is he all right now then? I thought he was broken down."

Steve glanced at Chloe and said nothing. Chloe smiled. "Yes it turned out just to be a minor knock so we should be able to get him out and about soon."

"I suppose you'll be wanting me to ride him in this competition?" Steve asked slowly.

"Of course, you're getting along famously with him," beamed Chloe.

Steve took a drink of his coffee. " I've not really done any horse trials, to be honest."

"Oh don't worry you'll be fine." Chloe said.

Jade looked at Ella. "Isn't that kind of stuff really dangerous though?"

"Yes." Ella agreed nodding solemnly at her.

Chloe sighed, "we'll just have to get him kitted out with all the protective gear. Steve too," she added with a smile.

Jade nodded. "Bet that'll be expensive though."

Chloe rolled her eyes. "Well we'll just have to raise some money."

"How?" Steve asked looking at her questioningly.

Chloe paused and looked up at the ceiling in frustration.

"We should get someone to sponsor him." Jade said brightly.

Chloe's expression brightened. "Excellent idea! Right we'll have to start canvassing," she looked at Ella. "You'll have to tell us who's got some money round here and we can go and knock on their doors."

Ella nodded this was all sounding rather fun she thought. Shame she was stuck at miserable Celia's yard. It was much cheerier here.

Steve took another swallow of his coffee. "We need to find a competition first and get some schooling in."

"Absolutely. We'll see if we can find something for you two to try out at first." Chloe agreed

Ella piped up. "There's a horse trials in a few weeks time it's at Berryford."

Chloe frowned. 'A few weeks!"

"Yes," continued Ella, "some of our yard are going. It's not affiliated but apparently they use all the proper cross country fences and it's a really big event. A lot of the pros take their young or novice horses there to get them started. " Ella paused for a moment and then added quietly, "they're having training with Lucinda Lilac there too."

Chloe looked up. "Lucinda Lilac? Is she coming here?"

"Yes, she's doing a clinic at Berryford." Ella said with a small sigh. "A one off apparently, next week. I will be grooming for Paul," she finished, frowning at the table.

Jade looked away biting her lip and then turned to Steve,

"who's Lucinda Lilac?"

Steve raised an eyebrow. "Only one of the greatest eventers in this country, or even in the world."

Chloe nodded in agreement. "Yes, she's won European gold medals and world championships and even an Olympic medal. She won Badminton six times!"

Jade was staring at Chloe blankly. She licked her lips. "Well she sounds good," she said finally.

Steve smiled at her and turned back to Chloe. "We still need to fund this whole thing. We're going to have to get some good sponsorship. We may need more than one sponsor."

"Yes, I think I'm going to have to do some networking and not just around here." Chloe agreed. "We'll need to get to know people and try to persuade them to sponsor us."

Jade had an idea, "why don't you have a party here and invite some of your contacts from the City. They might buy in to sponsoring us when they see how nice it is here."

Chloe laughed. "Jade! You are having rather good ideas today. Yes, I think we should do that. I mean we can ask around here too, you never know they might help support a local horse and every little will help. If I butter them up a bit and invite them to a bash here they might be more forthcoming."

Jade was beaming now, Steve smiled as he saw her happy expression. Jade smiled back at him. "We could have lanterns in the garden, it would look so pretty," she said dreamily.

Chloe nodded. "I think that you should plan this party Jade." Chloe stopped and frowned suddenly to herself.

Steve noticed her look. "What's up?"

Chloe sighed and looked around for the biscuit barrel. She walked over to the table and reached into the barrel, only to find nothing more than a few crumbs. She raised an eyebrow at Jade who gave a sheepish shrug in response. Chloe looked back at Steve. "Well I'm going to have to go back to the office. I told Carl that I'd have this wrapped up in a week."

Chloe stopped and stared at Jade, "How would you feel about staying here with Steve and helping out around here."

Jade looked at Chloe in astonishment. "What? Me? By myself?"

"Yes Jade you're a big girl."

"Well I'll have to ask my mom."

Ella couldn't stifle her giggles. Steve gave her a stern look but then found himself also smiling.

Chloe looked at Jade and spoke slowly. "Jade, I'm sure your mother can cope for a little while without you. If she has any problems let me know and we'll sort them out. It's not going to be for long."

Jade bit her lip. She really would love to stay here as long as Steve was around. He would make sure everything was safe and fix anything that went wrong. She looked at Chloe questioningly, "what about your work? Who's going to sort everything out?"

"Well you can do some stuff from here and I'll get Carl's assistant to help me out with the rest for now." Chloe said as she walked back to the other side of the kitchen. "I just need to make sure we've some money coming. If I speak to Carl I'm sure I can persuade him to give me some more time to sort things out."

Steve looked at Jade who was now staring dreamily into space. He shook his head with a smile. "Well you need to tell me what you want me to do with Sam," he said to Chloe.

"Get him ready for the horse trials and I'll get you on this training day with Lucinda Lilac before the trials to iron out any issues, although hopefully there won't be any. You need to take him out for some jump schooling when he's ready."

"We haven't got any transport." Steve said flatly. "In fact, I may need to borrow Ella's bike to get to the yard. Are you okay to sit on the back with me Jade?" he asked her giving her a wink.

Jade felt herself reddening again but couldn't help but smile.

Chloe rolled her eyes. "I'll sort something out tomorrow. I'm sure we can hitch a lift from Sam. I'll bet there are some people from the yard going, they all seem to be quite competitive."

Steve nodded. "Well they need to be at their best, especially with all of those cameras about, you never know who's watching," he said staring pointedly at the table.

Jade's eyes widened and Ella looked at him curiously. "What? Are there cameras everywhere?" Ella asked.

"Yes," Steve replied, "they're all over the place."

Jade couldn't believe her ears. "Why do they have cameras all over the place?"

Steve shrugged. "Perhaps that Sarah is worried about what her liveries are up to. Just be careful what you say when you're there," he said nodding at Jade and Ella.

Chloe said nothing. She had wondered whether Steve had noticed the cameras at the yard. She had thought that there seemed to be rather an excessive amount of them herself.

"Okay, so we need to get the sponsorship and get the entries done. Oh and you need some more shopping." Chloe said holding up the empty biscuit barrel and waving it at Jade. "And another thing. Has anyone seen my paperwork from the Solicitors? I can't find it anywhere. I'm sure I left it in the sitting room."

They all shook their heads. Ella gave a sigh and rose from her chair, "time for me to go I suppose," she said.

Ella had seen Steve wink at Jade. He'd not done that to her in the time that he was at Celia's she thought with a sinking heart. She might as well go back and tell Joanne all the gossip she thought morosely. They certainly seemed to be having more fun over here than she did at Celia's. Ella wondered if she would get an invite to the party.

Chloe looked at Steve. "Why don't you give Ella a lift, she can put her bike in the boot. You two can get some food from the shop for us," she said. "I need to make some phone calls," she added as she walked out of the kitchen.

"Oh by the way Steve," Chloe suddenly peered back around the doorway to the kitchen. "How much experience have you had competing in horse trials?"

Steve got up from the table and reached for the car keys. "Up until this one you mean?"

"Yes"

"None." Steve said as he walked away.

CHAPTER 19

Saturday dawned bright and clear. The sun rose slowly across a cloudless sky. Ben had the car window open as he drove along. He took a deep breath of the fresh air and exhaled with a smile. This was going to be a wonderful day he could feel it. He was so excited that he was actually going to Lucinda Lilac's clinic.

He had combed Gatsby's mane and tail out to within an inch of their life and they looked so splendidly fluffy he was sure that she would be impressed. He smiled in the mirror at his two young girls who had come along to watch their dad in action. They were squabbling in the back of the car over which Barbie would get to ride the plastic pony. His wife Gill sat next to him filling the passenger seat with her ample behind. He smiled again, yes this should be a super day.

Gill turned around. "Will you two behave!" She shrieked at the two girls, who both sat back in their seats, observing her with wide eyes. Gill turned to Ben. "For God's sake shut that bloody window will you, it's blowing a gale in here." Ben nodded and closed the window, still smiling. "I hope that that woman is giving you something for taking her horse with you," she added, nodding back towards the trailer.

Chloe was driving along behind Ben. Steve was sitting next to her and Jade was in the back of the car admiring Steve's fair hair. Jade felt as if she should reach out and touch it. His hair looked so touchable. Jade mulled over the last few days. Chloe had gone back to London but had returned within two days. Apparently Carl had been quite supportive of her venture with Sam. Still, the two days spent with Steve had been the best ever.

Steve had shown her how to hold and lead Sam and how to brush him. She was feeling much braver now around horses now. She had even toyed with the idea of asking Steve to let her have a sit on Sam. Steve was just so amazing with Sam. He was so quiet and confident, yet so gentle. Sam looked lovely when he rode him. Even better had been the evenings she had spent with Steve. They had sat together talking on the sofa and had watched the television both laughing in unison at the same daft sit com. Jade hadn't even had her mother nagging at her yet to come home. She had been surprised at how calm her mother had been about her being away. She wished things were always like this.

Chloe saw Sam look around behind him as he travelled in the trailer. She couldn't help but smile. He was coming along so well. She had been giving him conditioning food as liberally as was safe for him and his build had picked up enormously. She thought that they could just about get away with taking him out now without someone reporting her.

Chloe pondered for a moment on her return to the City. Carl had needed to make a visit to Europe to wind up some apparently extremely lucrative deal in Strasbourg so she had ended up Skyping him to talk. She had been pleasantly surprised when he had advised her to work from home as much as she could. He had also eased her workload saying, "you're too good for me to let go Chloe, I never know when I might need you to close something I can't get to."

Chloe had also been startled at her own feelings. She had actually looked forwards to returning to her late aunt's house. When she had first arrived back at her apartment in the City she had suddenly noticed how cold it felt. Yes it was clean and contemporary with all the latest gadgets at her disposal but the plain walls and minimal furniture suddenly made her feel empty. She had a sudden yearning to return to the large rambling house in the country.

Chloe surveyed the rolling fields as they finally arrived at

Berryford. Ben parked the trailer and jumped out of the car. Chloe parked next to him and they all piled out too. Ben looked around with widened eyes. "My this is some place," he said.

There was a huge out door all weather arena, which had a full set of show jumps all ready to be used. Next to that was an equally large all weather warm up arena. If you followed the wide track next to it, you came to some large fields where you could see cross country jumps of all types scattered around their length and breath.

Chloe was also looking around with interest. "Well this is certainly well equipped," she said "You and Sam should have some fun," she added giving Steve a slap on the shoulder.

Steve stared across the fields, at the cross country jumps. He hoped that he didn't let anyone down. Chloe had been good enough to let him ride Sam even though he hadn't competed in a horse trial competition before. He had been spending time schooling Sam around the ropey old jumps that Sarah had randomly scattered around the fields but these fences were much more solid and spooky looking.

As they unloaded the horses from the trailer to get them ready they could see that some of the other liveries were already here.

Big Jayne was strapping Heather into her body armour. Jane had shared a lift in Big Jayne's trailer and watched as Britney tacked up Whitney. Britney had a big smile on her face, she was so looking forward to this. She couldn't wait to jump some real jumps. She just hoped that Whitney would wake up a bit more. At the moment she had her eyes shut and her head was nearly on the floor.

A silver Freelander arrived, towing another trailer. Ben waved at Lyn and she parked next to them. Kelly was sitting next to her. Lyn had managed to borrow Sarah's trailer as Sarah had wanted Kelly to bring Chester to the clinic. Sarah had thought that the experience would be good for Chester and it would be good to see if he took a liking to cross country. Kelly had been thrilled at the idea. She would be less thrilled if she knew that Sarah only wanted to see if Chester was any good at cross country so that she could sell him for an over inflated sum of money.

Steve shook his head as a large lorry arrived. "That's Celia's truck," he said to Chloe as he tacked up Sam. Chloe smiled. "Well this should be fun then, all good buddies back together for a reunion."

Steve smiled and gave Sam a pat. Sam was looking around him with interest. Chloe turned to Jade. "Go and find out where we have to go," she said. Jade nodded and trotted off in what she hoped was the right direction to find someone in charge.

Jade returned a while later to find nearly everyone mounted. They were standing in groups chatting excitedly. She saw Ella tacking up a horse by the lorry. Joanne was standing behind her holding another horse with her good arm.

Jade found Chloe. "We have to go over there," she said pointing to the far end of the field. "We just ride along this track and it takes us up to it," she finished.

As the group set off along the large sandy drive, Chloe noticed Rory's car pull up. Rory had decided to come along for the entertainment value. There were sure to be some interesting scenes with this lot. Fortunately he had managed to wriggle out of taking part in the clinic himself, saying that he didn't want Ted to get excited by doing cross country as it might spoil his dressage training.

Paul mounted the horse that Ella had been holding and another lad mounted the other. They rode off after the rest of the horses along the track.

Chloe had set off with along the track with Steve but Jade paused and waited for Ella. Jade smiled at Ella but her smile froze as she saw the look on Ella's face. "What's up?" Jade asked her.

"I could have been doing this but instead they let the new lad do it!" Ella said sharply, gesturing at the riders in front of them. "I've been there longer than him and he doesn't even ride that well, but they still let him come and ride and I'm just the bloody dogsbody again," she seethed.

Joanne nodded in agreement. "It's terrible, Ella is such a good rider but she keeps getting ignored. I reckon it's sexism in the workplace. Mind you, Celia probably fancies the new lad too."

Ella looked at her in surprise "She's old enough to be his mother!"

Joanne smiled. "Bet it wouldn't bother her. He's got that Spanish look about him don't you think? Tony's is his name. Wonder where she found him? Bet she poached him from some livery yard. Luring him in with talk of fame and fortune and his own place and then giving him a cheap wage and an ancient caravan."

Ella rolled her eyes at Joanne. "That doesn't make me feel any better you know."

Jade sighed. "Oh Ella that's such a shame. We can still watch and listen though, I'm sure you'll pick some tips up from watching the clinic."

Ella looked dismally back at Jade. "I suppose that's all I can do," she said. Ella was getting so fed up with being ignored and Paul had been even more unbearable since their sexual encounter. He had started grabbing her around the waist when no one was around and pulling her against him so that she could feel his stiffness against her. Then he would just push her away with some sarcastic remark like; "You need to work a bit harder before you get another seeing to from me, slapper."

The trouble was, every time he did pull her against him she felt that deep longing start to rise in her. She had to fight off that feeling. Thank God she had got the morning after pill after last time, at least she hadn't got pregnant. She had made sure that wouldn't happen again by a visit to her Doctors. She had complained that she needed something to ease her terribly painful period pains as a subterfuge to get on the pill.

They reached the end of the sandy track and walked across to the fields where the horses and rider were milling about. Steve walked Sam quietly around. He had seen Celia glaring at him from across the way. He looked up as another horse suddenly appeared alongside him. It was Paul.

"Don't know why you've bothered coming here on that bag of bones," snarled Paul. "He was a rubbish race horse and he'll be rubbish at this."

Steve turned around and gave Paul a warm smile. "Good to see you're here. I'll be able to see you ditched into a fence. That horse you're on hates solid jumps," he said. Steve quickly trotted Sam across the diagonal away from Paul who was left seething.

"You're just trying to worry me because you know that I'm better than you." Paul muttered as Steve rode away. He suddenly wondered if there was any truth in what Steve had said. His horse could be a bit stuffy to jump sometimes after all.

Chloe was standing further away from the horses with Gill who was trying to stop her two young girls from pulling each others hair out as they fought over the now one legged doll. Those girls were so loud. Chloe wished they had a volume switch so that she could mute their shrieking. Gill was making no effort to quieten them as she pulled them apart. Chloe had noticed that Gill never did make much of an effort to calm them down when they were out though. She had brought them to the yard a couple of times and Gill seemed to think that once they were at the yard it was like dropping them off at a crèche and someone else would look after them while she strolled off for a chat.

Chloe slowly edged away from Gill and the girls and over towards where Jade was standing with Ella and Joanne. Celia was standing with Rory and Sarah. Celia had already given Chloe several filthy looks, causing Chloe to smile widely back at her in response. Chloe noted Celia's face seemed to become redder with each smile.

Chloe thought that Ella seemed rather tense. "I thought that you were going to be riding today, " she said as she approached them.

Jade shook her head. "Oh don't say anything you'll only wind her up," she said quickly. Chloe nodded and looked back to see what Steve was up to on Sam. He was cantering him quietly in a large circle. Sam looked like he was going very nicely. Chloe found herself smiling as she watched them.

Steve took Sam over to a small log fence and Sam popped over it easily. They both looked so comfortable together. Chloe had definitely made the right decision in taking on Steve to look after Sam. Chloe noticed that Jade's hand went to her mouth as she watched Steve jump. Jade obviously still had a crush on him. Chloe hoped that he wouldn't hurt Jade's feelings. Although when she had returned back from the City she had been surprised to find that Jade had been helping Steve with Sam at the yard. Jade had even learnt how to muck out and groom Sam. At least she seemed to be getting over her fear of horses.

She looked back at the horses and winced as she saw Firefox following Sam over the fence. Heather's face was in a grimace of terror as Firefox flew over. She hadn't intended to jump it but had found it impossible to stop Firefox from tearing off after Sam once she'd seen him cantering past. Firefox had taken quite a liking to Sam and was always whickering to him from across the stable block. Big Jayne was nodding as she watched with a smile on her face. "That's the way Heather, get her warmed up nicely," she shouted.

Chloe's thoughts were interrupted as she heard a car pull up behind her. She turned around to see a Range Rover continue off the track and drive on to the field. Jade's eyes widened. "I thought you weren't supposed to drive on here," she stated.

Ella gave a small smile. "Oh, she's allowed to. It's Lucinda Lilac."

They all watched as the car parked on the edge of the field and Lucinda Lilac jumped out. Lucinda stopped and watched the horses and riders. They were milling around now, unsure of what to do now that she had arrived. Some of them had halted and were just staring across at her waiting for instructions.

The passenger door opened and Lucinda's daughter jumped out from the car. She smiled at her mother. "This is nice mum, not too many."

Lucinda nodded. "Yes, I think doing it as a last minute thing has thrown a few people out, Lucy. Well, let's see what this lot can do then," she said brightly and walked across to where the Berryford head groom; Simone was waiting for her.

Lucinda smiled at Simone who beamed back at her. "Oh how nice to meet you Mrs Lilac." Simone gushed. "Where do you want them?"

"Well, let's line them up and I can have a chat and then we'll see what they can do."

Chloe watched as Simone called the riders into a line in front of them. Lyn and Kelly were looking nervously at Lucinda as she approached them. Lyn was thinking perhaps she shouldn't have bothered coming. Quickstep seemed to be even more lethargic after the trailer journey and she had needed to give him the biggest pony club kicks just to get him to canter a circle.

Kelly was hoping that Chester's wind would hold out for this. Although Chester had been hobdayed he still made quite a wheeze when he exerted himself too much and she had already heard the faint whine coming from him when she had been cantering him around. She wished that Sarah would spend the extra money to sort him out properly but she was too tight for that. Kelly suspected that Sarah had only sent him here to see if he had any potential to event and then she'd probably sell him. Sarah hardly ever rode either of her horses these days and when she did all she ever did was go for a plod around the lanes.

A silence descended as Lucinda approached the group with a small smile on her face. She stopped a few feet away before addressing them. "Hello, I'm Lucinda Lilac. Now why don't you each tell me why you're here."

CHAPTER 20

Celia was scowling at Chloe from across the field. She was so annoyed with that woman. Who did she think she was? She'd been going around the village trying to get money from everyone to sponsor that awful horse. Celia had heard that they'd even gone to the local village shop to try and get money from Mrs Patel. The nerve of her! Celia turned and looked across at Steve. She was hoped that sly little shit would get himself in a fix today. As far as she knew he hadn't done much cross country riding. Although from what she'd seen so far she had to admit he looked quite at home out there.

When Lucinda had finished speaking to the riders, she sent them all off so that she could watch them schooling by themselves. She strolled around looking at each of them in turn.

Lucinda raised an eyebrow as Firefox flew across the field with Heather clinging on. Lucy nudged her, "I take it that's her mother over there," she said nodding in the direction of Big Jayne who was shouting at Heather. "Pop Foxy over a fence, show this lady what you're made of."

Lucinda pressed her lips together managing not to laugh out loud. "Poor child, she looks terrified," she muttered to Lucy.

Lucinda paused and narrowed her eyes as she watched Steve schooling Sam. She smiled and nodded to Lucy and they walked on. They were just in time to see Ben tearing across the diagonal at a rapid trot. Ben's two girls had plaited Gatsby's hairy feathers earlier on in the morning. The plaits bobbed merrily about around his legs as he trotted.

Lucinda and Lucy exchanged glances. This time they both had to stifle their grins. Lucinda smiled politely at Ben as they passed. She paused as she saw Lyn managing to kick Quickstep over a small log fence. Quickstep made an over exaggerated leap over the little log.

They wandered further over the field, pausing as Paul came flying past them. He cantered on rapidly and took the log from the fast canter. Tony, who took the small fence in the same rapid style, quickly followed him.

Lucinda looked further across the field to where Kelly was trotting slow circles on Chester. She had sloped away from the others hoping that Lucinda wouldn't hear Chester's wheezing, which had become increasing louder as she moved him up a gear. Lucinda bit her lip as she observed them. She was just close enough to hear a faint whine coming from Chester.

Lucinda turned around as she heard Britney pleading with her mount. "Please get on!" She said as she tried to boot Whitney over the log fence. Whitney trotted up to it and then trotted over it. The mare had decided that it didn't warrant the effort of a jump.

Lucinda called to Simone who managed to get the riders attention. They came back over and formed a line in front of Lucinda who stood in front of them with a small smile fixed on her face. "I'm going to split you into two groups," she announced. "The first group will go with Lucy for a while who will give you some training and then I shall come back to you. I'm not sure if you know this, but Lucy is the current Junior European Eventing Champion so do feel free to pick her brains."

Lucy smiled warmly at them. Lucinda divided them into their groups and set off across the field with her group; Steve, Paul, Tony and Kelly

Lucy signaled her group over and had them follow her to

where a few small fences were laid out. Heather was sweating in her body amour as she tried to keep Firefox from spinning around to head off after Sam

Lucy turned and inspected them. She had them all canter a circle again first. Then she lined them up and spoke briefly to each of them in turn. She then told them that she wanted them to jump over a small tiger trap fence.

Britney managed to wake up Whitney by giving her a small whack on the rump. Lucy had told her that she needed to get her going a little more forward. Whitney took a deep breath and decided she'd better get her act together. Britney seemed to be in a serious mood today. She swished her and cantered nicely over to the fence jumping over it with a flourish.

Ben came next. He had to give Gatsby a bit more of a dig in the ribs than he would have liked. Lucy had also advised him that he would need to rally Gatsby around some more. Gatsby cocked an ear on Ben and also popped easily over the fence. Heather followed Ben. She merely had to point Firefox in the direction of the tiger trap and she was on the other side of it before she knew what happened. Lucy had told her to use less rein and more leg but she was too terrified to do anything but cling on and hope that she didn't fall off.

Lyn gritted her teeth as her turn came. She gave Quickstep a sharp slap and cantered him in a small circle, trying to get him as bouncy as she could. Quickstep gave a grunt and decided he'd better be careful today as Lyn was being a bit handy with that stick. He reluctantly jumped over the fence without any over exaggerated theatrics, landing easily on the other side. He did, however let out a grunt as he landed. He wanted Lyn to know much effort he was putting in for her.

Lucy smiled. She sent them away again. This time it was over a double of two small poles. There were no ditches underneath. Lucy decided that they were going to need way more schooling before she risked their necks over ditches. After they had finished, she lined them up and spoke to them. "I'm glad that you know each other," she smiled, "I'd like to make a couple changes amongst you, as long as you're agreeable that is." Lucy looked across at the two mothers standing watching on the sidelines. Big Jayne and Jane exchanged glances.

Across the field, Lucinda led her group over to a complex of fences. They included a water that could be jumped into and out of in a variety of different ways. She looked at them as they arrived at the complex. "As you can see we have a range of fences here and I'd like to see you over each one individually before we put them together as a course. You can see that there is a larger or trickier option as well as an easy option at each one. I want to see you and your horses in your comfort zones first so if there is anything that you're not happy about then give it a miss or jump another one instead."

Lucinda smiled at them. They all stared back at her unblinking. Lucinda cleared her throat. "Have you all much experience of cross country riding?" The group shook their heads in unison.

Paul hoped that Steve hadn't seen him shaking his head, mind you he'd shook his head too. "Lots of practice over the sticks though." Paul quipped quickly.

Tony tried to avoid Paul's gaze. Tony had limited experience over anything higher than a cross pole. He'd been working at the riding school in the next village before he came to Celia's yard. Celia didn't realize that he'd been more of a handyman who just hacked the horses out sometimes to help out. He'd only taken the job at her yard as the riding school was cutting back his hours. Tony was lucky though. The mare he was riding had been very obliging with him so far. Mary was an Irish thoroughbred but she looked more like a bog trotter compared to the other race horses. She certainly wasn't built for speed but she loved jumping.

Lucinda nodded. "Okay, well let's see you over that small brush fence first," she said nodding at Pau. Paul kicked his horse, Solly into life and cantered away so that he could get a good run up to the brush.

They watched in silence as Paul flew over the fence at little short of a gallop. Lucinda walked across to Paul and started trying to explain that he didn't need to take every fence at the gallop. Finally she sent him off again and summoned Kelly, Tony and Steve to also each go over the fence. She watched as Tony booted his mount along grabbing a piece of mane as she took off over the brush.

Kelly cantered away and back over the fence. Chester had been given the time he needed to recover and managed to complete the task with just a subtle wheeze at the end. Chester enjoyed jumping but he found it all very tiring as he struggled to for air.

Finally, Steve cantered Sam around and over the brush fence. Lucinda smiled as she watched Sam's easy jump over the fence and the way he fell straight back into his rhythmic canter afterwards. Steve sat quietly, giving Sam a squeeze of encouragement and a little more of the rein so that he could drop his nose and pop up over the fence.

Lucinda wandered over to each of them individually and gave them some tips on their riding and then sent them off to try the other fences. Tony avoided the bigger ones. Paul took them all on. He was still taking everything at the gallop. Lucinda was becoming increasingly concerned. He seemed to be going even faster and Solly looked like he was starting to get rather over excited. She decided to send them off to the water.

After giving them some tips on how to ride into the water, Lucinda sent Steve off first on Sam. Steve had not ridden Sam through any water yet, so he decided to start him off gently. He walked him to the waters edge and asked him to continue on through it. Sam paused and looked at the water. He gave a small sniff. This was a new experience.

Sam was enjoying himself. He was being asked to do all sorts of curious things lately and he was finding this new life very interesting. He gave another sniff and walked into the water. Steve gave him a few more firmer squeezes with his legs and Sam trotted on through the water and up out of it, via the bank on the other side. Steve turned him around and this time trotted him straight into the water and off out again. He returned to the group with a smile.

Paul saw his smile and sneered back at him. "That was pathetic. You'll never get anywhere if you ponce about like that," he spat as he kicked Solly off away to the water.

Paul cantered around and sent Solly off towards the water. He decided that he would jump into the water over the drop fence and then jump out over the other side. Lucinda watched him with a frown on her face. "Slow down," she shouted as he resumed his usual gallop and headed towards the water.

Solly pricked his ears, he was enjoying all of this galloping around and jumping over these unusual fences, it certainly made a change from being on the gallops. Solly speeded up as he saw the fence that Paul was pointing him at. This was easy. Solly arrived at the fence and poised himself ready to spring over it. Suddenly he saw the vast expanse of water behind it. Solly froze in shock. He hadn't known that was there, and it was right behind the fence. He didn't want to get wet and he certainly didn't want any water in his ears.

Solly reacted with the speed of a truly terrified equine and slapped the brakes on. He managed to stop himself from falling over the fence. Thank goodness, he wouldn't have to swim! He felt a sudden moment of lightness from his back, as Paul sailed over his head. He landed in the water with a splash. Solly peered over the fence apologetically. Paul looked okay, albeit soaking wet and covered in mud. Solly could see he wasn't hurt so he started grazing happily on the tasty grass beside the fence.

Lucinda's hand went to her mouth as she heard the splash. Fortunately Paul was on his feet quickly. Thank goodness, he didn't look hurt. She walked over to him as he sloshed out of the water. She looked him up and down as he paused in front of her. Lucinda shook her head at him. "See. Speed kills," she said and grabbed Solly before he could tread on his reins.

Paul was seething as Lucinda handed Solly back to him. She pursed her lips, "you'd better let yourself dry out a bit before you get back on," she said. "Well as long as you're in one piece, I'll crack on with this lot while you dry off," she added managing not to smile.

Paul turned and walked Solly away and stood him by Kelly who tried to avoid his gaze. They were all stifling giggles. Even Tony was trying not to laugh. He was staring fixedly at his horse's forelock.

Steve looked over at Paul. "Good plan, worked really well for you," he said and couldn't help but smile. Paul turned away and was horrified to see that the other group had also paused in the distance as they heard his splash. They were all staring at him now.

Paul felt himself start to glow. Big Jayne had waddled over to see what had happened. Celia and Sarah looked mortified and that bitch Ella was laughing out loud. Joanne and Jade were clinging on to each other. He could hear that Joanne's stupid guffaws from where he stood. Paul was furious. Bloody stupid horse, he'd never live this down.

Sarah thought that she was coping magnificently as she stood next to Celia. She had managed not to burst out laughing. Celia was fuming. She had already been cursing Paul for riding too fast to the fences. Tony was doing a better job than Paul was. Celia had a customer who was looking for a horse to event and she could hardly palm Solly off to her if Paul was going to teach him to take anything cross country as if he were running in a Derby. She noticed that Rory was grinning from ear to ear. Celia felt like punching the arrogant twat.

Chloe smiled, she just couldn't help it. She managed to compose herself to continue to watch as Kelly and Tony also took the same route as Steve had through the water. After they had all done this a couple of times without problems, they came back to the water and actually jumped into it from the smallest drop fence next to it. It didn't take long before they had all started to jump in and out of the water.

Chloe was delighted with Sam's progress. He seemed to be taking everything in his stride. She was also cheered up by the fact that Steve seemed to be handling all of this so well, despite his claims to knowing little about cross country riding.

The two groups swapped to different areas and Lucinda soon had them cantering easily around the complexes of fences. Except for Paul that is, who sulkily said he was too wet to get on again.

Lucinda glanced across to Lucy and smiled She had swapped Heather and Britney's mounts over. Heather was also smiling. For the first time she didn't have to worry about when Firefox would tear off, taking her into some scary obstacle that she didn't really wish to go near, let alone jump. She found Whitney's laid back temperament much more enjoyable. All she needed was a little bit of an extra kick and Whitney popped nicely over the fences. Big Jayne had been watching her daughter with a frown plastered across her forehead, why on earth did Heather look so pleased to be on such a ploddy pony?

Britney was also beaming. She loved riding Firefox. She felt like she could jump the moon and she had been going over all of the bigger fences, much to her mother's horror. Jane had resorted to closing her eyes when it was Britney's turn. That Firefox was a lunatic. Jane couldn't wait until all of this was over and she could get her daughter safely back on her quiet pony again.

Paul was still sulking and wouldn't even speak to Lucy. He merely nodded or shook his head when she spoke to him. He finally, begrudgingly rode Solly over the rest of the fences. He had seen that Celia looked like she was seething and thought that it would be wise to get back on.

Finally Lucinda drew the clinic to a close. Ben walked back with Lyn. Ben was grinning as he had just completed a jump into the water. Gill watched him as she tried to screw Barbie's head back on whilst the girls still squabbled beside her. Gatsby's plaited feathers hung around his legs like rat's tails and his long tail was soaking and muddy as it trailed along behind him.

Lyn felt newly inspired. Quickstep had jumped most of the fences. Admittedly, they had been the easy options but he'd still had a go. Perhaps he would make a jumper after all. Quickstep flattened his ears as he plodded along. He was exhausted. At first it had been fun, but then it was just tiring. There was no way he was going to get conned into doing this stuff again.

Lucinda smiled as she brought the groups back together. "Well, I hope that you have enjoyed today and please feel free to ask me any questions when we go back to the yard." Her gaze rested briefly on Paul whose clothes were still sodden. She turned and looked at Steve. "Good luck to you all. You've all been terrific."

With that Lucinda turned and walked away with Lucy back to her Range Rover. "Well mum, that was an interesting bunch," said Lucy. Lucinda nodded, "that's an understatement," she said with a smile.

CHAPTER 21

Chloe was feeling slightly nervous as she drove home. She had managed to get away from work earlier than normal, but she was still apprehensive about the party tonight. She had invited some of her business clients as well as practically all of Diddlecot.

This was an important night. She was struggling to finance this whole venture with the house and Sam. The house was so big it cost a fortune to run, and then she had to pay for Steve's wages. Sam was also a money pit. She should have remembered what it was like having to pay for a horse's keep. Her aunt and uncle had always been forking out for things when she lived with them, just to keep her and the horse going.

Chloe felt a sudden deep pang of sadness as she thought of her aunt and uncle. Well, this was why she was doing all of this, she reminded herself. To try and show them some respect. Hopefully things would be sorted out soon. She still hadn't caught up with Carl either, which was a bit worrying, although he seemed to be being quite positive about her working from home a lot of the time. She hoped he wasn't trying to palm her off and move someone else in to the company to take her place.

Chloe arrived back at the house in time to see a flurry of activity. Jade and Ella were hanging lights around the garden. Steve was blowing up balloons and Joanne was unraveling some bunting, which she was finding quite difficult to do with one arm in plaster and Jerry attacking the end of it.

They all looked up as she approached. Jade beamed at her. Chloe smiled back as she wandered over. "How are things going?"

Jade nodded enthusiastically. "Oh great, we've got loads to put out and we've done some lovely food. Most of it's ready. "

"Good, do we have any idea of how many are coming?"

Ella laughed, "everyone in the village!"

Joanne also smiled. "Most people just want to come over for a nose around the house."

Chloe shook her head. "Well I hope that we can get some sponsorship out of this. We really need it."

Jade looked at her with excitement in her eyes. "Oh we've got some sponsorship already."

Chloe stared at her in amazement. "That's wonderful, who and how much?"

Jade licked her lips. "It's only a hundred pounds I'm afraid. It's from the village shop, but it's a start."

Chloe sighed, "I suppose it's better than nothing. I'd better see what food and drink you've concocted," she said as she walked into the house.

Chloe paused in the hallway and looked around. Jade appeared behind her. "We've tried to have a good tidy up and moved some things out into the garage in case they got broken." Jade said with a smile. Chloe looked back at Jade with a raised eyebrow. She had really planned ahead. She hoped that she had done a good job with the food too.

Chloe walked on through the house with Jade following behind her. Jade hoped that Chloe didn't mind them having a tidy up. They had been so worried about any of those beautiful things getting broken they had all agreed that it would be best to put them away just for one night.

Chloe peered around the doors to the sitting room and then moved on to the study. Finally, as they reached the kitchen she turned back to Jade, "yes, it was a good idea to move things. You've done a good job Jade," she said as they walked in to the kitchen.

Chloe stopped and stared at the kitchen table as Jade hovered behind her. Chloe slowly turned around in time to see Jade's humble expression. "You've bought everything from the village shop?" Chloe asked.

Jade nodded, "oh yes, we bought it from her Farm Shop section." Jade scurried around to the table. "We've got some fancy bread and thought we could toast it and cut it up and put cream cheese and smoked salmon on it." Jade glanced across to Chloe who was observing her silently.

Chloe walked across to the fridge and opened the door. She shut it quickly and looked back at Jade. "What on earth are you going to do with all those sausages?" She asked raising an eyebrow.

Jade smiled feebly, "sausages on sticks?"

Chloe was inspecting the wine on the table. "This is all made in Britain. Have you any idea what it tastes like?"

Jade shook her head slowly. "Mrs Patel said it was very popular," she murmured.

Chloe put down the bottle and fixed Jade with an interrogative gaze. "Is this how you got her to sponsor us?"

Jade looked sheepishly down at the floor and gave a small nod. Chloe sighed and rolled her eyes. "You've probably spent more three times more than she sponsored us."

Jade chewed her bottom lip and continued to gaze at the floor until Steve arrived. Chloe turned as Steve walked into the kitchen. She fixed him with a stern look. "I

suppose you helped organize this sponsorship deal too?"

Steve grinned at her. "All your guests will be pleased that we are supporting local businesses," he said and tipped a wink at Jade who beamed back at him.

Chloe shook her head. "We had better get ready I suppose, then we can do something with this banquet."

Jade smiled. "Yes, I'll get Jo and Ella and Anne said she will help too. We haven't got any music though."

"That's okay, there's some on my laptop." Chloe said. "I've brought my sound system from home. Where is my laptop by the way?"

"Oh, it's in the study." Jade replied.

Steve turned to Jade. "I'll put out a few more decorations before I go and change. You can go and get ready if you want, I know a lady likes to prepare," he smiled as he left the kitchen.

Jade, Ella and Joanne all headed up the stairs to go and get ready in Jade's room. Chloe collected the laptop and went up to her own room. She suddenly felt incredibly weary. Chloe smiled at Jerry who was sprawled across her bed like a great big grey sausage. Jerry flexed a paw at her as she tickled his forehead. Chloe turned on her laptop. After she had showered she changed into an emerald green fitted dress with diamante detail across one side of it, which matched the diamante on her high heels.

Chloe gave Jerry another stroke as she sat next to him on the bed inspecting her laptop. She watched the fur puddle around her hand as she touched him. She smiled to herself, it looked like she was going to be wearing cat fur accessories.

Chloe always found it irritating when programs were left on when you turned on computers. Jade must have not shut it down when she used it last. Chloe moved to quit the program and paused as she did. What the hell? Chloe looked again at the screen, it was confirming an order for the morning after pill. Chloe's eyes widened and she opened her mouth in disbelief.

Chloe was still for a minute as she double checked the page. She put her laptop on the dresser and walked down the stairs where Steve was hanging some lights in the hallway. She stopped in front of him. Steve froze as he saw her face, she looked furious.

Chloe leaned close to him, "get your things and get out," she said quietly.

Steve stared back at her. "What? What's wrong?"

"You heard what I said. I will not have Jade being used by men like you. She is

vulnerable and naïve and you should be ashamed of yourself. Now go." Chloe hissed.

Steve's eyes widened. "What? Look, I've no idea what you're talking about. If I've done something wrong tell me."

Chloe glared back at him, she remained still for a moment and then she grabbed his arm. She marched him up the stairs gripping his arm tightly and dragged him in to her bedroom. She pushed him towards the laptop, tapping it into life as she did so. She pointed at the screen. "That is what I'm talking about." Chloe could not contain her anger any longer. ""How could you? I thought I could trust you and this is what you do.

That girl deserves better.' Chloe's voice had become raised, making Jerry suddenly look up from his bed.

Steve looked at the screen and frowned. "I don't know anything about this."

Chloe rolled her eyes. "Well of course you would say that, anything to save your own arse," she shouted.

Steve was shaking his head when Jade popped her head around the door. Jade saw Steve's confused expression. She then noted Chloe's angry face and shrank back visibly as Chloe turned to her. She had not seen Chloe looking so angry before. "Everything all right?" Jade squeaked, moving further back around the door.

Chloe looked at her for a moment and took a breath to calm herself. "Jade I know that Steve has slept with you and I'm sorry. If I'd known that he would take advantage of you I would never have hired him. Don't worry though, he is leaving."

Jade's eyes widened as what Chloe had said sunk in. "No, you can't."

Chloe nodded. "Yes, look Jade I'm not having someone like him mess around with your head any more," she said walking towards Jade who had edged further back around the door.

Jade shook her head. "No, but we haven't done anything wrong!" She said loudly as Chloe took her hand. Jade looked at Steve who was staring at her with a distant look on his face.

Chloe looked at Jade sympathetically, "it's al right Jade you don't have to stick up for him.

"I'm not! We haven't done anything!" Jade wailed as Chloe

pulled her into the room.

Steve shook his head. "Chloe thinks I've been using you," he looked at Chloe angrily "She obviously thinks that's the type of person that I am, so I'm going any way." Steve said turning to leave.

"No!" Jade shouted

Chloe glared at Steve. "You've completely brain washed her haven't you!" She shouted. She turned back to Jade. "I know about you having to take that morning after pill, I saw the order on the laptop, but don't worry I won't tell your mother."

Steve paused for a moment awaiting Jade's response. Jade looked uncomfortably at Chloe and then at Steve. Chloe shook her head.

Suddenly Joanne and Ella peered round the door. Ella's eyes widened. "Er, is everything all right?" We heard shouting." Ella asked cautiously.

Chloe continued to glare at Steve "You might as well know that he is leaving now. I've found out what a shit he is."

Jade looked at Ella. "Chloe found the order for the morning after pill on the laptop."

Ella swallowed and moved towards Chloe. "You don't understand," she said, looking uncomfortable. She gave a sideways glance at Jade. She couldn't drop Jade and Steve in it she decided. "It wasn't for Jade it was for me."

Joanne gaped at her in in astonishment. Why hadn't Ella mentioned this to her?

Chloe was taken aback and looked at Ella silently, blinking.

Jade looked at Steve, he was shaking his head at them. He started to move again to the door. Chloe looked back at him. "Wait."

Steve glared back at Chloe. "I'm off, I'm not staying if you don't trust me," he said and headed for the door.

Ella, Joanne and Jade all stood looking at him open mouthed. They all thought the same thing. No way could he go he was too nice, in all ways. In unison they all started to shout at Chloe and Steve. Pleading with Steve not to go and for Chloe to make him stay. Steve tried to push around them but Jade and Ella grabbed his arm while Chloe grabbed at the girls shouting to at them to let him go. Joanne decided to go for his waist. Unfortunately her rugby tackle knocked him bringing Jade and Ella with him and tripping Chloe over in the fall. They all landed in a heap on the floor, still shouting. Joanne screamed as her bad arm hit the floor as she landed.

Jerry had had enough of this. He was not used to humans behaving in this manner. The shouting had become unbearable. He stepped forwards and squatted on the bed. With a big push he passed a large chocolate brown stool on to the bed. He added another smaller one to it for good measure. Then paused and looked at the group who were still rolling around on the floor.

"Chloe," a voice suddenly said from the doorway. "Is this a good time to introduce you to a potential sponsor? This is Simon Clark."

Chloe managed to look up to see Carl standing in the doorway. The gentleman with him was observing the scene with one raised eyebrow. He looked at Carl. "Perhaps I'd better wait downstairs," he said.

CHAPTER 22

Jerry patted at the quilt with his paws, in a half hearted attempt to bury his droppings. He decided that was sufficient and that he was top dog round here anyhow, so it wasn't really necessary to hide his stools. He jumped off the bed and trotted off down the stairs without so much as a backwards glance.

Anne was in the kitchen. She had been starting to prepare the party buffet but had decided they needed some fizzy wine or some decent red. She wondered why they had bought all of this local rubbish? Anne knew that Sophie had her own much tastier selections tucked away in the cellar. She had shared a tipple on occasions with both Sophie and Harry. Anne decided that it would be prudent to open a few bottles. After all they were trying to get people to part with their cash they should be given something decent to drink.

Jerry paused as he reached the kitchen. He suddenly smelt something very interesting. He trotted into the kitchen and looked up at the work surfaces that were laden with food. He jumped deftly up onto on end and sniffed at the artisan bread laid out before him. He could smell cheese in it. He took a careful mouthful. Not enough in it cheese he decided. He took another quick nibble and then moved on. He had spotted something far further ahead.

Jerry started to purr to himself as he looked at the large salmon sprawled before him. Yum, he liked fish. He observed the salmon and stared at the head for a moment before touching it deftly with a paw. It was dead. Shame he thought he could have played with it for a while. Jerry licked at the salmon before chewing on its flesh. It was delicious but a bone stuck in his mouth. He picked at his face with a paw and sniffed the air again. He had caught a whiff of something even better. His purring increased in volume, he couldn't believe that his new friends had left him such a feast.

Jerry moved along the work surfaces and started to eat the chicken drumsticks that were cooling on a plate. They were still a little warm but after a few shakes of his head they went down nicely. He looked further across the surface. What was that? Jerry moved further along and observed some cream cheese. He sniffed at it and then gave it a lick. It was divine. Jerry stuck his head into the cream cheese and lapped it down. He put a paw in and scooped a pile out, eating it like ice cream. He sniffed at it again rubbed his head across it lovingly. Jerry decided that this was insufficient in showing his appreciation. He moved farther over the cream cheese and lay on top of it. He rolled his front paws lovingly around it and then rolled over it relishing its delicious smell.

A man suddenly appeared in the room. Jerry paused, he wasn't sure who this new visitor was. He rolled on to his back again and waved his paws at him exposing his cream cheese covered tummy. With half closed eyes and a big cat grin he stretched a front paw towards the man in greeting.

Simon observed the scene for a moment. He had decided to wait in the sitting room whilst Carl sorted the mayhem out upstairs. After a while he'd decided to get himself a drink and had wandered to the kitchen. Simon stared at the mess in the kitchen and at the cat languishing in cream cheese. This was a mad house.

A sudden shriek behind him made Simon jump out of his skin. Anne had returned from the cellar. She nearly dropped the wine bottles she was carrying when she saw the mess on the units. She put the wine down and hurried to Jerry. "Oh no Jerry what have you done?" Anne wailed as she saw the half chewed food and chicken drumsticks on the floor.

Jerry smiled at her and purred loudly in response. Anne

turned back to Simon. "Oh my manners. You're that other young man's friend aren't you? Sorry, what was your name again? I was thinking of other things when I let you in. this is Jerry," she said cocking her head at the cat.

Simon gazed at them both, for a while and then cleared his throat. "Yes, I've already met Jerry. I'm Simon," he said with a wry smile.

Anne smiled back at him. She observed his face. His dark brown hair was combed away neatly and he had lovely white teeth. He was rather a dashing young man, Anne wondered if Chloe had met him yet. "Why don't you let me get you a drink and you can relax in the sitting room until our hosts decide to show up, she said."

Simon smiled. 'That sounds delightful," he replied looking at the bottles on the work surface with interest.

Anne looked back at the wine she'd brought with her. "Here don't you have any of that rubbish, try some of this. This is good stuff," she said reaching for a corkscrew.

Simon pulled a chair out from the table. "Why don't you have one with me and I'll help you clear up the mess," he said looking at Anne earnestly.

Anne smiled back, thinking what lovely grey eyes he also had. She patted her hair net into place. "Well I only drink the odd sherry usually, but what the heck." Anne turned back to look at Jerry who was languishing in his cream cheese bed. He stretched out a front paw and hooked another chicken drumstick towards him and rolled over to eat it.

Anne sighed and moved forwards to take it from him. "Jerry you shouldn't eat things with bones in," she chided. She surveyed the mess along the units and sighed again. "Oh dear, now what is everyone going to eat? They'll be arriving soon." Anne reached across for some paper towel and started dabbing at Jerry with it, trying to clean off the cream cheese. She didn't want him dragging it all around the house.

Simon had taken the corkscrew and found a couple of glasses. He opened a bottle of red wine and poured two glasses out handing one to Anne. Simon clinked his glass against hers. "Here's to a good party then," he said brightly.

Anne nodded, "well it's not getting off to a brilliant start," she said. She froze as she heard a knock from the front door. "Oh no, they're arriving already. Where is Chloe?"

Simon shook his head. "I believe she is otherwise engaged. Would you like me to get the door?"

Anne smiled weakly. "Would you? I need to sort this mess out and get something else out for people to eat. Where are the rest of them? They're supposed to be doing this and I'm helping them, not the other way around."

Simon paused. "Let's just say I think we need to give them a moment," he said and walked quickly away to answer the door.

Simon opened the door to see Celia, Duncan, Sarah and Mark standing in front of him. Mark beamed at him. "Hello we've come for the party, " he said grasping Simon's hand and shaking in vigorously. "Don't believe we've met. I'm Mark and these are Duncan, Sarah and Celia," he said nodding at the others.

Celia and Sarah said nothing as they looked back at Simon. Duncan gave a small nod in Simon's direction. Simon wondered which one was Sarah and which one was Celia. Either way, they both looked as miserable as sin.

Celia was fuming. She hadn't wanted to come here in the first place. She didn't see the point. Celia had thrown the invitation in the fire when she had seen it. How that Chloe woman had the nerve to send her an invitation, she didn't know. She had no intention of giving her anything to help with that useless horse that should have been put down. However, Duncan had thought that it would be good to go to as it was a local event and after all, everyone else in the village seemed to be going. So he had managed to talk her round and Sarah and Mark said that they were coming too so she finally supposed that she might as well go. Unfortunately, Celia had felt more annoyed at them all, as they got closer to the house. If that bloody woman started lording it over her with her condescending manner, then she would be straight home.

Simon paused as he saw another two cars pull up at the house. Oh dear, the hosts had better put in an appearance soon he thought. He ushered Celia, Sarah, Mark and Duncan into the sitting room and went back to let the others in. Simon paused to pop his head around the kitchen door to Anne as he passed. "Could you be a love Anne and put some drinks in the sitting room while I get the door, then I'll give you a hand with the food," he asked.

Anne smiled nodded and reached for the wine.

Celia looked around the sitting room and gave a sniff. "Looks a bit dated in here. You'd think they would have tarted it up a bit," she said as she plonked herself down on the sofa.

Duncan was wandering around the sitting room. He paused to look at the shelves and inspected their contents. Sarah sat down on the sofa next to Celia. She hoped

that Celia would be in a better mood soon. She had felt her seething in the car. She didn't want there to be any trouble.

Mark was standing in front of the French doors, gazing out at the garden. "My what a super gaff," he breathed.

Anne came in to the sitting room with some bottles of wine and glasses, which she placed on the coffee table. "Here's something to keep you all going. I'm sure your hosts will be here shortly. They're, er just performing their ablutions," she said.

"What, all of them?" Celia asked reaching for a bottle. She poured herself and Sarah a large glass each and sat back with a sigh.

Anne was in the kitchen pulling some pizzas from the freezer when Simon arrived back and sat down at the table. "They're coming thick and fast now," he said tickling Jerry's neck who was now sitting on the table.

Anne breathed a sigh of relief when Jade walked in to the kitchen. "You look nice dear," she said, admiring Jade's gold dress.

Jade took in the scene for a moment and her eyes widened in a watery stare. She put in her contact lenses for the evening. She didn't wear them very often as she found they just made her eyes water. They had already started to irritate her, resulting in her teary eyed look.

Jade turned to see Jerry licking the remains of the cream cheese off his paws on the table. "Oh Jerry, have you done this?" Jade asked despairingly.

Anne looked back at her. "It's my fault I shouldn't have left the food unattended. It's going to be pizzas and garlic bread with potato wedges now. Why don't you see if we've got some pickled onions, we can stick the them on some sticks with some cheddar from the fridge."

Simon nodded at Jade who gave him a shy smile. "I take it you've all ironed out your issues now?" He asked raising an eyebrow.

Jade nodded. "Yes Chloe and Steve are just working things out. I don't know what we'd do without Steve. He rides Sam so well, they really get along," she said as she headed for the food cupboards

"You may need to entertain your guests." Simon said, stopping her dead in her tracks. "There are quite a few in the sitting room now,"

Jade froze. "Me?" She squeaked. "I wouldn't know what to say to them."

"Don't worry Jade." A voice piped up behind her. "I'll sort them out." Jade gave a sigh of relief as Chloe entered the kitchen. Chloe paused as she stared across at the work surfaces. "What on earth?" Chloe looked at Jerry who was lying on the table now purring. She looked back at Jade. "I think it would be a good idea if you took Jerry up to bed for the evening. I don't think he'll like the noise. Put him in one of our bedrooms and shut the door."

Jade nodded in agreement and went to pick up Jerry.

"Jade," Chloe said quickly, "put a towel around him first, you don't want to ruin your dress. Oh and best take him a litter tray up, we don't want another "incident"."

Jade grabbed a towel and quickly gave Jerry a rub down and scooped him up in her arms. She paused as she left the kitchen and turned back to Chloe. "Er, Chloe about Steve?"

Chloe sighed. "It's okay Jade he's staying, he's just getting changed that's all."

Chloe shook her head as Jade beamed and skipped out of the kitchen. Chloe hoped that she wouldn't trip over in those heels otherwise Jerry would be in for a shock. Chloe looked at Simon for a moment. "What are you doing in here?" She asked suddenly.

Anne turned around. "He's been helping out. He's let the guests in and served them drinks and he's been helping me too."

"Oh God." Chloe groaned, "I'm so sorry," she held out her hand. "I guess you know that I'm Chloe Marcus."

Simon smiled as he shook her hand. "Yes, you certainly know how to make an impact."

Chloe rolled her eyes. "Oh dear that was awful. How embarrassing," she said. Chloe looked up suddenly as she heard another car arrive. "I haven't set up the music yet! I need to get going."

Simon laughed. "Why don't you answer the door and show me where the music is and I'll sort that out for you," he said getting up from the table.

Chloe beamed at him. "That would be so helpful," she said with a smile.

Anne watched as both they left the kitchen and started smiling to herself. She heard the music start to play. The speakers were all along the hallway so that it could be heard all over the house. The lights were dimmed and the fairy lights switched on. It was finally starting to look like a party.

Celia was annoyed. She was sulking on the sofa with Sarah. Duncan had disappeared and Mark was chatting up some young woman from the City. She took a slug of her wine and shook her head. Sarah patted her hand and gave her a smile.

"Don't worry I can smell food, we can have a little nibble in a while."

Chloe had finally managed to escape from hosting for a while. Everyone seemed to be enjoying themselves. Even Celia was smiling now that she devoured half a pizza. Steve had calmed down after she had conceded her mistake and done some serious groveling. Chloe was someone who was always able to see when she had done something wrong and misjudging Steve had been a major error on her part.

Chloe saw Carl and Simon across the sitting room and wandered over. She smiled at Simon. "I hope this is making up for earlier," she said looking at his face to see if he was annoyed.

Simon laughed. "Don't worry about earlier, it makes a change from the other parties that I normally go to."

Carl glanced at Chloe. "Do you know, I think this is the first time that I've ever seen you at a party." He turned back to Simon. "She only attends social functions if she absolutely has to, don't you Chloe?"

Chloe shook her head. "Well I suppose I'm not very sociable," she admitted.

Simon raised an eyebrow. "You could have fooled me," he said, "look around, this is one heck of a party."

Chloe did and admitted to herself that it was. There were plenty of people chatting away and some were in the hall having a little dance. Even the substitute food seemed to be a hit. Chloe paused as she suddenly saw Jade gesturing to her from the doorway. She excused herself and went over to see what she wanted.

Jade grabbed her hand and pulled her out to the hallway.

"Chloe, you'll never guess what we've found," she said excitedly.

Chloe stared back at Jade's excited face. "What? What one earth's wrong?"

Jade turned and dragged her along quickly beside her, past a few milling guests and across to the far end of the hallway in to the study. As they went inside Chloe saw Steve, Ella and Joanne huddled in the corner of the room, they turned around as she entered.

"Shut the door." Steve said. He looked back at Chloe. "Joanne was dancing and she fell over."

Chloe glanced at Joanne. She wasn't surprised she looked a bit the worse for wear.

Steve continued, "she hit the book case and this opened."

Chloe walked around and peered at where he was pointing. She paused and looked at Steve for a moment in surprise. "I don't believe it," she murmured. "It looks like you've found some sort of a secret passageway."

CHAPTER 23

Ella and Joanne were staring curiously at the opening behind the bookcase. Chloe turned to Steve. "Have you seen where it leads?" She asked. Steve shook his head. "We haven't been in yet, thought we'd better show you first."

Jade nodded. "Plus it's really, really dark in there."

"And it could be booby trapped." Joanne added. Ella looked at her with a frown. "Oh, that's just silly," she exclaimed. Joanne was quick to retort, "no, this house is really old, there might be all sorts of things left over from the olden days."

Ella stared at her for a moment. "Such as?"

"Well, there could be stuff stashed away from the war, or you never know, maybe someone who used to live here was into witchcraft or something." Joanne replied.

Jade's eyes widened in horror. "Oh no, you don't think that do you? You mean that there could be dead bodies and all sorts in there?"

Chloe rolled her eyes. "Oh for goodness sake, it's like living with the Goonies." She looked back at Steve. "Can you fetch a torch and I'll have a look inside." Chloe looked around at the crumb littered desk and random glasses scattered around. "What have you been doing in here?"

Jade looked sheepish. "We were just having a chat with Steve."

Ella chipped in. "We wanted to make sure he still felt welcome, we don't want him clearing off."

"So, you were having some kind of team building exercise." Chloe said, shaking her head.

Steve appeared, he practically ran back into the room. He was clutching a large torch. He thrust it in Chloe's hands and looked back at her eagerly. "Do you want me to go first? Just in case there's anything dodgy in there."

Chloe stared back at him and shook her head. "It's okay, I think I can manage. You can come along though, just in case there are any zombies in there," she added rolling her eyes. She looked back at the girls. "You lot stay put until we return, and if anyone asks I'm powdering my nose."

Chloe flicked on the torch and stepped into the passageway. It was a fairly narrow space she thought as she shone the torch around it. The torch was not providing as much light as she would have hoped, it would seem that the batteries were getting flat. She shone the torch forwards and saw that the passage went along a few metres before dropping away into darkness. She moved forwards, walking carefully. She paused to pull some cobwebs from around her head.

Chloe could hear Steve walking along behind he. She realised that she felt glad of

his presence, as the dim light from the room subsided and she moved further into the dark passageway.

As she walked further forwards the passage seemed to come to an abrupt end. She shone the torch upwards and yes there was nothing but a wall up ahead. She felt strangely disappointed. Was that it?

Chloe's was distracted as Steve suddenly grabbed her around the waist and pulled her towards him. "Stop!"

Chloe gasped in surprise. "What on earth are you doing?"

Steve spoke into her ear. She could feel his warm firm torso against her back. "Look down," he said, still holding her around the waist. Chloe did as she was bid, shining the torch further down. The dim orange glow showed her the narrow stairway that dropped away about a foot in front of her. If Steve hadn't stopped her she would probably have fallen down the stairway.

"Well spotted, " she muttered. "Saved me from ruining a perfectly fine dress." She added giving him a small smile.

Steve let go of her waist and she moved forwards and carefully stepped on the stairs. They seemed stable. Steve put a hand on her shoulder. "Careful Chloe, perhaps I should go first, we don't know how safe the stairs are."

"It's okay, I think they're fairly solid," she replied as she moved down the first step. As Chloe stepped downwards the wall widened away. She began to feel a little giddy and was relieved to feel a rail to hold on to as she moved further down the steps.

They walked carefully down the stairway, which spiraled downwards, until finally Chloe felt herself step on to a firm floor. She shone the torch down again and was relieved to see that there appeared to be no more stairs. She walked forwards slowly and looked around. They seemed to be in a large corridor, there were a few a good few feet of space on each side of them.

As they moved along Chloe thought she could see something in the left of the passageway. She moved toward it and shone the torch on it. "What's this?" Steve was looking at it in the dim light. "I think it's a light fitting," he said, after staring at it for a few moments. "We just need to find out how to switch it on." He started to feel around the fitting. Steve could not find any way of turning the thing on. "It must be controlled centrally. There must be a box somewhere," he looked around and then continued feeling the wall, trying to find something in the dim light.

Chloe shone the torch and walked further along the corridor. "There's something else up ahead," she said, straining her eyes trying to see beyond the torch's amber glow.

Steve walked carefully after her. "Slow down, I can hardly see you Chloe." His voice

had a slight edge to it. Chloe ignored him and carried on along the passageway. She walked further on towards the shape that she had made out in the dull light from the torch. She stopped and shone the torch on it.

Chloe took a sharp intake of breath as the corridor was suddenly filled with light. She span around to see Steve smiling at her. He pointed at the box on the wall that he'd found. "Fuse box," he said as if any explanation was needed.

The corridor lights were not particularly bright but both Chloe and Steve felt more at ease now that the pitch blackness had been replaced by this warm glow.

Steve walked over to where Chloe was standing and they both looked along the corridor. The corridor was littered with the lights that they had just found. The lights were not overly bright but there was just enough illumination to see that there were several doors along the corridor. The doors were all dark oak, as was the one that they stood in front of. Chloe was looking at it with bright eyes.

Chloe looked back at Steve. "Shall we?"

"Ladies first?" Steve said raising an eyebrow at her.

But of course." Chloe said with a small smile. She turned the door handle and pushed the door slowly open. She paused and shone the torch into the room. There were no lights on inside this one. Chloe felt around the wall at the side of the door inside the room for a light switch, finally she found a large brass switch that she pulled downwards.

The room was flooded with light. Chloe stopped again and blinked as she looked at the interior of the room. She moved forwards, trying not to tread on the papers that were strewn around the floor. Steve followed her into the room. They both paused and looked around at the room in which they stood. It had a mass of bookcases around its walls, which were bursting at their seams with the amount of papers and files that were stuffed inside them.

Chloe walked over to one and picked up some papers. "This must have been the stuff my uncle used to work on." She said as she saw the symbols that were all over the papers.

Steve was also looking at a bookcase. "Why didn't he keep it in the study in the house?" He wondered aloud.

Chloe turned back to him frowning. "I don't know." She continued looked around the room. Not only were there papers all over the bookcases but there were also papers scattered all around the floor of the room. She also noticed an overturned table in the corner and the remains of a smashed paperweight were on a large desk in the centre of the room. "Looks like someone had a bad day," she murmured.

Steve nodded. "It's strange that this is in such a mess. I wonder what went on in here?"

Chloe shook her head. "Shall we see what else lies down the rabbit hole?"

Steve nodded and they walked back out into the corridor and along to the next room. Chloe opened the door switching the light on as she entered. She stopped as she looked around.

The room looked like a large tack room. It had saddle racks and free standing saddles holders around it and bridle hooks. There was a rug rack in the corner. A two seater sofa was positioned comfortably close to a small stove and there was a table positioned against a wall.

Chloe stared with widened eyes at the dusty saddles and bridles that adorned the room. Then she looked up, she couldn't help but be drawn to the photos that were also all over the walls.

Steve walked over to one of the pictures. It was of a young girl jumping a cross country fence on a bay horse. "This is you isn't it?"

Chloe nodded silently, she was looking at each of the pictures in turn and every time she looked she felt a lump rise further in her throat. Finally her gaze settled on a photograph of her sitting on a horse. The horse was adorned in garlands of flowers and leaves. Two other people were also smiling at her from each side of the horse.

Steve looked at the photograph that seemed to have captivated Chloe. "Where was this taken?"

"It was at Ravensthorne. I'd just won the three star. That's aunt Sophie and uncle Harry with me," her voice barely more than a whisper.

Steve's eyes widened in surprise, "you won a three star?" Steve paused, he had noted Chloe's watery gaze. He bit his tongue he could see that Chloe was getting emotional looking at the photograph. She turned and fixed Steve with a slightly steely stare. "I didn't win it she did," she said and pointed at the horse in the picture. She paused and stared at the photograph again, she looked as if she might cry and indeed she felt as if she should. "Her name was Roxy. She was amazing," she murmured.

Chloe took a silent deep breath and straightened herself back up. She looked around the room again. Steve also looked around. His eye was caught by the array of rosettes and cups that filled the table. He walked over to them to examine them closer. Chloe gazed at them for a moment and then turned back to look at the sofa by the fire.

Steve picked up a rosette. He read the venue and placing from the front of it and then turned it around to read the writing that had been excitedly written in green ink on the back. "These are all yours too aren't they?" Steve took another look at the rosette before slowly replacing it. He turned back to see that Chloe had sat on the sofa by the fireplace.

Chloe stared at the fire for a moment before picking up the book that had been placed down on the arm of the sofa. Steve walked over and also looked at the book. "Black Beauty. I'd have thought your aunt and uncle would be a bit old for that," he said quietly.

Chloe shook her head. "They used to let me clean tack in the house by the fire. When I first lived with them. They used to like to read to me. That was the first book they ever read to me." She smiled fondly at the book for a moment. "My uncle got a bid carried away later though. I think he was trying to convert me to science. He started reading deeper stuff to me when I got older. I wasn't really interested but I used to let him carry on. I liked to humour him."

Chloe smiled at Steve now and stood up. "This must have been some kind of basement at one time and someone's converted it to this." She gestured around trying to find the words to describe what this was.

"Den?" Steve filled in for her.

Chloe nodded, she saw a pile of rugs in the corner and walked over to them. As she bent down to pick one up she saw the brown fur on it and felt her throat catch again as she remembered her beloved horse.

Chloe pulled at the rugs. "We should hang these on the rug rack, they might fit Sam. I suppose I'd better come back for them or I'll be covered in fur," she said, laying them back down.

Ever practical thought Steve. He frowned as he noticed something behind the table where the rugs had been. "What's that behind the table?" He asked and walked over to where the rugs had been lying. He pulled out the table and stared at the safe that was built into the wall behind the table. "Not only a secret den but locked safe in the secret den. What was your uncle up to?"

Chloe shook her head. "Oh he was always worried that someone would be trying to steal his work and abuse it. That's probably why he put that stuff next door."

Steve stood back up. "So what was this room for?"

Chloe looked away. It looks like this is where they put all of my stuff when I left. They probably wanted to forget about me."

Chloe turned around and walked away to leave the room. Steve took a final glance around and then followed her. Chloe turned off the light and closed the door as they left. She walked towards the final room in the corridor.

Chloe paused at the final door. She looked at Steve before she opened the door "Well what do you think is in this one?" She asked with a raised eyebrow.

"You'd better just open it before I start getting over imaginative," he replied quickly.

Chloe smiled and pushed open the door, flicking on the light as she did so. They both stared around the room. There was a moment of silence and then they exchanged glances.

"What on earth were they up to?" Chloe asked.

Steve shook his head, frowning in puzzlement. Chloe gave him one more glance and stepped inside the room.

CHAPTER 24

Jade peered down the corridor, squinting through watery eyes, trying to find a better view. "I hope they're all right in there," she said finally, turning back to Joanne and Ella who were sipping glasses of wine. Joanne smiled back at her blearily. 'As long as there are no vampires in there they'll be all right. Mind you, I'll bet Steve would sort 'em out." Joanne grinned at Jade who shook her head and looked away.

Joanne had been slightly upset to find that Ella had not confided in her about her fling with Paul. She had been feeling down and so she had decided to cheer herself up by getting into the party spirit. She poured some more wine into her glass and offered the bottle to Ella and Jade. Jade shook her head and Ella rolled her eyes. "You've had too much of that, I don't want to have to carry you to bed." Ella said, fixing Joanne with a stern gaze.

Joanne grinned. "You could get Paul to carry me to bed, maybe he'll give me some extra tuition too," she slurred. Ella bit her lip and looked away in embarrassment.

Jade gave Ella a watery stare as a silence suddenly descended on the house. They could hear some laughter and chattering in the distance now. "The music's stopped." Jade said with a frown. "Oh dear, I'd better go and sort something out."

Ella shook her head. "I'll go and do it. Jade. I really think you should take those lenses out, your eyes are getting really red, you look like you've been up for a week."

Jade nodded. "They are driving me nuts," she paused and glanced at Joanne who was sitting down leaning on the table now, staring morosely at her drink. "Do you think she'll be okay? What if Chloe or Steve calls us?" jade asked.

Ella nodded. "She'll be all right and I'm sure Chloe and Steve would want us to keep the party going. Besides, they could be ages down there if they find something of interest."

They made their way out into the hallway and Ella headed off to re start the music, which was soon echoing around the house again. She turned to go back and paused as she passed the sitting room as she saw Tony and Paul standing in a corner chatting and laughing with one of Chloe's guests. She hoped that Paul wasn't corrupting him.

Ella saw that Celia and Sarah were also in the room in conversation with Simon and Carl. Oh dear, perhaps she should go and call Chloe back to rescue them she wondered. She peered in for a moment. Maybe she had better bring some more wine or food in to keep them occupied.

Celia had been giving Ella the cold shoulder for a while now and she suspected that she didn't like her hanging around with Jade. Celia had not even hinted that Ella would be allowed to do much more that stable duties at the moment and Ella was now getting fed up of it. She wished that she could get to compete for once.

Ella marched off to the kitchen she grabbed a loaf of bread and spread butter on some of the bread. She filled the slices with grated cheese and whacked them together. Perhaps a cholesterol overdose might finish off that old bat Celia she thought, scowling at the sandwiches as she sliced them up. Ella took a deep breath and told herself off for being evil. She found a large plate and heaped the sandwiches on it and headed back to the sitting room carrying them and some bottles of wine on a tray.

Ella swept in o the sitting room. "More refreshments?" She asked and laid down the sandwiches and wine on the table. Paul and Tony stopped talking at the sound of her voice and looked at her. Ella was wearing a fitted silky pale blue dress which had thin straps encrusted with crystals. Her golden locks hung around her shoulders. Tony couldn't help but take a large swallow. "She looks amazing," he murmured to Paul. Paul stayed silent he felt a pang of irritation that Ella had not even spoken to him yet.

Paul felt in his pocket and smiled to himself. He turned back to Tony. "She looks like butter wouldn't melt in her mouth but don't let looks deceive you, " he said with an evil grin. Paul also nodded at the other man Richard who apparently was some stockbroker, loaded of course, no doubt he just got lucky.

Celia gave Ella an evil glare before catching sight of the sandwiches. "Go and grab us some food Sarah before these gannets wolf it all down," she said, giving Sarah a prod in the ribs.

Sarah rolled her eyes and pulled herself up from the sofa. They were having such a nice talk with Simon and Carl she didn't want to move. Not to mention how easy on the eye they both were.

Ella paused as she turned to leave Paul and Tony and the fair haired, middle aged man who was with them, they were all looking at her in a strange way. Paul was grinning salaciously across at her. She felt a shiver go down her spine. Tony was just gaping at her, his mouth ajar like a fish out of water. The other man was also staring at her with wide eyes. He looked slightly flushed. Ella felt a sinking feeling in her stomach. What had Paul been up to?

Ella strolled over to them, trying to appear casual. "Don't you want any more refreshments?" She asked glaring at Paul.

Paul gave her a small smile. "Are you being the host tonight then? Must be another one of your talents," he said, taking a sip from his bottle of beer. He had something in his other hand that he waved around his head as if he expected her to try and grab it.

Ella stared at them all. Tony now looked uncomfortable and wouldn't meet her gaze. The other man excused himself and made a hasty retreat to the bathroom. Ella glared at Paul. "What's going on? Why are you looking at me like that?"

Paul put his beer down on the floor and opened up what he was holding in his other hand. It was a page from a magazine showing a photograph of a naked wet Ella straddling a saddle rack, clasping the whip in her teeth.

Ella froze in horror. "What the hell?" She suddenly felt as cold as ice. She reached forwards and tried to take the page from Paul, who whipped it away from her, waving it mockingly in front of her nose. Paul grinned maliciously at her. "Looks like you've found your vocation in life," he said nastily.

Ella felt a sudden wave of fury rise inside her. She glared angrily at Paul and suddenly punched him squarely in the nose with her right hand. Paul staggered back with an expression of surprise and pain on his face. He grabbed at his already swelling nose. "You silly little cow, you could have broken it," he hissed.

"Good, it's the least you deserve," said Ella and snatched the page from the floor where Paul had dropped it. She turned and walked briskly out of the room, aware of the eyes of the other guests that followed her curiously.

Paul was still clutching his nose. He looked around briefly, only to see that everyone in the room had witnessed him being punched in the face by Ella. Tony was standing next to him with a slightly dazed expression on his face. Paul turned to him. "You saw that, completely unprovoked. I'm going to have her arrested for assault."

Tony blinked and looked at Paul levelly. "You really can be a shit sometimes," he said and walked out of the sitting room.

Paul clutched his nose again, aware that he had been abandoned. He felt acutely embarrassed. Celia was smirking at him from the sofa as she stuffed a sandwich down her throat.

Celia was starting to enjoy this party. She had been having a nice chat with Carl and finding out all about Chloe. She had managed to pretend that she was genuinely concerned for Chloe and interested in her cause. Carl had been quite happy to waffle on about Chloe at length.

Celia smirked at Paul through a mouthful of sandwich. "Had a lover's quarrel?" She shouted across at him, winking evilly.

Simon was standing next to the sofa with a raised eyebrow. He had noticed Celia seemed to be giving practically everyone that she saw extremely filthy looks. She looked like a pissed off middle aged woman who was not happy in her skin and she was also asking Carl a lot of questions about Chloe. Simon had also witnessed the altercation between Ella and Paul but he wasn't the slightest bit surprised. This evening had already been far from the usual party norm.

Carl watched as Ella left. He took a sip of his wine and decided it was about time that he had a chat with the hostess. He turned to the others. "If you'll excuse me, I think I need to have a word with Ms Marcus," he said. He nodded to Simon and gave him a wink as he left. Celia and Sarah failed to notice this. The also failed to notice the commiseratory pat that he gave Simon on his shoulder as he passed him.

Ella stood in the hallway and looked at the photograph of her. How could he have done this? She felt a sudden pang of despair. If Paul had this then everyone in the village would soon have seen it. She felt herself well up suddenly. Ella took a deep breath and went into the kitchen to pour herself a drink. She sat down at the table and looked at the bottom of the page of the picture. There were some paragraphs of writing.

Ella read the page and shook her head. "I don't believe the nerve of that bloke," she murmured to herself.

"Are you all right?" Tony was peering around the kitchen door nervously. "I wanted you to know that I had no idea that Paul had that picture and I would have taken it from him if I'd known he would do that. That's just not right," he said quickly.

Ella gave a sniff and took a slug of her gin and ton. She eyed Tony warily. "I though you two were BFFs," she said icily.

"I wouldn't say that. " Tony said walking over and helping himself to a bottle of beer. He opened the bottle and took a sip before turning back to Ella. "Are you two an item? Or should I say were you two an item?" He said tentatively hoping that Ella wouldn't tell him to get out.

Ella suddenly gave a shriek of laughter. "I wouldn't go as far as to say that," she said when she had stopped laughing. She stared into space for a moment. "I wish I'd never met him."

Tony walked over and pulled a chair out to sit next to her. "You're better off just trying to forget about it. If you ignore him he'll get fed up and leave you alone."

Ella stared at him with raised eyebrows. "He sent that picture to some sleazy magazine just to earn himself fifty quid. And he's made up a whole lot of crap about me, saying I'm his fiancé and that I like doing weird sex with animals. Particularly horses." Ella said, placing the written part of the page in front of Tony.

Tony glanced down. Ella had discreetly covered up the picture of herself by folding the page in half and holding her hand over any part of her that would have showed. Tiny swallowed. "Can't you sue people for that kind of stuff?" He said quietly as he read through the lines.

Ella gave another shriek of laughter. "Oh please, I just want it to go away!"

"Want what to go away?" Jade asked as she walked into the kitchen. She paused as she scrutinized Ella. "Oh what's happened now?" She asked rolling her eyes.

Ella handed her the page and shut her eyes placing a hand over each ear. Jade gaped at the page for a moment, eyes wide behind her glasses. Her mouth dropped slowly open as she read the write up accompanying the picture. It was named "Erotic Ella"."

Jade finished reading and slowly folded the page up. "That was him wasn't it? Why would he do such a thing?" She muttered looking back at Ella who had now opened her eyes and uncovered her ears.

Jade sat down opposite Ella and Tony. "Look Ell, he's just being spiteful. You should just ignore him, he just wants to try and make you do what he wants."

Ella nodded and gave a big sniff. "I know. But everyone in the village is going to end up seeing this. I'll never live it down and what about my parents? They'll have a heart attack!"

Jade patted her hand. "Look try and stay calm. We'll think of something won't we?" She said, nodding hopefully at Tony who nodded enthusiastically back.

Jade got up. "I'm going to make you something to help calm you. My mom makes things for me when I get upset," she said patting Ella's hand. She went to over to the cupboards and started opening them up. "We've got some chamomile tea that I brought with me, that's a good one. Where the heck is it?" Jade said, more to herself than anyone.

Jade swore by her chamomile tea. It was a remedy that always made her feel better and she had used it frequently. Although admittedly she usually accompanied it with a piece of cake. She continued to root through the cupboards. As she bent down to look below the sink she suddenly noticed something gleaming on the floor underneath the end unit just behind the bin.

Jade paused and walked over to see what was shining on the floor. She picked it up and smiled to herself. She was holding a slightly moth eaten cat collar. It was made of thin black leather and had a piece of elastic set half way around it. It had a few small brass stars placed around its circumference. A slightly faded brass name barrel hung from it. "Jerry," she said with a smile.

Jade waved the collar at Ella and Tony. "Look, I found Jerry's collar."

Ella rolled her eyes. "Oh please," she sniffed and turned back to her gin and tonic. Tony placed a tentative arm around her shoulder. His heart skipped a beat when Ella did not try to pull away from him.

Jade looked at the collar. She picked up a cloth and wiped the dust from it. "Naughty Jerry," she said smiling. She looked at the name barrel and paused. She wondered if they had put any information about Jerry in there. She unscrewed it and was delighted to find that it did indeed have something inside it.

Jade pulled out the paper and scrutinized it. It had Jerry's address on one side. She turned it over. It just had a number on the other side. Must be the number of Chloe's late aunt she thought. She wondered why he hadn't got his name on it. Suddenly she understood. "Ah" she nodded to herself. "You're not supposed to put animals names in their collars are you? " Jade said to Ella and Tony who ignored her. They had no idea of what on earth she going on about? Jade continued talking regardless, "it's to stop people taking your pets. That's why. So they don't think that some stranger knows them."

Jade smiled again and put the collar back together. She fastened it and looped it through her wrist. She would put it back on Jerry later. She turned back to resume her search and opened another cupboard. At last, right at the back of it there was her chamomile tea.

Jade paused as she realised that she hadn't needed the tea for some time now. She smiled again to herself, she was sure that this would help Ella feel better. She turned back to Ella and Tony. "Tea then?"

Ella and Tony both looked back at her Ella frowned "You have got to be kidding!" Ella said and took a large swig of her drink.

CHAPTER 25

Chloe and Steve stood inside the room. Their eyes were wide as they looked around. The room had several tables dotted around it. They all held TV monitors. There were also laptops placed on the tables. There appeared to be some sort of other electronic equipment that was also placed on the tables next to a few of the monitors.

Chloe shook her head, "It's like some kind of communications centre." She walked over to one of the tables and inspected the monitors. She reached forwards and tapped at a keyboard but nothing happened.

Steve also inspected another monitor. He stared at a laptop and then switched it on. Chloe walked over to him and watched the laptop flicker in to life. She sighed as she looked at the screen. "Password protected. How the heck are we ever going to find out what was on these things?" Chloe leaned over and switched the laptop off.

Chloe looked around the room. There were also boxes of discs in the room. She plucked one of the discs from a box. "Well at least we can take this back and see what's on it," she said to Steve. Steve nodded at her and looked around the room again. "Did you ever see anything like this in your relatives house before?" He asked.

"No, never," answered Chloe. She looked around the room again and sighed. "We may as well go back up before we are missed. We can have a good look at all of this another time. I need to try and raise some Sam funds."

Chloe turned around and nearly jumped out of her skin when she saw someone standing in the doorway. She placed a hand on her chest. "Carl, you nearly gave me a heart attack."

Carl was looking around the room with wide eyes. "What on earth have you been up to? You've got a secret hideaway down here."

Chloe smiled. "Yes, it's something else isn't it? We only just discovered it."

Carl nodded. "Yes your, er, helper said something to that effect when she sent me down here. Although, to be honest she didn't make much sense," he said. Carl remembered Joanne slurring something about Chloe and Steve having an adventure down the stairs, before she slumped across the desk and started snoring loudly.

Carl had already come across the two other rooms. He had shut the door on the first one but paused in the second one when he saw the pictures of Chloe. He had looked at the pictures for a few moments. He hadn't realised that Chloe used to ride horses. She had never mentioned it, but then again she probably wouldn't. She rarely disclosed anything personal about herself. She always seemed somewhat guarded. This was the most relaxed he had ever seen her.

Chloe closed the door quietly as they left the room. Steve turned the power off and they made their way back up the stairs by the dim light of Chloe's torch.

They returned to the study to find Joanne still lying across the table. Chloe rolled her eyes. "Oh dear. Steve do you think you could take her upstairs and put her somewhere to sleep it off?"

Steve nodded and roused Joanne enough to help her to her feet. Joanne smiled at him. "Steve, are you getting fresh with me? I don't mind if you are."

"No, I'm getting you somewhere that you can recover. Now

lean on me and I'll take you upstairs." Steve replied as he propped her up with an arm.

Joanne grinned at him. "Oh Steve, at last."

Chloe shook her head as Steve almost carried Joanne out of the room. She put the disk on the desk and sighed. "Honestly Carl it's like looking after a bunch of kids sometimes."

Carl smiled at her. "You seem to be managing it though. I would never have pictured you in a situation like this before."

Chloe raised an eyebrow. "Neither would I."

Carl paused for a moment before speaking. "I think that Simon may well give you some sponsorship. He's taken quite a liking to you."

Chloe's face brightened. "Oh that would be wonderful. We really need the cash."

Carl frowned, she had missed his point of course. "Chloe I mean that he likes you."

Chloe stared at Carl and he saw the expression change on her face as she suddenly understood what he was saying. "Oh really? Well I suppose if it would help Sam I suppose I'd better go and butter him up," she muttered.

Carl smiled. "Chloe please don't string him along, he is a friend of mine."

"Is he? How come I've not met him before then?"

Carl raised his eyes to the heavens. "Because you hardly ever come to any social functions when I ask you. I mean this is the first time I've seen you outside work in goodness knows how long." Carl hesitated for a moment before continuing as

Chloe stared at him with wide eyes. "And I must say Chloe how lovely you look," he finished with a smile.

Chloe looked away, she suddenly felt embarrassed. Carl had never spoken to her like that before. She looked back at him, he was still smiling at her. She thought that he looked rather appealing in his dark jacket and crisp white shirt. She quickly pushed that thought from her mind. "Carl, I know that I don't socialize much, but I just never really want to these days. Honestly the thought of having to go out and have to force a conversation with people, most of whom I probably won't like, well I just can't be doing with it," she said with a shake of her head.

Carl laughed suddenly. "Oh Chloe, well at least you're honest," he reached forwards and took her hand gently. She didn't pull away from him. "Well Chloe I hope that you don't feel like that with me?" He said looking at her intently.

Chloe looked back at Carl. She felt confused. She had known Carl for a while and had always liked him but had never thought of him in a romantic sense. Why did she suddenly feel attracted to him? She had not looked at anyone in that way for some time now. Not since her husband had died.

Chloe studied Car's face. His handsome features were caught in a gesture of tenderness and concern as he looked at her. Chloe felt a warm flutter inside her stomach. She squeezed his hand gently. "Carl of course I like your company. I wouldn't work for you if I did now would I?" She said with a small smile.

Before she knew what was happening Carl had pulled her towards him and was kissing her gently on the mouth. She felt herself submit to his kiss as her lips responded gently back to his warmth.

Carl touched her face. "I've wanted to do that for so long," he said, running his hand softly across her cheek.

Chloe looked back at him. She wasn't sure how that had happened but she knew that she had liked his kiss. "Carl, I really should go and speak with my guests. They'll be wondering where on earth I am."

Carl dropped his hand and gave her a small smile. "Yes, you need to carry on with the fund raising."

"Yes, perhaps I should have a word with your friend."

Carl rolled his eyes. "Oh Chloe, please," he shook his head as she smiled back at him.

"It will be strictly business," she said and walked from the study.

Chloe was pleased to see that the party seemed to be in full swing. She smiled as she saw Ben and Lyn chatting in the hallway. Ben was wearing a tuxedo, he'd obviously made an effort bless him. Lyn was wearing a long halter neck silver dress that clung to her in all the right places. Her sandy hair cascaded around her shoulder. She looked stunning

Ben turned to Chloe, "Ah Chloe, what a lovely party and what an amazing house this is," he said with a grin.

Lyn nodded in agreement, "yes, it's a beautiful house, are you going to stay here?" Chloe shook her head, "too expensive I'm afraid."

Chloe felt a gentle tap on her shoulder and turned around to see Robert Morecom standing behind her. "Hello Ms Marcus. I see that you have settled into the swing of things," he said with a small smile. He was wearing a tweed jacket and a red bow tie.

Chloe smiled back at him, "well I'm still trying to sort everything out, it's a bit of a nightmare actually."

Robert nodded. "Well, I'm sure you'll fathom it all out eventually," he said and turned around as Anne appeared at his shoulder.

Anne gave Robert a prod, "I want a word with you," she said taking his arm. She gave Chloe a small smile and a wink as she turned away.

Chloe smiled, she really must try to get some sponsorship money for Sam. She headed for the sitting room, stopping at the kitchen for a bottle of wine to take with her. She thought that if she could get a few guests a bit tipsy then they might be more forthcoming with the funds. She assumed that some people would be staying the night at the house and they could always make up a few extra beds downstairs if it helped the cause.

Chloe stopped as she walked in to the kitchen. She took in Ella's glassy face with Tony patting her on the shoulder and Jade fussing around her with a cup of tea in one glance.

Chloe took a deep breath, she'd only been gone ten minutes and they had obviously been up to no good. "Okay, so what's happened now?"

Jade jumped and turned around. "Oh, er, Ella's had a bit of a shock," she mumbled.

Ella looked up at Jade. "You might as well tell her, everyone will know soon," she said and took another gulp of her drink.

Jade stepped back from Ella and walked over to Chloe. She leaned close to her and spoke quietly in her ear. "I'm afraid that Ella has been caught in an inopportune moment and someone has done the dirty on her," she whispered.

Chloe blinked at her. "What in God's name are you talking about?"

Jade sighed and leaned closer. "Paul took a rude picture of her and sent it to a magazine and now it's their main feature."

Chloe shook her head. "Oh. Well there's no point in going to pieces over it. There's nothing you can do about it,' she said firmly to Ella. "Why don't you just tell everyone that you sent it in? Say you want to be a glamour model or something, be open tell people about it and turn the tables on him."

Ella sniffed. "You haven't seen the picture," she said and waved the magazine page at Chloe.

Chloe took the page from her and opened it up. She stared at it for a moment before speaking. "Okay maybe you should just emigrate," she said finally and handed it back to Ella.

Ella gave a sniff. "You see, everyone will think I'm a right slapper."

Chloe picked up a couple of bottles of wine. "Oh it will soon blow over. You know what they say, tomorrow's fish and chips and all that.

Jade looked up suddenly. "What happened in that passageway?" She stopped suddenly, "where's Steve?"

Chloe waved dismissively at her. "Oh it appears that they converted the cellars in to some extra rooms. We'll have a good look around them tomorrow." Chloe started to leave the kitchen and then paused. "Oh yes, Steve has taken Joanne to bed. She was rather tipsy." Chloe looked at Ella and then at Jade. "Don't let her get in the same state please," she said nodding at Ella.

Chloe circulated with the wine, making sure that drinks were topped up and chatting with the guests. They all seemed to be enjoying themselves. Chloe went back to the large sitting room where Paul was standing staring out the French doors at the garden. He was sipping on a bottle of beer. Chloe shook her head that young man seemed like trouble.

She nodded to Sarah, observing the crumbs scattered around her and Celia. Chloe held up a bottle of wine. "Anyone need a drink?" She asked. Celia lifted her glass at her in response. She didn't meet Chloe's gaze as he poured her drink and she didn't thank her either.

Simon gave a small smile as Chloe offered him some wine. "Don't mind if I do," he said moving his glass forwards. "Now Ms Marcus, how is your fund raising going?"

Chloe smiled back at him. "A bit slow to be honest. I'm hoping that it will pick up now though?" She said, pointedly raising an eyebrow at him.

Celia shook her head at Sarah. "I don't know she's got the nerve," she hissed quietly.

Simon had seen Celia's black look. "Perhaps we should have a chat somewhere quieter," he said gesturing away from the sofa. Chloe gave him a warm smile and nodded and they moved away. Paul looked up as they walked away and then took a large drink of his beer. He put the empty bottle on the table and walked out of the sitting room.

Simon looked at Chloe as they walked along. She looked positively radiant. "Well now I have you all to myself at last. What have you done with Carl?"

Chloe smiled to herself, "he was in the study but I've a feeling he'll be here to keep an eye on me soon. We might as well see what he's up to," she replied.

Carl had paused for a moment in the study as Chloe left. He was pleased that she had not turned him away from her. He had not planned to kiss her like that, it had been a sudden impulse. He had realised how much he had missed her these past few weeks and not just from a work point of view.

He sighed and paused as he saw the disc that she had left on the desk. He picked it up wondering what could be on it. Carl decided that he would have a look while Chloe was busy networking. He might save her some wasted time by looking at it first.

There was a television in the corner of the room. Carl switched it on and pushed the disc into it. He picked up the remote control from the desk and fiddled with it until he found the play button.

Carl waited for the disc to load. For a moment it was quiet and the screen stayed black. Perhaps there was nothing on it after all. He was about to switch it off when suddenly the screen lit up. Something was playing, the picture quality wasn't the best he'd seen it certainly didn't look like it came from Universal Studios.

Carl watched as a title came up on screen. "Juicy Julia Gets Her Oats". He cleared his throat. Perhaps he should put the film back, he pondered. He moved towards the screen to remove the disc but paused. He would just wait a moment in case this was some sort of a joke.

Carl watched as the scene unfolded in front of him. Yep it was exactly as the title depicted. He pressed the stop button on the remote. He had better put this away. "What on earth will I tell Chloe? She must have had no idea what her relatives had been up to," he muttered to himself

"What do you mean Carl? What were my relatives up to?"

Chloe asked. She was standing in the doorway of the study with Simon. Carl smiled and flicked off the television quickly. "I was just checking that disc. I think they liked their home video," he said quickly.

Chloe frowned at him. "As long as I'm not in any of them," she said looking at him questioningly.

Carl shook his head quickly and pulled the disc from the monitor. "Certainly not," he said firmly and slipped the disc into his back pocket. He would have to have a word with the others. He would have to tell them to check out the discs discreetly, he didn't want Chloe getting upset.

Carl looked at Simon and Chloe. "Now are you two cutting a sponsorship deal or not?"

CHAPTER 26

Berryford Spring Horse Trials always pulled in quite a crowd. It was one of the most prestigious unaffiliated horse trials in the country. Many professionals took their novice horses there in order to get a feel as to how they would progress on the professional eventing path, before the season got into full swing.

It was also an opportunity for competitive amateurs to ride around a course that would later in the year be modified for professional riders. This took the form of Berryford Autumn Horse Trials, where the course as vastly more arduous.

There were several levels of competition available at the horse trials catering for most levels and ages. Most of Sarah's yard had attended the Lucinda Lilac clinic at Berryford so they had also decided to try out at the horse trials. This resulted in a small convoy from Sarah's yard turning up together at Berryford.

Chloe parked her car next to Ben's trailer and took a deep breath. They had thought that they were early but already around the large field was a sea of lorries and horse trailers. It looked like there were loads of people here. Riders were already warming up their horses and ponies. It wasn't even eight o'clock and it was a hive of activity.

There was an announcement over the tannoy calling a rider up for their dressage test. This was interrupted by a sudden screech of feedback as the tannoy system was diverted to another commentator. A very upper crust sounding gentleman spoke, "would the owner of the blue lorry registration number Nag 22 please shift it from next to the lake. You're supposed to park in the designated area and we won't be blamed if you get stuck. You won't get to the burger van any quicker form there you know."

Chloe raised an eyebrow as Ben came to her side and smiled. "That'll be Colonel Nick Nipper on the tannoy,' he said. "Apparently he owns the estate and he loves the eventing, but I heard that he's going a bit, er non compos mentis so to speak. He allows this to go on at the estate as long as he's allowed to add a bit to the commentary. He likes the unaffiliated trials to be a bit more relaxed, so to speak."

Chloe stared at him curiously. "Seriously?"

"Yes, he used to be all right a few years ago but he gets a bit carried away these days. He sits in a horse trailer somewhere and improvises, apparently."

"I hope to God he doesn't improvise about Sam," muttered Chloe as they went to the trailer to unload the horses.

Steve emerged from the car dressed in his new riding jacket. He looked very smart thought Chloe. Fortunately Simon had come up with some sponsorship money quickly so they had also bought Steve the latest in body protectors for the cross country and Sam some new boots to protect his legs. Simon had said that he might provide some more funding depending on their performance He also said that he would probably come to watch. Chloe hoped that Sam and Steve would put on a good show.

Jade was holding Sam. She looked a tad nervous but not of Sam. Chloe smiled at her. "Don't worry Jade everything will be fine." Chloe said, touching her shoulder. Steve walked over to them and Chloe gave him a leg up on to Sam. Chloe gave a small sigh as she read the logo on Sam's saddle cloth. "Mrs Patel's Tea Mart." Jade had promised to do a bit of advertising for Mrs Patel in exchange for her donation and had been true to her word. She had spent several hours carefully sewing the logo on in order to save further costs.

Chloe could hear Ben's two girls bickering behind the trailer. Gill was leaning against the front of the car smoking a cigarette now that Ben had mounted Gatsby. Ben had plaited Gatsby's mane and tail. He had also given him a good wash, using some expensive shampoo to try and really whiten up his white bits. He had then rugged him up and to the eyeballs to try to keep him clean.

Unfortunately, Ben had put a burgundy traveling rug underneath Gatsby's stable rug while Gatsby was still wet. This had resulted in Gatsby having rather a pink sheen to his coat that was particularly noticeable on his white patches. Ben hadn't had time to wash him again and just hoped that no one would notice.

A sudden screech erupted again from the tannoy and the clipped tones of Colonel Nipper reverberated around the grounds of Berryford. "Just remember everyone, there are cakes now on sale next to the secretary's office. They're all hand made by our staff and friends of the W.I. and I can certainly vouch for what fine ladies they are, so don't miss out!"

Jade looked at Steve. "Do you think I should get one now, before the rush?" She asked.

Steve eyed her for a moment and managed not to laugh. "Yes sweetheart, why don't you get one now we can have it after our dinner tonight," he said sweetly. He checked Sam's girth. He was feeling a little apprehensive about this and was hoping he wouldn't forget the dressage test. He was already going through the motions in his head.

They made their way over to the warm up area. Big Jayne was standing with her hands on her hips watching, as Heather warmed up Whitney who was trotting quietly along. She was still unconvinced about the girls swapping over their mounts.

Firefox had been an expensive buy and she had hoped that she would take Heather to the top of the competitive tree. She was still living in hope that Heather would ask to ride her again, but ever since the two girls had swapped mounts they both seemed to be getting on far better with their new rides than previously. Big Jayne had to admit that Heather seemed a lot more comfortable and relaxed on Whitney and she was certainly a lot brighter in herself. These days Heather couldn't wait to get to the yard whereas before she had made all kinds of excuses to get out of riding Firefox.

Jane also watched as Britney managed to curtail Firefox's efforts at cantering on the spot and drew her back to a working trot. Jane just wasn't happy about Britney riding this pony, it seemed like an absolute lunatic. She had to admit however, that Britney seemed to be loving every moment that she rode her. When she wasn't riding Firefox she was constantly chattering about how she wanted to show jump her and event her and try to qualify for some big championships. Jane tipped her head back and poured half a bottle of bach flower remedy into her mouth. She seemed to be getting through a lot of this stuff lately she thought with a sigh.

Lyn was booting Quickstep into a trot as they left the ring. They had completed their dressage test and she thought that she had managed quite a respectable performance. She had taken Steve's advice and spent some time tickling him with her stick before the test. She'd also been giving him a few sharp digs in the ribs to wind him up so that he entered the arena with a bit more energy than normal. He had actually performed the test quite obligingly.

Quickstep actually didn't mind dressage. Quite frankly today he had been glad to get into the arena and have Lyn stop nagging at him all of the time to get a move on. Of everything his rider asked him to do this he found dressage tests the least strenuous. Trotting around in circles and being asked to do the occasional lengthening of stride was much more relaxing than all that jumping marlacky. He really didn't see why he should continually be asked to throw himself over silly looking obstacles, it was a complete waste of his energy. He reached down to try to have a nibble at the grass as Lyn pulled him to a halt, he was feeling rather peckish now, but Lyn pulled his head back up, typical.

Lyn watched as Kelly completed her dressage test on Chester. He was also doing a nice test. Kelly had been working hard on his flat work to improve his self carriage. Chester always preferred to carry his head quite high but he was now cantering in a nice soft outline looking very balanced and relaxed. Lyn could see Sarah watching with Celia over by the ring. Rory was also standing with them, no doubt picking Kelly's riding to pieces.

Since Steve had been at the yard Lyn was beginning to think that Rory didn't really seem to know what he was doing. Steve had been giving her a lot more tips that seemed to work with Quickstep than Rory ever had. Lyn was about to head off to see what time that she was show jumping when something caught her eye. Oh no, what on earth had Ben done? Gatsby's white patches were now pink. That's why Ben had kept him under wraps until he had needed to tack him up. Lyn couldn't help herself she burst out laughing.

Chloe was also trying to avoid looking at Gatsby. Every time she did, she also started grinning like a fool. She turned back to watch Steve as he entered the ring to do his test on Sam. She hoped he wouldn't forget the movements.

Jade suddenly appeared panting. She was clutching Sam's rug, she looked at Chloe with wide eyes, "I thought I'd miss him. You should have seen the queue for those cakes. You wouldn't believe it at this time of day. Apparently they're really popular."

Chloe stared back at Jade for a moment and then turned back to continue watching

Steve. Unperturbed Jade continued babbling, "I didn't know which one to get. The lemon drizzle looked nice, but then I thought that Steve would need something stodgier to reboot his energy levels after today so I went for the chocolate fudge. Then I thought it's going to melt. It's warm now and they reckon it will get hotter. So I put it under the car just by the wheel. Make sure you don't..."

"Jade! Please! I'm trying to watch." Chloe said, a little sharper than she intended.

Jade stopped and bit her lip. "Sorry," she whispered, looking at Steve and Sam cantering a circle. "I'm just a bit nervous."

Chloe raised an eyebrow and smiled but her eyes did not leave Steve and Sam. She watched as they completed their test, finishing with a halt in front of the judge. She was pleased to see that Sam stood perfectly squarely. Steve had been doing some work with him.

Chloe patted Sam as they walked away the ring. "Well done, that looked a nice test."

Steve leaned forward and gave Sam a pat too. "Thank goodness that's over, now we can have some fun," he smiled. He couldn't help but notice Paul scowling at him from aboard Solly as he walked by.

Jade saw Ella as they arrived back at the trailer. Celia's lorry was parked across the field from them. She waved and Ella gave her a wave back. Ella had decided that she was not going to bother watching Paul competing. The shit didn't deserve her attention. Since the party she had not gone out of the caravan unless she absolutely had to. When she had finally needed to go to Mrs Patel's to get some milk- as Joanne had been unable to ride the bicycle- she had felt as if everyone was looking at her.

Mrs Patel had been her usual chatty self but as she left the shop and hopped back on to the bike a couple of local lads had seen her and shouted, "on yer bike Erotic Ella." Another one had added, "thought you'd want a better ride than that. Why don't you come here and I'll put a smile back on your face." She had cycled furiously away, feeling herself go crimson.

Ella had also been avoiding her parents. She wasn't sure if they knew about the picture. Perhaps not, she knew that they would be furious when they found out. They would probably drag her back home and refuse to let her out of their sight, saying that she couldn't be trusted to be left alone unsupervised. Ella sighed and picked up a rug.

Lyn was now trying to warm Quickstep up for the show jumping. Quickstep had been disgusted to find that she also wanted him to do this pointless rubbish again. He had rolled his eyes as soon as he saw the practice fence and had stopped in his stride as he spied the show jumping arena in the background. Surely not? Did she think he was stupid?

Lyn gave Quickstep a dig in the ribs as he ground to a halt and gazed at into the distance. He had become sluggish again. Lyn felt her heart sink. Perhaps doing the dressage test had tired him out too much? On the other hand, she had spent a lot of time getting him fit lately. Surely it shouldn't have taken that much out of him? She gave him a tap with her stick and sent him forwards.

Lyn gave an internal groan as she saw Rory, Sarah, Celia and the others from the yard come over to watch the showjumping. Their show jumping times were all scheduled quite closely together so they would probably end up watching each other's rounds.

Lyn perked up as Ben came trotting over. He smiled at her. "That dressage was fun wasn't it?" Lyn nodded back at him. "Probably the only thing we'll get round to finishing today," she said morosely.

"Oh don't be silly, you'll fly around," said Ben, crossing his fingers.

Lyn paused for a moment, "by the way, what's with the pink colouring?" She asked nodding at Gatsby.

Ben shook his head. "Oh we've just had a wardrobe malfunction. I hoped that it would brush out," he said slightly sheepishly, "do you think anyone's noticed?"

Lyn stifled a laugh and shook her head, "oh no, I'm sure they haven't," she said and kicked Quickstep away into a canter before her giggles could escape.

Rory watched as Quickstep stag leaped over the cross pole in the warm up area, clearing it by four feet. He laughed out loud and shouted to Lyn. "My he's got his jumping head on today!" Sarah winced as Lyn came round again, this time Quickstep ground to a halt in front of the fence at the last minute sending Lyn sprawling up his neck.

Lyn turned him away trying to avoid their stares. She felt like crying. Why one earth had she bothered even thinking they could compete in a horse trials. Suddenly Steve appeared next to her. He saw her tear filled eyes and leaned across to her, "don't worry," he said reassuringly, "try it again but just wind him up a bit first, get him cantering on the spot." Lyn nodded and took a deep breath before she went off again to try to motivate Quickstep.

Steve cantered away to continue warming up Sam. It wasn't long before Chloe shouted across to him, "Steve you're in next but one."

Steve brought Sam back to a walk giving him a pat. It wasn't long before the steward called his number into the ring. Steve took a deep breath and spoke quietly to the horse as they walked into the ring, "this is it boy don't let us down."

CHAPTER 27

Chloe watched as Steve cantered Sam to the first fence. She felt unbearably nervous. She held her breath as Sam pricked his ears and jumped over the upright. Thank goodness, he was moving forwards. She had been worried that Sam might be fazed by being in this large ring, with all the banners flapping along its sides and all of these people watching, but he seemed to take it all in his stride.

Chloe had a hand in her mouth as Sam continued with his round. She held her breath as he approached each obstacle and found herself unwittingly lifting a leg every time he jumped over the poles.

Sam popped over the planks and over a triple bar and turned towards the double. Chloe gave a small gasp as she realised that he was on the wrong stride. "Oh no," she said as Steve asked him to take off too early but Sam just opened up, putting in a huge jump over the oxer. He still managed to put in his two strides and easily cleared the upright coming out of the double.

As Steve turned him to the last two fences Chloe could barely watch. She could hear Jade mumbling, "come on," repeatedly as she stood next to her, clutching Sam's rug as if it were a worry blanket. Sam popped over the last two fences with inches to spare and cantered through the finish. He pricked his ears as Steve walked him out the ring, showering him with pats as they went.

Chloe ran up to Sam and threw her arms around him, "you were wonderful," she said. She looked up at Steve "and you weren't too bad either," she added patting him on his boot.

Steve beamed back at her, "he was so good, especially going into that double."

"Yes," Chloe agreed, patting Sam, "don't ever do that to me again."

Jade jogged along on the other side of Sam beaming happily, "you were so good," she said smiling up at Steve, "you made it look so easy."

Steve gave her a wink and smiled back as he brought Sam to a halt by the side of the ring. He dismounted and patted him again. He would have to think about the cross country now.

They paused to watch, as Lyn went cantering into in the ring on Quickstep. She had been tickling him with her stick outside the ring and prodding him with her spurs and now he was positively buzzing.

Quickstep was actually pretty horrified that Lyn had the audacity to think that he would jump around those awful fences, but she had been nagging at him so much with her leg, spurs and the stick that that his adrenalin had shot up and he bounded into the ring.

Lyn turned him into the first fence and with an almighty boot sent him sailing off towards it. This was either make or break time and she was going to give it her all.

Quickstep hesitated for a moment and then decided he didn't want another smack. He could easily clear these fences and he supposed he might as well keep going now he was in canter mode.

Lyn managed to navigate Quickstep around the course, although it wasn't a pretty sight. Quickstep hesitated at practically every fence and ended up doing the most ridiculous over exaggerated jumps over most the fences.

As Lyn turned him to the last fence Quickstep was flagging. When was this going to end? He decided that he'd had enough and ground to a halt at the second last. Much to his horror Lyn immediately gave him a sharp whack on the backside. Quickstep shook his head at her in disgust and shot off away from the fence. Lyn managed to wheel him around and booted him into the last two fences again. This time he clambered over them over resulting in him having the last fence down.

Chloe shook her head, "I don't think I've ever seen a horse shake his head at someone like that before," she said in wonder.

Lyn came out of the ring and walked over to them with small smile on her face. Steve nodded at her, "well done, you really had to work for that one."

Lyn smiled back, "I can't believe I got the bugger round, that's a first."

Chloe laughed and took Sam from Steve, "you'd better go and get your cross country kit on," she said to him. Steve nodded in agreement and gave Sam a final pat before trotting off towards the car.

Jade held Quickstep so that Lyn could also go and get changed. Chloe observed her from the corner of her eye. Jade was holding Quickstep and still clutching Sam's rug. She had certainly got her confidence up around horses now.

They watched as Paul jumped Solly around the show jumps. The round was not as fluent as Steve's. Paul was still tackling everything at racing pace and they had three fences down. Celia was glowering at him as he left the ring.

Ella suddenly appeared next to Jade, "how are we doing?" She asked cautiously.
Jade beamed back at her, "Steve's gone clear," she said

excitedly.

"Good," said Ella with a nod. They both watched as Tony brought Mary into the ring. They cantered around and despite Tony's steering being a bit haphazard Mary jumped all of the fences. Mary just caught the planks as Tony steered her into them from a hair pin bend.

Ella smiled, "that wasn't bad. That'll piss Paul off."

Chloe laughed, "would you be able to see if there are any dressage results yet?" She asked Ella.

Ella nodded, "of course, this should be interesting," she said and ran off towards the Secretary' tent.

Steve and Lyn returned dressed in their eventing colours. Steve's shirt was bright orange and gold. They had decided to pick something cheerful when they selected his shirt to try and make him and Sam stand out. Jade thought how dashing he looked and tried not to stare.

Chloe was studying the dressage sheet that Ella had brought back. She looked up and smiled at Steve, "Ella fetched your dressage test. You got 25." Steve nodded back at her, "how does that look compared to the others then?" He asked cautiously.

Chloe shook her head "Apparently it's the best! In fact, as you have a clear round show jumping you are currently leading your section."

Steve stared at her for a moment with wide eyes. He couldn't believe this was happening. He tried not to grin but couldn't suppress his smile. "We've still got the cross country though yet," he said firmly.

They made their way over to the cross country course as Ben

trotted merrily into the show jumping ring on Gatsby. He seemed oblivious to the ripple of laughter that went around the ring as they entered. Gatsby plodded obligingly around the course but didn't quite have the momentum to manage a clear round and had two fences down, much to the despair of Ben's two girls who let out loud shrieks of dismay each time a pole fell to the ground.

Steve warmed Sam up quietly until it was finally his turn to go to the starting box. Sam seemed quite relaxed and was looking around with interest. Chloe Felt butterflies in her stomach as Steve walked Sam into the starting box. She stepped away from the box. She had decided to run up to the top of the hill by the starting box. Hopefully she would be able to see more of their round from that vantage point.

Chloe turned around and walked straight into Simon who was standing next to Carl. They were both beaming at her.

"How's my investment doing?" Simon asked.

Chloe nodded at them, "we must be quick or we'll miss his cross country," she said pulling at Carl's arm, "come on," she said and turned to run up the hill.

Carl exchanged a glance with Simon and they both followed Chloe up the hill with Jade running along behind.

The starter counted down and then they were off. Sam cantered off from the start box as soon as Steve asked him and was soon flying towards the first fence. Chloe had her hand in her mouth again as he approached it. Sam pricked his ears and had a look at the fence but showed no signs of hesitation. He took the fence easily in his stride.

They watched as Sam jumped over three more fences before he disappeared out of sight. They now had to rely on the commentary to give them an update of his progress until they were able to see him again. Unfortunately the tannoy remained silent for what seemed like an age.

Chloe waited anxiously, "oh this is so nerve wracking," she moaned to Carl who gave her hand a squeeze.

"Don't worry he looked like he was up for it," he smiled. He had never seen Chloe so excited or so nervous before and he found it quite charming.

Steve and Sam finally came into view and Chloe gave a shout of excitement. She watched as they jumped into the water and splash across it. Sam jumped easily out over the other side. Chloe held her breath as they loped along to the last few fences. Sam looked happy and relaxed as he popped over the final obstacles.

Chloe raised her hands in triumph as Sam cantered across the finish She let go of Carl and tore across the field towards Steve and Sam. Jade thrust the fur covered rug into Simon's hands and set off in hot pursuit of Chloe.

Simon stood for a moment in silence and then looked at Carl, "I don't think we knew what we were letting ourselves in for," he finally said.

Carl nodded, "crazy horse mad women and deranged locals," he said with a wry smile. He still had not shown Chloe the contents of the disc that he had secreted away. He would have to think about that one.

Chloe was patting a sweating Sam while Steve loosened his girth. Steve was grinning from ear to ear, "that was amazing, " he said giving Sam's ear an affectionate rub. "He was so good he just did everything he was asked."

Chloe and Jade couldn't stop smiling either. Steve paused as he looked across to the start to see Lyn walking Quickstep into the box. Quickstep was observing the grass around him with interest. It was about time he had a nibble on some of that. He didn't mind going into the box and stood quietly contemplating the greenery in front of him.

Suddenly it was their turn. Lyn kicked him away from the start waking him from his reverie. Quickstep trotted reluctantly from the start box. Another few boots and Lyn had got him cantering. Quickstep was still hungrily observing the rolling grassy hills in front of him. Hopefully he was going to be allowed to eat soon.

Quickstep now looked straight ahead and suddenly realised that Lyn was booting him towards a fence. He couldn't believe it! Not once but twice in one day she was expecting him to jump. Had she gone mad? Quickstep decided that enough was enough. Lyn just didn't know the boundaries and he would have to teach her the rules. He eyed the fence and flew at it with enthusiasm. He waited until he was nearly there and then slapped the brakes on at the last minute, cleverly dropping his left shoulder at an angle in order to assist Lyn's expulsion from the saddle.

Lyn flew over Quickstep's shoulder and straight on to the log fence. There was a united gasp from the observers. Several people ran quickly to the fence. Quickstep looked at Lyn. She'd be fine, she was moving about. Now he could finally have some lunch. He lowered his head and tucked in to the grass around the fence.

Jade gasped as Lyn fell from Quickstep and they all caught their breath as she landed. Fortunately she was soon back on her feet. Steve gave a sigh of relief, "thank goodness she looks all right," he said as she led a munching Quickstep from the course.

Lyn walked over to them looking dismal. She shook her head. Chloe looked at her pale face, "are you all right? Have you hurt yourself?" She asked.

Lyn shook her head and gave a big sigh, "I should have known it was too good to be true, him even doing the show jumping was a miracle," she said, taking off her hat and shaking her hair loose.

Steve looked at her sympathetically, "look, there was nothing you could do about that. He did a really dirty stop," he told her.

She nodded and gave a small sad smile. She might as well put Quickstep away now and watch Kelly and Chester. She pulled him around pausing when she saw Carl and Simon. She remembered them from Chloe's party. She gave them a small wave. Why did she have to fall off when they were there? She had been getting on famously with Simon at the party. Typical. He probably thought that she was a right useless twit now.

Carl and Simon had arrived and stood a little distance away observing them with interest. Carl raised an eyebrow at Simon, "I'm not sure that we should be getting involved with these horses, it looks a bit dangerous to me." Simon nodded in agreement looking at Lyn's mud grass stained jodhpurs and watching as she removed pieces of bark from her vest. He looked back at Carl, "but the scenery's quite nice," he said with a smile. Carl nodded in agreement.

The tannoy announced Ben and Gatsby and they set off to the first fence in a steady canter. Ben was beaming as he clucked at Gatsby who clambered politely over the fence. There was a sudden spluttering over the tannoy as Colonel Nick Nipper observed Gatsby from his seat in the horse trailer that was parked at the top of the hill.

Colonel Nipper was half way down a bottle of Jack Daniels accompanied by a truly deliciously moist slice of lemon drizzle cake. He was having a super time. He always loved this event. It made all the aggravation of organizing these things worthwhile. He took another bite of his cake. Better have something to soak up that alcohol, he didn't want to get tipsy now, he would only have his daughter nagging at him again.

He took another sip of his whiskey and looked down at the next competitor who was cantering up the hill. Colonel Nipper nearly choked on his cake. Good Lord! What the hell was that? He grabbed his binoculars and stuck against his face. "I say it's a pink peril," he muttered. Colonel Nipper threw his head back and started chortling with laughter. He continued chortling as Ben kicked Gatsby over the log fence.

Chloe winced at the sound of the tannoy screaming in protest as Colonel Nipper intercepted it. His daughter Kate was at the start box, she cringed in embarrassment. She really wished she could pack her father off somewhere when this event was on but he just wasn't having any of it.

"Warning, warning, there is a pink panther loose on the course," Colonel Nipper announced. This was followed by a guffaw of laughter that descended into pig like snorts as his laughter became uncontrollable. "Call the turn out police, there is a pink panther on the course."

The tannoy shrieked in protest again as the commentary was diverted back to the correct box. "Er, please disregard that last announcement and our apologies if any offence has been caused," declared a crisp female voice.

Chloe and Jade exchanged glances before falling into fits of giggles as they clutched Sam by the neck. Even Lyn managed a small smile, good old Ben. Chloe's smile was short lived however as the tannoy blared out again. She looked at Jade in despair as she heard the words. "We have an up date of our previous competitors, Sam Seven ridden by Steve Bradshaw. Unfortunately I have to announce that this pair have been eliminated."

CHAPTER 28

Chloe froze as she heard the announcement. "What the hell is going on?" She turned to Steve, "why have you been eliminated?"

Steve shook his head frowning, "I don't know. I thought that we'd gone clear."

"I'm going to find out what on earth is going on." Chloe said and marched resolutely away towards the secretary's box.

Steve's mind was in a whirl as they walked back to the trailer. What had he done wrong? He thought that Sam had jumped everything correctly. Jade smiled at him tentatively and reached across to pat his arm, "don't worry, Chloe will sort them out. It's just a mistake."

Jade was holding Sam when Chloe arrived back after what seemed like an age. Chloe's was stony faced. She paused as she observed Steve who was leaning against the car. He looked at her quizzically, "well?"

Chloe shook her head, "you took the wrong bloody course."

Steve jumped away from the car, "no I didn't!"

"Yes you did, you stupid twit," admonished Chloe, "apparently when you came out of the wood and up the hill you jumped the fence on the right. The one on top of the hill."

"Yes of course. It was the next fence." Steve agreed.

No, you were supposed to jump the fence on the left and not the one on top of the hill. Didn't you think that it was a bit big and spooky for a novice class, with that big drop on the landing side and a massive ditch under it?"

"I did think it was quite tricky when I walked the course but I just thought that they were testing us," Steve said quietly.

Chloe rolled her eyes, "that fence is a permanent fixture on the course. They use it in the advanced class later on in the year. It's not used in a novice class. No one would enter if it was."

Chloe turned away for a moment trying to curtail her annoyance and then turned back to him, "honestly Steve it hadn't even got a number or any bloody flags on it. Didn't you notice that either?"

Steve shook his head sheepishly. When he walked the course he had left the wood and walked up the hill the fence had been virtually right in front of him so he had assumed that it was the next one. He hadn't realised that he was supposed turn to the left. He felt awful. He had let everyone down and Sam had been so good, jumping around doing everything he had been asked. Steve shut his eyes for a moment. What a mess he'd made.

Chloe observed his expression. She could see that he was in despair. She felt herself relenting slightly. "I suppose I should be impressed that you jumped such a scary fence."

Steve opened his eyes and looked back at her, "it just seemed like the natural route after we left the wood," he muttered. "I'm sorry, I should have checked the course plan."

Chloe nodded, "too right you should. You've just cost Sam winning that class.'

Steve nodded, "I know, perhaps you should get someone else to ride him. Someone who won't make stupid mistakes."

Chloe sighed, "no, you ride him fine. Next time we'll all walk the course together," she said firmly.

Steve brightened slightly and reached across to give Sam a pat as he munched on the grass. Jade was holding him waiting for Steve and Chloe to finish their conversation. Jade felt sorry for Steve. He'd had so much to remember today no wonder he'd taken the wrong course. She was glad to see that Chloe didn't look as if she was going to tell Steve off any more, she hated it when they had disagreements.

Carl and Simon had been observing the proceedings with interest. They had decided that it would be best not to get involved in the matter. It all seemed far too complicated. They moved closer to Chloe now that she seemed to have calmed down. Carl looked at her questioningly, "so does that mean he won't get anywhere in the competition then?"

Chloe widened her eyes and then paused. She gave a slight smile. "Yes, I'm afraid it means we're stuffed on this one," she smiled at Simon apologetically, "sorry, I can only promise you that it won't happen again."

Simon was momentarily distracted as Lyn returned. She had changed into her jeans now and combed out her hair. "What was the result then?" She asked.

Chloe let Jade and Steve explain what had happened to Lyn. She walked over to Sam and gave him another pat. What a shame, he had done so well. It might have meant that she could have re homed him pretty quickly and could then have wound up the estate and returned to her normal life.

"I say that was a shame," a voice called across to Chloe. Chloe looked up, Lucinda Lilac was walking along behind her daughter who was leading her horse back to their lorry. Chloe blinked and then nodded, suddenly taken aback. Lucinda paused and smiled at her, "he's a super young horse. You should enter him for the young horse classes, he's good enough to qualify for the finals," she said nodding at Chloe.

Lucinda gave her a wave and continued on to her lorry.

Chloe stood still, staring into space. Jade looked at her for a moment before speaking, "wow he must be good if she says so. What about those young horse things? Can we go to one of those?"

Chloe turned to Jade, "well, I suppose I'd better find out." Chloe stopped as she saw Paul riding past on Solly.

Paul was grinning evilly as he looked across at Steve, "maybe we should have a whip round and get you some glasses Bradshaw. Stop you screwing up this poor lady's horse's chances," he shouted and then laughed loudly.

Ella was following him some distance away carrying Solly's rug. She shook her head as she walked past them and mouthed, "sorry," at them.

Chloe sighed she just wanted to go home now but they would have to wait for Ben first. Gill had dragged him away to buy her some cup cakes from the cake stand. She glanced across at Carl and Simon who were chatting to Lyn.

Steve walked back over to Chloe, "I'm really sorry about messing things up," he said quietly.

Chloe nodded, "I know you are. I've done the same thing myself," she said with a wry smile, "one thing I can guarantee though, is that you won't do it again."

As they waited for Ben they saw Tony riding past returning to the lorry on Mary. Celia and Sarah strolled along behind him along with Rory who was looking his usual smug self. Rory paused as they walked by and wandered over to them to speak to Chloe. "Dam balls up he made with your horse, he could have won that class," he said loudly.

Chloe glared back at him, "it happens" she replied sharply.

Rory gave a small smile and leaned closer to her, speaking in a whisper, "Celia's lad has just gone clear on that mare over there. Perhaps you should think about giving him the ride?" He gave Chloe a conspiratorial wink before heading off after Celia who paused to glance around at Chloe. Celia gave Chloe a frosty smile arching an eyebrow at the same time before turning around to continue walking. Chloe shook her head. She would be glad when they could leave.

They were all getting bored when finally the competitions drew to a close. Ben had also wanted to watch Britney and Heather compete in the under sixteen section so they had to wait even longer. They had put Sam and Gatsby back in the trailer with large hay nets for them to munch on to pass the time.

Britney stormed around the cross country on Firefox who was in seventh heaven at being allowed to jump at top speed. They had a near miss at the seventh fence that involved a tight turn away from a ditch but Britney managed to haul Firefox around to it. Firefox leapt deftly across at a sharp angle to clear it.

Jane was so relieved to finally see them cantering towards the last fence. She removed her hand from her mouth and ran over to give them a pat. Her heart was lifted as she saw that Britney was beaming from ear to ear, "she was so good mum, that was amazing!" Britney cried out as they trotted over to her.

Jane gave her a relieved hug and helped her off Firefox. They waited to hear how Heather and Whitney were doing. Jane moved closer to Big Jayne who was standing, hands on hips straining to look for any sign of Heather.

Big Jayne threw her hands in the air as Heather and Whitney appeared over the hill, "give her a kick Heth! You're going too slow," she shouted at them.

Heather was too far away to hear her mother's cries and would not have taken any notice anyhow. She and Whitney were having a very nice time going around the course at their own pace. It was turning out to be far more enjoyable than Heather could have ever have imagined. Whitney was no where near as fast as Firefox but all Heather needed to do was give her an extra kick as they came in to the fences and Whitney pricked her ears and popped quietly over the obstacles.

Whitney was enjoying Heather's company. This girl was a much quieter rider than Britney. Although Whitney liked Britney, she had been getting rather fed up of Britney's constant nagging at her to get a move on. Sometimes she had even resorted to slapping her with her stick. Whitney didn't understand why she was expected to do everything at such a fast pace. She wasn't a racehorse and she wasn't high on oats. She was much happier with this steadier canter.

As they went through the finish, Big Jayne marched over. She really had to tell Heather that she needed to get a move on. It was called cross country for a reason and she didn't necessarily have to take all the longer routes and easier options around the fences. Big Jayne hesitated as she saw the look of delight on Heather's face. Heather reached around Whitney's sweaty neck and hugged her firmly, planting a kiss on her neck. "Oh what a good girl," she beamed. Big Jayne shook her head in disbelief but reached forward and patted Whitney gently on the neck. "I suppose she'd better have some carrots in her dinner tonight," she said quietly. Heather looked up at her mother and smiled happily.

The tannoy gave a whistle and the slurred tones of Colonel

Nipper reverberated around the grounds of Berryford. "Thanks you ladies and gents for coming to this delightful occasion. Now we will give you the results."

Jane sighed as she rolled up manure stained tail bandage. She had forgotten to bring a spare bandage and now her hands were tinged with a hint of green. She looked up as Britney and Heather gave a sudden shriek, hoping no one had been trodden on. Britney ran over to her, "mum we won!" She shrieked and continued jumping up and down now holding on to Heather who was bouncing around with her.

Jane nearly dropped the tail bandage. "No way?" She exclaimed.

Big Jayne appeared. "Come on we need to and get her rosette." She ordered and dragged Whitney from the grass to load her into the trailer.

Jane realised that she was trembling as they ran over to the secretary's tent. A large crowd had assembled inside the tent to hear the final results. Ben grinned at them as they arrived, "well done girls," he said loudly. Jane pushed Britney forwards, "go on love, get your rosette," she said with a smile.

Britney walked shyly forwards and smiled at Kate who presented her with a rosette and a trophy. There was an envelope stuffed inside the trophy. Jane felt herself welling up as she watched her daughter. She couldn't wait to ring her husband. He would be thrilled. Perhaps he might start taking more of an interest in his daughter's hobby now. She might even be able to persuade him to buy Britney that fancy new hat that she wanted. The one that had the crystals along its brim.

Big Jayne gasped suddenly startling Jane from her reverie. "I don't believe it," she said with a smile. "Heather came seventh!" Big Jayne clapped her hands together enthusiastically as Heather collected her rosette, she was grinning from ear to ear.

"Bravo," shouted Ben from across the tent, raising his hands in the air to clap as she returned to her mother.

Kate moved on to the results for the seniors. The competition had been split into two groups. Ella and Joanne looked at each other in surprise as Tony and Mary were announced in fourth place. Tony was in a state of shock as he collected his rosette. He hadn't been keeping an eye on the scores and didn't realize that Mary had finished on one of the best dressage scores of his group. Only their four faults in the show jumping had gone against them. He must remember to thank Ella for helping him with her flatwork.

Paul took a deep breath. How the hell had Tony managed to pull that off on that donkey? He gave Celia a sideways glance. The old bag was grinning like a loon. You'd think she was the one that had done the riding. Paul gave a quiet snort. Personally he thought that those dressage marks were fixed. Tony must have given the judge a backhander. That was the only explanation for why his own mark was so low.

As Kate continued with the second group Kelly was thrilled to hear that she and Chester had come third. She gave a small squeal as it was announced and beamed at Lyn who gave her a hug before pushing her up to collect her rosette. Sarah grinned as she clapped loudly next to them, she might be able to make some money on selling him now.

Ben sighed as Kate wound up the results and prepared to leave. His exit was stopped as his name was called and he realised that he had just sneaked into the ribbons coming tenth on Gatsby.

Ben blinked in surprise. Chloe standing next to him smiled at the stunned expression on his face. "It's because you went clear on the cross country. There were hardly any clear rounds," she explained. "You had a few time faults but you didn't get any major penalties," she added as she gave him a push forwards to collect his rosette.

As they left the secretary's tent there was quite a buzz in the air. Although Sam hadn't won Chloe was pleased with how he'd gone and was mulling over her options with him. Ben was completely dazed at coming tenth. It was the first rosette he'd won with Gatsby at a proper event. The only other thing he'd won so far was for a clear round. The dressage judges had also been very complimentary about Gatsby's rhythmical gait and quiet obedient transitions.

Jane was clutching the envelope from the trophy in one hand and Britney's rosette with the other. Britney was leaping around with Heather. She was waving her cup in the air in delight and they were throwing high fives at each other as they walked along. "Calm down Britney." Jane said quietly.

"What's in the envelope?" Big Jayne asked as she tore her eyes away Heather's delighted face. She was wearing her rosette around her neck laughing happily with Britney.

Jane paused, "oh I suppose I might as well find out," she said and tore it open. They stopped as Jane opened it up. She found a voucher for fifty pounds for the Berryford Saddlery Shop inside. They both exchanged glances and smiled.

Berryford had a reputation as being one of the best shops for equine related goods in the county. It carried a wide range of designer labels as well as the basic horsey essentials.

Jane laughed. "Brit will love spending this," she beamed. She looked at Big Jayne. "You should have half of this after all she's your pony," she smiled.

Big Jayne smiled back, "well perhaps the girls can share it, that would be nice."

They returned to their cars and prepared to leave. Chloe sat in her car waiting for Steve and Jade to jump in. She could hear the distant sounds of Ben's girls bickering in the back of his car.

"All ready?" She asked and reversed away from the hedge. She turned the car around to drive away. Suddenly there was a shriek from Jade. "The cake!"

Chloe stopped the car and Jade leapt out and ran off to where they had been parked. She soon returned looking rather crestfallen. She was carrying what looked like a large cow pat in her hands.

Steve stared at the remains of the squashed cake trying to stifle a laugh. You could see a vague tyre print across it where the car had rolled over it. He looked at Jade's worried face. "Don't worry Jade, we'll just put a bit of cream on it and no one will even notice," he smiled.

Chloe couldn't help but laugh out loud, "let's call it our consolation prize," she said. She paused before looking at Steve, "don't get too relaxed you. I've got plans for you two. You've still got plenty of work to do."

CHAPTER 29

At the yard the next day, Chloe watched as Steve cantered Sam around the manege. Sam maintained his rhythmical gait and easily managed to canter on a smaller circle when Steve asked him. He changed rein without protest and obligingly went down to a walk without any fuss.

Chloe did not turn around as she heard someone approach her, she knew who it was and managed to stop herself from frowning.

Rory leaned against the fence next to her and watched Sam for a moment before speaking. "You should really think about getting someone more experienced to ride him you know. You surely don't want a repeat of Berryford?"

Chloe managed to stifle a sigh, "that won't happen again. Steve is perfectly capable of competing Sam. You only have to look at them now to see how well they've clicked."

Rory shook his head, "well I can always have a word with Celia for you if you change your mind. She's got some good lads riding for her."

"I won't be changing my mind." Chloe said firmly. Thankfully, Jade then wandered over. She was clutching Sam's head collar. "I've cleaned his stable out and left the bed up for it to dry out," she said.

Jade observed Steve riding Sam for a moment, "do you know what time the photographer is coming?" She asked Chloe.

Rory smiled, "he should be here any minute. I'd better give Britney a shout." He said and marched off towards the stable block.

Chloe rolled her eyes, "you'd think he was Britney's agent the way he's been smarming all around her and Jane."

Chloe turned and looked at Jade, "I haven't seen any sign of Sarah this morning. I'm surprised she's not on the yard getting ready for the photo shoot."

Jade nodded in agreement. Jade was quietly excited about the photographer coming to the yard. After Britney had won the class and the others had also done so well at Berryford, Sarah had been contacted by the local newspaper that had caught a whiff of the yard's success.

The newspaper journalist had asked if they could come and take a photograph of the yard members and publish a small article about them for their Friday feature. Sarah had been delighted. It was good publicity for the yard. Everyone else had also been keen to have a claim to fame.

Steve finished Sam's schooling session and walked him off. Chloe and Jade wandered back to the stables where Britney and Heather were hopping around excitedly, waiting for the photographer to arrive.

Kelly was sweeping the stable block. She wanted to go and tidy herself up before the pictures were taken but she had seen no sign of Sarah this morning. Surely she hadn't forgotten?

Chloe took Sam from Steve as they returned to the stable and stroked him while Jade and Steve removed his tack. She picked up a brush and started to brush out the tack lines from his coat.

Chloe had decided to take Lucinda's advice and had entered Sam and Steve into a young horse class. Fortunately their sponsors had been understanding about the error at Berryford. Simon had even said that at if Sam could jump the bigger fences then they should affiliate him and find some proper classes to take him in.

Chloe had thought that this was a sound idea. If they could get Sam to win an affiliated class then she could re home him and finishing sorting the estate out. She had still not had the chance to go through the files that were in the basement rooms of the house. She realised that a part of her was reluctant to venture down into those rooms again, particularly the one with the photographs of her inside. That had been a little too much.

Chloe still wanted to find out what the formula was that they had given Sam. It was obviously something that her uncle had been working on. She was sure that he must have recorded its ingredients some where in the house.

Chloe had asked Jade to try to have a look at the discs from the basement rooms when she had time, but Jade had not mentioned that she had found anything of any significance yet. It seemed that Jade and Carl were investigating them. Chloe was glad that Carl was being so understanding about all of this. He was still allowing her to work from the house and had even said that he would try to call in today to see how the photo shoot went.

Chloe finished brushing Sam and looked up as Britney and Heather let out shrieks of excitement, "they're here!" Britney cried, clapping her hands together. Chloe smiled as they both ran out of the stable block with their mothers walking along behind them trying to maintain a dignified slow pace.

Chloe walked outside to find the yard members gathered together trying to contain their excitement. Ben couldn't stop smiling and his glasses looked as if they were steaming up.

Ella and Joanne had asked if they could come along and were

chattering with Jade who was standing next to Steve. Steve was looking around uncertainly, "I shouldn't be included in this as I cocked things up," he muttered.

"Nonsense! " Big Jayne replied, "you jumped the biggest fence on the course and besides, this is supposed to be about the yard doing so well not just about one person."

Lyn nodded in agreement, "if you shouldn't be in it Steve, then I definitely shouldn't. I didn't even get past the first fence," she said forlornly.

Jane shook her head, "don't be silly Lyn, you've done wonders with that horse. He wouldn't jump a stick before you had him. Like I said the article is supposed to be about us doing well with our horses and how we've all improved," she said smiling at Britney who was now clutching Heather excitedly.

They waited as the photographer and the journalist approached them. Rory looked around. "Where is Sarah? She should be here to meet and greet them."

Kelly nodded, "I'd better go and fetch her," she said and ran off towards the house.

A dark haired lady of around twenty five introduced herself as Sian Westbury and the tall dark man of around thirty five who accompanied her was Derek Sharman.

Derek surveyed the group for a moment. "Can we feature one of the horses in the picture?" He asked.

Big Jayne nodded eagerly, "oh yes, we should have Firefox in, seen as how she was on the winning side." Big Jayne sent Britney and Heather off to bring Firefox over from her box. "Make sure she's clean girls," she shouted after them.

Simone turned back to the group who were all looking at her

eagerly. She gave a small smile. "I'd like to have a little chat with each of you so that you can tell me how you are all progressing and what your goals are." Her eyes rested on Steve. A picture of him should help sell a few newspapers she thought. She beckoned him over, "let's start with you."

Chloe raised an eyebrow at Jade who shook her head in response. Chloe looked up as Kelly came trotting back, she looked rather worried. Chloe caught her eye and Kelly jogged over to her. She looked at Kelly's concerned expression, "what on earth's wrong?"

Kelly leaned close to Chloe. She didn't want the others to hear her. "It's Sarah, she's having a big argument."

Chloe shook her head. "What do you mean? Where is she?"

"She's in the house with Duncan. They're having a right barney. I didn't dare interrupt. I knocked and she didn't answer and so I went in and there they were shouting and screaming at each other. I don't think they even noticed me so I left them to it."

"Unbelievable." Chloe muttered. "Why is she having a row with Celia's husband? Did you catch any of it?"

Kelly shook her head. "Not really. I was too scared to stay, they seemed so angry."

As Sian worked her way through the other yard members Derek started organizing them into various poses ready for the photograph. Heather and Britney emerged with Firefox who was placed in the middle of the group.

Derek had another idea. He stepped back and looked at the group. "Let's have a picture of you all running towards the camera, as if you're running for your mounts."

Rory rolled his eyes, "now this is just getting silly," he muttered."

Heather and Britney shot forward in delight as Derek gave them their cue to run forwards. Firefox was left standing in the yard looking bemused as they all tore off in the opposite direction towards the camera.

Sian looked up from her notes and stopped her dictation. "So who is the yard owner? We need her to give us a few words," she called across to the group.

Rory looked up, "she's in the house. I don't know why she hasn't shown her face." Rory stopped as they heard a sudden shriek coming from the direction of the house. This was followed by the sound of Sarah shouting at the top of her voice. "Don't you walk away from me! You get back here you pathetic excuse for a man!"

Everyone stopped and turned towards the house. Ben's eyes widened behind his glasses as he saw Sarah grabbing Duncan's coat as he tried to leave.

Big Jayne stared at them in in fascination. "What on earth are those two up to?"

Duncan tried to free himself from Sarah's grasp but she hung on. Finally he turned around and gave her a hefty shove, "let me go you crazy fucking cow!"

Sarah tumbled to the ground and landed heavily on her backside. Chloe winced as she watched, "that must have hurt," she murmured.

Sarah clambered up from the ground and for a few moments she just glared at Duncan. She looked as if she wanted to kill him.

Sarah suddenly sprinted after Duncan. She was trying to head him off before he got to his car. Duncan heard her approach and ducked sideways away from her under the manege fence. He decided that he would run around to the other side of the yard and get out that way. He ran across the manege to make his escape but as he turned around to check Sarah's progress his trousers flapped around his ankle and sent him flying.

Sarah watched Duncan sprawl across the arena and gave another shriek. She sounded like a Mohican going into battle. She sprinted across the manege and grabbed one of the plastic trotting poles that had been left out. She gave a grunt and hoisted it into the air directly at Duncan who was struggling to get to his feet.

Steve stared at them with a slightly open mouth. What on earth was going on? Had they gone mad? He watched as the pole connected with Duncan who managed to deflect a direct hit to his face by throwing an arm out in front of him.

Duncan yelled out in pain as the pole whacked his arm. "You stupid fucking witch!" He scrambled to his feet and turned around. Right now she was going to get it. He leaned down and grabbed another pole from the ground.

Big Jayne had covered Heather's ears. She turned to Jane. "We should take the girls away from here, this really isn't suitable for young ladies."

Britney shook her head, "no mom this is great," she said straining to watch as Jane tried to cover her eyes.

Sarah had smiled in satisfaction when the pole hit Duncan. Her eyes widened when she also she saw that Duncan had picked up a pole himself. She quickly turned around and grabbed another pole and started advancing towards him with half of it held out in front of her like a light sabre.

Duncan saw her coming and paused for a moment before gripping his pole more firmly. "Right you want to play rough you little slapper," he snarled at her.

Chloe looked around to see that the photographer was grinning with delight. He zoomed in on the pair and started snapping away. Sian had her recording equipment held out in front of her. Her eyes were wide with excitement.

Steve caught Chloe's eye as Sarah heaved the pole around at Duncan. It whacked him firmly across his other arm. Duncan cried out and retaliated by whacking Sarah across the backside with his pole, sending her to her knees with a shriek.

Steve and Chloe exchanged glances. Steve nodded at her and turned and ran across towards the manege where Sarah was clambering back to her feet.

Sarah glared at Duncan venomously. "Right you stringy piece of shit let's see what you're made of," she snarled. She grinned evilly at him and then and swung her pole around with all of her might. She was aiming right for Duncan's head. Duncan's eyes widened in panic as he realised what was coming.

Before Sarah managed to make contact with Duncan's head Steve grabbed her around the waist, pinning her arms to her side. Sarah cried out in anger and surprise. She had not even noticed that there was any one else around. She had been so focused on pulverizing Duncan.

Duncan paused for a moment as the realization that his head was still intact dawned on him. He glared at Sarah and then scrambled away across to the arena to his car.

Sarah turned around to glare at Steve who had let go of her arms now. "Get your filthy hands off me," she hissed.

Steve held his hands up in front of her in a placating gesture, "calm down, you two were acting crazy. What on earth is wrong? The newspaper people are here and they've been taking pictures of you two fighting."

Sarah's face flushed as she glanced around quickly to see that everyone was still standing watching her in amazement. She paused for a moment and then glared at Steve again. She gave one last glance in Duncan's direction. He had fired up his car and was reversing rapidly away from the house. Sarah shook her head before turning on her heel and marching back in to the house.

Derek took a few more snap shots of her before turning back to the group who were now staring at Steve as he returned from the manege. Derek smiled, "one last shot for good measure," he shouted. A silence descended as they all turned back and stared at Derek. The sound of his camera clicking seemed overly loud.

Sian looked at Derek, "I guess you could say that's wrap. Thanks guys," she said waving at yard members as they turned and walked away towards their car.

Sian smiled at Derek, "wow, you couldn't have written that. I told you this horse lot were a right bunch of nutters. The editors going to love this." she said as they strolled past Firefox who was nibbling happily on Sarah's pansies.

CHAPTER 30

Chloe sat at the desk in the study. She had completed Sam and Steve's entry form and sent it off on line. She hoped that they weren't going to be out of their depth.

Chloe had checked out the classes for five year olds that qualified for national championships. She had found one an hour and a half drive away. She had also found a company that they could hire a trailer from. It was pricey but she didn't want to ask Ben. He had been kind enough already giving them lifts, besides she had decided to keep this under wraps for the time being.

Chloe sat back for a moment and Jerry took his cue to jump on to the desk. He tried to walk across her laptop and she pushed him gently away. "No Jerry you can't sit on that, even if it is a nice warm spot."

Chloe paused and stared at Jerry. "What on earth are you wearing?" She reached over to him to touch the collar that Jade had placed around his neck.

Jerry shoved his head into her hand for a stroke and Chloe obliged him with a caress across his head and ears. He rewarded her efforts by purring loudly.

Chloe removed the collar and looked at it for a moment. She shook her head. It looked rather worn out the elastic in it was quite stretched. She decided that it would be safer for Jerry if she bought him a new one. Jerry reached out a paw and started grabbing at his collar.

Chloe smiled at him, "you like this do you?"

Jerry responded by trying to pat at his collar again. Chloe sighed and replaced it back around Jerry's neck, "try not to lose it then," she said giving him another stroke.

Chloe turned back to her laptop. She needed to send the entry in as the competition was only next week. Fortunately they were still taking entries, but only until the next day. The other qualifiers were much further away and later on in the year and she needed Sam to try and do well in something, then she could get him re homed and get back to her old life.

Chloe stopped and looked out of the window. Strangely her old life was becoming more distant the longer that she stayed here. She really needed to get back to normal. All of this kind of country living and messing about with horses was in the past now. A past that had far too many sad memories for her to want to return to it.

Chloe's jumped as her mobile rang. She saw that it was Carl, she hesitated a moment before answering it.

"How are things on the homestead?" Carl asked.

Chloe smiled to herself, "we're surviving."

Carl asked her about her client bookings for the week and she relayed her diary to him. When they had finished their conversation about work Carl paused for a moment. "Chloe, would you like to come to dinner with me on Friday?" He asked.

Chloe froze for a moment and bit her lip. "Yes," she said suddenly, "why not? It'll make a change from Jade's cooking I suppose."

Carl laughed, "don't sound too keen will you." He replied, "all right, I'll see you then."

Chloe sat back with a sigh after they had said their goodbyes. She was surprised that she had accepted his invitation. That was another thing about being in this place. Since she had been staying at the house she seemed to be making too many irrational decisions on the spur of the moment.

She had always liked Carl, there was nothing not to like but she had not wanted to become involved with anyone again. When she had lost her husband she had decided that she would concentrate on her career. It seemed that everyone she cared about always had to leave her. It was easier to simplifier her life by not having anyone in it that she might worry about losing.

Now she had accepted a date with Carl. She would have to be careful. She didn't want to put herself through any more worry and pain. Not again. She would have to tell him that once they had this dinner then that would be the end of it. Yes that was what she needed to do.

Chloe took a deep breath as she remembered her aunt and uncle trying to comfort her after she lost her husband. Jeff had been the love of her life. She had met him in Diddlecot. He had been a gardener and quite in demand locally. He loved his work and being out in the fresh air.

Chloe tried not to think of him but suddenly the memories came flooding back and she felt a tear trickle down her face. She had been so happy with him. She had not been able to believe it when she found out that he was dead. She remembered and shut her eyes.

The Policeman had banged on the door of their little house in Diddlecot that had been just within a short walk of uncle Harry's and aunt Sophie's own home. She remembered how the expression on the Policeman's face had made her realize that something terrible had happened. He had explained to her that Jeff had fallen from a ladder when he was pruning old Mrs Vale's ivy Chloe had just gaped back at him thinking that this must be some sick joke. Jeff was always so careful.

He had told her that Mrs Vale had accidently backed her car into the ladder while Jeff had been up at the top of it. This had resulted in him falling very badly. Unfortunately he had landed on her car in such a way that he broke his neck instantly. Chloe had felt sick.

Apparently Mrs Vale had heard a thud but not realised what it was. She had parked her car and wandered off into the house to make Jeff a cheese and ham sandwich and a cup of tea. It was only when she had emerged from the house some time later that she had caught sight of poor Jeff straddled across the roof of the Rover. Unfortunately it had then been too late to help him.

Chloe remembered how her aunt and uncle had tried to console her, but she had been consumed with grief. That was when she had decided to move away to the City and maximize her degree in marketing that her aunt and uncle had funded her through college to gain. At the time of taking the degree she had thought it had been a waste of time and just the best choice of several mediocre topics. After Jeff's death she realised that it was the way forward.

Chloe felt a lump in her throat as she remembered how she had left the village without even saying goodbye to her aunt and uncle. She had just needed to get away as soon possible.

Chloe took another deep breath. On reflection perhaps it had not been the right thing to do. She had put all thoughts of these events to the back of her mind for such a long time, but now as she reflected on those events here in her aunt and uncle's domain, the memories seemed to be coming back to haunt her.

Chloe was startled from her thoughts as she heard a loud shriek. It sounded like Ella. She got up from the desk and went into the hallway where she found Steve, Jade and Ella crowded around each other. They were all looking at the newspaper that they had open in front of them.

Jade was frowning and shaking her head, "I look like I'm in shock."

"We all look like we're in shock," answered Steve.

Ella was staring at the newspaper with wide eyes "I look like I'm not even with you lot," she exclaimed.

Jade was reading the article, "oh my God, look at that other picture," she said stabbing at the paper.

Steve frowned at it, "the one titled fun and frolics down on the farm? Oh dear."

Chloe walked over to them and cleared her throat. "What's happened now?"

Jade looked at her apologetically, "you won't like it," she said with a grimace.

Chloe raised an eyebrow and held a hand out for the paper. Steve handed it over to her. Chloe surveyed the photographs and the editorial that accompanied it. She read the article out loud. "How enlightening it is to see what really goes on at successful yards. It is a miracle to comprehend how this particularly successful yard has achieved such great heights in light of its idiotic inhabitants." Chloe paused and looked up at Steve who gave her a grim nod.

Chloe silently read the rest of the article. It gave an in depth report on Sarah and Duncan's fight and then went on with a scathing piece on the lack of organization that seemed apparent in the yard members. It described Steve as model material but a typical blond who couldn't even remember a course. Ben was the short sighted over ambitious hairy cob lover. Heather was an excellent example of the product of the "pushy parent" and Rory was an overly arrogant know it all.

Lyn was the entertainment factor who was perfecting her falls on her lazy horse and Britney was the overly brave, bordering on stupid, money pit of a child whose parents would end up mortgaged up to the hilt in order to fund her dreams. Kelly was the horse loving loser who would permanently be put upon by penny pinching bosses like Sarah who would take advantage of her horse loving nature to work her into the ground in defiance of any work time legislation that other employers had to adhere to. Jade was the dopey groom to the townie who was trying to impress her friends by being an event horse owner.

Chloe stopped reading and rolled her eyes. "Bloody cheek. I've a good mind to sue them for this."

Ella nodded, "how the hell have they got the cheek to call me another blonde bimbo? "

Steve shook his head, "It's the part that mentions locals inter breeding that worries me," he muttered

Chloe folded up the newspaper and tucked it under her arm. "Let's hope that this doesn't get noticed by too many people," she said firmly. "Come on let's have a cup of tea and think about getting some dinner."

They trudged off to the kitchen and Jade started making tea while Chloe rummaged through the cupboards. "By the way Jade have you been moving things about? I can't find the papers that I left in the sitting room again"

Jade shook her head, "you've said that before, I always put things back honest."

Ella and Steve sat at the table. Ella sighed, "I don't believe this, I'm in another derogatory photo. My parents are going to go mad."

Steve gave her hand a pat, "I'm sure they won't, it's not your fault, it was that rotten journalist. No wonder she was asking me strange questions. They just wanted to find some dirt on us. How were we to know that they would print the worst photographs and turn the whole thing into a comedy piece?"

Chloe looked up, "by the way, did you find anything of interest on those DVDs?" She asked Jade.

Jade froze for a moment and bit her lip. She shook her head. "No it was just some film of the village fete," she murmured, feeling her face go red. She couldn't tell Chloe that and Ella had started to play one of the discs and found that it had contained some rather explicit sexual scenes. Carl had spoken privately to Jade and specifically told her not to tell Chloe if she found anything that may be considered lewd. He had indicated that this may well happen and that he didn't think that Chloe should have any dispersions cast on her late relatives. After all what they did in their spare time was no one's business really as long as it was legal.

Carl had said that he would sort them out when he was next at the house. He wanted to check things, just in case there was another reason that they were there. After all Chloe's aunt and uncle might have had a lodger and the discs might not have even belonged to them for all they knew. Once he had looked into things then perhaps he would break the news to Chloe

Ella glanced up at Jade and looked away quickly to avoid her gaze. She had been sworn to secrecy by Jade and would not break that oath. Steve saw her expression and looked at her curiously. What had those two been up to? He would ask Jade later, he was sure that she would tell him what was going on if he asked her nicely.

Chloe stared at Jade for a moment. She decided that she would interrogate her later she was obviously lying about something and would soon spill the beans under pressure.

Jade was given a welcome distraction as Jerry jumped on up to the kitchen unit. "Oh Jerry you're so naughty, you know you're not supposed to jump up," she chided, giving his chin a tickle.

Chloe looked at Jerry, "we should get him a new collar that one's stretched to its limit, we don't want him getting stuck on something," she said as she pulled out a sachet of food for a loudly purring Jerry who was now twirling around Jade's legs.

Jade nodded, "I'll take it off for now then," she said and reached down to remove his collar as Jerry tucked into his food.

Jade held the collar up and studied the worn leather. "I must remember to put his phone number in the new one, that's a good idea isn't it?" She asked Chloe who stopped opening a jar of Spanish chicken sauce to look at her curiously. "What do you mean?"

Jade handed her the collar, "In the barrel they put his number," she smiled.

Chloe took the collar from Jade and unscrewed the barrel. She unrolled the paper out and stared at the numbers. "That's not the house phone number you daft nit," she said shaking her head. She stared at the numbers again and then looked up at Jade. "That's definitely no phone number not with that configuration of numbers."

Jade stared back at her curiously, "what could it be then if it's not the phone number?"

Chloe stared at the numbers again frowned as she concentrated. Finally she looked up, "If I'm not mistaken, it looks like it's a combination number."

Jade now shook her head frowning in confusion, "what do you mean."

Steve looked up at Chloe. "I think Chloe means that it is a combination number for opening a safe?" He said raising an eyebrow at Chloe.

Chloe nodded firmly. "Yes, I do believe that this may be the key to where my uncle kept his most important work. Now all we have to do is find out what safe this is the combination for. In the meantime, you'd better not lose this." With that, she rolled up the paper and placed it gently into the barrel of the collar.

CHAPTER 31

Chloe nervousness had increased steadily as they drove to the young horse qualifier. Steve had also become quieter and quieter as they became closer to the venue. Jade was her usual cheerful self. Her answer to dealing with nerves was to just keep talking and so she had maintained a steady stream of pointless banter for most of the two hours drive. Fortunately this meant that Chloe didn't have to engage herself in any conversation apart from the occasional nod in Jade's direction.

They qualifier was being held at one of the country's premier eventing venues and was slotted in alongside a three star eventing competition. This meant that most of the top event riders were at the trials.

Jade looked around in amazement as they parked their hired trailer, "goodness, look at the size of those trucks," she exclaimed. "Look at that one over there," she said pointing at a huge gold lorry, "they've got a sitting room in it and they've got a telly on!

"Probably hoping to catch a glimpse of themselves on it," muttered Chloe as she turned off the engine.

Steve said nothing. He had a feeling of dread in the pit of his stomach. He hoped to God that he wouldn't let anyone down this time. He was determined to study the cross country course avidly. There was no way that he could mess this up, he had to prove that he was up to the job.

Chloe ran off to check the show progress leaving Jade and Steve with Sam. Jade was still looking around with wide eyes. "Steve do you think there's anyone famous here?" She asked excitedly.

Steve couldn't help but smile, "yes, probably, but I'm not sure you will know who they are. They will probably be famous horse people."

"Oh." Jade nodded looking a little disappointed.

Steve shook his head, "don't worry, I'll point them out to you when we've finished."

Jade brightened noticeably, "okay, I need to tell Ella and Jo. See if I can do a bit of name dropping," she beamed.

Chloe returned. "Just twenty minutes behind so we had better go and check the courses they'll be starting soon," she informed them.

Chloe and Steve marched off leaving Jade to keep an eye on Sam. Jade clucked in Sam's ear and told him how handsome he was until they finally returned. After a few moments of talking about the course they fell into a silence. Jade gazed at the sign on the side of the trailer, "Truckers and trailer hire" it read. She stared at it dreamily, picturing a scene of Steve holding a large cup on a podium sharing a winning smile with her as she applauded by his side.

Steve finally looked at Chloe. "I really will try my best for you and Sam you know. I know the dressage test inside out and I've got the course's set in my head," he said, tapping the side of his forehead.

Chloe smiled at him. "Steve, I know you will do your best. You always do. I think you should stop worrying and relax and enjoy it. I have every faith in you."

Steve looked back at her for a moment trying to decide if she was teasing him. She wasn't. It was the first time that anyone had ever said anything like that to him. Steve looked at the ground for a moment, feeling a sudden rush of nerves and anticipation. "I think I'll give Sam another brush," he murmured and walked away to unload Sam from the trailer.

After what seemed like an age it was finally time for Steve and Sam to go and warm up. Chloe watched as Steve eased Sam into his rhythmic gait and then pushed him forwards into some extended strides. Sam obliged willingly. Steve gave him a pat when he had finished and waited for the steward to call them forwards.

"Good luck." Chloe said her voice was barely a whisper as Steve trotted Sam away to the dressage arena.

Chloe and Jade watched as Steve and Sam performed the dressage movements. Chloe thought that they looked wonderful. Jade's eyes were bright. "They look so nice." Jade said, "is that good? Because it looks good."

Chloe nodded. "Yes it does look a good test, but you never know what the judges are thinking with the dressage."

Steve and Sam left the dressage ring. Steve smiled at Chloe and gave Sam a pat. "Did that look okay?" he asked.

Chloe nodded. "From where we were standing it looked very good," she said with a small smile, "let's just hope the judges agree."

They walked back to the trailer to wait for their show jumping time to come. Jade was fondling Sam's ears while Steve was going over the cross country course again and again in his head.

Finally it was time for their show jumping round. Steve and Sam walked across to the ring and set off in that soft canter to warm up over the practice fences. Sam's ears pricked as he saw the show jumps, time for some fun.

The steward called them in and they were off. Chloe could barely watch as they went around the show jumping fences. She felt her leg lifting up again as they approached the first fence.

Jade clapped her hands together as Steve and Sam jumped around the course. "Oh I hope they go clear, they must go clear," she said excitedly.

Chloe bit her lip as they went to the double with no faults yet. She knew that if she said anything good they would have a fence down, it was the commentators curse.

Chloe held her breath as they went clear through the double. Steve turned Sam towards an oxer that was followed by some planks. The planks had been catching a lot of people out. They only seemed to need the slightest touch to send them flying. Chloe sucked in again and felt her leg rising in the air as they took off over the oxer. Jade suddenly clutched her arm, "come on, come on." she was chanting.

Chloe watched frozen as they cleared the oxer. Steve now asked Sam to come back and shorten up to meet the planks. For a brief moment she thought that Sam would throw his head up and dash forwards but Sam obligingly rounded back to Steve and they cleared the planks with ease.

As they headed for the last fence Chloe didn't want to watch. The nerves inside her stomach were out of control. She just wanted this to be over. It almost didn't register when Sam cleared the fence by a foot and cantered easily through the finish.

Chloe and Jade couldn't move. They both stood perfectly still for a moment. Jade broke the silence by giving a loud, "whoop," and leaping into the air with her arms held aloft. "They did it, they did it, they went clear," she shrieked.

Chloe shut her eyes for a moment and then grinned back at Jade before grabbing her in a bear hug, "shush Jade, you'll scare the horses," she said with a smile. Jade was momentary taken aback at Chloe's sudden hug but was soon hugging her back delightedly.

They walked hurriedly over to the ring's exit. They were both trying to keep themselves from running. Their eyes were bright and they were both grinning like fools as they rushed up to Steve and Sam.

Steve smiled at Chloe, "we still have the big one to do," he said. He was trying not to be too pleased about the show jumping round. He knew that the cross country could go completely differently.

Chloe nodded as she took Sam. "Just keep it together. I know that you two can do it."

Time seemed to slow down as they waited for Sam's turn on the cross country and when they were finally walking into the start box Chloe had the most terrible butterflies in her stomach. This was agonizing. She never thought that she would feel this nervous. If she were riding Sam herself she probably would feel less apprehensive. Fortunately Steve seemed calm and collected as they headed off.

The countdown started and they were off. Sam galloped away from the start box towards the first fence with his ears pricked. Steve collected him for a moment and they sailed over it easily.

Chloe watched as they jumped over the third and fourth fences and then headed out of view towards a double of ditches. This was unbearable. She turned to Jade and saw that she looked as anxious as she felt. Chloe bit her lip and strained to hear the commentary. They turned and hurried across the field towards the finish where they could at least see them jumping the last few fences.

Chloe took a short deep breath as the commentator announced, "number seventeen Steve Bradshaw and Samson Seven have gone clear with nice jumps over fences five and six and are heading into the coppice."

Chloe and Jade listened in silence as they heard the updates on Steve and Sam's progress. They appeared to be going clear so far. Chloe frowned as the commentary switched to another competitor on the course and she stood on her toes straining to see any sign of Steve and Sam.

Suddenly they could see Sam galloping along the top of the hill. Jade's mouth dropped open and she smiled in delight as they could just make out them jumping over the fence at the top of the hill and then turning to sweep back towards home.

Jade grabbed Chloe's arm as they saw them galloping across towards them, "here they come," she gasped. Jade was suddenly breath taken at how lovely they looked galloping along the field, Steve looking so dashing in his colours.

Chloe's hand went to her mouth as they flew over the last two fences and through the finish. They headed towards Steve and Sam but Chloe paused as she tried to listen to the commentary to find out whether they had actually gone clear or not.

Chloe nearly choked when the commentator announced, "that's a good clear round for Steve Bradshaw and Samson Seven, completed within the time, well done."

Chloe suddenly couldn't stop smiling as she and Jade dashed over to Steve and Sam. She showered a panting Sam with pats, "well done you two that was wonderful," she cried.

Jade threw her arms around Sam and looked up at Steve who was also grinning as he patted Sam, "aren't you both so clever," she said smiling at Steve shyly.

Chloe gave Sam another pat and looked again at Steve. "Result!" She said and high fived him, now he was now grinning even more.

Steve jumped off Sam and loosened his girth giving him another pat. "He's such a good horse Chloe, I really don't have to do anything. You wouldn't think he was still just a baby."

Chloe took Sam's reins, "it takes two to tango, I'm sure you give him confidence," she smiled as she led him back to the trailer.

After giving Sam a drink and then treating him to carrots, they put him back in the trailer. He had huge hay net and the top door on the trailer was open so that he could enjoy the view. Sam seemed to be quite happy to stand on the trailer quietly munching on his hay and watching his equine cousins. He gave the occasional whicker when one of particular interest caught his eye as they walked past.

Chloe decided to take Steve and Jade for some lunch after they had gone to the Secretary's tent to have a look at the results. They stood in the tent studying the board intently. Chloe felt a sudden sense of disappointment, "they're not up yet." She shook her head, how much longer would they have to wait.

Steve saw her face, "why don't we get our lunch and have a look around. I'll check on Sam in between." He turned to Jade, "I can show you some of those big cross country fences that they're competing over today and point out some names for you."

Jade nodded enthusiastically and looked at Chloe eagerly. Chloe shook her head. "I think I'll go and stay with Sam. Why don't you two get something nice to eat and I'll see you later," she said pressing some twenty pound notes into Jade's hand. "Bring me a sandwich back and maybe a slice of cake," she said as she left. Although she realised that she didn't really feel particularly hungry.

"Is she all right?'" Jade asked looking at Steve. Steve nodded. "I think she's just a little nervous about the results." He looked at Jade. "She wants Sam to get somewhere so that she can re home him and get back to her life in the City."

"No!" Jade looked horrified. "I thought that she might keep him and stay here."

Steve shook his head. "I don't think that she can afford to. The Estate has some debts to pay apparently."

Jade looked downcast as they walked on. Steve pointed out a few famous event riders to her and they picked up some rolls before heading back to find Chloe sitting on the floor by the trailer. She had taken Sam off it and tied him up outside with his hay net so that he could admire the view more easily.

Steve noticed Chloe's morose expression. "Everything all right?" He asked.

Chloe looked up at him and frowned. "They finally put the results up and I've had a good look," she said simply.

"Oh, are they not good?" Steve asked tentatively.

Chloe looked straight at him with slightly wide eyes. "You've only gone and won it. "

Jade gasped and shook her head. "Oh that's amazing," she said looking at Steve excitedly. Steve paused for a moment and then smiled. He suddenly picked Jade up and swung her around him with a shout of delight.

Chloe watched with a smile as Jade clung to Steve giggling. She looked around at the horses and the rolling fields and felt a sudden unexpected pang of sadness. She supposed that now this was the beginning of the end.

CHAPTER 32

There was an air of solemnity in the house as Chloe cracked open the bottle of champagne that she had brought from Mrs Patel's. She wiped off the dust from the bottle before she poured it into the glasses that Steve, Jade, Ella and Joanne held out.

Joanne was grinning happily. "Do you think there will be a write up about you anywhere?" She asked Steve.

"Perhaps we should let the local newspaper know, especially after that awful article that they wrote," nodded Ella.

Steve shook his head, "I honestly don't know, there are a few other qualifiers around the country."

"But you got the best score that they've had so far,' said Jade.

Chloe finished filling up their glasses and then held hers up. "To Sam and Steve." She announced and they all clinked glasses. "Sam and Steve." They said almost in unison.

"So what happens now with the qualifier?" Jade asked nervously.

Chloe paused as she sipped her champagne. "Well the final is not for a while yet so..." She tailed off and took another sip of her champagne relieved at the distraction of Jerry marching into the room mewing loudly. "Hasn't anyone fed you Jerry? Oh, Jade look at him, his collar is over one ear! I told you that we mustn't lose that number."

Jade put her glass down. "Oh poor Jerry, and I forgot to feed him."

Chloe put her glass down quickly. "Don't worry, you sit down I'll see to him," she said and headed off to the kitchen with

Jerry in hot pursuit.

Jade looked at Steve as Chloe left and shook her head. "She seems a bit evasive. It must be true what you said," she muttered.

Ella and Joanne looked across at them. Ella saw Jade's expression. "What is it? What's going on?" She asked.

Jade sighed and looked at Steve who shrugged. She may as well tell Ella and Joanne they would find out soon enough.

Chloe walked to the kitchen. She really must now move Sam on and get the house sold she thought. There were bills and debts to pay and they wouldn't hold off forever.

Chloe stopped as Jerry headed off in the other direction. Jerry paused for a moment and turned back giving a loud mew as he looked at her.

"I thought you wanted some dinner? Come on Jerry you know that it's this way," she said and gestured a hand towards the kitchen

Jerry looked at her and gave a rather loud wail.

Chloe looked at him with concern. "What on earth is wrong with you boy? Are you feeling poorly?" Chloe said as she walked towards him.

Jerry hesitated, shook his head and then trotted away down the hall. Chloe stopped and frowned. Jerry turned back to her again and gave a loud mew.

"Why are you going that way?" Chloe asked Jerry who looked at her intently. His amber eyes were wide and almost imploring. As if he wanted her to do something, but what?

Chloe walked over to Jerry and as soon as she got close he padded off again. This time he glanced briefly over his shoulder to check where she was. Chloe walked after him. "Okay you have it your way, I'll follow you and see what you want," she said as she walked after him.

Jerry gave another mew and continued along the hall with Chloe following a short distance behind. Jerry trotted along checking over his shoulder every now and again just to be sure that she understood that she must keep up.

Finally he turned into the study doorway. He jumped up against the door to give it a push open and went inside. Chloe followed him as instructed.

Chloe stopped as she entered the study and frowned. Jerry had gone over to the secret passageway door that was standing wide open. He sat in front of it and gave a loud mew before giving a shake of his head and glancing back at Chloe.

Chloe watched as Jerry's collar finally fell over his other ear and landed on the floor beside him. She picked up the collar and held it fondly. She looked back at the door. Why was the door wide open? They always kept it shut. It had been agreed that it was always to be kept closed. They didn't want anyone seeing what was down there yet and they certainly didn't want Jerry trotting off down there and perhaps being shut in.

She walked towards it and paused. Chloe looked at Jerry who gazed back at her and then turned his gaze towards the open door. Chloe paused for a moment. "I suppose I may as well go and have a look down there," she murmured.

Chloe walked forwards and made her way down the passageway. Jerry observed her but made no effort to follow her, instead he decided it was time for a face wash.

Chloe walked carefully down the stairs in the darkness. She felt relieved when she made it to the bottom and felt around on the walls until she found the power switch. She flicked the switch and the basement was instantly showered in its dull yellow light.

Chloe walked along the corridor. She paused at the first door fingering the collar that she held in her hands. She peered along to the end of the corridor as something caught her eye. Something looked different at the end of the corridor, or was it the light casting a dark shadow there? It almost looked as if another door had appeared there, right at the very end, it must be a trick of the light.

Chloe stopped and thought for a moment. Her eyes suddenly widened as she remembered the room with the rugs inside. It had a safe inside it. She marched quickly down the corridor and opened its door flicking on the light as she entered.

Chloe paused in the doorway, what on earth? She looked around the room. It appeared as if someone had been fooling about in here. The room was a mess. She would have to have a word with Jade. Everything was strewn all over the place. The photos were on the floor or on their sides. The rugs appeared to have been thrown all over the room and bridles and saddles were all over the floor.

Chloe shook her head and stepped across to the corner where the safe was sunk into the wall. She stopped and frowned as she looked down at it. It had a mark in it that she hadn't noticed before. It was almost a dent but the steel on the thing was so thick you could hardly tell.

Chloe opened the barrel on Jerry's collar and took out the piece of paper inside it. She put the collar down on the floor and bent down to look at the safe. It did indeed have a combination lock.

Chloe took a deep breath and grabbed hold of the dial. She looked down at the paper and ticked off the numbers as she simultaneously turned the dial. She finally clicked it around to the last number and held her breath.

She stared at the safe, nothing happened. Then suddenly she felt something click inside the dial. She almost fell backwards onto her backside but grabbed on tighter to the dial. She felt a feeling of excitement rising inside her as the safe door swung open.

Chloe peered inside the safe. It was quite small, not much room inside. There were two envelopes inside and nothing else. She pulled them out and stood up, looking at them curiously.

She turned them over and gasped as she read the writing on them. One envelope had, "Formula" written on it. The other had, "Formula Composition," written along its length.

Chloe moved over to the desk and placed the "formula" envelope down on it, along with Jerry's collar. She looked at the other envelope and felt its weight in her hands. She opened it quickly and pulled out some folded papers and a disc.

Chloe unfolded the papers and looked at the writing on them. She rolled her eyes. She didn't understand it. It was all mathematics and some kind equations. She pulled put another piece of paper from further inside. She recognized her uncle's writing on it.

Chloe stared at the page. Her uncle seemed to be writing an introduction as to how he came upon his formula. It stated that the disc gave detailed process as to the function of nanobots in the use of bio chemical technology and reciprocites. The formula was the result of his research into enhancing your own body's ability to repair itself.

Chloe frowned at the paper. She had no knowledge of such things and no idea as to what this meant. She sighed and turned around. Duncan Morcross was standing in the doorway watching her.

Chloe almost jumped out of her skin. Yes it was Duncan! What in God's name was Celia's other half doing in here? Chloe had a sudden uneasy feeling as she remembered the strange incidence with Duncan and Sarah.

Chloe swallowed. "What on earth are you doing here? How did you get in? Did Steve and Jade send you down here?"

Duncan gave a small tight lipped smile and shook his head. "No Ms Marcus. I arrived here of my own volition, and it appears to have been perfect timing," he said and gave a nod at the envelope and papers that she was holding.

Chloe stared back at him. "I really think you should leave now Duncan. If you haven't been sent down here by Steve or Jade then you have no business being here," she said slowly. She wondered how the devil he had got in and why she was feeling so uneasy.

Duncan's smile tightened and he took a small step forward. He stopped and held out his hand, "the papers Ms Marcus. Hand them over to me and I shall be out of here before you know it."

Chloe gaped back at him. Was he serious? Yes he certainly looked it. She shook her head. "These are nothing to do with you. Now get out of here before I call the Police."

Duncan sighed, "I had a feeling that things were not going to be simple. He pulled something out of his pocket with his free hand. Chloe could see the beads of sweat starting to form on his forehead.

Duncan held up his hand to reveal the hypodermic needle that he had been carrying. "I hoped I wouldn't have to use this but you have given me no option."

Chloe's eyes widened as he took another step towards her and took the plastic cover from the end of the needle. Duncan surveyed her once more and waved his other hand at her again. "Now we can do this the easy way or you can have a very long sleep which of course will look completely natural to anyone who finds you"

Chloe stepped backwards, "are you mad? If I give them to you I'll just report you to the Police anyway. You'll get a very long time for this Duncan."

Duncan shook his head. "I hoped that you wouldn't say that. Now you do realize that you're going to have to have that little nap anyway."

Chloe gave a gasp, "Duncan! Surely you aren't serious. You would kill me for these papers?" She moved backwards again and felt the desk behind her blocking her retreat.

Duncan nodded. "Oh yes. I've been looking for those for a long time. When you found that safe for me I thought that I had finally found what I was looking for but I couldn't get the bloody thing open. Even when I shot it with a rifle it still wouldn't budge. Your uncle was so pedantic about his security."

"How do you know what's in the papers?" Chloe asked trying to buy some time.

Duncan paused and stared at her sternly. "Oh I've known what your uncle was up to for years. That's why I came to this village. I heard about this genius that was working on bio chemical engineering from a friend of mine who works for the Government. Apparently your uncle worked out how to reproduce red blood cells that had a lifetime three hundred times longer than normal human cells. Do you know what that means?"

Chloe shook her head and tried to slide slowly across the desk. Duncan raised the needle at her and waved it from side to side. "Don't try anything funny. You might as well hear the rest seen as you won't have much more time. Your uncle could have prolonged the human life span. He could have made us live for two maybe three hundred years. He could cure practically anything on the planet with what he knew. But you know what? "

Chloe shook her head.

"He was a sentimental fool!" Duncan spat. "He didn't think that it was ethical to allow his research to be shared with anyone. He didn't think that we should be allowed to live that long. He said it wasn't natural, bloody idiot. That's why he left the Government. Apparently there was a fire at the lab after he left. Destroyed his work. Strange coincidence eh? The only development of his research that he allowed was in that formula that you gave that horse and he kept that to himself. But that will do to start off with and I have a feeling that there's more in that disc you're holding. Once I have hold of that I won't have any more worries and I won't have to keep flogging those sordid films on the internet any more."

Chloe blinked she felt herself go cold. "What do you mean? What films?"

Duncan rolled his eyes. "Well when I finally managed to find the back door to this basement," he said gesturing over his shoulder "and that took some doing believe me. Still, when I got to that other room I realised that it could be a little gold mine. All the equipment is there to make those sleazy films that sell so well and what with cctv cameras you can always catch someone up to something. It's pretty easy to change their features so they can't be recognized and then you have a nice little earner. You don't think that my job funds Celia's yard to you? It's a bloody money pit but the bitch just won't let it go."

Chloe couldn't believe what she was hearing. She shook her head in disbelief. "How could you?"

Duncan rolled his eyes, "oh please. I've been trying to find this formula for months, that's why I had that horse of yours fixed. I knew that your aunt would use something of your uncle's on him if he was hurt badly enough."

Chloe now froze and stared at Duncan with widened eyes. "You did that to Sam?"

Duncan shook his head "Not me directly. I paid that head lad of Celia's and he took him off and hammered the horse until his legs couldn't take any more. That lad's a nasty piece of work you know. He didn't ask any questions just took the money and did the job." Duncan gave a thin smile. "Hadn't you ever wondered how he got injured?"

Chloe looked away, suddenly she felt so angry. How could he have done that to poor Sam?

Duncan stared at her for a moment, "good lord you didn't even think did you? My, my, people are so stupid. I was hoping that your aunt would come out to give him something so that I could analyse it but she snuffed it. Bloody typical." Duncan's eyes narrowed, "I never caught you giving him anything but you did and you must have been real sneaky about it. Perhaps you're not as stupid as you look." Duncan's thin smile widened into a predatorial grimace, he glared at her malevolently, "now it's time for a sleep," he snarled and advanced towards her, needle held aloft.

CHAPTER 33

Chloe shrank away grabbing at the desk behind her. There here was nowhere for her to run, to she had to stop him. Suddenly she felt her hand connect with something on the desk. It was a riding crop.

Duncan was almost upon her as she grabbed the whip and whacked him as hard as she could across the face. Duncan reeled away in shock, grabbing at his face and dropping his needle. "Aaargh! You bitch!" He yelled.

Chloe didn't hesitate. She kicked as hard as she could, aiming right between his legs. Duncan screamed as her foot made contact with his testicles. He fell forwards cupping his hands between the legs. Chloe grabbed the other envelope and the cat collar and ran out of the room as fast as she could. She tore along the corridor checking once behind her to see if he was following her. There was no sign of Duncan. She shot up the stairs and slammed the door behind her. She grabbed a chair from behind the desk in the study and shoved it in front of the door to hold it in place.

Jerry was now sitting on the desk. He sat up as he saw her and mewed loudly. Chloe picked Jerry up with one arm and ran out and into the sitting room. Steve, Jade, Joanne and Ella were sitting there completely oblivious of the fact that someone had just tried to kill her.

Steve looked up as he saw a sweating, scared looking Chloe enter the room. She was carrying a mewing Jerry under one arm. Steve jumped up quickly, "Chloe what's happened?"

Jade went to her and quickly took Jerry from her, "sit down," she said to Chloe. Jade glanced nervously at Steve who came over and took Chloe's arm. Chloe pulled away, "no we must stop him," she gasped.

Steve stared at her, "who? What in God's name has happened?" Steve had never seen Chloe look so afraid.

Chloe quickly told them what had happened in the basement. There was a moment of shocked silence as they all took it in. Jade's eyes were wide in disbelief. "I can't believe he could be so horrible," she murmured clinging on to a now purring Jerry.

Chloe looked at Steve. She remembered the shadow at the end of the corridor. "We must go outside. There's another door he found that he used to get into the basement. It must lead outside, there has to be an exit out there somewhere," she said thrusting the envelopes and collar at Jade's hands and grabbing Steve's arm.

Steve stopped Chloe and looked back at Jade, Ella and Joanne. They were all staring at him with wide eyes. "Stay here and phone the Police," he said to Jade who managed to nod back at him. "Be careful," she said quickly as they left the room.

Chloe ran ahead and threw open the front door. She slipped through and started to run out but instead ran straight into Carl who was about to knock the front door. Simon was at his side.

Carl caught hold of her. He looked at her expression and was instantly concerned. "What's going on?' He asked.

Chloe froze and looked up at Carl. "Thank goodness. You can help us. It's Duncan, he tried to kill me and now he's escaping, we need to stop him." She pointed franticly down the drive, "he'll get away."

As if on cue they heard the sound of a car engine. Duncan must have parked off the road and down by the track where the drive from the house ended and woodland grew next to it.

Chloe shook her head in despair. "No! He's getting away, we have to stop him."

Steve strained his eyes and ears to track the car. "It's too late," he said "we'll never catch him now." He turned back to Chloe. "Don't worry, I'm sure the Police will find him.

Chloe realised that she was shaking and took a deep breath. She looked up and could see the concern in Carl and Simon's eyes. Carl looked at her and touched her face gently. "Are you all right Chloe? He didn't hurt you did he?"

Chloe noticed that she had been gripping Carl's arms quite tightly. She pulled herself back and stood up. "I'm okay," she nodded. "We'd better go inside and see what the Police have to say."

They walked back in to the sitting room where Jade was standing nervously holding on to Jerry with the envelopes and collar clutched to her chest.

Ella looked up as they came into the room they seemed subdued, "you didn't catch him then?"

Joanne was sitting on the sofa drinking a glass of champagne that she had topped up from the bottle. "Well, you just wouldn't think it of Duncan," she said as she stared into space.

Ella frowned, "Jo, please."

Joanne looked back at her, "well, honestly, he seemed such a nice quiet man, you wouldn't think that he would say boo to a goose."

Chloe looked at Carl. "By the way, what are you doing here?"

Carl raised an eyebrow, "that's some welcome."

Chloe closed her eyes, "I didn't mean it like that, I'm glad you're here, especially with that maniac on the loose."

Carl smiled at her. "When you called to tell us of Sam's and Steve's victory I rang Simon and we decided that we should come up and celebrate their victory with you," he said nodding at Steve. "Seems like it's a good job we did come over."

Chloe froze as a sudden thought crossed her mind. "Oh God."

Steve stared at her, feeling a surge of nervousness as he caught sight of her face. "What is it?"

Chloe turned to him her eyes eyes wide. "What if he's gone to do something to Sam? He said something about cctv and filming people to make sordid films. He and Sarah had that big fight. What if she's in on this?" She looked around her eyes alight with panic. "We have to get Sam, before he does something."

Carl touched her arm, "we'll go to the yard and make sure he's all right. I'm sure he wouldn't be that stupid though," he said glancing at Simon.

Simon nodded, "Carl you stay here with Chloe, I'll go and check the yard."

"I'll come with you." Said Steve firmly. He suddenly felt a rising panic in his stomach. What if that crazy fool did hurt Sam?

"Take my car, bring him back here." Chloe said suddenly.

Steve paused, "what, are you sure? I can stay with him if you like."

Chloe shook her head, "no, I want him here where I can keep

an eye on him. We'll fix up a stable in one of the out buildings. Give Ben a call, I'm sure he'll let us borrow his trailer, if not ride him here."

Steve raised an eyebrow and gave a small smile. "Consider it done Ms Marcus," he said and left walking swiftly to the car with Simon.

Chloe turned back to Carl. "We need to check the exit from the basement so that we can secure it in case he comes back."

Joanne spluttered on her drink. "You don't think he's coming back do you?"

"You never know." Chloe said. "We should secure the place just in case."

"Perhaps we should go home." Joanne said to Ella. Her eyes widened suddenly. "Oh blimey, what if he's waiting for us at Celia's yard? "

Ella chewed her bottom lip. "Do you think Celia is in on this?" She asked looking at Chloe.

Jade's clung on to Jerry even tighter and he started purring and curling his front paws. His loud purr was the only sound in the room for a moment.

Chloe looked at Ella and Joanne thoughtfully. "I have a feeling that Celia doesn't know about this. I reckon that Duncan and Sarah were up to something because of that fight they had."

Jade nodded enthusiastically, "yes, if those two were up to something Celia and Sarah surely wouldn't have stayed friends if Celia had known."

Ella and Joanne exchanged glances. Ella nodded, "I'm going to call Tony, I need to warn him that something could be up."

Chloe looked up quickly. "Tell him not to mention anything to Paul, he knows what Duncan is like. Duncan paid him to break Sam."

Ella froze and stared at Chloe in disbelief. She knew Paul had a mean streak in him but surely he wouldn't stoop that low?

Chloe nodded at her, "tell him not to trust Paul and you'll explain later."

Ella walked to the end of the room to make her call. Carl looked at Chloe. "Come on sit down. You've had a traumatic time. Just how did you get away from him anyway?' He asked as she melted down onto the sofa.

Chloe told him about her actions in the basement and Carl couldn't help but grin. "What a wild cat, good for you."

They all jumped at the loud knocking that suddenly came from the front door. Carl went to answer it and returned with two Police Officers.

Chloe felt herself start to relax as she went through the incidents of the evening. She led the Police officers down to the basement along with Carl and showed them the rooms where everything had taken place. She felt herself shiver as she entered the room with the safe inside. The hypodermic needle was lying on the floor and one of the officers carefully placed it into a bag with gloved hands.

When they came out they inspected the door at the end of the corridor. It was indeed exit. It blended perfectly into the wall and Chloe would never have found it if Duncan had not left it slightly ajar, casting a small shadow across the wall.

Chloe watched as the Police pulled open the door. Carl glanced across at her anxious face and took her hand, giving it a reassuring squeeze. She gave him a small smile in response. They waited for the Police officers to investigate the exit. The stairs looked even steeper than those that led down to the basement from the house and there were no lights. The Policemen muttered to each other and suddenly the stairs were flooded with light.

Chloe and Carl watched and waited until the Policemen said that they could follow them up the stairs. Chloe went first and blinked in the light as she stepped from the stairs into the outside world.

Chloe looked around her. The door was set right into the side of the house next to the utility room was. It blended in almost perfectly with the wall of the house and was covered in ivy. She stared around in surprise. "No wonder we didn't see this?"

One of the Police officers raised an eyebrow. "This exit door is pretty well disguised," he said closing the metal door and locking it back into place.

They returned back to the house and Chloe finished giving the Police her statement. Carl went off to find something to secure the passageway door with.

Joanne looked nervously at Chloe as the Police left. "Are the Police going to Celia's?"

Chloe nodded. "Yes and to Sarah's, I told them everything and that Sam was coming here." Chloe noticed Ella and Joanne's worried expressions. "You can stay here if you like girls."

Ella and Joanne looked relieve and exchanged glances. Joanne gave a nod. Ella spoke first, "thank you I think we would like that."

Joanne nodded in agreement. "Yes I'd rather be where there are more people around in case that nut case comes back. Besides, God only knows what Celia will do about all of this."

Chloe looked up as she heard another car pull up on the drive. She ran out of the room and across the hall and flung open the front door. Steve had jumped out of her car that was towing Ben's trailer. Chloe looked at Steve anxiously. "Is he all right?"

Steve nodded and smiled. "He's fine and no sign of Sarah or Duncan."

Chloe felt a surge of relief as she walked around to unload Sam. She led him from the trailer and gave him a pat as he looked around with pricked ears. She buried her head in his mane, breathing in his sweet equine scent and smiled. "It's all right Sam, you're home now."

CHAPTER 34

Ben grinned as he looked around the yard. It was a nice turn out. He took a sip of his lager and lime and nodded at Chloe. "I say they've done a nice job on tidying this yard up don't you think Chloe?"

Chloe nodded. "Yes it looks much smarter. It's amazing how sometimes you don't realize things need tidying up until it's actually done."

Ben raised an eyebrow quizzically. "Are you generalizing?" He asked with a small smile. Chloe smiled back at him. "Well perhaps I am." Chloe looked over to where Carl was chatting with Simon and Lyn. Simon had his arm around Lyn's waist. Ben noticed Chloe's gaze. "Don't you think that it's wonderful that those two are an item? Lyn deserves a break. She's been bored to death in that insurance job and desperate to get out for ages now and she's so into the horses."

Chloe nodded. "Yes and she'll run the yard much better than Sarah did. She's far more enthusiastic. Ben nodded. "That Simon must be quite smitten to buy this place for her and to put her in charge as well. It was a good idea to have an open day too, its good publicity for the yard. That was Lyn's idea," he smiled.

Chloe saw Carl glance across at her and she gave him a smile and a nod to say that all was well. They both jumped at a sudden shrieking and turned around to see Ben's two girls were at it again. This time Lily had a handful of Milly's hair that she was holding proudly aloft while brandishing Ben's horse clippers threateningly. Lily was shrieking in fear.

Ben sighed as Gill tried to pull them apart and they both flew at each other. "I'd better go and help," he said apologetically to Chloe who was trying not to laugh.

Chloe took a sip of her champagne and wandered over to where Jade, Steve, Ella, Tony, Joanne and Kelly were all standing chatting. Kelly had been handing out some curried pasties that were now sitting on a tray on the floor. She looked up as Chloe came over and picked up the tray quickly. "Like a nibble?'" She asked as Chloe arrived.

Chloe shook her head. "Not yet thanks," she said looking at the pasties dubiously. "Did Jade make those by any chance?" She asked as she noted that they looked more like puddings than pasties.

Jade nodded happily. She looked radiant. She had stopped dying her hair that awful unnatural burgundy red colour and let it grow out. It now hung silkily around her cheeks, shining a vibrant chestnut red in the sunlight. She had replaced her glasses with some much nicer silver ones and even had a little lip gloss on. Steve had an arm laid casually across her shoulders. Chloe felt herself smiling again. She was glad that she had been right about Steve and even more delighted when Jade's mother had given her blessing on Jade remaining at Diddlecot to help her to sort out the estate.

Chloe also noticed that Tony also had a protective arm around Ella. Chloe looked at her she also looked radiant. "How's the modeling going?" She asked.

Ella beamed, "oh it' going wonderfully. I can't believe I've been head hunted."

Joanne laughed, "you see something good came from that sleazy mag."

Ella frowned at her and then smiled back at Chloe. "I suppose that you're right. If he hadn't seen my picture pinned up in that garage and then found me through his friend showing him our local rag with that awful write up then I would never have got that lingerie contract."

Joanne grinned at her. "You could end up as one of those Play Bunnies. Living in the lap of luxury."

Tony shook her head. "Ella's only doing stuff with her clothes on Jo, she doesn't need to strip off now." Tony stroked Ella's arm gently. He had enjoyed the horse riding and was surprised at how well he managed to get on with it but he was more relaxed now that he was working with his uncle. His uncle owned a chain of shops that bought people's jewelry and gold. Tony had been doing quite well too, at this rate his uncle said that he would have his own shop to run soon and even could be a partner."

"Well I'm glad it all worked out." Said Chloe, she looked back at Joanne, "how are things at the yard?"

"Much better now that Celia's gone. The new owner is into show jumping so the horses aren't quite as mad, well most of them anyhow. The owner is much more laid back than Celia was and not half so angry. I was lucky they kept me on I'm actually enjoying it now."

Chloe nodded, "well that's good."

Joanne smiled. "Funny how Celia went off with Sarah though, don't you think? Especially after Sarah was having a fling with Duncan. How weird is that?"

Chloe smiled grimly. " A marriage made in heaven. I still can't believe that Sarah didn't know what Duncan was up to."

Jade looked thoughtful. "Joanne's cousin in the Police station said that she claimed that she only knew that he was on to some business deal to raise some cash. She said that they were supposed to be going away together. I feel sorry for Sarah's husband, apparently he's gone to live in Spain with his sister."

Steve shook his head. "What a strange set up. Still, at least Lyn is running the yard now and that awful Rory has done a runner too."

Ella laughed, "just because he got a crap mark in a dressage test, mind you he probably felt lonely when Sarah and Celia left him."

Jade nodded. "It's good that Kelly got kept on though and at least she gets to keep riding Sarah's two that she left behind. I'm glad that Lyn got Ted off Rory too. She's been getting on great with him."

Chloe smiled "Yes Simon decided that he might as well invest in another horse to compete and Ted was certainly a good choice. That reminds me, I have a little something for you Steve. I thought that you deserved it after you and Sam did so well to qualify for the young horse finals, which is only three months away by the way so you'd better get schooling."

Steve stared at Chloe. "Does this mean that you're staying?"

Chloe nodded, "suppose I'll have to. Now that we have the recipe for the formula we can market it for animal medicines. In its diluted version of course, as my uncle would have wished."

Steve grinned and hugged Jade close to him. "Does that mean that Jade can come to stay here?"

Chloe nodded solemnly. "If Jade would like to stay then she can stay full time if she wants. She can continue to help me when I'm working from home and keep the house tidy. In fact if you teach her some more about horses she can do more in that department so that you can have more time to do your free lance work. As you seem to be in demand after your success with Sam."

Jade beamed excitedly, "oh I'd love to stay. Mum has come round to me being away and she even said it might be nice to move somewhere quiet like here."

Steve gave Jade another hug to and she put her arm around his waist affectionately. Steve gave her a kiss on the head. "Looks like you could be stuck with me sweetheart. Perhaps you'll let me take you out to dinner to celebrate?"

Jade glanced up and managed not to let her eyes fill up with tears. She never thought that she could feel this happy. She couldn't believe that someone like Steve would look twice at her.

Joanne rolled her eyes, "oh please, not you two as well. Honestly I'm beginning to feel like a right gooseberry."

Ella laughed, "well you should give Paul a call. I'm sure he'll be grateful of any friends. Since he left the yard."

Joanne sighed. "Apparently he went back home and his parents are trying to get him back to University to study for a degree. They were disgusted when they found out he'd been involved with Duncan."

Chloe shook her head, "I'm surprised he didn't get sent to Prison for cruelty."

"His parents paid for an up market lawyer to make sure he didn't get sent down said Joanne. His mom and dad are very well off.

Ella looked at Chloe. "What will happen to Duncan now?"

Chloe shrugged, "I don't know, it depends on how the trial goes. Duncan is denying everything of course but the Police found various incriminating discs and newspaper cuttings when they went to the house. He hadn't the time to destroy them all."

Ella was shaking her head "I still can't believe he was such a sly, sleazy man."

Chloe sighed, "well it's in the past now and at least all of those stupid cctv cameras have gone from the yard now." Chloe looked back at Steve and reached into her bag she handed Steve a package.

Steve handed his drink to Jade and opened the package. He looked at it for a moment and then grinned at Chloe.

Chloe smiled back. "I thought that you would find it handy especially for the young horse finals," she said brightly.

Steve held it up so that the others could see it. "Ms Marcus I do believe that you have a sense of humour?" He said with a wry smile.

Jade read the cover out loud, "Brain Training Exercises For Young Professionals," she gave a small laugh.

Chloe gave Steve a wink. "No pressure though," she said and walked away towards Carl.

She paused as she heard someone call her name from behind her. "Ms Marcus. "

She turned around to see Robert Morecam standing behind her. She nodded at him "Hello Mr Morecam, how are you? I didn't expect to see you here."

"I am fine Ms Marcus. Just supporting the locals and I assumed that you would be here. I gather from your phone call that things are going well with the estate?"

"Yes, I'm getting on top of things now." Chloe smiled

"Good. Your aunt and uncle would be proud. I'm so glad that you decided to stay." He said nodding slowly. "I trust that I will be seeing you soon to sort out the paperwork?"

"Yes very soon."

"Good then I'll leave you with this," he said handing her an envelope.

Chloe looked down at the envelope it simply had her name written on the front.

"What's this?" She asked staring at it.

Robert stared back at her for a moment before replying. "It's something that your aunt wanted me to give you. When it seemed the time was right, so to speak."

He smiled again and gave her another nod as he turned and walked away. Chloe jumped as she felt a hand suddenly grasp her arm. "Anne! What are you doing here?"

Anne nodded at her, "oh I got a lift from my neighbours. Their daughter is horse mad and wanted she to come and show them the yard. She's trying to persuade them to get her a pony. Bless her, If only they knew what they were getting into eh?"

Chloe shook her head, "if only."

Anne stood back and smoothed her hair net down. "Well I just came to say that if you still want me to come around then I can manage to do most days."

"Yes that would be nice,'" said Chloe "but I still haven't paid you for what you've done already."

"Oh we'll sort that out some other time. " Anne said, with a wave of her hand. "I like to keep an eye on things. Promised your aunt I would." She gave a small chuckle. "Honestly, at one point I thought you'd never find that safe combination. I left the collar lying in front of you enough times and even Jerry was trying to drop you hints," she said.

Chloe's eyes widened. "What? You mean you knew about all of that?"

Anne touched her arm, "your aunt was my dearest friend, we became very close especially after dear Harry passed away and she was left all alone."

Chloe felt a lump rise in her throat. Anne gave her arm a squeeze. "That's life though isn't it dear? Well I'll be off, we'll catch up later." With that she was off across the yard patting her down hairnet again.

Chloe gazed after her in wonderment. She nearly jumped again as Carl suddenly appeared next to her. "Are you all right? You look like you've seen a ghost," he said staring at her in concern.

Chloe swallowed and nodded slowly. "Yes I'm fine," she said as he took her hand. She looked up at Carl, "I'd like to go home if that's all right. I feel like I need to be there."

Carl smiled and nodded. "Of course, I'll take you home," he said and put an arm around her shoulders.

Chloe smiled to herself. She had called the house home automatically and strangely, she felt quite elated about it.

Chloe stood in the bedroom looking out of the window. She could see Steve and Jade. Jade was sitting on Quickstep who was resting a hoof with his eyes half shut. Jade was clinging onto his mane and had her feet thrust too far into the stirrups.

Chloe sighed. Steve might find this pupil a little more challenging than most she thought with a smile.

Steve pulled at Quickstep's head as he leaned forwards to try to nibble on a rose bush. Chloe rolled her eyes and shook her head. She hadn't liked Sam being here by himself and as Lyn now had Ted to ride she had said that Quickstep could come here to keep him company. To be honest, he was perfect for Jade to learn on. He was so lazy he couldn't be bothered to play up and he was a plod on a hack. He didn't bat an eyelid at anything.

Chloe turned around as she heard Jerry jump on to the table with a quiet thud. Jerry looked at her from his perch. His beautiful eyes didn't move as he gazed up at her.

Chloe walked over to him and stroked him along his head and around his chin. She smiled as his loud purr filled the room. She looked down and saw that his front paws were resting against the envelope that Robert had given her.

Chloe picked up the envelope and looked at it for a moment. She looked back at the still purring Jerry who was still gazing at her intently.

"I suppose you're trying to tell me to open this now? Eh, furrball?" She said ruffling his chin.

Chloe looked back at the envelope and slowly tore it open. She pulled out the paper from inside it. It was a letter. Chloe read it.

Our Dearest Chloe

If you are reading this then it means that we are no longer alive. Please do not be sad about this. Just remember our happy times together. They were times that we will always cherish.

Chloe you are like a daughter to us and we have never stopped loving you. We know that we've had a few problems, but we were always there for you. We just wish that we could have had more time with you.

We understand that you wanted to move on with your life when you lost Jeff and we could see how consumed by grief you were, so we are not angry that you did not want to see us. We knew that you just needed time.

The fact that you are reading this also means that you have decided to stay at the house and keep Sam. That was our dearest wish. The house we have left to you as part of the estate.

We are sorry that you have some financial restraints in the estate. It's just that your uncle Harry's research got a bit costly at the end. All that bio mechanics materials gets rather expensive don't you know. As I'm sure you have found out. It was worth it though and you should be able to pay off any debts and then some with the income from the formula.

There is also something that we wanted to tell you that we have never told you before.

When you left, we always hoped that you would change your mind and come back and ride your beloved horse Roxy again. She still used to look out for you over her stable door you know after you left. Her eyes were always so bright and expectant we think she loved you as much as you loved her.

Because you didn't come back and Roxy was so lonely we decided to put her in foal and this we did. She had a lovely foal that we named Samson because he was so big and strong.

We are sorry that Roxy had to be put to sleep. She came

down with severe colic when Sam was just eight months old. At least she had a little time with him though and would have seen how lovely he was. That was the last time we wrote to you wasn't it? We felt that it was only right that you knew about Roxy's death. We were hoping that you would get in touch and then we were going to tell you about Sam, but time just caught up with us and before we knew it he was grown up. We were going to try and race him and were going to tell you in the hope that you might come and watch him run. Sadly it appears that we ran out of time.

Don't be sad when you read this. Just remember that Roxy lives on in Sam and we live on in you. As long as we have our memories no one is truly gone.

We will always love you our darling Chloe.

Aunt Sophie and Uncle Harry

PS Give Jerry a tickle from us. Xx

Chloe looked up and a tear fell down onto the letter. It smudged the writing and she patted it away quickly. She looked back at Jerry who was staring at her silently.

"What a fool I was. I should never have run away should I?" Chloe said to him.

Jerry suddenly raised a paw at her as if he were waving at her. Chloe gave a small smile. "Oh Jerry you're such a darling," she said, running her hand along the back of his head.

Chloe turned around as she heard a squeal. She walked across to the window and looked out to see Steve running alongside Quickstep who was doing a slow trot along the drive. Jade was clinging on, bouncing around on his back with a huge grin on her face.

Chloe looked up and gazed away at the view. The open fields rolled away in the distance and the sun was going down, sinking away into the horizon. She smiled to herself, what a beautiful place. Who would want to be anywhere else?

ISBN 978-0-9926379-6-5

www.ingramcontent.com/pod-product-compliance
Lightning Source LLC
Chambersburg PA
CBHW061933170626
46813CB00006B/2384

* 9 7 8 0 9 9 2 6 3 7 9 6 5 *